WHEN THE SMOKE CLEARS

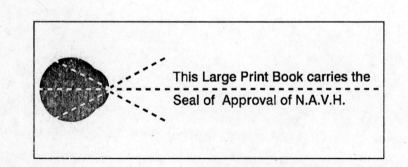

This Large Print Book carries the
Seal of Approval of N.A.V.H.

WHEN THE SMOKE CLEARS

LYNETTE EASON

THORNDIKE PRESS
A part of Gale, Cengage Learning

Detroit • New York • San Francisco • New Haven, Conn • Waterville, Maine • London

GALE
CENGAGE Learning®

LIBRARY OF CONGRESS CATALOGING-IN-PUBLICATION DATA

Eason, Lynette.
    When the smoke clears / by Lynette Eason.
        pages ; cm. — (Thorndike Press large print Christian
    fiction) (Deadly reunions ; book 1)
        ISBN-13: 978-1-4104-4969-6 (hardcover)
        SBN-10: 1-4104-4969-6 (hardcover)
        1. Large type books. I. Title.
    PS3605.A79W47 2012b
    813'.6—dc23   2012013870

Published in 2012 by arrangement with Revell Books, a division of
Baker Publishing Group.

Printed in Mexico
1 2 3 4 5 6 7 16 15 14 13 12

Dedicated to my Savior, Jesus Christ,
who allows me to do all that I do.
Thank you for the words.
May the readers see you on every page.

So do not fear, for I am with you;
do not be dismayed, for I am your God.
I will strengthen you and help you;
I will uphold you with my righteous
right hand.

— Isaiah 41:10

PROLOGUE

June 6, 2002

Flames licked higher, swallowing everything in their path. The curtains, the recliner . . . her father and sister.

Blinking the nightmare away, eighteen-year-old Alexia Allen clutched her diploma and looked out over the audience.

The families of five hundred students hovered around their proud teens in the downtown auditorium. Camera flashes nearly blinded her, and she decided she didn't care a bit that she didn't have even one family member in the audience.

She had her diploma. That was all that was important. That and the bus ticket she had in the back pocket of her only pair of jeans. She would've worn a dress if she'd been able to afford it, but the graduation gown and cap had already taken enough of her savings. A dress wasn't a necessity.

Jillian Carter sidled up to her. "Are you

going to the graduation party?"

"For a few minutes. Then I've got a bus to catch."

"Where are you going?"

Alexia sucked in a deep breath and looked around. "Anywhere that's not here."

The flash of pain in her friend's eyes made her bite her lip and regret her bitter words. The thumb and forefinger of her right hand went to the little silver ring on the pinky of her left hand and twisted it.

Round and round. A nervous habit she'd picked up right after the fire.

"Sorry. You and Serena are the only good things left in this town, but even you guys can't keep me in that house a minute longer. Every day it's a constant reminder of . . . well . . . you know. And my mother told me the other day not to let the door hit me on the rear on my way out." Alexia swallowed and studied her fingers.

"I'm so sorry."

Jillian's compassion brought Alexia's emotions to the surface. Emotions she didn't want to deal with. "She's just turned into this bitter old woman and I can't take it anymore. I tried to help her. I did." She sighed. "But she doesn't want help. At least not *my* help."

And still she couldn't seem to lose the

10

guilt. If only she'd had more control over her actions. If only . . .

"I don't blame you." Jillian's soft words brought Alexia back to the present.

"I know you don't." She paused. "There was something in her eyes when she told me to leave . . . something . . . I don't know . . ." She let her voice trail off, forced her mother's face from her mind, then whispered fiercely, "I won't let him hit me again. I can't stay there one minute longer. If I do, it's going to kill me. *He's* going to kill me." A shudder wracked her. "I need to get away. Tonight." She now understood the desperation her brother, Dominic, had felt when he'd run away. She'd been angry with him for a long time, but now . . . she empathized with him. She just wished she knew where he was.

Wished she could take back the spiteful, hurtful words she'd hurled after him as he stomped out the door, and out of her life.

"I wish I had the guts to come with you," Jillian murmured.

Hope brightened Alexia's heart for a brief moment before she could stop it. She knew Jillian wouldn't leave. Her mother needed her too much. However . . . "Call your aunt. Tell her she needs to come help with your mother."

11

"I can't do that and you know it. She's got my two little cousins to take care of." Jillian gave a sigh and shook her head. "No, I'd love to go, but . . ." She shrugged and the pain returned to her eyes along with a flash of desperation.

Alexia put a hand on her friend's arm. "What's wrong, Jilly?"

"Nothing. Nothing. I'm fine."

The forced smile said otherwise, but before she had a chance to question her friend further, she spotted Serena Hopkins pushing through the crowd and heading their way.

Giving a rare squeal, the usually dignified Serena waved her diploma and then gave each girl a massive bear hug. "We did it!"

Alexia couldn't help laughing. Serena could always make her laugh, even when she thought she had nothing to laugh about.

Midnight black hair that looked almost purple danced around her shoulders. Tall, poised, and runway gorgeous, Serena was confident in the dark good looks her Spanish mother had bestowed upon her, not to mention her serene personality and flashing chocolate eyes that drew guys to her like a moth to the flame.

And she made it impossible to hold her wealth against her. Although Alexia often wondered what attracted Serena to the two girls from the wrong side of the tracks, she'd never worked up the courage to ask her. It was enough to bask in the friendship and Serena's loving family.

So different from her own.

"Are we going?" Serena demanded. "The party's starting."

"I'm in," Alexia said.

"I'll be there too," Hunter Graham said over Alexia's shoulder.

She shivered as his breath caressed her left ear. And his bright blue eyes had that little glint in them that she'd started seeing every time he looked at her. The little swoop in her stomach failed to take her by surprise this time. But she'd sworn off guys forever after Devin's betrayal.

She frowned as she pictured her ex-boyfriend. She'd thought Devin was different.

Obviously, she had lousy judgment in guys and wasn't to be trusted when it came to picking one out. Although she had to admit, if she were interested in trying the whole boyfriend thing again, Hunter would be the one she'd choose.

But she wasn't.

Besides, he was only going to the graduation party to keep an eye on his brother and sister, who'd just graduated with Alexia. Chad and Christine Graham were twins who had a penchant for trouble. Which was why Hunter often drew the short straw and got chaperone duty. She wondered how they felt about his big brother eye now that they were eighteen.

She considered him again. He was already a junior in college. Alexia knew she'd never be worthy of his interest.

Not that she wanted his interest, her mind insisted.

Right?

Right. Besides, she was on the next bus out of here.

Frowning at him, she started to tell him to get out of her space — in a nice way, of course — when Jillian said, "I'll be there in a little while. I have to run an errand first."

The girl's voice trembled and Alexia shot a glance at Serena to see if she'd caught it. The frown on her face confirmed she had.

Glancing at Hunter, Alexia said, "Excuse me." Taking Jillian's arm, she pulled her to the side.

Serena followed.

Hunter got the hint and walked off.

Alexia rubbed her hand up her friend's arm and gave her shoulder a reassuring squeeze. "Tell us what's wrong, Jilly."

Jillian waved a hand. "Later. I need to go. I'll catch up to you at the party, all right?"

Serena grabbed Jillian's hand. "Promise?"

"Promise."

Jillian whirled and headed for the door.

Alexia looked at Serena. "What's her problem?"

"I have no idea. We'll get it out of her when she gets to the party. Now let's go!"

They raced for Serena's car — a sweet little BMW Roadster — and within ten minutes arrived at the school gym.

Alexia looked around and smiled. The decorations looked great, the music was loud, and her friends were at her side. Life was good.

Soon she'd be on a bus to wherever, USA, and she'd never have to come home again. No more living with the craziness of her home life. The thought of her mother shot pain through her. She really didn't care if she never saw her dad again, but her mother . . .

Memories of her mother's arms around her when her dad had been gone — or passed out — flitted through her mind. Whispered words of her mother's brand of encouragement flickered.

But the woman didn't want her at home. Had been pretty definite when she'd told her she needed to leave.

She shook her head and focused on the music.

Life had just improved 110 percent. And the fear churning in her gut had no place in that new life.

Serena danced with Jacob Styles, her on-again, off-again boyfriend. Alexia gave a regretful sigh as she watched Serena fold her head into Jacob's shoulder.

Even though she'd just convinced herself that she wasn't interested in having a boyfriend, she couldn't help wondering what it would be like to be able to lean on someone. To let yourself go enough to trust another person with your heart. To believe that person would never betray you. Alexia blinked back tears.

Allowing someone that close hadn't been an option. Not with her home life. The one time she'd allowed someone to cross the barriers to her heart, he'd betrayed her. Devin Wickham. It hadn't taken him long to show his true colors.

But now?

No. She had a life to make for herself. She had goals. Plans. Dreams . . .

But maybe one day.

Her throat clogged. Would she ever find someone to love her? To believe in her?

Alexia's eyes strayed to Hunter, dancing with his sister, who didn't seem to care that he was there. He caught her eye and winked. She flushed and looked away.

Then back.

If he was interested . . .

A hand gripped hers and she turned to see Jillian standing beside her, wide-eyed and frantic, tears streaking her cheeks. "Jillian! What's wrong?"

"I need your help," she gasped. "I don't know what to do . . . I saw . . . I've got to leave!"

Alexia looked for Serena, snagged her attention, and motioned her over with a mouthed "Help!"

Frowning, Serena whispered something to Jacob and moved to join them. Alexia pulled Jillian into the relative quiet of the hallway. Serena followed two steps behind. "What is it?"

Jillian burst into tears and sank to the floor. "I'm dead," she whispered. "I'm so dead. I can't believe this. I don't know what to do."

"What happened?" Serena ignored her expensive dress and sank to the floor beside her friend.

"He's going to kill me. He's going to . . . because I was there and I think he saw me and what I saw . . ."

Jillian stopped and slapped a hand over her mouth. Her eyes darted to the door as the tears flowed. Frustration with Jillian started to sprout inside Alexia — not to mention a sprig of fear at her talk of killing. "Spill it, will you? You're talking in circles. How can we help you if we can't understand you?"

The girl went still. Her tears stopped as though turned off with a switch. She looked up, horror on her face. "I can't. I can't be here and I can't tell you. He knows we're friends . . ."

"Wh— ?"

"I'll just put you in danger too." She jumped up, eyes wide with sudden renewed horror. "Oh no! I can't believe I didn't think . . . I didn't —" She shot a desperate look toward the exit. "I've got to get out of here. They'll find me. And then they'll find you. They'll think I told you . . ."

"Who? What?" Alexia nearly yelled.

"I can't go home . . . I'll need some money." Grief and terror flowed from her. "Please, I'm sorry to ask, but . . ."

"Here." Alexia dug into her purse and pulled out a hundred dollars.

"Never mind, I have to get out of here." Jillian started for the door and Alexia grabbed her arm.

"Here," she said, shoving the money into Jillian's hand.

Serena did the same and handed her a handful of fifties. Jillian didn't even blink as she grabbed the cash and took off.

"Hey! Come back!" Alexia called.

But Jillian's feet pounded down the hallway toward the exit at the other end.

"Jillian!" Serena yelled. "Wait!"

Jillian didn't even turn as she hit the door at a full run. The alarm sounded and Serena and Alexia took off after her.

By the time they got the door open again, Jillian was nowhere to be seen.

1

Ten Years Later
April 6, 2012
5:45 p.m.
He suspected what was in the envelope. Shaky fingers opened it and pulled out the single white sheet with the block-style printed words.

I KNOW.

Senator Frank Hoffman leaned back in his plush leather chair and drew in a deep breath.

It was Jillian; he knew it. She'd decided to come out of hiding. He'd searched high and low for the girl ten years ago, when she simply dropped off the face of the earth.

But the letter proved she wasn't dead. She was back, taunting him with the skeleton in his closet.

Jillian Carter. The one person who could kill his career, ruin his shaky marriage, and sabotage his future.

He'd rather put a bullet in her brain than let that happen.

Again, he read the words.

I KNOW.

Amazing that two small words could instill such terror.

Jaw tight, he started to crumple the letter into a ball, then thought better of it.

Pulling out a large brown envelope, he added it to the one that had come two weeks ago. The one that said, "HELLO FRANK. I'LL BE IN TOUCH." The one he'd been praying was from anyone but her.

He shoved the envelope into the top drawer of his desk, shut the drawer with a snap, and twisted the key to make sure it was locked. He did *not* want his wife finding those notes.

What did Jillian want? There'd been no blackmail demand, no reason given for the subtle threat.

Just, I KNOW.

And only two people on this earth knew his secret.

Of course one wasn't talking. Were there others?

He doubted it. The fact that the last ten years had flown by without a peep from anyone was proof of that. With dread in his heart, he knew the truth of his situation. A truth he had avoided facing for ten years. Now that truth stared him in the face, mocking him. Letting him know that his comfort zone had just been penetrated.

He had to find Jillian Carter.

There was only one way to restore peace to his life. He picked up the phone and called the one person he trusted with absolute confidence to bury this secret so deep it would never stir again.

2

April 10, 4:35 p.m.

The flames reached for the ceiling, consuming everything in their path. Sprawled on her belly and forearms, staying as low as possible in the burning house, Alexia paused and listened. Visibility was almost non-existent. She heard an ominous creaking and raised her eyes to the ceiling. It splintered, cracked. The fire had been burning up there a lot longer than reported if the ceiling was ready to go.

"Joel! Get out from under there!" She shoved herself toward him, still staying low and knowing she wouldn't reach him in time to push him out of the way.

On his knees, testing the door in front of him, Joel looked up — just as the ceiling caved, sending a large piece of wood crashing down on his shoulder, then glancing off the side of his helmet.

With a cry, he went down flat against the

24

rapidly heating floor.

"Joel!" She made her way back through the smoke to reach him. Into her radio, she called, "Joel's down, Captain, I need help!"

"On the way," he reassured her. "Lex, the mother just showed up. Little girl, three years old, name's Maddy. In the back bedroom, last door on the left."

Alexia froze. A kid?

She scrambled over to Joel, grabbed him under his arms, and started hauling him to the exit, her exertions using more air. How much time did she have left? Plenty. They'd been in the building less than two minutes. "Joel, there's another kid in here somewhere. I've got to find her." But she couldn't leave her partner. Not yet, not ever. She made sure his air tank was functioning. He looked dazed, stunned, but not seriously injured.

Looking up, she made out the shape of another firefighter. "Get Joel, he's hurt. The girl's in the back! I'm going to look."

"I've got him." Alexia recognized Snoop's voice.

"I'll be right out," she said.

"I'm coming with you." Sanders. Great. The one man in the department she didn't want to work a fire with.

Another groan sounded from above.

Alexia looked up just in time to jump back from the crashing beam. Sanders muttered a curse and dove to help cover Joel. "Get back, Alexia! RIT'll be coming for you!"

The Rapid Intervention Team. Two firefighters whose only duty would be to get her out. But until they reached her, she still had a job to do. She was trapped between a wall of flames and the back of the house.

"I'm looking for that kid!"

Without waiting for a response, she turned and crawled toward the bedroom. She paused and listened.

Nothing but the sound of the burning building.

Pounding on the closest door, she hollered, "Maddy?"

No answer.

Raising up on her knees, she tried the knob.

Locked.

She rose to her feet and stepped back. Lifting the axe in her right hand, she brought it down on the knob. The door shuddered and the molding around the door cracked as the knob fell to the floor. Lifting her booted foot, she gave the door a hard kick and it slammed in against the wall. Smoke swirled out, but no flames. Breathing in the life-giving air from the tank strapped to her back, she used the thermal imager device in her left hand to search for anything that pumped blood and put off heat.

Nothing.

She filled her lungs again and headed for the closet.

Flames licked down the hall behind her. Great, she'd have to find another way out. She reported in. "I'm in the small bedroom on the left."

"We've got Joel, Alexia. You find the kid?"

An alarm sounded. Alexia pulled in another breath of air. And stopped. No air. She looked at her gauge. Out of air. That was the alarm going off.

Panic hit her. "Captain, I'm out of air."

"What?" His voice roared in her ear.

Dizziness hit her.

"Get out, Alexia. Now!"

"Just going to check the closet first, sir."

"Get your tail outta there. Immediately!"

She needed air. She reached up to disconnect the hose from her tank, then shoved it up under her heavy turnout. The coat would protect her as much as possible from smoke inhalation. And she sure didn't want a blast of hot air in her lungs. She caught a breath. The dizziness receded.

The countdown was on.

The decision: leave or check the closet?

She scanned the imaging device over the door. Bingo. "I've got something. Definitely a child."

"Alexia! Get out!"

"She's here, sir. Can't leave without her."

Alexia went to the door and turned the knob. A little girl. "Maddy?"

The child looked up at her, eyes wide, stark terror stamped on her tear-streaked features. Then she coughed and her eyes rolled back. Alexia slung the imager over her shoulder and leaned in to pick up the little girl.

Alexia took another breath and coughed.

Dizziness returned full force and she went to one knee. Vaguely, she felt the sweat roll down her back. "I'm in trouble," she said into her radio, keeping her cool, refusing to panic. Help was just a second away. "Where's RIT? No air."

Lights flashed in front of her eyes and she blinked. Tried desperately to fill her lungs. How had she run out of air? She should have had plenty of time left.

She pulled in a lungful of smoke this time. Coughing, sputtering, she turned with the child, frantic to get her out before the flames caught up with the smoke.

And then she had no more time to think

as the spots before her eyes merged into one big black dot.

Then nothing.

3

May 8, 8:16 p.m.

The letter had arrived at one o'clock this afternoon.

Seven hours and sixteen minutes ago.

Alexia picked it up and studied it once more, as though rereading it might change the contents.

It didn't.

She tossed it back onto her bedside table. It had been four weeks since the fire. Four weeks of giving her statement and waiting on pins and needles as the investigation progressed at a snail's pace. Four weeks of wondering if she had a job or not.

Well, now she knew.

She'd disobeyed a direct order from her captain. He'd been livid.

But she should have had time. Should have had enough air.

The investigation showed one thing that really concerned her. She had tiny little holes in her air hose. That explained why she'd had to replace her tank so soon. She'd brought out a nearly unconscious six-year-old boy and handed him over to the paramedics. He was mumbling a girl's name over and over. They could only guess it might be a sister still inside, and Alexia started to head back in. That's when she glanced at her air gauge and saw she was low on air. A quick trip to the truck and she shrugged on her new tank before heading back inside with Joel. But still using the same air hose, she had again run out of air too fast.

Confusion filled her as the horror of her suspicions hit her once more. Holes in her hose meant someone had deliberately put them there.

Which meant — someone had tried to kill her? Why?

Unless she could prove it, she was stuck. She was officially suspended from both firefighting and smokejumping until further notice. After all, it wouldn't look right for a suspended firefighter to be smokejumping, would it?

Not according to her boss.

"Argh!" Alexia grabbed the nearest pillow and punched it. The depression morphed into anger, and she flexed her fingers before curling them into another fist. Unfurling them, she twisted the ring on her pinky as she thought.

Okay, she'd disobeyed a direct order from her captain. But she'd saved a child's life. That had to count for something, didn't it?

Apparently not.

Her stomach churned. She'd worked hard to get where she was. Straight out of high school, fresh off a cross-country trip to a new city, she had started training to be a firefighter. She worked her way up the ladder — literally. From secretary to firefighter to smokejumper. She sweat blood and tears for her current position. She was proud to be a member of the North Cascades Smokejumpers.

And now she was in danger of losing it all.

Normally, she wouldn't have even been at the Washington Fire Station No. 2, but her old chief, Corey Burnham, had called and asked her to fill in. The flu had wiped out half his crew and he needed her if she could spare the time.

It wasn't supposed to happen this way. She'd been doing a favor and now her life had fallen apart.

Again.

The letter glared at her like the accusing

eyes of her captain when she'd finally regained consciousness in the hospital.

Alexia swung her legs over the side of the bed and stood.

Another piece of mail caught her eye.

A postcard announcing her ten-year high school reunion to be held in September. Four months away. Her eyes bounced back and forth between the letter and the postcard. Did she dare go back?

She remembered the night she left. And Jillian's frantic plea for help before her dramatic disappearing act. She remembered her mom's not-so-subtle push out the door.

The phone rang and she jumped. A glance at the caller ID told her it was Serena Hopkins.

Alexia picked up the phone and dropped back down onto the bed. "Hello, Serena. Are you a mind reader now?"

"You're thinking about the reunion."

"I am." She flopped back onto her pillow.

"And you're coming, right?" Serena didn't sound at all sure, just hopeful.

"I don't know. When I left there, I sure never planned on going back. Too many bad memories."

"You think it might be time?" A pause. "Your mother's in the hospital."

Alarm clanged through her in spite of the

33

fact that she didn't want to care. "What's wrong with her?"

"They're not sure. They're running tests to find out."

"Come on, Serena, you and I both know there's nothing wrong with her. It's most likely another anxiety attack." Her friend didn't say anything, and Alexia drew in a deep breath. "But she's all right?"

"For now." Serena paused. "She's really changed, Alexia. You would be amazed at the new person she's become over the last few years."

"You keep telling me that. But why would she change? How does someone grow a spine at the age of fifty-six? And why now?"

"God can do amazing things when he has a willing heart to work with. You used to believe that."

"I used to *want* to believe that. There's a difference."

"You *still* want to believe that," Serena countered.

Yes, she did. Desperately. But it was a moot point.

Time to change the subject. She didn't feel like churning up emotions that took too much time to calm down. "How's the morgue?"

"Dead."

"Cute."

"Seriously, I'm so not busy right now."

"Which is why I get the phone call." Silence. Alexia frowned. "Hey, you okay?"

"I heard from Jillian."

Alexia sat straight up in the bed. "Where is she? How is she? What's she been doing all this time?"

"She said she's fine, but not to tell anyone she'd been in contact. She's been living under a different name all these years. Can you imagine?"

Memories bounced in her mind. "She's still scared, isn't she?"

"Sounds like it. I told her about the reunion, but I don't think she'll even consider coming back." A pause. "She still refuses to talk about that night."

Alexia remembered Jillian's frantic desperation to escape. Even now, she could hear the echo as the exit door slammed behind her fleeing friend. "I always wondered what she saw. What she was so scared of that she wouldn't risk telling us about."

"I know. Me too. When I asked her why she was calling, she just said, 'It's time.' "

"It's time?"

"Yeah. Then she said she'd be in touch and hung up." More silence, then, "So, are you coming home?"

35

Alexia drew in a deep breath, forced herself to think about what Serena called home. Columbia, South Carolina, held so many bad memories, but Serena was there. And the fact that her mother was in the hospital concerned her more than she wanted to admit.

Why *did* she care? Her mother had never done one thing in her life to *make* her care. And yet . . . she was still her mother. Some part of Alexia wanted to believe the woman had changed.

"Yeah. Yeah, I guess I am."

Serena's uncharacteristic squeal nearly pierced her eardrum. But for the first time in a month, Alexia smiled. Serena did not squeal unless she was extremely pleased.

Then Alexia frowned as her thoughts circled back to her faulty equipment. If she stayed in Washington, she could fight back and figure out what had gone wrong with her tank. And she could appeal the decision and see how everything played out. But if she stayed, would she be in danger?

If she went home to Columbia, she wouldn't feel compelled to watch her back. Maybe she could forget there was the possibility that someone tried to kill her.

Maybe.

Taking a deep breath, she said, "I guess

it's time for me too."

As she hung up the phone, somewhere in the back of her mind, she heard a voice mocking her decision.

Running away again, huh, Alexia?

Why not?

It was what she did best.

4

Monday, May 14
5:32 p.m.

Senator Hoffman walked to his desk, pulled the key from his pocket, and used it to unlock the top drawer. The shaking in his hands hadn't eased since the first letter. If anything, it had gotten worse. And now the third letter joined the first two in the brown envelope.

This one simply said: SOON.

His pulse quickened as he thought about the election coming up. He had to take care of this and fast. Thank goodness his bank account could handle whatever he needed to have done.

Footsteps sounded in the hall. Pocketing the key, he considered whether or not to tell his wife everything. Their marriage wasn't exactly in the best place right now. It was probably best to continue to keep this to himself.

"Frank, are you in there? It's time to go."

"I'm coming, Elizabeth."

She appeared in the doorway. For the first time in a while, he studied her and found hints of the young woman he'd fallen in love with thirty years ago. Wrinkles had tried to invade her face, but she'd raced ahead of them with surgery and whatever it was women did to stay looking young. Not a touch of gray dared show itself in the brown hair she had cut in a stylish bob.

She looked like a senator's wife should. Poised, classy, confident, and wealthy. Everything she'd been reared to be.

And yet, lately, there was a look in her eye that made him wonder what she was thinking. Sometimes a sadness that she didn't blink away fast enough.

But they both enjoyed the perks of his job, so neither rocked the boat. "Did you have Ian bring the car around?"

Ian, their live-in handyman and gardener. He'd been with the family for two decades, and both he and his son, Joshua, were faithful, loyal employees.

"I did. He said he would have it waiting in the time it took for me to find you and get you out there."

Frank placed his iPhone into the front pocket of his tuxedo coat, then reached up to adjust his tie. "All right, darling, let's go mingle with the common folk."

Her left brow lifted. "Don't forget it's mostly those common folks who vote you into office."

His hand absently reached into his pocket to touch his phone. Sometime during the evening, he'd find a quiet moment to make a phone call.

5

Monday, 5:39 p.m.

Detective Hunter Graham folded his six-foot-two frame into the unmarked squad car and shut the door. He cranked the engine, pulled from the station parking lot, and headed down the street to meet up with Katie Isaacs, his partner.

When the phone rang and the caller ID popped up on the screen, his heart lurched into his throat.

Chad was at it again.

Hunter's brother, twenty-eight-year-old Chad Graham, couldn't seem to get his life together. Instead of turning to those who wanted to help him, he'd decided to turn to alcohol, drinking himself into oblivion. Fortunately, he usually chose the same bar every time he felt the need to toss a few back, and the bartender was good about calling Hunter's cell phone.

Wheeling into the parking lot of the Westwood Bar, Hunter clenched his jaw. Chad was already drunk and causing trouble, and it wasn't dark yet. And it was only Monday.

He climbed from the vehicle and drew a couple deep breaths. After all that Chad had been through, Hunter couldn't turn his back on his brother. He was family. And he was hurting.

Just outside the door, Hunter could hear the music and smell the smoke coming from inside. Before he could open the door, his phone vibrated. An impatient glance at the screen showed his father's number.

"Hello?"

"Hunter? Where are you? What's that noise?"

"I'm on a call, Dad, what do you need?" An unofficial call, but a necessary one nevertheless.

"Saturday night, your mother and I need the pleasure of your company."

"For what?"

A long, disapproving silence came through the line. Hunter wracked his brain. What had he forgotten?

"The dinner, Son, remember?"

Oh right. "Dad —"

"No excuses. I need you there."

His father had decided he was getting too old to work fires. Only retirement wasn't an option for him. Someone had decided Harper Graham would make a good mayor with his background in law and five years as a street copy before changing careers. Harper agreed with that assessment and now was working on getting elected to the office.

And he expected his family to put as much into the effort as he did.

Hunter would do his best if this was really what his dad wanted. "Fine. I'll be there."

"And bring a date."

"Dad . . ."

"Your mother made me say that. I've done my duty. See you Saturday."

Shaking his head, Hunter hung up. His father could be overbearing and autocratic, but he was a good man with a good heart. Hunter loved him. Respected him. And would do what he could to help him out.

Stepping into the smoky atmosphere, Hunter paused a moment to let his eyes adjust to the dark environment. Music pulsed, bodies danced. He ignored it all to zero in on the one he came for.

His brother slapped his glass on the bar and slurred, "I'm not done, yet, Zeke. I want another one."

Zeke's eyes met Hunter's and the bartender turned away as Hunter slid onto the stool beside Chad. "Hello, little brother."

43

Chad jerked as though he'd been shot. With a narrow-eyed glare, he slurred, "What are you doing here?"

"Thought I'd come by and check on you."

Chad sneered at his brother. "Rescue me, you mean?"

Hunter gave a nonchalant shrug. On the inside his gut churned. Was Chad going to go peacefully this time or would it be a struggle? "Whatever. You ready to go?"

Chad gave a dramatic sigh and dropped a twenty on the bar in front of him. "Fine. I have a headache anyway."

"You think you have one now, wait until morning," Hunter muttered as he led the young man from the bar.

Chad stumbled along beside him as Hunter kept a firm grip on his brother's upper arm. "Why do you keep doing this, Chad? You ought to realize by now this isn't going to make things any better."

Hunter got him into the front seat and belted in. He shut the door, rounded the car, and settled himself behind the wheel.

"She left me, Hunt," Chad whined. "She left me and won't forgive me. And she won't let me see Shorty."

Hunter blew out a sigh and clapped his brother on his shoulder. "I know, man. I know." Shorty was Chad's six-year-old daughter, Michelle.

"I'm gonna find me someone else." Chad sniffed and tried to punch a determined fist into his opposite palm. Instead, he managed to hit Hunter's elbow. "Someone who'll love me. You know? Someone who won't leave me and take my kid. And break my heart. She's mean and unfair and I hate her, man." He choked on a sob. "But I'm gonna find someone else. I am. Someone sweet and gentle and kind and . . ."

"Yeah, you will, Chad. As soon as you get over Stephanie." And sober up.

But Chad didn't hear him. A light snore drifted toward him. Raising his eyes heavenward, Hunter offered a prayer for his hurting sibling.

6

Monday, 6:24 p.m.

Alexia sat in her car and took a deep breath. She looked in the rearview mirror. An eerie glow reflected off the empty street, the setting sun casting an orange halo around the houses at her back. In less than an hour, it would be dark. Already the sun dipped in the west, causing a dusky hue to cover the area.

Shadows shifted, and memories surfaced.

Why was she here? What was she doing?

Ignoring the cramping in her stomach, she looked again at the white house with the black shutters.

She was home. For the first time in ten years.

She paused a moment to examine how she was feeling. And decided she felt . . . okay. Except for the part of her that felt guilty for not going straight to the hospital to check on her mother. Anxiety and fear mingled, twisting inside her, but she would get it under control. She had everything under control. She wheeled the Toyota 4Runner into the drive and shut off the engine.

The house looked dreary. Dead. Creepy.

Did she want to stay here? *Could* she stay here?

Memories flowed. Heavy clenched fists. Flesh striking flesh. Painful screams. Flames. Unbearable heat. Then the suffocating darkness.

She winced. Blinked back sudden unexpected tears. She would not cry.

Alexia shook her head. What was she doing? Her mother was in the hospital, and according to Serena, Alexia's father had divorced her mother and left home two years after her high school graduation. No one had heard from him since.

It was only a year ago that her mother had started calling her on a regular basis.

Whatever.

At least he wasn't here and couldn't hurt her anymore.

She had no reason to feel fear. No reason to feel antsy about entering her childhood home. Her worst nightmare was gone. Hopefully he was dead.

The thought made her feel like the worst sinner ever.

But her father had caused her more than one sleepless night. She'd lost track of how many times she'd wakened in a sweat, dreaming he was after her. His threat rang in her ears long after she climbed from her bed to rinse her face and catch her breath.

"I'll kill you one day," he'd promised. "You're too sassy for your own good, girlie. Cross me one more time and you'll regret it."

Well, she'd certainly crossed him one more time.

And he was right. She regretted it every day of her life.

Alexia climbed out of the car, shut the door, and made her way to the front porch. Fingers gripped the key she'd never thrown away. Absently, she wondered if it would still work.

"Only one way to find out, Lex."

She slid it in the lock and twisted. The door opened, and as the sky darkened even more, Alexia stepped inside her childhood home.

Memories besieged her from all sides.

The flames reached for the ceiling as though to embrace it in a dance. Only instead of holding it gently, the fire consumed everything it touched.

"Alexia! Alexia! Where are you?"

The screams echoed through her. But she couldn't move, couldn't breathe, couldn't believe what was happening. What they'd told her she'd done.

A sudden thump from downstairs brought Alexia back with a start, and she gasped. She hadn't realized she was holding her breath. Somewhere in the house, the floor creaked. Alexia froze, blood pounding in her temples; caution stiffened her spine. She knew that sound. It was the fourth step from the top of the basement stairs. Even with the fire and subsequent rebuilding of the house, the basement had been spared.

Including the step that squeaked when a foot landed on it.

She bit her lip and stepped back. Run or investigate?

Who would be in her mother's house? There were no cars in the drive. No lights on. Nothing to indicate someone should be here.

Her eyes darted. Everything looked different — yet the same. If she hadn't known a fire had done significant damage to the house a dozen years ago, she'd believe it had always looked this way.

To her left were the stairs leading up to the second floor. Straight ahead, she could see through to the kitchen sink. A pile of dishes peeked over the edge of the stainless steel. A mug looked forlorn all alone on the counter.

Alexia frowned and stepped back once more. Her mother was a neat freak. There was no way she would have let the dishes pile up like that. A glance to her right showed the empty living area. It looked just like it had ten years ago, only with different furniture. Nicer furniture.

But it was still empty. Soulless. She felt her lip curl. Some things never changed.

Alexia moved forward, her white tennis shoes silent on the floor. Maybe she'd been mistaken about the noise she'd heard. It was an old house. Old houses creaked and moaned.

Right?

Ten seconds passed. Fifteen. Then twenty.

When she heard nothing else, her pulse slowed.

Her mother was ill. She probably hadn't felt like doing the dishes. Passing the half bath tucked neatly under the steps, Alexia entered the kitchen and pulled in a deep breath. Then her thoughts scattered as another footfall sounded.

Again, she froze as her adrenaline tripped into overdrive and her throat tightened. Someone was in the house and it was *not*

50

her imagination. "Who's there?"

As soon as the words left her mouth, she wanted to slap herself.

She was an idiot. She'd just let someone know she was here.

Silence echoed for a moment, then she heard another step. And another. Until the footsteps ran together, fading away as they reached the bottom of the wooden basement steps.

Gathering her wits — and her courage — Alexia dashed back down the hall, to the front porch steps, and around the side of the house.

Just in time to see a dark-clothed figure dart from the basement door, right hand clenched around a glinting object.

"Hey! What do you think you're doing?"

The fleeing intruder froze, turned.

Alexia gasped as the black-masked person took one step toward her. And thanks to a gleam of light, she finally registered what he held in his right hand.

A knife.

Dark liquid flashed on the blade. Blood?

She glanced around. All alone.

With someone who'd just been inside her mother's house.

Someone who was heading straight for her, knife in one hand and . . . something in the other.

Breaking out of her frozen state, Alexia instantly realized her stupidity in giving chase. Heart pounding, she backpedaled, spun on her heel, and snagged her Blackberry from her pocket. "I'm calling the cops," she yelled over her shoulder.

Pounding footsteps echoed behind her. She raced for the front door as a car pulled into the driveway across the street.

Panting, she looked back as her feet hit the front steps and saw her pursuer pause under the next-door neighbor's motion light, masked head swiveling between Alexia and the woman getting out of her car. With one last threatening look, the person turned and disappeared into the surrounding darkness.

"Hello? 9-1-1. What's your emergency?"

She realized she hadn't answered the operator. "12 Lockwood Lane," she breathed. "Someone was in my house. He just ran out of my basement. He has a knife."

"Are you in a safe area?"

Alexia looked around. Was she? "Well," she cleared her throat and ordered her pulse to slow down, "he's gone, so I suppose I'm pretty safe at this point."

A glance across the drive showed the

woman who'd arrived at just the right time had gone into her house, unaware of the drama playing out across the street. "Yes, I think I'm safe."

Just saying the words calmed her.

"I'm dispatching a unit. Please stay on the line with me."

The operator's voice faded as Alexia walked back to the house. Once again, she stood on the threshold, wondering if she should wait on the police.

A stirring of anger swirled within. Her jaw tightened. Who felt like he had the right to just violate someone else's space like that?

She flashed to the incident that nearly took her life. Someone had messed with her air tank. Now someone was messing with her mother's house.

The anger built — and built. She *refused* to be a victim again. She stepped into the house and made her way into the kitchen.

"Ma'am, are you there?" The 9-1-1 operator. Alexia had forgotten about her.

"I'm here."

She looked around for a weapon. Nothing. A can of wasp and hornet spray sat on the counter.

That would do.

Ignoring the shouting of her common sense and clutching the can of spray, she headed straight for the basement door. She yanked it open and stepped down the first three steps, automatically skipping the squeaky fourth one, and arrived at the bottom.

What had the intruder been looking for? Her fingers found the light switch and she flipped it.

Brightness bathed the area. The door that led to the outside yard stood open. She paused and pressed a hand to her stomach, reason bullying its way to the surface of her mind. What if he came back?

Dodging the accumulation of junk blocking her path, Alexia cautiously made her way to the door to look out. Darkness, broken by the bright light over the door, greeted her.

Her nerves tingled, the hair on her neck stood at attention. What if he hadn't been alone?

Was there someone down there even now? Watching her? She whirled to face the basement.

Her breathing quickened, her adrenaline rushed as she realized she was framed quite nicely in the doorway with the light on. She stepped to the side behind a large box, looked down . . .

. . . and screamed.

7

Monday, 6:40 p.m.

Hunter pulled behind the nearest cruiser and got out of the vehicle. His partner, Katie Isaacs, followed. Chad was still sleeping it off in the front seat.

Keeping a lid on his emotions, Hunter took in the scene. Four police cars, an ambulance, and a fire truck.

And every available neighbor who happened to be home during all the commotion. Well, good. Maybe someone saw something.

Approaching the officer in charge, Hunter asked, "What do we have, Simon?"

"A dead body."

"Great." Hunter sighed and couldn't ignore the twinge of sadness he felt every time he walked into a situation like this. Even after years of working homicide, a dead person was never just another day on the job. It was a person with a soul. Someone he might have been friends with in another time and place. "Where?"

"In the basement. We're waiting on the medical examiner to get here."

"Serena Hopkins?"

"Yep. She's on her way."

Hunter felt a flash of satisfaction. Even in high school he knew Serena was smart. And now she was back, one of the best in the business. The best that he'd worked with, anyway. She'd moved back from Spartanburg, South Carolina, a year ago on personal business and accepted the offer of Chief Medical Examiner without hesitation.

Katie asked, "How do we get to the basement?"

"That way, through the kitchen." Simon waved to a young officer and the man trotted over. "The photographer is down there now. Officer Mays here was first on the scene. As soon as the photographer is done, show these detectives where the body is. Y'all don't touch anything 'til Serena gets here, please."

Officer Mays nodded. "The basement door was open when she found the body."

"She?"

The young officer consulted his notes. "Alexia Allen."

Hunter's lungs suddenly lacked air. Alexia

Allen? Home? He stared at the officer. "Are you sure you got her name right?"

"He got it right."

The voice from his past echoed through his brain.

So, she'd finally come home.

Memories flooded his mind and he paused a moment to get his bearings. Then he turned to see her standing at the top of the stairs leading from the basement. She had the same red hair and flashing green eyes. He said the first thing that came to his befuddled mind.

"You've got blood on your hands."

"I-I'm a first responder," she stammered, then bit her lip. Her jaw firmed. "I didn't have any gloves . . . I just . . . I did my best to see if I could stop the bleeding and revive him." Regret flashed across her face. "I couldn't."

His eyes dropped to her hands. They were shaking, but she was holding herself together, her expression flat, impassive. She'd also contaminated the crime scene, but he'd deal with that later. The victim always came first. "How'd he die?"

"He was stabbed in the neck and bled out," she stated, her voice now cold, eyes blank.

Shock? "Are you okay?"

"I will be."

Still very little emotion. Interesting. "What was he doing in your mother's house?"

"I have no idea." A small shudder wracked her frame. "I just got here a little while ago. When I walked in, I heard something." She grimaced. "I've already been through all of this with the first officer on the scene. You want me to go through it again?"

"If you don't mind," Katie said.

For the first time since he'd entered the house, Alexia took her eyes off of him. Her gaze landed on his partner with a blink. "I guess not. The noise came from the basement, then I heard him running down the steps. I followed and found —" she swallowed hard, "— Devin."

"The body?" Hunter's interest sharpened. She knew him? Wait a minute . . . "Devin? Your ex from high school?"

Her nose reddened, but no tears appeared. "Yes."

"And you don't know what he was doing here." Katie didn't bother to keep the skepticism from her voice.

She focused those gorgeous green eyes at his partner. "No. I don't know what he was doing here."

She'd picked up on Katie's disbelief, her response almost mocking as she repeated

Katie's words. He wanted to apologize for his partner.

But wouldn't.

Statistics showed more often than not that the victim knew the killer. He certainly understood his partner's immediate suspicion, even if Alexia didn't.

Katie grunted, nodded at him to take over, and disappeared down the steps while Officer Mays wrote something in his notebook.

The Crime Scene Unit had already arrived and was hard at work. Hunter recognized Sarah McCoy, the crime scene photographer, as she entered the kitchen from the basement. "All done?"

"Yeah. The scene's photographed and secured. Just waiting on Serena." She shoved her camera into the bag sitting just inside the door. Looking at Alexia, she said, "It looks like you made a good attempt to save him."

"Thanks."

Alexia's wooden responses concerned Hunter. Before he could pull her aside and talk to her in private, Serena arrived, black bag in hand. When she caught sight of Alexia, a small gasp escaped her.

And for the first time, Hunter saw Alexia's tough façade crack. Her lower lip trembled. Serena set her bag down and started to reach for her best friend.

Hunter held up a hand and said to Alexia, "Have you been processed?"

Both women froze. Alexia nodded. "Yes. Downstairs. One of the CSU guys did it."

Officer Mays nodded at his backup.

Serena cleared her throat, gave Alexia the once-over, and narrowed her eyes at the sight of the blood. "Are you all right?"

A small sigh escaped Alexia's lips and she waved a hand as though dismissing the question. "He was still alive when I got here. I tried to stop the bleeding, but . . ." Biting her lip, she pulled in a deep breath. "He was hurt too bad."

"Okay." Serena became all business. "You need to get cleaned up. We'll talk as soon as I finish, all right?"

"Sure."

Serena started down the basement stairs, then stopped to look back over her shoulder. "It's really good to see you, Alexia. I'm so glad you decided to come home."

Alexia responded with a smile that trembled. "Yeah, well, I'm not so sure it was the best idea I've had lately." Another deep breath. "Serena, it's Devin."

A blank look crossed Serena's face. "Who?"

"Devin Wickham."

Disbelief flared, then sorrow. "Oh." A pause and a frown. "Oh," she repeated as though searching for words. "I thought it was just some random intruder. Devin? Really?"

"Yes."

Officer Mays asked, "What was he doing here?"

Hunter noticed Alexia's flash of exasperation. Turning her green gaze in his direction, she said, "I don't know."

Even though the answer was in response to the officer's question, Hunter knew she was once again answering his own skeptical query.

Serena's gaze darted between the two of them. One of her brows shot north and she cocked her head as though she was going to say something. She must have decided against it, because she turned on her heel and made her way down to the man who'd been in the wrong house at the wrong time.

And bothered the wrong person.

Detective Katie Isaacs. Alexia had recognized her from high school. Three years ahead of Alexia, she'd been in Hunter's class. Her narrow-eyed suspicion said she didn't like Alexia and certainly didn't believe Alexia's accounting of what had happened.

What hurt was the doubt on Hunter's face. He didn't believe her either.

Why that should sting so much, she had no idea. Honestly, she hadn't seen the man in ten years, and within seconds of their meeting, she cared what he thought about her?

Now that made as much sense as . . . finding a dying man in her mother's house.

She pictured poor Devin's face and shuddered. In her line of work, she'd seen a lot of damaged people. Burned, hurt in car accidents, suicides. But to have this happen in the house she grew up in, to a man she'd once cared about —

"What made you decide to come home?"

His voice jarred her and she jerked. Then processed his question. "Serena called me and told me my mother was in the hospital." Well, that wasn't the only reason, but it would do for now.

"How's your mom doing?" he asked.

"I don't know. I haven't gone over there yet. I had to stop here first." The reason why she had to stop at the house first now eluded her.

His eyes hadn't changed in color or intensity, but he'd matured from the twenty-one-year-old junior in college into a thirty-two-year-old with a few lines around his eyes and a touch of gray at his temples. Probably due to the job.

She had to admit, he looked great. Really, really great.

Ignoring the sudden charge flowing through her veins, she raised a hand to rub at her aching forehead.

He asked, "Can you give me a description of the intruder?"

She closed her eyes, pulling the image of the person to the forefront of her mind. "I . . . he was tall. Taller than I am, but shorter than you."

Hunter wrote in his little book. "Eye color?"

"Um . . . no. I didn't let him get that close."

"Any odors? Smells?"

"No, I didn't pay any attention. I was running and calling 9-1-1 at the same time. I was just making sure he couldn't get at me."

Hunter nodded and quirked a sideways smile at her. "Good idea."

"Wait! He did have something in his left hand."

He cocked his head. "What was it?"

She rubbed her forehead. "I'm not sure. Maybe some kind of box? I couldn't make it out. I wasn't looking that hard at the left hand. The knife in his right hand pretty much had my full attention."

Another nod. "Understandable. How long did you and Devin date back in high school?"

She blinked at the change in topic. "About six months. Most of my freshman year."

"Any contact since then?"

"Not really. Well, yes. Sort of."

He lifted a brow. "Could you clear that up a little?"

"Can I wash this blood off first?" She lifted her hands and inspected them.

"Alexia."

"I'm serious, Hunter. Please. Then I'll answer all the questions you want to ask."

Hunter sighed and led her outside to the ambulance. They climbed in, and he opened a compartment to pull out a roll of paper towels, a bottle of saline, and some liquid soap. "Hold your hands out."

"I could have used the sink in the kitchen."

"Not until CSU is finished processing the house."

"Right."

Once she was rid of the blood, she felt better. Her mind began to work again. The fog that seemed to cloud her since finding

Devin's body faded.

"Hey, Hunter? What's going on? Where are we?"

The thick voice came from the car on the curb. The tall man who stumbled out of the vehicle tickled the recognition sensors in her brain.

She thought she heard Hunter groan. "Get back in the car and finish sleeping it off, Chad."

Alexia finally put it together. Chad Graham, Hunter's younger brother and twin to Christine. Tall and athletic, they'd been part of the "pretty people." The popular crowd. Alexia had known them mostly by reputation. She remembered Christine had been on the girls' basketball team and won a scholarship for her skills. Christine had always been kind, even just in passing.

Chad had been the wrestler and star of the soccer team. She couldn't remember if he went on to college or not. Probably.

Only right now, he wasn't very star-like. He ignored his brother and managed to put one foot in front of the other. As he came closer, she could smell the alcohol on him.

With a muttered "Excuse me a minute," Hunter reached for Chad's arm. "Come here."

Chad yanked away from the light hold and

turned toward Alexia. "Well, hello, pretty lady."

Alexia lifted a brow. "Hello, Chad."

"Wanna go on a date?"

She'd dealt with drunks before. Car wrecks mostly. It was the drunks who usually survived. "Not —"

"Come on, Chad," Hunter interrupted. "Back to the car."

Chad frowned. "Don't wanna."

Again, Hunter intervened. "Look, you understand how it is, I'm in the middle of an investigation —"

"Who cares about your stupid investigation? I'm talking to the pretty lady." He turned his eyes back to Alexia. "So, as I was asking before I was so rudely interrupted . . ."

Alexia sighed and placed a hand on Chad's forearm. "Why don't we walk as we talk?"

His countenance lightened and he followed her like a giddy puppy. She shot a glance at Hunter and the thunderous expression on his face made her gulp. She wasn't sure if his look was directed at her or the drunken Chad. Nevertheless, he kept his mouth shut and followed them.

Chad moaned and cupped his head. "I've got a headache."

"I know," she soothed, slipping into first responder mode for the second time that night. "Why don't you sit here and we'll see if we can get that taken care of."

Without further protest, Chad slid into the backseat of the car and Hunter activated the child locks. He shut the door and did the same to the other one. "Should have done that to begin with." He shook his head in disgust. "As much as he's had to drink, I didn't think he'd wake up for hours, much less be able to walk." Hunter gave her a slow smile. "Thanks for getting him back in the car. I was going to have a fight on my hands."

Alexia shrugged. "I thought you might be mad at me for stepping in."

"No. Just mad at myself for not locking him in when I got here. Hopefully, he won't be aware enough to climb over the seat and get out that way." He took a deep breath, glanced one more time at the once-again snoring Chad, and said, "Now, can we finish our discussion about Devin and how often you'd been in touch with him?"

She pulled in a deep breath and blew it out between pursed lips, looking back at the house. "Devin used to call every once in a while, just to talk and catch up. Like twice a year or something. Lately, it was more often

— around every other month. I'm not sure why he felt the need, but I know he kind of looked in on my mother because he would ask if I'd called her lately." Guilt pierced her. Devin had certainly done more than Alexia over the years when it came to caring for her mother.

But her mother hadn't wanted her care, she reminded herself. After a while, she'd stopped trying. A person could only take so much rejection.

"When was the last time you talked to him?"

She thought. "April. Sometime a little before Easter. He said he and my mother were now going to the same church and they'd love it if I'd come home for the Easter service." Alexia wrinkled her nose. "I really can't see either one as a churchgoer."

Hunter nodded. "I didn't know Devin that well. Why'd you two break up?"

Was it really any of his business? The previous doubt in his eyes still stung and she wasn't feeling real chatty at the moment. However, she reined in her initial response and simply said, "He hit me. I wasn't going to give him the chance to do it again." Even at the age of fourteen, she knew she wasn't interested in giving a guy another chance to beat on her. She got enough of that at home.

Hunter's jaw firmed and his eyes narrowed as he assessed her. Then his countenance softened. "Good for you then."

Serena exited the house and Alexia felt her stomach clench once more. She hadn't realized she'd started to relax in Hunter's presence — in spite of his questions.

The ME came straight to Alexia and pulled her into a hug. "I've missed you," Serena whispered in her ear.

"I know. I've missed you too."

Serena had come to visit whenever they could coordinate days off, but it hadn't been nearly often enough.

Alexia looked at her friend. "Why was Devin here, do you know?"

A hint of embarrassment dusted Serena's cheeks. "Your mother was letting him live here."

"No." Shock held her almost speechless. "When did that start?"

"About a month ago. He lost his job and she kind of took him in, I guess."

"Why didn't you mention it?"

Serena's flush deepened. "I don't know. I suppose I didn't really think it was that important. He's been doing yard work and odd jobs for people until he could find something permanent. I'm not real sure of the details, just what I picked up at church."

Alexia stared at her friend.

She knew exactly what Serena had been thinking and why she hadn't mentioned Devin's presence. Serena had been protecting her. Why rub salt in old wounds that had never really healed by telling her something that would hurt her?

Still, now that she knew, the hurt spilled over. Once again, she'd been betrayed by a parent.

At least that was how it felt. That her mother would choose to let Devin live with her after what he'd done to Alexia . . . well, it just went against everything in her to accept that.

Anger burned within her as she sucked in a deep breath and schooled her features. "Oh."

She had a feeling she hadn't fooled Serena or the man who stood silent and observant, taking in every detail of the conversation.

"Hunter? You coming?"

Detective Isaac's voice jarred her. Alexia blinked and ordered herself to keep it together. She'd learned at an early age not to show too much emotion. Steeling her facial muscles, she turned toward the steps where the detective stood waiting.

Hunter walked past her and into the house. Alexia started to follow when Serena took her hand. "You don't need to go back down there."

"Good." Breathing a harsh sigh of relief, she looked at Serena and gave a brittle smile. "Crazy way to see each other again, isn't it? I think I much prefer you making the trip to Washington."

8

Hunter stared down at the body of the man he'd known only in passing.

Katie joined him. "You think she did it?"

"I don't know." The coroner had already placed the body in the bag, he just hadn't zipped it. Serena would get Devin cleaned up and make the official call on how he died, but it was pretty obvious to Hunter. "Any sign of the weapon?"

Katie shook her head. "No. A knife is missing from the set in the kitchen. The killer must have taken it with him."

"Assuming there was a him," Hunter muttered.

"Right."

With everything in him, he didn't want to believe Alexia killed Devin, but he hadn't seen her in ten years. He didn't know what she was capable of. One thing he did know was that he was still attracted to her. Amazing that after ten years, he was still drawn to her haunting beauty. To the red hair that he was sure would singe his fingers should he touch it, and the eyes that looked like they'd been carved from the purest emeralds.

More than ten years ago, he'd noticed more than her beauty, though; he'd been fascinated by her strength, her character, and her dogged determination to rise above her family's lousy reputation.

Today, he was just drawn to her. Definitely something he would have to dig deeper into at a later time.

In spite of who his father was.

He winced at the thought. Yeah, that might be a problem.

Katie rubbed her chin. "I think we should search the house. You know, cover all our bases."

"We don't need a warrant." Hunter looked around, filing his personal thoughts away to be pulled out later and examined.

Katie nodded. "We've got probable cause. The murder weapon could be in the house somewhere."

"CSU hasn't found anything yet," Hunter stated. "And there's no evidence that says Alexia murdered Devin."

His partner snorted. "Except the blood

on her hands."

Hunter watched the coroner zip the black body bag, then turned and headed back up the steps to find Alexia in deep conversation with Serena.

Alexia was frowning. "I know I need to go, I just don't want to."

"Your mother's changed, Alexia. Give her a chance."

"So you've said a dozen times." Alexia didn't look convinced.

Hunter watched her, curious at the expressions flitting across her face.

She chewed her lip, looked at the ground, then back at Serena. "I've tried to call her."

"How often?"

"Often enough," she mumbled.

Serena pushed. "And how many messages have you left?"

Exasperated, Alexia threw her hands up. "A couple."

Serena lifted an eyebrow.

"Seriously, I've left several."

Hunter wondered how many *several* actually translated into.

"And when she called you back, you didn't answer, did you?" There was no condemnation in Serena's voice, just a soft question that carried a wealth of meaning.

Alexia groaned and bit her lip. "I . . .

couldn't," she whispered. "I just . . . couldn't."

"And I enabled that," Serena said quietly.

Alexia seemed to think about that for a minute. "I guess you did. You always kept me pretty well informed. I really had no reason to talk to her." She must have remembered that Serena hadn't told her about Devin, because she cut her eyes at Serena and added, "At least I thought you told me everything." She paced, lifted her head, and spotted him standing there.

"Sorry to eavesdrop," he said.

She simply stared at him with that blank expression that was starting to dig holes in his heart. What had she gone through as a child? What had her mother done that made Alexia cut off practically all communication? Instead of voicing his questions, he said, "Just thought I'd let you know, we're searching the house."

The blank stare morphed into a frown. "For what?"

"The murder weapon."

"But he took it . . ." Realization dawned and her lips thinned. "Oh. You still think I did it."

Hunter held up a hand. "Just call it covering all our bases." He used Katie's reasoning. "A knife is missing from the block in

75

the kitchen. Did you go in there? Move it?"

She frowned. "No. I heard something in the basement practically the moment I walked in the door. I didn't touch anything in the kitchen." Alexia bit her lip, then focused her gaze on his. "Do I need to call a lawyer?"

Letting out a sigh, he said, "That's certainly your right."

9

Monday, 8:57 p.m.

Alexia felt a surge of satisfaction. She'd passed on the lawyer. The fingerprint results would prove she'd been nowhere near the kitchen. And they'd searched the house — and her car — and found nothing.

She knew they wouldn't.

Serena had offered to let Alexia stay with her until the crime scene cleanup crew could get out to the house and take care of the basement. Alexia appreciated the offer and decided to take her friend up on it. Only she had one stop to make first.

The hospital.

She had to or the guilt would consume her.

Glancing at the time on her cell phone, she saw that it was pushing 9:00. And still her mother's neighbors watched the action from across the street. Some even stood just beyond the nearest cruiser. She wanted to holler at them to go home.

The need to escape made her nerves jump and her palms itch. She wanted to go straight to Serena's and crawl under the covers. Instead, she called the nurses' station and found she could come see her mother, even stay the night with her if she chose to do so.

She didn't. She couldn't. At least not yet.

But she did need to break the news to her about Devin.

And to avoid giving her mother a heart attack, she told the nursing staff to let the woman know Alexia was on her way to see her.

She wondered if her mom would believe them. She wondered if her mother would be awake. Alexia hesitated. Maybe she should wait until morning. But the guilt pressed in on her. Even if her mother was asleep, someone would pass the word on that Alexia had been there. She'd tried. Right?

Hunter watched her from the front steps, his eyes intense. He'd told her she could leave, go to the hospital, but . . .

Emergency vehicles still loitered at her mother's curb, and she felt weird leaving, even though she was no longer needed. She reached to open the door to her car.

"Alexia? Is that you?"

Spinning, she spotted the owner of the question. A fit young woman with a pony-tail, in jogging shorts and a tank top, stood at the edge of her mother's yard. "Yes, who're you?"

A smile crossed the woman's mouth as she approached. "I'm Lori Tabor. I graduated with you — we only had a couple of classes together."

Vaguely, Alexia was able to dredge up a memory. "Really shy? The photographer for the yearbook committee?"

Lori let out a small laugh. "Yes, that's me. I suppose I figured as long as I was taking pictures I wouldn't have to talk to people except to tell them to stand still and smile. Fortunately, I've matured a little since then." She nodded to the house where the children played. "My brother, Avery, lives there. I keep his kids for him sometimes when he has to work late at the hospital. He's a doctor."

"Ah." She really wanted to get going. "Well, it was nice seeing you. Maybe we'll run into each other again soon."

"Sure." She glanced at the still-active house. "Is everything all right? The officer who came to question me said someone was killed. I'm so sorry."

"I am too. It was Devin Wickham."

Shock lifted the woman's brow. "You're kidding! Devin? That's horrible. I knew your mother was letting him live there."

"Yes, just until he could get back on his feet."

Lori nodded. "When I heard she let him move in, I wasn't surprised. She's always helping someone. When do you think they'll release her from the hospital?"

"I . . . uh . . . I'm not sure." The need to hurry bit at her while the desire to question Lori about Devin had her pausing. But she had to see her mother. "In fact that's where I'm heading now. And while I hate to rush off, it's already late and I really need to try and see her tonight."

"Oh! Sure, I didn't mean to keep you. Tell her I'll be by to see her tomorrow sometime."

That stopped Alexia. "You're good friends with my mom?"

Lori smiled, her even white teeth flashing. "Yes. She makes the best pot roast. I think she feeds my brother and his kids at least twice a week. Since I'm the kids' nanny, I generally benefit from her generosity. And I drive her to church sometimes. The kids just love her and she dotes on them like a grandmother."

Really? Her mother did that? Keeping her shock from showing wasn't easy, but she did her best. "Wow, that's really sweet of her."

"I know. We just love her. Please let me know if there's anything I can do for her."

Alexia offered a reassuring smile. "Well, thank you. I'll be sure to let you know. If you plan to visit Mom, I'm sure I'll see you around."

"Probably." The right corner of Lori's lips quirked up. "I'm on the reunion committee, so I might be knocking on your door asking you to volunteer some time. If you have it."

Alexia paused. That might actually be a good idea. It would give her access to people who knew Devin. If she was on the committee, she could ask questions without being too obvious. "I'd love to." Digging in her purse, she pulled out a loose grocery receipt and a pen. "Here's my cell number. Give me a call before the next meeting and I'll try to be there."

"Great!" Lori snatched the slip of paper like she expected Alexia to renege on her offer. "I'll call you."

Climbing into her car, Alexia waved good-bye and headed down the short road that would lead her out of the subdivision. She thought about Lori and wondered how the woman stayed in such great shape. Whatever it was, it kept her toned and fit. Which reminded her that she needed to make time to stay in shape. She planned to get back to work as soon as she was allowed. Because the more she thought about it, the more she realized she couldn't just let it go. She hadn't been negligent in her duties — but someone had wanted to make it look that way. As soon as she had things wrapped up here with her mother and the reunion, she'd go back and fight to clear her name.

With that resolved in her mind, she focused on her surroundings. Turning left, Alexia noticed the dark streets, the area of town that even ten years ago had been the one to avoid. Now, it looked much worse.

Her phone rang and she frowned as she looked at the number.

Hunter. Make that Detective Graham, she reminded herself. She pressed the button to take the call. "Hello?"

"Hi, Alexia, this is Hunter. I was wondering if we could meet. I have a couple more questions for you."

"What kind of questions?"

She looked around. Two young men stood on the corner under a streetlamp making an exchange. Money for drugs? Probably. When her headlights framed them, they jumped and turned cold, suspicious eyes in her direction.

She checked the locks. Heard their reassuring click. Why had she come this way? She hadn't been thinking. But truly, there was no easy way to get to the hospital from her side of town. And she'd been in a hurry, so she'd gone the shortest way.

Telling herself she'd take a different route back, she eased her way through the streets. Rolled up to the stop sign.

Wham!

Two fists slammed against her driver's window, and she let out a scream as the face leered at her with a wicked grin. Her phone flew across the car and bounced off the passenger window. Greasy hair slapped alongside the gap-tooth mouth. The door shook as the man grabbed the handle and yanked. Alexia pressed the gas pedal, pulse thumping, heart pounding.

Her breath came in panicked pants as she left the vagrant behind screaming curses at her.

"Hey! Alexia, answer me. Are you okay?"

His voice sounded far away. Keeping her eyes on the road, she leaned over and snatched the phone from the seat. "Yes, yeah, I'm sorry. Some guy came up and pounded my window and then tried to get in my car while I was at the stop sign."

She nearly choked while trying to slow her jackhammer heartbeat. Almost through with the bad part of town, she reassured herself. Almost. Hang in there.

Headlights came up behind her and reflected back at her from the rearview mirror. Flipping it so the lights didn't hit her eyes, she pressed the brake. The headlights eased off even as her stomach turned a flip.

Keeping one eye on the car behind her and one on the road before her, she finally breathed a sigh of relief as she left the neighborhood behind.

"Where are you?"

"Just pulled out of Crosstown."

"Crosstown!" Disbelief echoed in her ear. "Are you crazy? Most cops don't even want to go there during the day."

She shivered. "Yeah, it was a little worse than I remembered."

Hunter muttered something she missed and she thought she might be better off not knowing what he said. Back to the reason he called. "What kind of questions?"

"Just routine ones. Ones I'd like answers to so I can get some sleep tonight."

Biting her lip, she scanned the street again. "I'm on the way to the hospital to see my mother. I don't know how long I'll be."

A pause. "Do you mind if I meet you there?"

The questions were that urgent? She frowned. "I guess not. Where are you now?"

"About five minutes from the hospital. I dropped Chad off at his house and I'm on my way back to the station to finish up the paperwork, but that can wait. Where are you going to park?"

"In the garage on the fourth floor if I can find a spot."

"I'll look for your car."

"Fine. I'll wait for you at the elevator."

She hung up and tossed the phone onto the seat beside her, his voice still echoing in her ears. Memories of her high school attraction to him flooded her. She was still drawn to the man in spite of the fact that he believed she had something to do with Devin's death.

Great. Just one more complication in her life she really didn't need.

Clutching the steering wheel, she suddenly wished she prayed. Wished she felt like she could talk to God about everything, spill it onto his shoulder and let him take care of it. She'd heard of people who did that. She'd even tried church a few times, but it just didn't seem to work for her.

Alexia simply couldn't wrap her mind around the concept of a loving God. A father who loved her.

But Serena was right. Alexia wanted to.

With a sigh, she pulled into the hospital parking deck and started for the fourth floor, circling up. A car turned in behind her and headlights tracked her progress. Squinting against the brightness reflected in her rearview mirror, she finally reached the fourth floor.

Pulling in to the nearest vacant space, she cut the engine and chewed on her bottom lip. Staring at the building, she took a fortifying breath and opened her door.

As she headed for the exit door, her senses tuned to her surroundings. Although the deck itself was well-lit, the darkness pressed in from the outside, the emptiness surrounding her.

Footsteps followed her.

She stopped walking. Glancing over her shoulder, she let her eyes probe the shadows.

Her stomach twisted. Was that someone hiding behind the post?

An engine sputtered to life, startling her. She spun and gave a relieved half-laugh as a car pulled out from the space about three yards in front of her. The driver lifted a hand in greeting, and Alexia resumed her trek toward the elevator as silence echoed around her again.

Footsteps sounded a steady rhythm on the concrete, and again she jumped, spun, and looked. They stopped. A car door opened. Shut.

Chill, she told herself. Someone was here to visit a patient, just like she was. Or was getting in the car to leave.

She picked up the pace.

The steps behind her resumed too — at a faster clip, drawing closer.

Her heartbeat thudded and she darted behind the nearest post, pressing her hands to her stomach. She shivered in spite of the heat. Fear clumped in her gut and she took a deep breath.

The footsteps stopped.

Alexia held her breath, waiting to hear a car door open.

Nothing.

No doubt about it. Someone was following her. Adrenaline rushed through her, her hands shook and her knees felt weak.

Pushing the fear aside, she searched for an emergency button.

She spotted one about twenty feet away.

Alexia beelined for it, hand outstretched.

Almost there.

A wicked laugh echoed just behind her.

She whirled.

Blinding white pain streaked through her as something clipped her on the side of the head. Before she had a chance to scream, she found herself facedown on the fioor of the parking garage. Terror pounded through her, shortening her breath, making her head spin. "Wh-what do you want?"

No answer. Just breath against her cheek.

Then she felt the cold barrel of a gun kiss her already-aching temple.

10

Monday, 9:24 p.m.

Hunter took a left instead of the right that would take him home. It was late, very late. And he'd taken a chance on catching Alexia. Katie had already taken herself off the clock to grab a few hours of sleep before they would be back at it in the morning. While Devin's murder had moved to the top of the stack, he and Katie still had other cases they were working on. He should have followed Katie's example and gone home.

But he felt restless and couldn't put Alexia Allen from his mind. So, he'd called her. On the pretext of asking her more questions about the murder. That was a new low for him.

His conscience bothered him only slightly. He'd apologize later. Maybe.

Approaching the parking garage, he glanced upward toward the higher levels. From their conversation, he'd gathered that he was only a minute or so behind her. As he swung into the fourth level, his headlights captured a person in a mask standing over something. The masked head snapped up, and for a moment, narrowed eyes locked with Hunter's.

Then the attacker raced to a nearby car, hopped in, and squealed from the garage. Hunter started to gun his own vehicle and go after the rapidly disappearing taillights when he spied a body lying on the ground, still, unmoving.

A body he recognized.

Slamming on the brakes, he pushed against a surge of panic as his shoulder harness locked into place. He ripped his seat belt off, bolted from the car, and raced toward Alexia.

Alexia reached up to touch her head as she took a mental inventory and double-checked to make sure she was still alive. Her heart pounded in her throat and she swallowed a wave of nausea.

"Alexia!"

Warm hands wrapped around her upper arm and relief flooded her. Hunter.

Tears flooded her eyes, shocking her. Blinking hard, she forced her emotions into a corner of her mind and let Hunter help her to her feet.

His arms went around her and she caved in to her need for comfort. His voice sounded in her ear. "I've called for backup and gave a description of the guy and the car."

"You saw him?" Her tongue felt too heavy for speech, but she managed to get the words out.

"Yeah. He had a mask on, but I was able to give some height and weight details. He's tall, with a light, athletic build. I got the make and model of the car, but the plate had been removed."

Pulling out of his arms, she gave herself a shake. His fingers grazed her temple and she winced. "That's where he hit me before jamming the gun into it."

"You'll have a bruise and a headache."

Two police cruisers pulled onto the fourth floor, lights flashing.

"No kidding." Alexia grimaced. "It'll heal." Her hands still shook. She clenched her fingers into fists to gain control.

One of the officers approached and Alexia recognized him. It was Officer Mays from her mother's house just a few hours earlier.

He nodded at her and Hunter. "So we meet again."

Hunter gave the man the rundown on

what had happened. Officer Mays took notes in his little book, and Alexia said, "I thought I heard him following me. When I turned around, he knocked me in the head."

"Did he say anything?"

Did he? "I think he whispered something before Hunter pulled in and scared him off."

"What was it?"

Alexia closed her eyes and concentrated, but all her stressed mind could come up with was the terror she'd felt. "I don't know."

Hunter kept a hand on her back and was rubbing little circles in a spot just below her shoulder blade. His touch set off sparks even in this situation.

Clearing her throat, she ignored the throbbing in her head and said, "I guess I still need to go see my mother. Are we done here?"

"Do you need medical attention?" Hunter asked.

Alexia considered the pain level. "No, I'll have a few bruises, but I'll be all right."

"Okay then." He looked around. "I see cameras in here." He pointed to one on the column directly in front of them and another two rows over. "We'll see what we can see, but even if the cameras caught everything, I'm not sure they'll tell us anything since he had a mask on." He ran a hand through his hair, then pinched the bridge of his nose. "But yeah, I would say we're done here." He looked at Alexia. "I know you said you didn't need anyone to look at your head, but I'd feel better if we got it checked." Without waiting for her to answer, he placed a hand beneath her elbow. "Let's go get that done, then visit your mother."

Surprise zinged through her. "You're coming with me?"

"Is that all right?"

Was it? She shrugged. "I — yes, sure. I guess."

Hunter signaled the lead officer that they were leaving.

Officer Mays caught her eye. "I'll be in touch."

"Thanks."

Together, Hunter and Alexia headed to the parking garage elevator. Once inside and moving toward the bottom floor, Hunter pushed the first-floor button, then gave her a measured look. "Trouble seems to follow you everywhere, doesn't it?"

"Excuse me?"

"First your mother's house, then this personal attack. Looks like you've made someone pretty mad. Any ideas who?"

Alexia frowned. "Not that I can think of."

At least not here in Columbia. She sighed. "I just got home, Hunter. As in today, a few hours ago. The only person who knew I was coming was Serena."

"Would she have told anyone?"

Alexia shrugged. "I don't know. It's not like I was keeping it a secret." She felt the flush rise in her cheeks. But she hadn't called her mother to let her know either. Every time she picked up the phone, she froze when it came to dialing the number. More guilt pierced her.

The aching in her head didn't help matters. It hurt to think.

Hunter's astute gaze noted her discomfort and his sympathy flashed at her. "But Serena could have mentioned it."

"Sure she could have."

The elevator doors slid open, but instead of getting off, Alexia reached across Hunter and pushed the fourth-floor button.

Hunter frowned at her as he let the doors close. "This isn't the way to the ER."

"I'm not going there."

"Alexia . . ." He shook his head and sighed.

The doors opened, and as they stepped into the hallway, Hunter touched Alexia's arm briefly to stop her. "Is there anyone in town who might not appreciate you coming back?"

Alexia bit her lip. "Well, I don't know that Devin would have appreciated it, but I guess we can rule him out."

Shockingly enough, she felt tears clog her throat at the memory of Devin on her mother's basement floor. She'd tried hard to stop the bleeding. His eyes had begged her to help him.

She shuddered and shoved the image from her mind. For now. She had a feeling it might return once she managed to fall asleep.

"Why would he not want you coming back?"

Shoving a strand of hair behind her ear, she said, "I suppose because he was living with my mother. Assuming he even knew I'd decided to come home for the reunion, he may have been concerned he'd be tossed out on his ear." She frowned. "Because there's no way I would be sharing the same house with him."

"Okay, well, if he were still alive, that might give him a motive for not wanting you here. Anyone else come to mind?"

"No, not off the top of my head. I haven't talked to anyone here other than Serena in about ten years. I've talked to my mother a handful of times. Mostly through messages left on voice mail. And before you ask, no, I didn't tell her I was coming home today. As far as I know, Serena's the only person who knew." She shot him a wry look. "And I know she didn't kill Devin or try to kill me in the parking garage."

"Well, if she's the only person who knew, then Devin would have no reason to worry about you coming home." He squinted in the distance, thinking. "We need to talk to Serena and see who she told about your arrival back in town."

"Fine. But right now, I'm going to check on my mother." The words nearly stuck in her throat, but she managed to get them out.

Hunter's eyes softened. "What about your head?"

"I'll get someone to look at it later if I think I need to."

He frowned. "Promise?"

Did he really care? "I promise."

"All right. I'm going to make a few phone calls."

"Thanks." Alexia turned to walk down the hall, looking at the room numbers. She pulled in a deep breath and, for the second time that night, wished she prayed. Frustrated at her cowardice, she ignored the emotions raging through her and schooled her face into a plastic mask. She came to the room, pushed the door open, and stepped inside.

Then stopped short and stared.

Her mother lay on the bed, face pale, heart monitor beeping, oxygen hooked up, IV tube running to the pole beside her. The woman looked completely helpless. Then again, she'd always looked and acted that way. Helpless, without a thought of her own, following her husband's commands with slumped shoulders and downcast eyes.

Serena seemed to think she'd changed over the years since Alexia's dad had left. Had she?

A toilet flushed, then running water sounded. The bathroom door opened. Alexia's eyes went wide when a tall man in his midfifties stepped out.

"Who're you?" she blurted.

He jumped and slapped a hand to his chest. "My word, young lady, you sure know how to scare a person, don't you?"

Alexia gaped.

An uneasy smile crossed the man's face. "I can see I've scared you as much as you've scared me." He held out a hand. "Allow me to introduce myself. I'm Michael Stewart."

Almost against her will, Alexia placed her

hand in his. Clearing her throat, she found her voice. "I'm sorry, but you're the last thing I expected to find in my mother's hospital room."

It was his turn to stare. "Daughter? Alexia?" Then amusement replaced the uneasiness. "I assure you, I am not a thing. I'm your mother's . . . pastor."

That stopped her cold. "My mother has a pastor?"

A gentle smile dented his cheeks when he glanced at the woman on the bed. "She started coming to my church about four years ago."

Right. Serena had said something about that.

Alexia turned back to see her mother's eyes open. Shock rippled across the woman's face and Alexia immediately forgot about the man behind her. Telling her legs to move, she took three stiff steps to the edge of her mother's bed.

"Hi, Mom."

"Lex," she whispered. Tears flooded her green eyes and flowed over.

Stunned at her mother's reaction, Alexia's gaze went straight to the heart monitor. It picked up speed. Alexia frowned. "They were supposed to tell you I was coming."

"They did, but I just didn't . . .

couldn't . . . believe it. Not until I saw you with my own eyes."

"What are you doing here?" Alexia swallowed, trying to make sense. "I mean, what's wrong? Why are you in the hospital?"

"They're not sure." Pastor Stewart spoke up from behind her. "They're running tests and keeping Hannah for observation."

Alexia cocked a brow at him. This was her mother's pastor? Sounded like he was a lot more than that to her. At her questioning look, the man flushed. "Sorry. I'll just wait outside until you two are done."

"No." Her mother's hand reached out in supplication. "Stay. Please."

Pastor Stewart reached over to squeeze her mom's hand, then sat in the chair next to the bed. Alexia watched her mother's hands tremble as she clutched the sheet. Was she nervous? Scared? Was her stomach flipping with dread the same as hers?

"I can't believe you're here," her mother whispered again.

"I decided it was time to come home."

"Serena talked you into it, hmm?" A slight smile trembled on her lips, and to her surprise, Alexia felt one tug in response.

"Yes."

Her mother drew in a deep breath and then looked into Alexia's eyes. "I owe you . . ."

"What?" Confusion drew her brows together.

"I owe you an apology."

Alexia simply stared at the woman who'd given birth to her. Her mother's eyes flicked to the window, to the man sitting silent and still in the chair. Then back to Alexia. "I was a terrible mother and I owe you an apology." Tears hovered on her lashes, her chin wobbled, and she swallowed twice before she said, "I know an apology can't make up for the past, but I've missed you, Alexia, and I was hoping —" her voice broke — "hoping we could somehow have a future. Together. As mother and daughter."

Alexia wasn't sure whether to laugh or run screaming from the room. Surely, her mother had developed some sort of dementia or something. She stood on legs that threatened to collapse. "I'm sorry. I . . . I . . . need some air."

She fled the room.

11

Monday, 10:47 p.m.

"I'll take care of it," the voice promised.

"How?"

"If she knows where Jillian is, she'll tell. We've just got to get our hands on her. She's proving elusive. And now she's on her guard."

The senator felt his jaw tighten. "This can't come back to me, to us. You know that."

A disgusted sigh filtered through the line to echo in the senator's ear. "Of course I know that, Frank. I've got someone taking care of the problem. In fact, the plan is already being carried out."

"Who? What plan?"

"It doesn't matter as long as we keep a lid on your secret, does it?"

A pause. "I suppose not. I'm probably better off not knowing anyway." Frank pulled in a deep breath and changed the subject.

"I got another letter."

"How? When?"

"It came through the mail today. Addressed to my wife." Outrage filled him. Along with fear. "Do you know what would have happened if Elizabeth had gotten to it first?"

"What made you open it?"

"I recognized the writing on the envelope. It's the same as the other letters. Sort of a block style, like someone's trying to disguise their handwriting."

"Look . . ." The voice paused. "Just keep an eye on things on your end. Concentrate on your campaigning, pleasing the people, and getting votes. I'll take care of this mess. Just consider it done."

"It won't be done until I know for sure this won't ruin everything I've worked so hard to build."

"We."

"Excuse me?"

"*We.* What *we've* worked so hard to build."

The senator stilled. "Of course. I'm sorry. I'm just not thinking very clearly at the moment."

"Then let me think for you. You just focus on what you're good at while I do what I'm good at."

"Fine, just keep me updated, will you?"

102

"Of course. Now put that note with the others and let me get on with this."

The senator hung up the phone, hating the trembling in his fingers as he lifted the latest note.

HOW ARE YOU SLEEPING AT NIGHT?

12

Tuesday, 7:50 a.m.

"How are you doing this morning?"

Serena's calm voice jarred her as a golden retriever bolted to the edge of the bed to swipe Alexia's face with her tongue. Alexia laughed and cringed at the same time. "Ew."

Yoda, Serena's two-year-old retriever, sat on her haunches and cocked her head, tongue lolling sideways. Alexia looked at her friend standing in the doorway holding a cup of steaming coffee.

Alexia's nose twitched. "I'm not sure. I think I'm just numb." She used the sheet to wipe her face and looked at the dog. "Although, Yoda's greeting has me waking up a bit." Slanting her eyes at Serena, she said, "You know Yoda is a really dumb name for a female dog. Why not Princess or Leia or something?"

Serena simply grinned. She'd never apologize for her Star Wars fever.

Flopping back on the bed, Alexia thought about the night before. Somehow she'd managed to escape the hospital last night, avoiding Hunter and everything else in her path, to arrive on Serena's doorstep asking for a bed to sleep in.

Serena had welcomed her without hesitation, led her to her spare bedroom, and told her they'd talk in the morning.

Now it was morning and Alexia didn't want to talk. She wanted to forget the last twenty-four hours ever happened.

Then it occurred to her she hadn't told her mother about Devin's death.

Which meant another trip to the hospital. She'd rather try to figure out who killed Devin and why.

"Hey, I need to talk to you about something."

Serena's serious tone brought Alexia's attention back to her friend. "What's that?"

Sipping her coffee as she walked, Serena sat on the edge of the bed. Yoda edged closer and placed her nose on Serena's feet. "I've been asked to go to China."

"What? Why?"

Sadness creased her friend's brows. "Because of the earthquake last week. There were a lot of US citizens there." She waved a letter Alexia just now noticed. "I got notification from Washington, DC, that I'll be working with Robert Douglas, one of our local ME investigators, to help identify and return the remains of those US citizens to their families."

"When do you leave?"

"Tomorrow morning."

"So soon?" Alexia swallowed hard and reached out to grasp Serena's hand. "I'm sorry. That's going to be tough."

"Yes. It will. But it has to be done, so . . ." Serena drew in a deep breath and stood. "I don't know how you feel about staying in your mother's house after all that's happened, but you're welcome to stay here if you like."

Alexia blinked at the offer. Surprisingly enough, her mind didn't flash to Devin's bleeding body but instead to the fire.

The flames greedy and grasping, swallowing everything in their path. Her father's hoarse yells, her sister's screams cutting through the roar —

"Lex?"

Alexia shook her head to force the memory away. "Sure. I'd love to stay here. I'm guessing you have an ulterior motive for asking, though."

A gleam appeared in her friend's eyes.

"Well, it would help if you would dog and cat sit."

Alexia lifted a brow. "Cat? When did you get a cat?"

Serena flushed. "She just kind of showed up about six weeks ago. Skinny and no tags. I fed her and now I think I'm stuck with her."

"What's her name?"

"Chewbacca. Chewie for short."

Alexia rolled her eyes. "You've got to be kidding me."

"It seemed to fit."

"Huh." She thought about it. "Sure. I'll stay here. And even if I decide not to sleep here, I'll still take care of your critters." That wouldn't interfere with her decision to find Devin's murderer.

"Good." Serena's eyes brightened. "Then you won't mind feeding the fish and watering the plants?"

Alexia huffed a long-suffering sigh. Then grinned. "Naw, I don't mind."

"Yoda has her own doggie door, she can come and go as she pleases, so you don't have to worry about getting over here at a certain time. She and Chewie have hit it off and keep each other company."

Even as the words left her mouth, the animal that could only be Chewie strolled into the room. Alexia's eyes widened. "I understand now."

The long-haired brown and gold cat stared at the occupants of the room with unblinking eyes, then sat on the floor by Yoda and began grooming her front left paw.

Stretching, Alexia wondered what she'd committed herself to, even as she swung her legs over the side of the bed. "Oh, I meant to ask you. Did you mention to anyone that I was coming home? Hunter seemed to think he might need to know that piece of information."

Serena frowned. "No, I don't think I mentioned it." Her eyes went wide. "Why? Does he think Devin's death has something to do with you coming home?"

A groan escaped Alexia and she tossed her hands in the air. "He doesn't know. He said he was just making sure that he went through as many scenarios as possible. And one was questioning whether you said anything to anyone."

"Wait a minute." Serena snapped her fingers. "I did mention it to Christine. She's on the reunion committee and I told her you would probably be glad to help."

Alexia shot her a dark look. "Thanks."

"Now, now." Serena laughed. "It'll be good for you. Keep you from wallowing."

"In what?" Alexia asked with an indignant snort.

"Whatever it is you might want to wallow in." Serena patted Yoda's head and the dog gave a contented groan.

"I'm not going to wallow in anything." And she really wouldn't mind helping. Alexia paused and returned to Serena's comment. "Christine." Alexia swallowed hard. "Hunter's sister? That Christine?"

"Yep. She and Lori Tabor are heading up the reunion committee. She asked me to help, but I told her I couldn't. Now that I'm off to China, it's a good thing I said no. Hopefully I'll be back in a couple of weeks."

"Oh right, Lori. She keeps her brother's kids while he's working. They live in Mom's neighborhood and had a front row seat to the chaos last night. I gave her my number and told her I'd help." Alexia let out a sigh. "Okay, I'll let Hunter know you told Christine, although I don't think that's going to be much help. I guess I need to get going. I need to check in with Mom and . . ." She flailed a hand. What did she really need to do?

"And?"

"I don't know. I want to go back to Mom's house. I noticed her grass needs cutting. I might as well do it. I feel like I have ants crawling under my skin. I'm restless. Maybe doing something physical will help. Plus I want to see if I missed anything from yesterday, see if I can figure out anything about Devin."

Serena frowned at her. "The police will figure that out."

"I know. I just . . ." Once again she trailed off. "Something really feels wrong."

"A man died. Of course something feels wrong." Concern etched itself on Serena's face.

Alexia stared at her friend. "I need to remember what happened that night."

"The night of the fire?"

"Yes. I get bits and pieces, but I can't remember what started it, why my dad would blame me — other than the fact that he hated me."

Serena didn't bother to object to Alexia's statement that her father hated her. She'd seen for herself the bruises on Alexia's back, stomach, and shoulders.

"I don't know, Lex."

"And —" Alexia drew in a deep breath — "I think I need to do something I really don't want to do."

"What's that?"

"Find my father."

Serena lifted a brow. "Are you crazy?"

"Probably." Alexia spotted her overnight bag on the chair. Before leaving Washington, she'd packed a big suitcase for her stay and an overnight bag that held her toiletries. Serena had already dug a clean set of clothes from the suitcase and draped them across the back of the chair. "Thanks for getting these out for me."

Serena shrugged. "No problem. I didn't figure you wanted to put those back on." She gestured to the pile of clothes by the bed.

Alexia grimaced and shuddered. "I think I'll burn them."

Understanding flashed across Serena's face.

Desperate for a change of subject, Alexia asked, "What's up with my mother and Michael Stewart?"

A faint smile curved Serena's lips. "I think they have a mutual attraction for each other."

Alexia didn't know why the words carried such a punch. She'd suspected as much. "My mother? Interested in a man? A man interested in my mother?" She snorted. "Now that's just weird. After the number my father did on her, I would have figured she'd run screaming if another man even looked at her."

A light hand settled on Alexia's shoulder. "Your mom's had a lot of counseling over the last few years. She graduated from school with an administrative assistant degree. She's going to church. I'm serious. I've been in a few Bible studies with her and gotten to know the new Hannah Allen. She's not the same woman you're picturing from ten years ago. Give her a chance."

Pausing, Alexia studied her friend. Then blew out a sigh. "All I can do is promise I'll try to see what you see in her. Okay?"

"It's a start."

Alexia's head ached from her run-in with her attacker in the parking garage, but she felt the need to return to the house. Plus, the grass needed cutting. Her mother loved a neat yard. Why Alexia felt compelled to give her one she couldn't say. She just remembered her mother's comments on the rare occasion her father cut the grass. "I love the yard, Greg, it's beautiful."

Most of the time, the job fell to the teenaged Alexia. And she loved it. It got her out of the house and gave her time to think.

Pulling into the driveway, she parked her car and noticed the crime scene tape. Should she go in? Were they finished processing the house? Unsure, she pulled out

112

her cell phone and dialed Hunter's number.

He picked up on the third ring. "Hello?"

"Hi, Hunter, it's Alexia."

His voice warmed. "Hi there. How are you this morning?"

"I'm doing all right, thanks. I'm at my mom's house. Is it all right if I go in? Has it been cleared?"

"Hold on a sec. Let me check." Shuffling in the background came over the line. A minute later, he said, "Yeah, it's cleared. They finished up late last night."

"Thanks."

"Sure. You need any help with anything?"

Did she? "No, not right now. I'm . . . not going in the house or down to the basement or anything. I just want to cut the grass for her."

Silence on the other end. Then he said, "All right. I'll let you know if there are any new developments in the case."

"Sounds good." She was stalling. Sounded like he was too. Clearing her throat, she said, "I've gotta go. Talk to you later."

"Right. Later."

She hung up and stared at the house. The back of her neck tingled and she shivered at the sensation. When she turned, she didn't see anything out of the ordinary.

A door slammed and she whirled back in

the other direction to see Lori Tabor walking down the front steps of her brother's house, following two small children. The kids laughed as they ran to the swing set at the edge of the yard. Lori saw her and waved.

Alexia waved back, hopped out of the car, and headed for the carport.

The lawn mower sat in the corner. Alexia grabbed it and wheeled it to the edge of the lawn, feeling like she was once again a fourteen-year-old desperate to escape her life for the next hour, losing herself in the roar of the engine and the precision of neatly cut rows of grass.

Leaning over, she grasped the starter and pulled. The engine sputtered and died. She tried again with the same result.

"I bet you need some gas."

Alexia looked up to find Lori standing at the edge of the yard. She smiled. "You think?"

Lori shrugged. "Sounds like it. If you don't have some, I'm sure Avery has a can in the garage."

Alexia nodded. "Thanks." She went back into the carport and hunted around. Opening the storage room, she checked.

A gas can huddled in the corner. She hefted it, deciding it probably held about half a gallon. Surely that would be enough.

Walking back to the lawn mower, she noticed Lori had returned to her charges. Alexia filled up the gas tank. Before she had a chance to start the mower, an older man who looked to be in his late sixties walked up the drive. Placing his hands on his hips, he said, "Glad to see someone's taking care of this place while Mrs. Allen's in the hospital."

Alexia straightened. "I'm her daughter, Alexia."

His eyes cooled. "Ah. So you're the one. Heard you all had some excitement around here."

"Yes sir. And you are?"

"Harold Yarborough."

"Did you know Devin Wickham, Mr. Yarborough?"

"Not very well." He clicked his tongue. "A real shame, though. He sure did help your mom out quite a bit."

"So I understand."

He might as well have shouted, "Unlike Hannah Allen's irresponsible daughter." She refused to allow this man to see how guilty she felt.

"When's your mother expected to come home?" he asked.

"I'm not sure."

"Have you even been to see her?"

Alexia gaped, then caught herself. "Yes sir, I have. Now, if you don't mind, I think I'll get on with cutting the grass."

He didn't take the hint. "My wife, Annie, and your mother are good friends. Annie's been up to the hospital every day since she was admitted." He nodded in Lori's direction. "Her too."

"I'm sure Mom appreciates that, Mr. Yarborough." Would the man never leave? His hostility was beginning to grate.

"She does. Talks about you all the time, though. Your brother, Dominic, too."

"Really?" Now that did interest her.

"Annie says Hannah talks about how bad she wants to see her kids again, to have them in her life."

Was he for real? Why did he feel so comfortable chastising her? "Well, we'll have to see what happens, won't we?"

Mr. Yarborough grunted and narrowed his eyes. "If you're going to hurt that woman again, you might as well get on back to where you came from."

The urge to tell the man exactly what he could do with his unwanted advice had her opening her mouth. Then she shut it. He and his wife were friends with her mother. Of course they'd want to look out for her.

Alexia calmed. "I'm going to do my best to make sure that I don't do anything to hurt her."

Her words seemed to surprise him. And mollify him. Giving her a small smile and a crisp salute, he nodded. "Good then. Be seeing you around." He walked off and Alexia watched him enter the house next door.

She shook her head and muttered, "See you." She bent back over the lawn mower just as something slammed into the garage post behind her.

13

Tuesday, 9:12 a.m.

Spinning, she saw . . . a dart? After the incident in the parking garage, she didn't think twice about falling to the cement drive. Another dart whizzed over her left shoulder.

In disbelief, fear thudding through her, she scrambled to her knees and dove for cover behind the large white freezer. Shaking, her fingers fumbled for the cell phone she had shoved in the back of her shorts pocket. She punched in 9-1-1.

Huddled behind the freezer, she was trapped. If the person shooting the darts came looking for her, she had nowhere to go.

"What's your emergency?"

"I . . . someone's shooting darts at me. I need help!"

Once again, Alexia found herself in terror mode but managed to relay the information the man needed. Fighting fires had taught her how to fight panic and win.

"Help is on the way, ma'am. I've dispatched a unit that's only a minute or so away."

All remained quiet. No more darts came flying in her direction.

Sirens sounded in the distance.

Alexia stayed put.

Hunter heard the call over the radio. Someone was shooting darts at Alexia? He'd been on his way to check on Chad but decided his brother could wait. Adrenaline spiking, he made a left turn, then a right. Soon, he was racing toward the Allen house, punching the speed dial number he'd assigned to Alexia's phone as he slowed to make his way through an intersection.

It rang. Then went to voice mail.

He grabbed the radio, patched through to the dispatcher, and requested an update.

"Officers are on the scene now," she said.

"Any report of injury? A request for an ambulance?"

"Not at this time."

Hunter felt his pulse slow slightly. If the officers were there, and no one had called for an ambulance, then Alexia was probably all right.

Two minutes later, he pulled in front of the house. The area looked much like it had last night. CSU would arrive soon, Hunter would make sure of it. This was no coincidence.

Alexia finding Devin dead in her mother's house, then being mugged in a parking garage? Yeah, okay, that could be coincidence.

Add this incident into the equation and no.

He saw her sitting sideways in the back of a police cruiser. The door was open, her feet on the ground. She looked both vulnerable and mad, with a tight jaw and narrowed eyes. One officer hovered over her. The other examined the area around the carport.

Hunter approached and flashed his badge. Alexia saw him and gave him a tremulous smile.

Touching her shoulder, he asked, "Having a hard time staying out of trouble, aren't you?"

She sighed. "At least I'm not bored."

A king cab truck pulled in beside the cruiser and Hunter blinked. "Chad?"

"What's he doing here?" she asked.

"I don't know. Let me go find out."

Hunter left her watching his back as he rounded the front of the cruiser and approached his brother. Chad pushed the sunglasses to the top of his head.

Hunter eyed him. "What are you up to, Chad?"

"Heard the excitement and the address on the scanner. Thought I'd come by and see what it's all about."

"You off today?"

"Yep."

Seemed Chad was off more than he was on these days. "Then why don't you go enjoy your day and let me worry about what's going on around here."

A hard glint turned Chad's blue eyes as cold as ice. "I guess I can come by if I want."

Not in the mood for his brother's antics, Hunter decided to let it go. "Right. Sure. Why not."

Chad jerked his chin in Alexia's direction. "She all right?"

"Scared, but not hurt."

"Tell her I'll call her, check on her later."

Did his brother think Alexia really wanted him to do that? Instead of asking, Hunter simply nodded. "Sure."

Chad's eyes thawed a few degrees. "I'm heading over to see Dad. He wanted me to help him plant some bush or something."

"Okay. Catch you later." Their father loved to work in the yard. Hunter shuddered.

Give him a murder to investigate any day.

"You coming to dinner tonight?" Chad asked.

"If I can."

Chad smirked. "Why don't I go over and invite Alexia?"

Hunter resisted rolling his eyes. Barely. "I don't think that's a good idea right now."

"Yeah, probably not. See ya." With that, his brother stepped on the gas and sped off.

Hunter gathered his thoughts and turned back to finish working the investigation.

Alexia watched the exchange between the brothers. Chad seemed angry, hostile toward Hunter. Hunter looked frustrated. But he quickly wiped the expression from his face as he walked back over to her just as the CSU van pulled up.

Hunter looked at Alexia. "As soon as they get one of the darts bagged, I'm going to take it to the lab myself. I've got a friend who might have time to run it while I'm there."

"Do you mind if I go with you?"

Before he could answer, an officer approached from across the street. "I've knocked on a lot of doors. Almost no one's home. Guess they're at work. The lady across the street and a few doors down said she saw a dark-headed guy with a backpack walking his dog." The officer shrugged. "Could be a cover. Why would somebody carry a backpack on their morning walk?"

Hunter nodded and looked at Alexia. "You remember anyone like that?"

"No. I talked to Lori Tabor and another neighbor, Harold Yarborough."

"Yeah, I talked to him too," the officer said. "He didn't have anything interesting to add other than he wished you'd leave and take all your trouble with you."

Alexia flinched. "That's pretty much what he said when I talked to him a little while ago."

Hunter frowned. "He has something against you?"

"He and his wife are friends with my mother. He thinks he's protecting her."

Hunter raised a brow at that. She refused to explain. He nodded at the officer. "Let me know if you find anything else." To Alexia, he said, "I'll be right back."

She watched him walk over to one of the CSU team members. Climbing out of the car, she decided to follow him and got close enough to hear him ask, "Hey Shelly, do you mind if I take one of those darts to Rick?"

"Now?"

"Yep."

Shelly shrugged. "Sure, you know what to do." She handed him the computer. "Sign there." Then she handed him a clipboard. "And there."

Hunter complied and Shelly handed him the bag.

"Thanks."

"Gonna hit Rick up to process your stuff first, huh?"

He grinned. "I'm taking the fifth."

Shelly rolled her eyes and went back to work.

Hunter turned and spotted Alexia hovering behind him. She said, "So? Do you mind if I go with you?"

"That should be all right. I'll have to call ahead and let them know I'm bringing you. There's a lot of security and restricted places in the lab. You can wait in the waiting room or maybe Rick's office. All right?"

"Fine. I just want to be involved. I'll go crazy if I have to sit around doing nothing."

"I understand. Plus," his lips tightened, "you might just be safer with me than anywhere else right at this moment."

She grimaced at the truth of his statement and didn't bother trying to deny it.

Hunter pulled into the parking lot of the

state crime lab. One of the perks of working in the capital of South Carolina. Another plus was the fact that his tennis buddy Rick Shelton was head of the lab. Hunter tried not to take advantage of the relationship but had to admit when he needed something fast, he didn't hesitate to ask. And Rick came through for him when he could.

"Come on, follow me."

He got her through the security checkpoint, obtained a visitor's pass, and together they walked as far as Rick Shelton's office. The lab would be off limits.

He found his buddy munching a ham sandwich and rummaging in his desk. "You got anything yet?"

Rick looked up. "What makes you think I'm working on your case?"

"Because you want to date my sister and you need a good word from me?"

Unfazed by the comment, Rick simply lifted a brow. "The last thing I need is a good word from you. Christine and I can handle our own relationship, thanks."

"Aha! So, you admit there is one. A relationship, that is."

"I admit nothing." He went back to his desk. "Bingo. I knew I had a package of pepper in here somewhere." He opened it and looked back at Hunter. "This your friend you called about?"

"Alexia, Rick Shelton."

Alexia nodded and smiled. Rick held out a hand and she shook it.

Hunter dropped the bag with the dart in it on Rick's desk. "How fast can you find out if there's anything on the tip of that dart and if there are any fingerprints to run?"

Rick simply stared at him over his black-framed glasses.

Hunter couldn't read the man's face. A fact that frustrated him often.

Taking pity on his friend, Rick finally sighed and said, "Can you give me thirty or forty minutes?"

"Sure."

"I assume this has something to do with her?" He gestured toward Alexia.

Alexia said, "Someone tried to plant one of those in me this morning. I'd like to know what would have happened if I hadn't moved fast enough."

Rick frowned. "Well, that's just plain mean."

"I kind of thought so," Alexia murmured.

"Come back in thirty to forty minutes."

Hunter took her arm and led her from Rick's office. "Let's go down to the little café and grab an early lunch. The food here's actually pretty good."

"I take it you come here often?"

Hunter smiled. "Rick and I went through high school together. I bug him often enough. Are you telling me you don't remember him?"

She frowned. "Nope, can't say I do."

"Not surprising. Rick was always in the biology or chemistry lab. A major nerd."

"And you, the captain of the football team, hung out with him?"

"Yep. I liked him."

The look in her eye changed from teasing to admiring. "So you weren't just a shallow jock back then?"

He felt a flush start at the base of his neck and cleared his throat. "Nope. Not all the time." And if she'd given him half a glance, he would have been glad to prove it to her.

But she hadn't. And now that he had an idea why, he supposed he couldn't hold that against her. They entered the café and ordered their food.

Tucked away in a corner booth, Hunter watched Alexia pick at her tuna sandwich. "Can you think of anyone who'd want to shoot at you?"

"I have no idea."

They ate in silence for the next few minutes, then Alexia said, "Back in Washington, I was on a call at a fire and I ran out of air.

Someone messed with my fire gear. Punched itty-bitty holes in my hose. I didn't know it and went in to save a kid. My captain ordered me out when my alarm went off indicating my air was low. I ignored him and saved the kid. I ended up running out of air and passing out. All ended well, but the reprimand was pretty harsh and I'm on leave until I can appeal the decision."

"So, what you're saying is someone tried to kill you — or at least cause you serious harm — in Washington. And you're wondering if this person followed you here?"

She shrugged. "Maybe. I think the incidents could be related but have no idea how to connect the dots."

Before he could answer, his phone rang. "Hello?"

"I got your answer. Want to meet me back in my office?"

"Sure. We'll be there in five minutes."

When they entered, Rick looked at Hunter. "I ran tests on some of the more common narcotics used in tranquilizer darts and got a hit. These particular ones have midazolam on them."

Hunter's brow creased in thought. The name sounded familiar, but he couldn't place it.

"It's a fast-acting drug that's usually used

for treatment of seizures," Rick explained. "Sometimes it's used for inducing sedation before medical procedures."

"So, it's a knockout drug?"

Rick rolled his eyes. "In layman's terms, sure, a knockout drug."

"But nothing that would kill her?"

Rick shrugged. "Depends on how many darts hit her."

"Fortunately none did."

"Then no, they won't kill her," Rick deadpanned.

Alexia snickered.

Hunter rolled his eyes. "Wise guy."

Hunter took Alexia back to get her car. Then he followed her to Serena's house. She parked in the drive and Hunter pulled in behind her. When he got out, she asked, "You want to come in for a few minutes?"

He nodded. "Is Serena here?"

"Yes. Probably packing." She explained about Serena's unexpected trip to China. "She heads to the airport first thing tomorrow morning."

Alexia opened the door and they stepped inside the foyer. Hunter shut the door behind him.

He glanced around and gave a low whistle. "Nice." Then he frowned. "So you're going to be here alone?"

"Yes." She shrugged. "I've lived alone for the last ten years. It doesn't bother me." Much.

"You haven't had someone taking shots at you for the last ten years."

"So what do I do? Crawl in a hole and hide?"

He shook his head. "No. You just be extra careful. Watch your back."

Footsteps came from the kitchen. Alexia turned to see Serena, dressed in blue jeans and a knit T-shirt, coming toward them, Yoda at her heels.

Serena smiled. "Hey there."

"Hey. You all ready to take off?"

"Almost." Her eyes narrowed on Alexia's long pink T-shirt. "What happened to you?"

Glancing down, she saw an oil stain on her hip. Probably where she hit the concrete in the carport. "Oh. I didn't even notice that. I had a bit of excitement at Mom's house this morning." She filled her in.

Serena paled. "You're kidding. Who would do that?"

"I don't know."

"But we're going to find out," Hunter promised.

Concerned, Serena looked at Alexia. "You need to make sure you activate the alarm each time you get here and when you leave."

"I will. Come on, guys." She scratched the dog's left ear. "I'll be careful. Now quit worrying."

"What's your schedule like for tomorrow?" Hunter asked.

She thought. "I plan to go back to Mom's house. I still have to cut the grass, and I need to look around. I want to just be there and see if there's anything I missed yesterday. Some kind of clue or hint as to what Devin was into."

Hunter nodded. "All right, I'll see you in the morning."

"What?"

"After what happened today, I don't think you should go back alone. We'll go together."

"But —"

His raised finger stopped her. "I'm serious." Then he glanced at his watch and said, "Now, I've got a meeting about Devin's case. I'll be here first thing in the morning."

14

Wednesday, 8:16 a.m.

Hunter watched Alexia descend the front steps of Serena's house and head for her car. She looked tired, stressed — but very, very good. He wondered how she would feel about the fact that he still found her attractive.

How did *he* feel about that?

He wasn't sure but decided it was worth investigating. At some point. He'd not been interested in pursuing a woman in over a year. Not since Heather had decided she couldn't live with a cop's hours. And now Alexia appeared on the scene and his attraction radar went haywire.

Interesting.

Scary, but definitely interesting.

He saw the moment she caught sight of him. Her breath hitched and she stumbled on one of the stepping-stones leading out to the curb where he waited. "Good morning."

"Hi." A wariness that wasn't there yesterday afternoon emanated from her and he winced. He supposed he couldn't blame her. He wasn't very subtle about his suspicions with her involvement in the death of her ex-boyfriend.

However, he'd done some research on Devin and was itching to share it with her. "You ready?"

"I suppose." She bit her lip and looked at him. "You don't have to drive me. I don't mind taking my car."

"I want to do it."

"That's not in the job description, is it?"

"No." He left it at that.

Intense green eyes studied him. For some reason, he wanted to squirm like a kid caught doing something wrong.

But he hadn't done anything wrong.

"You might be stuck with me all day if you do that," she warned.

He felt a smile curve his lips. "That wouldn't be so bad."

Satisfaction curled through him when the wariness easing from her face was replaced with a questioning look. "No?"

"Nope." He opened the passenger door for her, and with one more lingering look at him, she slid in and he shut the door.

As he climbed into the driver's seat, she

asked, "Won't your father have a problem with you being stuck with me?"

He cut his eyes at her as he cranked the car and pulled away from the curb. "Probably." His father wasn't happy that Alexia was back. As the investigating deputy state fire marshal, he had insisted that the fire that burned down the Allens' house had been deliberately set and that Alexia had done it. And even though the evidence gathered at the scene was inconclusive, he'd always blamed Alexia simply because her father did.

Hunter wasn't so sure.

Friends, neighbors, gossips — even her own family — had placed the blame squarely on Alexia's shoulders. And she'd never denied it. Or confirmed it.

The girl he remembered from high school simply wouldn't do that. He'd watched her for almost his entire senior year of high school, waiting for her to offer him the slightest bit of encouragement after her breakup with Devin.

But she'd never given it. Holding herself aloof from everyone except for the two friends who'd stood by her side. He had a couple of buddies that he considered pretty good friends, but he had to admit, none of them had been through anything like Alexia

134

and her family. Alexia, Serena — and Jillian. The troublesome trio.

"Whatever happened to Jillian Carter?"

A sigh slipped from her. "Now there's a mystery you could put your talents to good use on solving."

"Rumor was that she just disappeared one night. I remember her boyfriend was a zombie when he realized she was gone for good."

"Graduation night." Her eyes flickered and he wondered at the secrets behind them. "I'm not sure what happened."

Alexia paused so long that he wondered if she was going to continue or not. She did.

"Jillian came to the dance that night at the school gym. She was crying, scared. Said she saw something but couldn't tell us what or we'd be in danger too. I haven't seen her since."

"That's weird."

"No kidding."

Hunter watched her very expressive face. A face he'd been entranced with his senior year. "So she was fine at graduation?"

"Seemed to be."

"Then she came to the dance upset?"

Alexia thought about it. "No. She was beyond upset. She was terrified."

"And she was too scared to tell you what

she saw."

"Exactly. But I think it was more like she was afraid of what might happen to *us* — Serena and me — if she told."

Hunter tapped the wheel as he drove, his thoughts whirling. "I wonder what she could have seen."

"I don't know." Alexia rubbed her eyes. "I don't even know where she'd been before the party."

Hunter made a mental note to do some checking into any criminal activity that may have happened that night. At least the stuff that was reported. It was very likely Jillian could have witnessed something that had never come to light. Still, it wouldn't hurt to check. But first, he had a murder to solve.

15

Wednesday, 8:26 a.m.

Alexia watched her mother's house come into her line of sight. Hunter parked in the drive and she started to open the door. A warm hand on her forearm stopped her. She raised her eyes to his. "What?"

"I did some research into Devin's background last night."

"Last night? Have you slept at all?"

A smile curved. "I don't need much sleep. Anyway, turns out he came from a pretty good home. His parents are still together, but they've been out of town on a trip to California. As soon as they got the word about Devin, they began making arrangements to head home."

"When will they get here?"

"Around seven tonight. I'm going to meet them at their house about seven thirty."

Alexia easily pictured the nice house in the middle-class neighborhood about five miles north of her mother's house. "I used to go home with Devin after school."

Hunter nodded. "They seem to be a nice couple. Quiet, reserved, but nothing that made the radar blip."

"Then why was he living with my mother? Seems like if he was having financial trouble, he would have moved home with his parents."

His brows furrowed. "I'm not sure. That might be something you want to ask your mom. And it's definitely on my list of questions to ask when I see them tonight."

"I'll ask her if I get a chance."

He nodded toward the house. "What do you think you're going to find in there?"

"I don't know." Biting her lip, she studied the structure. Crime scene tape still wrapped the front porch. "Maybe the reason Devin was living here and why everyone seems to think my mother is a changed woman — and if she is, what changed her."

"God can change people."

She was quiet for a moment, then said, "I have a hard time picturing the popular, life-of-the-party football star Hunter Graham as a . . ." She paused, not wanting to be rude. "Well, as someone who is now into religion."

A slight flush dusted his cheeks. "I know. In high school, I enjoyed being in the limelight. And you're right, I could party with the best of them. But" — he shrugged — "I was also going to church with my parents and listening to the teachings of the youth pastor. One day, in college, I woke up and realized I wasn't so interested in being hung over every weekend and wanted something more out of life."

She eyed him, seeing his sincerity. It made her even more curious about him. "I guess I can understand that."

"Thanks."

Taking a deep breath, she pulled out her key and had a moment of déjà vu. Blinking, she gave her head a shake.

Hunter's hand came up to rest on her shoulder. "What's wrong?"

"I keep picturing Devin in the basement, his life slowly seeping through my fingers." She could still see the blood on her hands.

His hand slid from her shoulder to grasp her left hand, letting his fingers entwine with hers. She jerked, but not away from him. She blurted, "Why are you being so nice to me all of a sudden?"

His flush deepened. "I decided you were innocent until proven guilty."

"In spite of what your partner thinks?"

He gave a rueful smile. "In spite of what she thinks."

"But I'm still guilty in your father's eyes, aren't I?"

Without taking his gaze from hers, he sighed. "He's always believed you started that fire on purpose because your father said you did." A pause, then a searching look. "Did you?"

She stared at him, trying to find some righteous anger at his query. But she couldn't.

"I don't know."

His left brow raised. "You don't?"

She looked away, back at the house that held so many memories. "No. I don't." Pulling in a shuddering breath, she said, "I remember the fire. I remember my sister screaming. I remember my dad's anger and my mother . . ." She frowned. "I don't remember much about her. And I don't remember what started the fire."

"Then why were you blamed for it?"

She looked at him. "Because my father said it was my fault and your father believed him."

"But my dad couldn't prove it."

"Apparently that didn't matter."

Her abrupt answer didn't faze him. "You were never charged with anything, so that meant even though my dad may have believed your dad, he didn't have proof."

Alexia arched a brow. She hadn't thought of it that way.

"Where was your brother?" he asked.

"He'd already left home."

After a minute of intense silence, Alexia finally climbed from the car.

This time, Hunter didn't stop her.

"I thought you were trained for this kind of thing." The voice turned cold, hard. Dangerous. "Attacking her in the parking garage wasn't part of the plan. I don't need her dead yet, I need information from her."

"I know, I wasn't going to kill her. I just thought —"

"That's the problem. You don't need to think. That's my job. When you think, you do stupid things like killing Devin Wickham."

"Devin was an accident. He was in the wrong place at the wrong time. I had no choice. He saw me and recognized me even with the mask on. No more stupid mistakes, I promise."

Good. He inhaled slowly, then exhaled, taking on the role of parent once again. "Now, are you using the prepaid cell I gave you?"

"Yes."

"Good, just keep —"

"Look, I didn't know Devin was going to be there. He was supposed to be at work. He got a new job, you know, and I thought it was her and —"

"It's over and done with. Here's the way we're going to do this from now on, all right?"

"Yes sir. I'm listening."

The house had been cleared by CSU and released back to the owner — her mother — so Alexia's returning here wasn't a problem. However, Hunter wondered at the emotional toll the visit would take on her.

"The grass still needs cutting," she said as he watched her step inside the house. He monitored each expression that flitted across her face.

After a brief pause in the small foyer, she went straight to the kitchen. "I noticed these here yesterday. Mom would have a fit if she saw these dirty dishes stacked in the sink like this."

He stepped behind her. "Then let's wash them."

Alexia looked around for a dishtowel, then gasped when her eyes landed on the stainless steel appliance. "She got a dishwasher!"

Nearly laughing at the expression on her face, he managed to swallow the chuckle and ask seriously, "And that's shocking?"

She grimaced. "That sounded crazy, didn't it?" Running her hand over the dishwasher, she shook her head. "Dad would never put one in. Said it kept her busy. Idle hands were the devil's tools."

"Ah."

She cut him a glance. "Yeah. A bigger hypocrite you've never met."

"I'm sorry."

A shoulder lifted. "Doesn't matter now, I guess."

"You said your brother, Dominic, was gone before the fire. Whatever happened to him?"

She froze. Pulled in a deep breath, then let it out slowly as though sifting through the information in her mind, trying to figure out what to share with him. Then again, he could go back to his office and pull any information he wanted. "When he was seventeen, he was arrested for dealing drugs. Shortly after that, he ran away."

"Why?"

"Because he hated our dad. And . . . I'm the one who turned him into the cops for dealing drugs."

A brow lifted. "I don't remember that."

"Well, it didn't make the eleven o'clock news, but it stirred things up around here pretty good." Her lips twisted in derision as she loaded the dishwasher.

She placed the last dish in the rack, reached under the sink for the detergent, and filled the cup. Shoving the door shut, she turned the machine on and a low hum filled the air.

"So, what's Dominic doing now?" he asked.

Alexia shrugged. She grabbed a rag to wipe out the sink. "I don't know. I tried to find him about three years ago, but I didn't have any luck. A private investigator was too expensive and —" another halfhearted shrug — "I took that to mean he didn't want to be found, for some reason."

"So you quit looking."

"Yep."

She tossed the rag onto the counter and looked around the house, eyes studying every detail. He could only imagine the memories flooding through her.

Taking another deep breath, she said, "But maybe it's time to start searching again. Maybe in order to find a measure of peace, it's time to try and lay all the ghosts in my past to rest." Alexia flushed and cut her eyes to the floor. "Sorry, I don't know why I'm sharing all this with you." She looked back at him. "When did you get so easy to talk to?"

It was his turn to feel the heat climbing up his neck. "If you'd been interested, you could have found out back in high school."

Her jaw dropped as she paused midstep toward the door, and he let out a laugh.

"What? You didn't know?"

"No, I didn't know. How was I supposed to know that?"

He felt a silly grin spread across his face. "You were a freshman, I was a senior. I was too cool to date a freshman." He ducked his chin and glanced at her from the corner of his eye. "I wish I hadn't been so cool."

The flush that graced her cheeks made him grin wider. Then he frowned and sighed. "And my dad would have killed me."

Alexia grimaced and tightened her jaw. "Yeah, couldn't go against Dad, could you?"

He ignored her bitter words. "Then the night you and Chad and Christine all graduated . . . I realized I wanted to get to know you more — regardless of what my father would say. Then you disappeared on me."

His confession seemed to knock her for a loop. She cleared her throat and said, "I had no idea, Hunter."

"I know." He shrugged. "I had just gotten

home from college. It was the first time I'd seen you in three years, and you didn't seem interested in me — or any other guy for that matter."

"Well, that's true. I'd pretty much sworn off men and dating by the end of my senior year. And," she twisted the ring on her pinky, a nervous habit she'd broken but seemed to have picked up again recently, "I've been running for the past ten years." She frowned and walked toward the basement door. Pulling it open, she looked down the steps, her shoulders hunched. "Now, I want to stop running. It's time to start fighting my own battles."

She headed down the basement stairs.

16

As she put one foot in front of the other, long-buried fears deluged her. The light tread of the footsteps behind her offered her more comfort than she wanted to admit. Part of her was relieved she didn't have to do this alone, but another part believed she didn't deserve to have company — or comfort.

Swallowing hard, she reached the bottom of the steps and flipped the switch. Just as before, the light illuminated the cluttered space.

Alexia walked straight to the area where Devin had died. His blood still stained the carpet. A dark brown spot with spatters on the wall. "The crime scene cleanup crew hasn't been here yet," she noted.

Then rolled her eyes at her statement. Duh.

But she felt better hearing her voice, trying to stay detached from it all, like she was working one of her fires. Noting details, doing what had to be done, but keeping emotion out of it.

"They'll probably be here sometime today," Hunter said.

Again his presence comforted her. And she was glad he didn't try to dissuade her from continuing. The memories threatened to overwhelm her, but she shoved them back with effort, refusing to let them in.

She studied the area, then moved on to the door. "He came in here."

"Yes, it looks like it." Hunter studied the lock. "Probably wasn't any trouble to either pick the lock or just jimmy it."

"Or she left it open."

"Or that."

"Or Devin let his attacker in because he knew him."

Hunter shot her a look, admiration glinting in his gorgeous eyes. "Or that."

A bolt of warmth shot through her and she realized how much she cared about what he thought about her. Clearing her throat, she made a mental note to be on guard. His father hated her and thought her guilty of arson. Whose side would Hunter take if it came down to making a choice between the two of them?

148

A no-brainer in her book. And by even thinking along those lines, she was jumping way ahead of things.

Or was she? After all, he'd just confessed to wanting to ask her out in high school.

She jerked her gaze from him and walked into the room Devin had used for the past several weeks.

"He was a neat person. Everything looks organized," she observed.

"Looks like he'd been living here for a while." Hunter looked around. "No boxes sitting around to be emptied."

Alexia walked to the nightstand and opened the drawer. "I feel weird doing this."

"CSU has been all over this place. What do you think you're going to find that they missed?"

Alexia shrugged. "Nothing probably. I just wanted to see . . . I don't know. If he was the same person I remembered."

"Probably not. It's been ten years. Are you the same person?"

"Goodness, no." She gave a little laugh and pulled out a picture. "Look. It's him and Marcie . . . Marcie Freeman." Hunter joined her to look over her shoulder, and she drew in a deep breath. "I like your cologne."

His eyes dropped to hers. A little smile

curved his lips. "Thanks."

Alexia felt mortification sweep over her. As well as a flush like she'd never experienced before. She really needed to get control of her tongue.

Settling her eyes on the picture, she frantically searched for a way out of the awkward spot she'd just landed in.

A thump sounded overhead and Alexia froze, shot a look back at Hunter, and narrowed her eyes.

"Are you expecting someone?" he whispered.

She shook her head.

Before she could blink, he had his weapon in his hand and was headed up the steps.

Jaw set, determined to do her part to figure out what was going on, she hurried after him. Keeping her steps light and soundless, she grabbed his arm and pointed to the fourth step from the top. "Step over," she mouthed.

He did. The door leading into the kitchen remained as they'd left it. Cracked. Feet planted on the second step from the top, his body edged sideways as much as possible, he swept the weapon in front of him. With a glance back at her, he motioned for her to mimic his pose — back flat against the wall.

No doubt, so if anyone shot into the basement, they would be out of the most obvious line of fire.

Fear reared its head, but she swallowed and complied. Alexia decided she much preferred the visible enemy of a good fire to murder, personal attacks, and home invasions.

Hunter eased the door open with his elbow.

17

Wednesday, 8:56 a.m.

When no bullets came tearing in their direction, Alexia allowed herself to breathe a little easier, although her nerves still hummed. Hunter eased his way into the kitchen. She stayed right behind him, eyes darting, probing, looking for anything that could be considered a threat.

Nothing.

Another noise from the direction of the den. So faint she wondered if she'd imagined it. Alexia swiveled her gaze from the kitchen to the opening that led to the living area.

Hunter sidestepped toward the noise. He'd heard it too.

The incident from the parking garage flashed through her mind, mingling with the fear she'd felt upon finding Devin's body. Was there someone in her mother's den? Had that person followed them? Or had he already been inside, lying in wait?

She wanted to grab Hunter, tell him to stop his slow move toward whatever lurked out of sight. She wanted to snatch her cell phone and dial 9-1-1.

Instead, she barely breathed as Hunter finally reached the door, edged to the side, and held his weapon ready. Again, he motioned her to move behind him.

She did.

His broad back blocked her view, shielding her from whatever lay before them. Heat radiated from him and she knew his adrenaline raced as fast as hers.

He moved, dropping to his knees. She did the same.

Hunter eased his head around the doorframe and pulled in a slow breath. "Clear in here," he whispered in a voice so low she had to strain to hear him. But she understood what he meant. There was nothing in the den area.

But that was where the noise had come from.

Hunter rose and entered the den on silent feet. Once again, Alexia followed.

She glanced around, nerves tight, tension knotting the muscles in her shoulders. What had they heard?

Her gaze fell on the one thing out of place.

A book on the floor by the end table nearest the front door.

The front door that was now cracked. She knew for a fact Hunter had closed it behind him when he'd followed her into the house.

Hadn't he?

Movement caught her eye and she sucked in a deep breath. "There," she whispered.

Hunter whirled, gun pointed.

A cat.

Just a cat.

Adrenaline still pumped. He kept his voice low. "Does your mother have a cat?" He didn't remember seeing any bowls or other evidence that would indicate a cat lived here, but that didn't mean the stuff wasn't upstairs. It also didn't mean there still wasn't someone in the house.

"Not that I know of," she whispered.

"Stick close."

He felt her behind him. His senses tuned in to react to any immediate threat, he still couldn't help noticing her light perfume. With her on his heels, he methodically checked the downstairs part of the house. "It's clear down here. Let's go up."

They started for the second floor. Two bathrooms and three bedrooms were upstairs. One by one, they checked and cleared each room until he was satisfied no one lurked, ready to pounce.

Hunter dropped his weapon to his side. "I'm going to have a look around outside real quick."

She nodded, still looking around the room like she'd never seen it before. "I'm going with you." He lifted a brow and she flushed, even as she offered a nonchalant shrug. "I don't want to be alone in here."

Together, they walked down to examine the front door. She hovered close by while he checked outside.

Nothing. He also noted he never heard a car drive up or drive away.

His gaze shot up the street then back down.

No one.

Hiding places abounded. There was no one to chase, nothing to indicate there'd been an intruder in the house only moments ago.

But his gut said there'd been someone there.

Retracing his steps, double-checking the lock on the front door, he turned and said, "I didn't see anything or anyone outside."

She followed him back up the stairs, quiet and subdued. Back in the room they'd just left, she finally found her voice.

"It's so different," she whispered.

He looked around. Pretty white curtains hung on the windows. A matching bed-spread covered the twin bed against the far wall.

"This was my room."

A simple statement. He wondered if he was supposed to respond. "Nice."

"Yes, it is." She sounded almost puzzled as she took in the decor. Then, "It didn't look like this when I was growing up." She shook her head. "Nothing's out of place anywhere else in the house. I guess you didn't close the door that well when you came in. The cat must have let himself in, then knocked that book off the end table."

"Looks like it." He agreed with her words, but his brain still flashed warning signals.

"I don't think the cat's Mom's. There's nothing in the house that says, 'Animal lives here.' "

"I noticed."

Her voice softened. "She kept these."

He stepped closer to look over her shoulder. Her light scent floated to him and he breathed deep. He'd be able to pick her out of a roomful of other perfumed women without trouble. Blindfolded.

"Look," she said and lifted several neck-laces for him to see.

"What's so special about them?"

"There are six of them. A separate chain with each letter of my name. When you line them up, they connect and spell my name."

Alexia demonstrated by slipping each silver chain over her head and around her neck. Soon all six silver letters interlocked to spell A-L-E-X-I-A. "The art teacher at school sort of took me under her wing my eighth grade year. She made these for me for my thirteenth birthday. I wondered whatever happened to them."

"So all your memories here aren't horrible."

With a sigh, she hung the chains back on the little tree on the dresser. "No, at least not that one."

Hunter turned to lead the way back downstairs when he saw something on the floor just under the edge of the white bedspread. Curious, he took the few steps he needed in order to lean down for a better look.

"What are you doing?" Alexia's voice came from the door.

"Something doesn't look right in here."

"Nothing looks right in here," she muttered. She came to stand beside him.

He reached under the bed and slid out a brown-and-black-striped box. Looking up, he noticed her wide eyes.

"What is it?"

"Put it back," she demanded.

"Why?"

She paced from the bed to the wall then back. "I can't believe she kept that."

"What do you mean?"

"That box. It survived the fire. One of the few things that did. I had hidden it downstairs in the basement. The fire started in the . . . the den. Yeah." Excitement flared in her eyes for a moment. "I didn't remember that. I mean people told me, but I never remembered it until now. Other than water damage, most everything in the basement wasn't touched." Shaking her head, she couldn't seem to take her eyes from the box. "That was one of them. And she put it up here. But why?"

"What's in it?"

"A lot of memories I'd rather not revisit right now."

Curious at her reaction, he cocked his head and studied her. "Like what?"

"Just stuff. Private stuff." She grimaced. "Now put it back."

"Sure." He started to push it back into place when something on the box's clasp caught his attention.

Pointing to it, he looked up at her. "I think that's either rust . . . or blood."

She blanched. "Blood? From what?"

"Can I open it?"

Biting her lip, she simply stared at him.

"What's in the box, Alexia?" He kept his voice soft, as unintrusive as possible. He figured she was taking a mental inventory of the contents.

She swallowed and he watched her throat work. "A letter from Devin . . ." She looked away. "He apologized and begged me to come back to him. Newspaper clippings of the fire. A few birthday cards from my mother when she could sneak a couple of dollars from my dad's wallet to buy one, a letter from a teacher who told me I had great potential." She shrugged and he could see the flush on her cheeks.

Then she pulled in a deep breath. "Fine. If you have to open it, then do it."

Hunter didn't want to touch the clasp with his hands. He didn't know why he was reacting this way to the box with what could be mud, rust, or any other substance on the clasp, but his instincts had kicked into high gear and he'd learned early on to listen to them. He looked at her. "In my car, there's a kit to process evidence. It's in the trunk. Will you get it?"

Puzzlement flashed across her face. "Why?"

"I want to take a sample of the stuff that's on here."

Realization marched in. "Oh."

He winced at the fact that she knew he didn't want to leave her alone in the room with the evidence. He could also tell she was hurt by it. He'd have to explain he was just protecting her. Hopefully, she would understand.

Within minutes, Alexia returned with the processing kit.

Hunter opened it and pulled out the necessary equipment, including a pair of gloves. He snapped them on. "Will you close the blinds?"

Again with furrowed brow, she did as he asked. With the flashlight, Hunter examined the box. Several prints leapt up at him. Working diligently, he dusted the outside of the box, using the graphite powder.

Following each step just as he'd been taught years ago, he expertly lifted the prints and transferred them to the white 3 × 5 cards he pulled from the kit.

When he was finished with the prints, he lifted the substance around the clasp. After a drop of luminol, he held it up for her to see, not at all pleased he'd been right. "It's positive for blood."

"But whose?"

"I don't know, but we'll compare it to Devin's." Hunter stored the evidence on the Q-tip in the tube and placed it in the kit.

Now, to open the box.

With a glove-tipped finger, he slid the clasp to the right and lifted the lid.

His stomach churned as he pulled out the blood-encrusted knife.

She felt faint. For the first time in her life, Alexia thought she might actually pass out. Okay, for the second time, if she counted the fire.

Pulling in a calming breath, she focused on Hunter's eyes. She had to know if he believed she put that knife there.

When she found no suspicion, the dizzying sensation passed and she said, "I don't know how that got there. I didn't put it there." She winced. That's what all criminals proclaimed when caught in the act, didn't they? Maybe, but the difference between them and her was that she was telling the truth.

But did Hunter believe her? For some reason, that was the most important question buzzing around in her brain right now.

Thoughtful blue eyes stared at her. "I don't think you did."

She nearly wilted into the floor. Felt tears

flood her eyes. Shocked at her reaction to his words, she simply stood still, fighting the emotion.

"I need to bag this, and it looks like I've got one big enough for the box, but I need another one for the knife." He held the weapon by the end of the handle. Even from where she stood, she could see it was the missing kitchen knife.

"Right." Grateful for the excuse to get out from under his watchful eye, she headed for the door. "Paper, right?"

"Yeah."

"Sure."

She bolted from the room, nearly tripping down the steps. The newly carpeted steps, she noticed. In fact, a lot of things looked kind of new around here now that she took the time to take in the details.

Without further thought of her mother's decorating habits, she searched the pantry for a paper bag. Finally, on the bottom shelf, she found one. She hurried back to the room she'd grown up in and handed it without comment to Hunter.

He took it and slid the knife inside. "I'll take these to the lab. They could be totally unrelated to what happened with Devin."

"But you don't think so."

He shook his head. "I . . . think that a

man was killed in your mother's basement with a knife. Up here, we have a bloody knife hidden away. Yeah. I think the two are related, but I'll let the lab confirm it."

"Why do you believe me?" She had to know.

He paused, then sighed. "A couple of reasons."

She lifted her right brow to encourage him to share those with her.

"One, I've developed pretty good instincts over the years I've been in law enforcement. I've gotten to know you a little bit and I don't see you as someone who could kill."

She breathed a little easier. "Thank you for that, but I'm not buying it. In order for you to calmly say I didn't do it, you'd have proof. So what is it?"

Admiration settled on his face, then he shrugged. "Yeah, true." He gestured toward the knife. "When would you have put it there? You spent all night at Serena's and were with me all morning."

"I could have snuck back here during the night."

He frowned, then flushed.

Knowledge hit her. "You had someone watching Serena's house, didn't you?"

The flush faded and his blue eyes bored into hers. "Yes." He held up a hand to stall her protests. "And yes, partly because I wasn't sure about you. And partly because I was worried whoever killed Devin would come back after you. After all, he knows you saw him. And even though he had a mask on, he's not going to be comfortable that there's a potential witness out there."

Her protests died a sudden death. "Oh."

He frowned. "I guess there is one time you could have done it."

Her eyes widened. "When?"

"When you came to cut your mother's grass."

She deflated, then brightened. "Lori can vouch for me. She was here the minute I drove up to a couple minutes before the person started shooting darts at me."

"Every minute? She can verify you never went into the house?"

Alexia frowned as she thought. "Yes, she can."

"Okay, I'll need to talk to her. But we have another problem."

"What?"

"While I believe you didn't put that knife there, I don't know that everyone else is going to be so easy to convince."

"Why?"

"Because . . ." He sighed. "Due to the blood on the clasp, it looks like the knife was placed in the box shortly after the murder. The blood was still fresh, wet, when the killer put it there."

Her brain processed what he was saying. "And the only person here right after the murder was me." Dread settled like a rock in the pit of her stomach.

"Pretty much looks that way." He touched her arm. "But I still believe you didn't do it."

"Okay." She pulled in a deep breath. "Then who did and why?"

18

With those questions still ringing between them, Hunter finished processing the room. He figured he wouldn't find anything new, but he did it anyway. When he finished, he took Alexia back to Serena's house. She wanted to pick up her car and visit her mother. He wanted to get the box and the knife over to the lab.

The more he thought about it, the more he felt the knife had been placed in the upstairs bedroom while he and Alexia were in the basement. The idea didn't sit well with him, but it nagged at him enough that he finally caved and gave it some merit.

However, if the box had been planted upstairs, that meant the perp had it in his possession. But how? And for how long?

Alexia said she'd hidden the box in the basement. Had the killer found it when he'd killed Devin?

Nothing was adding up and yet everything was.

The book on the floor.

The cat.

The cracked front door.

Someone had been in that house. The cat had just been a coincidence.

Or a well-thought-out plan in case something went wrong? Like knocking a book off the end table in a hurry to leave?

Had the person in that house been trying to frame Alexia? Possibly. In fact, with the appearance of the bloody knife, it's the only thing that made sense. But why?

And why come in while Hunter was there? The person had to have seen his car out front.

Unless the person had already been in the house when they arrived. The thought chilled him.

If he hadn't made the spur-of-the-moment decision to show up at Serena's house, Alexia would have gone home alone. And he might very well be investigating two murders.

That bothered him.

A lot.

He turned into the parking lot of the crime lab and climbed out of the car, taking the brown bag containing the knife. While he figured he knew whose blood was on the blade, he needed it confirmed. He also needed to know if Alexia's prints were on there.

Of course, if they were, would it mean much? She could come and go in that house as she pleased.

However, she said herself she hadn't done anything but walk in the door before she heard something in the basement. She said she hadn't touched the knives. If her prints were on it . . .

Pushing through the door, Hunter made his way to the elevator and pressed the button for the fifth floor. When the doors opened, he stepped out into a hub of quiet, well-run activity. Conversations buzzed, techs rushed evidence from one end of the lab to the other. Two cops hovered over the coffee machine, no doubt hoping to press for faster service on an urgent case.

Probably wouldn't happen. At least not for them.

Hunter hoped he would have a different outcome. Rounding the corner to the second office on the left, he saw Rick sitting at his desk, head bent over a stack of papers.

Hunter rapped his knuckles on the door. "Hey buddy, how you doing?"

Rick's head lifted. When he saw Hunter

with the paper bag held in plain sight, he raised a brow. "I take it you didn't stop by to set up a tennis date."

"We can do that too."

Rick snorted and waved him in. "What do you need?"

"I'm working the Wickham case."

"Ah." Rick nodded. "Yeah, that one came through last night." He frowned and motioned to the bag. "But what's that? I thought we had all the evidence."

"I found this a little while ago. In one of the bedrooms at the crime scene."

Rick's frown morphed into tight-jawed anger and his eyes narrowed. "Something CSU missed?"

"I don't think so. At least I hope not." He paused. "I honestly don't know but suspect this was planted after they left." Hunter explained the incident in the Allens' house, then threw in his theories for good measure.

"That's not good, my friend."

Hunter snorted. "Tell me about it. I'm just glad I was there."

"So, and this is just a wild guess, you want me to process this while you wait."

Hunter smiled.

Rick sighed. "Right."

"Just DNA and fingerprints."

"The DNA will take awhile, you know

that. Fingerprints I can do. Have a seat, I'll be right back." He walked to the door, then paused and turned back to Hunter. "Actually, you want to see something cool?"

Five minutes later, Hunter watched as Rick reverently pulled a machine from its box. "We just got this last week. They're relatively new but have proven effective at lifting prints. It's an EDAX Eagle II XPL MXRF instrument with a 40 W rhodium anode and a liquid nitrogen cooled Si—"

"Rick."

Rick looked up. "Huh?"

"English? Please?"

"Oh right. Sorry. Basically, it's a new-fangled way to lift prints. It uses a laser instead of powder. The laser detects sodium, potassium, and chlorine present on the ridges . . ."

An image appeared on the screen in front of them as Rick continued his lecture. "The fingerprints show up thanks to the chemical markers, displaying ridge patterns of prints, allowing a visible image to be seen. Like there."

The fingerprint stared up at him. "Awesome. Now can you match it?"

A heavy sigh blew through Rick's lips. "You really don't care at all about the techie stuff, do you?"

"Nope."

"Thirty-two years old and you act like you're one of the old fogies ready for retirement," his buddy mumbled — loud enough for Hunter to hear.

It was a long-standing argument between the two. Hunter just wanted the job done and he didn't much care how it happened. Rick wanted everyone to understand the technical side of forensics — whether they wanted to understand it or not.

Rick moved on to the next print. And the next. Finally, he said, "That's all that's on there. It'll take me awhile to match them up. I may have to call in our analyst."

"How long?"

"I can give you a list of possible matches before you leave, but until I — or an analyst — sit down and go over them point by point . . . well, you know the deal. It'll be awhile."

Hunter reached up and rubbed the back of his neck with his left hand. "All right. Give me the list and I'll see if I recognize any of the names."

19

Wednesday, 11:14 a.m.

Alexia made the trip to the hospital and parked in the same area in the garage. She'd have parked in the same spot if it had been available. Almost as though she wanted to dare her attacker to try again.

Almost.

She couldn't believe someone had been in her mother's house — *again*. And planting evidence in an attempt to frame her? Really?

The thought scared her and she had to admit she was doubly glad to be staying at Serena's home. The one with the nice fancy alarm system.

As she climbed out of the car, she stood and listened. Cars passing on the street below.

A conversation one aisle over.

Footsteps.

Behind her.

In disbelief, she turned and saw a young

mother carrying her toddler as she clipped her way to the elevator.

Stomach churning, Alexia hurried to the elevator behind the young woman and made her way to her mother's room. Just as she was about to knock, her phone buzzed. She glanced at the screen.

Hunter.

Her stomach flipped. Once again, she was surprised by her desire to talk to the man, see him, be around him. After all, his father thought she was guilty of setting the fire.

Guilty of causing her sister to commit suicide.

Guilty, guilty, guilty . . .

"Hello?" His voice tickled her ear.

Flushing — and grateful he couldn't see that she'd been standing there staring at the wall like an idiot — she said, "Hi."

"Just wanted to let you know that I talked to your mom's neighbor, Lori Tabor."

"And?"

"She verified you never went in the house the day you went over to mow."

Relief washed over her. *She* knew she hadn't put the knife there, but thank goodness she had a witness.

"What are you doing for lunch?"

His question made her blink. "Um . . . eating?"

His chuckle came through loud and clear. "Alone or with someone?"

Alexia looked at the door to her mother's room. Would she be eating with her mother? *Should* she eat with her mother? "I'm not sure yet. Do you mind if I call you back?"

Silence. Then, "That's fine. I'll look forward to hearing from you."

"Give me about an hour."

"Deal."

"Hey, Hunter?"

"Yeah?"

"I've been thinking about that box in my room. I think that could've been what the killer had in his hand. It's the right size. He could've put the knife in there right after he killed Devin, then returned today to set me up by putting the evidence in my bedroom."

He was quiet. She could picture him thinking. "It's a good theory. I'll give it some thought. Talk to you soon."

And then he was gone. Taking a deep breath, she placed her knuckles on the door and rapped.

"Come in."

The weak voice barely made it through the wood. Frowning, Alexia entered the room.

This time her mother was alone. And she still looked frail. Weak and washed out.

174

What was *wrong* with her? "Hi, Mom."

Her stomach churned. She still had to break the news about Devin.

"Alexia." The woman's eyes smiled even as her mouth trembled with the effort. "So glad you came back."

Alexia pulled the chair up beside the bed and sat down. "Sorry it took me so long." Should she tell her about Devin or not? "Mom, there's something I need to —"

"Did you go to the house?"

"Yes."

Her mother's eyes shut, then reopened after about half a minute. "I forgot to tell you that Devin Wickham is living there." She frowned. "He's had a really rough time of it and I offered him a place to stay. He's in the little room off the basement. Shouldn't bother you at all."

Just those few sentences seemed to exhaust her. She closed her eyes once more. At that moment, Alexia decided not to say anything about Devin. Her mother was just too weak right now.

A knock sounded and the door opened in a soft whoosh. Alexia turned to see the doctor. Without waiting for him to introduce himself, she stood and offered her hand. "I'm Alexia, her daughter. Have you figured out what's wrong with her yet?"

"I'm Doctor Howard Bales. We're waiting for the results of two more tests. So, until then, we're just trying to keep her as comfortable as possible."

Alexia frowned. "When will you have the results?"

"Sometime tomorrow, I hope."

She turned back to her mother. The woman had fallen asleep. "So, it's not her heart?"

"No, we've ruled that out. Along with some other things."

"Surely you have your suspicions as to what it could be."

He nodded. "I do, and I've discussed a few of them with your mother. But I don't know for sure. I'm not going to throw out any more diseases that'll scare both of you without those test results. We'll know what we know tomorrow."

Alexia looked at her mother. "Is she going to sleep the rest of the day?"

"Probably. We gave her something for pain."

Alexia chewed her lip, indecision warring within her. "All right. I'll be back later."

The doctor nodded and left. Alexia pulled out her phone and studied it. Did she want to eat with Hunter?

Definitely.

Should she eat with Hunter?

Probably not.

She dialed his number.

When Hunter saw Alexia's name pop up, his heart tripped over itself.

Shaking his head at his unusual reaction, he answered on the second ring. "Hello?"

"Is the offer for lunch still on?"

"You bet."

"Where can I meet you?"

Hunter suggested a local café and she promised to meet him there in fifteen minutes.

Fingering the page his buddy Rick had just printed out for him, he folded it and stuck it in his shirt pocket. It probably wouldn't hurt to run it by Alexia. She might recognize some of the names.

Hunter arrived first and got a table in the corner. Through the window next to the booth, he could see the parking lot. The sun shone and the heat beat down, making the asphalt shimmer. Fall could arrive any time, as far as he was concerned.

He glanced at his watch, then back up. His toe tapped the leg of the table. And he realized what he was doing. He wanted to see her again, talk to her, reassure himself his instincts were right and she had nothing to do with Devin's death.

He was 99 percent sure. And her reasoning about how the box got into her bedroom was sound. Even he wouldn't argue that someone hadn't been in the house. He knew it as well as he knew himself.

Unfortunately, another scenario had occurred to him as he'd walked out of the lab. What if Alexia had a partner? One who was afraid she'd squeal on him so he'd decided to plant the evidence in her house. Then if Alexia gave him up, he would simply say he'd taken the knife, then given it to Alexia to get rid of. How was he supposed to know she'd do something stupid like keep it?

Only, Hunter and Alexia had arrived at the house before the real killer could get out. Right?

Hunter snorted. It was a little far-fetched, but he'd come across stranger things. He definitely didn't want to believe it. Besides, his gut said she was innocent. And his gut was rarely wrong.

The scenario he'd just concocted wouldn't hold up anyway, because Alexia had either been with him or under surveillance since the murder.

Certainty filled him. She'd had nothing to do with Devin's murder.

A car pulled into the parking lot and

Hunter sat up. She was here. He watched as she parked and got out of the vehicle.

Another car pulled in beside hers and Hunter jerked with recognition. What was *he* doing here?

20

Wednesday, 12:06 p.m.

Alexia spotted Hunter sitting next to the window. A great spot that allowed him to keep his back to a wall and his eyes on the street. Typical cop seating.

She waved and started to cross the street that ran between the café and the parking lot.

The squeal of tires caught her attention and she looked left.

A blue van rounded the corner, striking the stop sign. Alexia froze, trying to determine which way the vehicle was going to go. She had a flash of the driver hunched over the steering wheel. Her mind shouted at her to move. Her feet refused to obey the command.

"Alexia!"

She heard the shout but still couldn't respond.

Couldn't move.

The van burned closer. From the corner of her eye, she saw Hunter bolt from his seat.

An arm clamped around her waist and yanked.

Tumbling to the side, she felt the blast of the van as it roared past. Heat rushed up at her as terror beat a new rhythm, magnifying the sounds around her.

"Alexia! Are you all right?"

Hunter's shout made her wince. The arm around her middle tightened, and she squirmed, desperate to draw a breath.

"I got it on video," a bystander offered.

Alexia pushed away from the arm that had saved her and sat up, grimacing at the new set of bruises she felt sure would show up.

Turning to thank her rescuer, she saw Chad Graham leaning in. His bloodshot eyes roamed her face. "Are you all right?"

Was she? "I think so."

A hand reached down and she grasped it. As though she weighed less than a feather, she was hauled to her feet and up against a hard chest.

A heart beat fast against her ear. Looking up, she saw Hunter's concern stamped on the lines of his handsome face. Swallowing, shaking, trying to control her harsh breathing, she stepped back and looked at Chad.

"Thank you."

What was wrong with her? Why had she frozen? She was used to reacting fast in a dangerous situation. But she'd felt paralyzed, unable to move.

"Sure." Chad's eyes narrowed as he took in the proximity of her and Hunter.

As she glanced back at Hunter, she saw his jaw tighten just before he asked, "What are doing here, Chad?"

"I saw your car in the parking lot. Thought I'd come in and join you." His gaze slid to Alexia. "Didn't realize you were expecting company."

Hunter seemed to brush off his brother's words as he turned and said to Alexia, "If you're sure you're okay, I'm going to call this in."

Nodding, she did another mental inventory. "I'm okay. Shaken, bruised, but okay." Her knee protested that statement, but she decided to ignore it. She could stand on it, so it wasn't a big deal.

With another worried look at her, Hunter turned to someone in the crowd, a crowd that was growing bigger by the second, and said, "I need your phone. I want that video. I'll make sure you get the phone back by tomorrow." The man offered it reluctantly.

Alexia took a step and stifled an involuntary groan. A scraped knee. A sore hip. She supposed it was a small price to pay for being alive.

"The back door of the van was open. It was one of those sliding kinds." Alexia looked to see who was talking. A young woman in her early twenties raked a hand through her straight brown hair.

Hunter scribbled in his notebook.

"And I tried to get a plate number, but it was covered up with something. Maybe mud or clay?"

More scribbling. Then Hunter slapped the phone to his ear and barked orders to whoever he had on the other end of the line. He was describing the van, hoping someone would spot it and report it.

Chad's fingers reached out to grip hers. "Anything else I can do for you?"

She squeezed his hand. "No."

"Come on, let's get you home. I'll drive you," he offered.

Straightening her spine, she balked. "Absolutely not. I'm hungry. I came here to eat and I'm not letting a little accident keep me from it."

But was it an accident? The driver had slowed, but the back door of the van had been open. She looked at the twenty-something woman. "Was there anyone in the back?"

"I couldn't tell if it was a man or a woman, but yes, there was definitely someone in the back next to the door."

Her stomach churned. After everything else that had been going on, she felt quite sure someone had just tried to kidnap her.

"He was waiting for me," she whispered to no one in particular. Then looked at Hunter, ignoring the fact that he was on the phone, and said, "Wasn't he? He was waiting for me."

A frown creased his brow as he pulled the cell phone from his ear. "I heard what she said. I've got the report in. It'll be on the news, so maybe someone will call it in. You can get your food while I talk to her."

Alexia shook her head as she headed for the restaurant. Chad fell in step beside her. She looked up at him. "Are you sure you're all right? You cushioned most of my fall."

He gave her a grin. "It was the highlight of my day."

Alexia flushed and felt a niggling of worry. She hoped Chad wasn't developing any romantic notions about her. Looking at Hunter, she saw he was on the phone again. She stopped and waited.

The conversation was short. He hung up and said, "The videotapes from the attack in the hospital parking garage are ready. As soon as we're done here, I'm going to head over to the hospital to watch them."

A police car pulled into the parking lot, followed by an ambulance.

Alexia ignored them and said, "I'll go with you. I want to watch them. I may see something important."

He hesitated and she narrowed her eyes and planted her hands on her hips. And winced. Her right hip throbbed, reminding her she'd just had a pretty rough landing.

Hunter shook his head. "All right, let's get this problem taken care of and then we can move on to the next. I've put out an ATL on the van. Maybe we'll be able to find it and get a clue about who was inside it."

"ATL?" she asked.

"Attempt to Locate. It was probably stolen. We'll check the reported stolen vehicles and see if one matches up to a description of the one that tried to run you down. From there, we'll get a plate number and send that out to every police officer in the state."

"Hey, what about lunch?" Chad's plaintive voice made her blink. She'd practically forgotten he was there. More guilt. The man had just saved her life.

Placing a hand on his arm, she said, "How

about another time? I really want to see those tapes."

Chad quirked a smile at her. "That's fine. I suppose I can't argue with that."

"Don't you have to get to work?" Hunter asked.

Chad's eyes darkened and his lips tightened. "No." He headed toward the restaurant, saying over his shoulder, "I'll get us something to eat. You can eat yours on the way to the hospital."

"Chad, you need to get checked out by the EMS . . ."

But Hunter's words were waved off as his brother never turned around.

An officer approached, followed by an EMS team. Alexia allowed them to bandage her knee but refused the offer of a ride to the hospital. And after she signed the form releasing them from any responsibility, they left her alone.

She wasn't hurt that bad. Besides, she wanted to make sure she was with Hunter when he left. She desperately wanted to see the videos of her attack. Silently analyzing her reasons for feeling so strongly about it, she decided she was just plain tired of being a victim. This was an opportunity to take some control and do something about it.

Hunter gave his statement to the officer,

then Alexia watched as he walked over to speak with someone who looked to be in charge of the whole scene.

As Alexia recounted the incident, suppressing a sick shudder as she relived the terrifying moment, she spotted Chad on his way back from the restaurant, a large bag of food gripped in his left hand and a smaller one in his right. She told the officer, "He's the one that saved me from being roadkill. He may have something to add."

"I'll be sure to ask him." The officer glanced at Chad as he approached. "I'll get your statement as soon as I'm done over here."

Chad nodded at the officer and sidled up to Alexia. He held out the larger bag. "Here. Wouldn't want you passing out from hunger."

"Thanks." Alexia took the bag.

"So, we'll do lunch another time." Chad gave her a wink.

Alexia wondered if her earlier comment had been a bad idea as she forced out a halfhearted smile. The awkward silence hanging between them was broken when Hunter walked up. He looked at the takeout bag in Alexia's hand and then at his brother.

"Thanks," Hunter said. "You didn't have to do that."

Chad gave them a brisk nod, turned on his heels, and headed toward the officer who wanted his statement.

Hunter looked at Alexia. "I think we're done here. Are you ready to head over to the hospital? Katie said she'll meet us there."

"Sure." More than ready to see the videos. Not so ready to see Hunter's partner, who probably still thought Alexia had something to do with Devin's death.

Alexia followed Hunter to his car. Once again, she'd be dependent on him to return her to her vehicle. He opened the door for her, and she slipped into the passenger seat, setting the takeout bag on the floor then buckling her seat belt.

When he was settled in the driver's seat, she asked, "Did you see the driver?"

"A glimpse, but I couldn't give you any details."

She'd been afraid of that.

"Hopefully, our tech guy at the lab will be able to pull something from the video."

"Hopefully." Shifting on the seat, she grimaced and decided she might need to pull out her old prescription painkillers to get some sleep tonight.

As he drove, Hunter tapped the steering

wheel with his left hand. When he realized what he was doing, he curled his fingers into a fist.

He was nervous.

"Are you okay?"

Alexia's question made him jump. He hadn't expected her to be that in tune to him. "Yeah. I just need to ask you something and I'm not sure how you're going to take it."

She lifted a brow at him. "Want to give it a shot?"

Blowing out a sigh, he glanced at her, then back at the road. "I have a dinner I have to go to."

He paused and felt her stare boring holes into him. "Yes? And?"

"I . . . uh . . . was wondering if you would consider going with me."

She shot him a suspicious look. "What kind of dinner?"

"My father's running for mayor. It's a dinner to raise money for his campaign."

"Seriously?" Suspicion went straight to disbelief. "Of all the people in this town, why would you ask me?"

Hunter cleared his throat. "I don't know. I'm not dating anyone and I like your company." He took his eyes from the road for a brief moment to meet hers again. "I like you. Why not?"

"Um, maybe because your father hates my guts?"

Hunter winced. "He doesn't hate your guts, he just needs to get to know you."

Disbelief colored her cheeks. "He was friends with my father who blamed me for burning down the house." Her eyes dropped. "Even my father hated me."

Hunter's heart squeezed at her very uncharacteristic, yet revealing statement. "My dad's not like that, I promise."

Alexia eyed him. "What about the case and the fact that I may be a suspect? Wouldn't me going to the dinner with you be a conflict of interest or something?"

He'd thought about that when he'd considered asking her to go with him. Now he shared the mental argument he'd had with himself last night. "You're not officially a suspect. There's no proof that points to you. You've not been arrested, you're not on the list of persons of interest." Although he had to admit, if she became a suspect, he could be in some serious trouble. It wasn't enough to deter him. He had a squeaky clean record. If he wanted to take Alexia to the dinner, he would take her. He was doing nothing wrong.

"I'm on Detective Katie Isaac's list." She

sounded a little bitter.

"Well, you're not on mine."

"Let me think about it," she hedged.

At the hospital, Hunter found a parking spot in the front, and they pulled out the sandwiches, making small talk in between bites. Hunter finished his quickly, while Alexia nibbled on hers and finally rolled up the leftovers. They headed into the building together. As they wound their way through the maze of halls, he noticed Alexia limping slightly.

"How's the knee?"

"It'll heal."

Her tight words told him she didn't want to discuss it. Hunter briefly wondered why he was so attracted to a woman who seemed to have no real interest in being in his company. *Lord, show me where you're going with this, please?*

They finally ended up in front of the room that said Security. Katie stood outside texting on her phone. She looked up at their approach. To Alexia, she said, "I hear you had a rough landing."

Alexia forced a smile. "Fortunately it was softer than it would have been if Chad hadn't knocked me out of the way."

"Chad, huh?" Katie lifted her brow to

191

Hunter, who frowned at his partner.

"Drop it," he ordered. Then lifted a fist to knock on the door.

21

Wednesday, 2:25 p.m.

Alexia followed Katie and Hunter through the door. Shivering in the cool building, she couldn't slough off the feeling of being watched. She looked behind her and saw nothing out of the ordinary. Just a hospital hallway full of people.

Telling herself she was just being overly sensitive, she pulled her gaze to her present location and took in the large room filled to capacity with monitors.

Ann Hyder, head of hospital security, was saying, "We have one of the best security systems available. Cameras are located all over the hospital that provide views of all building entrances and exits, in the hallways, elevators, and fire escapes."

"What about the parking garage?" Hunter asked.

"That too."

Alexia followed them into a side room

where Ann pulled a keyboard up onto the table and typed a few commands. A monitor to her left flashed and a picture came up.

Ann pointed and said, "You needed the footage from Monday night around 9:00 p.m. Correct?"

"A little after nine," Alexia said.

More tapping. Then the video started to play.

She leaned forward, determined to catch each and every detail offered by the video. "There's my car."

Hunter moved closer to her and she got a whiff of his cologne. She liked it. She liked his proximity. His strength, the way his eyes crinkled at the corners. In fact, other than his initial suspicion that she had something to do with Devin's murder, she really couldn't think of anything she didn't like about him. His father was another story.

Katie's voice intruded on her thoughts. "Can you switch cameras? That angle doesn't really give us a good view."

A few more clicks on the keyboard and Alexia saw her car enter the garage once more, this time from a different angle — and they watched headlights turning in to follow her. The vehicle waited while she parked. Then turned into a spot, pulling forward so all the driver would have to do was climb in and go. No wasting time backing out.

Alexia squinted. "I can't see inside the car. Can you zoom it?"

She felt a hand on her shoulder and then a light squeeze from Hunter's fingers. She looked at him and he smiled. "Good question. Ann?"

"I can give it a try." Her fingers flew over the keyboard and the car came closer. Along with a shot of the back of someone's head.

Hunter gave a grunt. "He was prepared for the cameras. He already had the mask on when he entered the garage. The parking spot was sheer luck for him. My guess is if that space hadn't been empty, he would have just jumped out and left his car running while he took care of Alexia."

She shuddered at the thought. Then wracked her brain trying to remember what he'd said. "Tell me."

"What?" Katie looked at her.

"That's what he said. 'Tell me.' Then you showed up and he didn't get to finish." In her mind, she heard the words clearly now.

Rubbing his chin, Hunter studied her. "So your attacker thinks you know something? He wanted you to tell him something?"

She shrugged.

"Or," Katie mused, "he was getting ready to play some sick game with you before he killed you."

Alexia shot her a black look. "Thanks."

Katie shrugged. "Sorry. I'm thinking out loud. But seriously, the hospital parking lot is a busy place. So is the restaurant. Seems to me that getting Alexia is a pretty high priority for someone or he wouldn't be willing to take so many risks by attacking her in such high traffic areas." Before Alexia could respond, Katie had already turned her attention back to the tape.

Alexia's nightmare unfolded on the screen before her. Her walk toward the elevator, the person behind her, hitting her as she spun, and then her fall to the floor of the parking garage.

When she watched him jam the gun into her temple, she flinched as she felt it all over again.

And then Hunter was there. Rescuing her.

Pulling in a deep breath, she just noticed that at some point during the viewing he'd placed an arm around her shoulders.

Katie's critical eye didn't miss his gesture of comfort. Uncomfortable under the woman's scrutiny, Alexia moved away from Hunter.

He shifted and said, "Not much help, is it?"

Katie shook her head. "But we now have a make and model. We can still send it up to the lab and see if our tech guys can get the license plate. I don't know how quick they'll be able to get to it, but it's worth a shot . . . I suppose."

Her last two words were said while eyeing Alexia, and Alexia wondered if the detective thought she'd set the whole thing up to throw suspicion from herself.

Eyes of blame. Feelings of guilt. Her past assaulted her . . .

"Come on, Alexia" — the deputy state fire marshal, Hunter's father, leaned toward her — "just tell me why you set the fire. Your dad was painting and you used the paint thinner as the accelerant."

"I didn't."

"Sure you did. Even your father says you did it. The father who's in and out of a coma. Why would you do that?"

Alexia jumped up from her seat. "I didn't! Okay? I wouldn't! I don't know!" She gripped her head as she struggled to remember exactly what had happened. How the fire had started. "We were arguing. I was getting Dad a beer . . . and I don't know. Then there were flames. And smoke . . .

and screaming." Tears streamed down her cheeks. "Please," she whispered, "I don't know. I can't remember. I . . ."

The memory made her blink. She hadn't relived that day in a long time. And this time the memory came with more details, bits and pieces she hadn't remembered . . . until now.

The beer. She'd been in the kitchen, getting her dad a beer. That was the first time that memory had popped up.

"Alexia?" Hunter's warm hand on her arm calmed her.

Her phone vibrated. "Excuse me." She stepped from the room before she said something to Katie that she'd regret. The more she was around the woman, the less she liked her.

Alexia pressed the talk button and lifted the phone to her ear. "Hello?"

"Hi, this is Lori Tabor. How're you doing?"

For a moment Alexia blanked, then her promise rushed back. Her classmate, the one on the reunion committee. "Oh, hi, Lori."

"Do you have a minute to talk?"

Did she? A glance back through the window showed Hunter and Katie in deep discussion. "Yes. A few minutes. What can I do for you?"

"We're having a meeting tomorrow night to discuss a few things. Would you mind meeting at my brother's house? He has plans with my nephew and I'm watching my niece."

Tomorrow? What was tomorrow? Wednesday? Thursday?

Thursday. She'd only been home two days? It seemed like a year.

"That should be fine. What time?"

"Let's say six thirty. That should give most people enough time to get home from work and eat a bit. I'll have some snacks here too."

"See you then."

Alexia hung up and turned back to see Hunter standing outside the door frowning at his phone.

"What is it?" she asked.

"My brother is once again up to no good."

"What's he doing now?"

Hunter sighed and slid his phone into its holder. He pulled out his keys from his pocket. "Getting ready to be arrested for drunk and disorderly. If his boss finds out about —" He stopped and shook his head. "Let me drop you off at your car and follow you back to Serena's. Then I'll go take care of Chad."

"I need to check on my mother."

"Right." He rubbed a hand down his cheek.

Alexia shifted, torn. She knew Hunter needed to leave and yet she didn't want to be stuck at the hospital. "Let me just call up there. If she's sleeping, I'll leave word with the nurse to let her know I called and then we can leave."

"Okay."

A minute later, she was on the phone with one of the nurses in charge of her mother's care.

"She requested something for pain only a few minutes ago. By the time you get up here, she'll probably be asleep again."

Alexia sighed. "All right. Tell her I asked about her, please?"

"Sure. Oh, here comes Pastor Stewart. She'll have some company after all."

Alexia swallowed. "Okay. Thanks."

She hung up and frowned. "I just really can't see this."

"What?"

"My mother dating her pastor. It doesn't compute."

Hunter gave her a slight smile. "Give it time."

Hunter felt his temperature escalating by

200

full degrees as he drove toward Serena's, his mind on his brother and his antics. The woman beside him remained silent.

"His wife left him," he finally said.

"What?"

"Chad's wife. She left him and took their six-year-old daughter with her. She rarely lets him see her. It's eating him up."

"Oh, that's awful." Compassion rang in her voice.

Hunter wondered why he was sharing such personal family information with her, but he wanted her to know. "I just want you to understand where he's coming from. What's going on with him."

"Did she leave him because he's a drunk?"

Her blunt words cut like a knife. Hunter shot her a glance. "He's not a drunk." At least not yet. "He's headed in that direction, I'll admit, but . . ." He sighed and rubbed his head. "This drinking thing is a new development."

The compassion in her gaze never wavered. Neither did the flat conviction in her voice. "He may not be an alcoholic yet, but much more of what he's doing and he'll be there shortly."

He blinked, not expecting that response. One minute she was full of sympathy, the next she was as blunt as his grandfather's old pocketknife.

"Why do you say that?"

"I lived with one for the first eighteen years of my life. I recognize a drunk when I come across one." A pause. "But I probably shouldn't have put it like that. I'm sorry."

She was comparing Chad to her father. As bad as his brother got sometimes, deep down he was a decent guy.

So what exactly had her father done to her? Visions of all kinds of abuse flashed through his mind and he shuddered. "Did he abuse you?"

"Yes. Emotionally and physically." She looked at him and sighed. "I see the question in your eyes. No. He never abused me sexually."

Relief threaded through him. Then compassion. "You're a survivor."

"I don't know about that." She shrugged. "I guess. I've done what I've had to do. If that makes me a survivor, then —"

His phone rang, cutting her off. He threw her an apologetic look and snatched the device from the holder on his belt. "Hello?"

"Chad's gone." The bartender's deep bass echoed in Hunter's ear.

"What do you mean he's gone?"

"Your sister came and picked him up."

Hunter's brows shot north. "Okay.

Thanks." He made a mental note to check on Chad later. For now, he found himself grateful for Christine's intervention.

Because the more he learned about Alexia, the more he wanted to know.

22

Wednesday, 4:26 p.m.

Alexia entered Serena's house and punched in the code to disarm the alarm. She planned to call to check on her mother, then take a warm bath to soak away the tensions of the day. Yoda greeted her with both paws to her midsection. She grunted and scratched her ears.

Hunter pushed against the door. "Will you let me come in for a few minutes?"

Yoda turned her attention to the newcomer and her ears dropped flat against her head until Hunter held out a hand for her to sniff. One whiff of the man and Yoda approved.

Alexia thought the dog had excellent taste; however, she wasn't so sure she wanted Hunter in her personal space. She bit her lip. Every moment in his company drew her closer to him. Made her like him more and more. And that made her nervous. Her track record with men didn't exactly inspire confidence in herself. If she was attracted to Hunter, there must be something wrong with him she hadn't figured out yet.

"Why are you bothering with me, Hunter?"

He stepped inside and shut the door. He cocked his head and studied her. Finally he said, "Maybe because I feel like you're worth it."

Alexia gave a short laugh devoid of humor — or belief. "Worth it? I'm not so sure about that."

Hunter took her hand and she let him. When he led her over to the couch and motioned for her to sit, she did. She also noticed that he didn't let go of her hand. Goosebumps popped up.

His blue eyes bored into hers. "You don't think you're worth it?"

"Hunter, come on . . . I . . ." She looked away, feeling emotion rise up in her. She wasn't ready to bare her soul to this man yet. If ever. Slipping into the place in her mind where she could gain control, she told herself not to let his compassionate eyes and strong shoulders lure her in. She couldn't depend on him for help. She'd learned early in life that the only person she could trust was herself.

And that didn't work out so great sometimes either.

"Seriously," he said, leaning in, "why don't
you think you're worth the trouble?"

She stood, her heart shaky, her emotions
on edge. Alexia had never had anyone be
quite so blunt with her before. "I don't want
to do this. Not now."

Hunter quit pressing. Leaning back, he
studied her and she wanted to squirm.
Finally she blurted, "Why is your partner so
hostile to me?"

He folded his arms across a chest she
wouldn't mind resting her head against and
pursed his lips. "I'm not sure," he admitted.

"Do you think you could find out? If she
and I have to be around each other very
much, it would be helpful if she didn't look
at me like I was something she'd like to
scrape off the bottom of her shoe."

A smile curved his lips. "Don't worry
about Katie, she'll come around."

She had her doubts about that. "What
time are you going to the Wickhams'
house?"

"After supper. Around seven thirty or so."

"I want to go."

"I don't think that would be a very good
idea." He frowned.

"Please, Hunter? I think I really need to

do this." She stared at her hands. "I couldn't save him. I couldn't stop what happened." She looked up. "But I can help find his killer. Mrs. Wickham liked me, but she's always been a timid, kind of shy woman. She'd probably feel more comfortable having another female there."

Hunter looked torn, then he stood. "I can always take Katie."

Alexia grimaced. "Oh yeah. She has such a gentle way about her."

He shot her a gently chiding look. "Let me think about it. I'll give you a call."

He headed for the door. She watched him step outside, then turn around to walk back to her and gently place a hand behind her head. Her stomach flipped as his head dipped. When his lips covered hers, she thought she might simply melt into the floor. The gentle sweetness of the kiss offered comfort . . . and maybe a promise.

He pulled back and stared down at her. "And for the record, you're worth it. I think so and so does God. One day you'll see that."

The door shut, but his words and his kiss lingered, leaving her reeling. Why did he have to bring God into it? Of all the things he could have said, that last statement hadn't been expected. Neither had that kiss.

Feeling antsy, she walked to the window and peered out.

Something swiveled around her left ankle and she jumped. Looking down, she saw Chewie, the cat, blinking up at her. "Hmm. Must be time to feed you."

As though the cat understood Alexia's words, she turned and headed straight for the kitchen.

Alexia turned to follow the feline. From the corner of her eye, she caught a hint of movement outside. She paused and stared, probing the scenery beyond. Serena's house sat on about an acre and a half of land. A few trees bordered the property, along with bushes and other shrubbery, giving it a feeling of isolation. Serena loved it. Alexia had found it peaceful at first.

Now, uneasiness with her isolation wiggled through her. She stood there for the next few minutes and saw nothing else that would account for the raised hair on her arms and her increased respirations.

Paranoia was not a feeling she was familiar with. Before the incident in Washington, she never worried that someone was out to get her or that she was being watched.

Now? She felt like something, someone, was out there, watching her. All the time. Just waiting for her to mess up and be alone so he could pounce.

Shuddering, she moved into the kitchen to feed the cat. Her cell phone rang, startling her, and she dropped the cat food can onto the floor. Grimacing at the sight of the splattered remains of Chewie's dinner, she grabbed the phone.

"Hello?"

Silence on the other end. She tried again. "Hello?"

More silence.

Just as she was about to hang up, she heard, "Don't think you can hide forever."

Chills swept over her. "Excuse me?"

"Your detective friend can't be with you all the time. I'll find you and you'll wish you'd never come back."

"Who is this?" she demanded. Her heart pounded in her chest. "Why are you doing this to me! What do you want?"

"Where's Jillian?"

"I don't know!"

"And what about Serena? Huh? Where is she?"

How dare he! Alexia snapped. "None of your business! I wouldn't tell you if I could."

"Then there's no reason to let you live. And this time I won't kill the wrong person."

Click.

Frozen fingers refused to cooperate. She

tried again and managed to pry her grip loose. She set the phone on the counter and backed away from it, then grabbed the landline handset and punched in the number she'd memorized when he'd given it to her.

It rang once.

She hung up. No, she had to collect herself. Her thoughts. Figure out what to do. Then she could call Hunter.

Shaking, she took a deep breath and paced from one end of the kitchen to the other, forcing her brain to work. She ran through what she knew.

Someone wanted to know where Jillian was. And Serena.

That someone thought Alexia knew where they were.

That someone knew Alexia's cell phone number.

The caller had seen Alexia with Hunter. The voice sounded similar to the one in the parking garage.

Her cell phone rang, jarring her once more, causing her heart to thump in anticipation of the whispery voice. Should she answer it or let it go to voice mail? She checked the caller ID. And let out a relieved breath.

Hunter.

"Hello?"

"Hi, did you just try to call me?"

She let out a wobbly laugh. "Sort of."

"Sort of?"

"Then I hung up."

A chuckle reached her ear. "I figured that out. What can I do for you?"

"I just got a . . . terrifying . . . phone call."

"You sound shaky. Tell me about it." His voice turned serious, all teasing aside.

She walked through the conversation word for word.

A swiftly indrawn breath was her only response for a few seconds. Then, "I'll have the call traced. I don't like it."

"Ha! *You* don't like it? I can't say I cared much for it either."

"At least you're keeping your sense of humor."

She sighed. "No. I'm really not. Sarcasm is my defense mechanism. I'm scared, Hunter. He said, 'Next time I won't kill the wrong person.' Sounds like Devin was killed because . . ." She swallowed, not wanting to finish the thought. "Someone seems to be after me and I'm not sure why."

"And it sounds like we need to find Jillian and let Serena in on what's happening. She told me that Jillian called her not too long ago when I asked what happened to her after high school, but as far as I know, Jillian hasn't been in touch with anyone since that last call."

"I haven't talked to her." Her concern for her friends deepened. "At least Serena's out of the country and safe, but Jillian . . . I just don't know about her."

"Well, somehow they seem to be connected to what's going on with you." A pause. "In the meantime, don't go anywhere alone."

"Then pick me up before you go to the Wickhams'. I'm coming too."

23

Wednesday, 4:48 p.m.

Hunter hung up the phone, concerned about the information Alexia had passed on to him. "And this time I won't kill the wrong person," she'd said. So Devin had been in the wrong place at the wrong time? And the killer had really been waiting for Alexia?

Maybe. It was something to consider.

But how would the killer have known Alexia would be home that day? Unless someone passed on that information? But who? And why? And why ask about Jillian?

Punching one number on his cell phone, he speed-dialed his partner. She answered on the second ring.

"Hello, Hunter."

"Katie, I need you to do me a favor."

"What's that?"

Hunter filled her in.

"You really think someone called her and

threatened her? What if she's making it up to throw suspicion off herself?"

"What if she's not?"

A sigh filtered to him. "All right. I'll run it."

"Thanks. And we need to see what we can find on Jillian Carter. Alexia said she hasn't talked to her since graduation night. But Serena heard from her not too long ago."

"Jillian Carter. Got it. I'll see what I can dig up."

"Thanks again."

Hanging up, he considered Katie's animosity toward Alexia and wondered at it. He'd never seen her act this way. Sure, she got hot tempered with some of the guys they put away, and she had a mouth that landed her in trouble occasionally. But when it came to an investigation, professionalism reigned. Usually. He made a mental note to question her. It was time he found out what was going on with her.

Hunter filed the thoughts in the back of his mind for later. Right now he was determined to check on Chad before he left to question the Wickhams. Not only that, if he had time in between, he wanted to do a little investigating into graduation night ten years ago.

Pulling into his brother's drive, he wondered how the man was making the mortgage payment. He hadn't worked much since the court had given Stephanie full custody three months ago.

Chad had made the mistake of picking a fight at the bar. He'd been arrested. Stephanie had pulled the trigger on both barrels, claiming Chad was an unfit father, violent and never there.

Although he'd never seen Chad violent and didn't agree with that accusation, sometimes Hunter wondered if Stephanie hadn't made the best decision. Then he felt guilty and disloyal for wondering. Hunter's parents were now in the process of filing for visitation rights. Chad wasn't the only one who'd been hurt in the process.

Hunter climbed out of his car and walked up the steps to bang on his brother's door.

Footsteps sounded.

The door opened and Christine stared at him with haunted, red-rimmed eyes. "Come on in."

Hunter entered the foyer and looked left into the great room where Chad lay sprawled on the sofa, snoring. Christine dropped into the chair opposite the sofa, and Hunter paced to the fireplace. The mantel was a shrine to the family Chad had lost. Michelle's sweet six-year-old face grinned back at him from a school photo.

He turned to Christine. "Is there any alcohol in the house?"

"I searched the house from top to bottom." Confusion buckled her brow. "I didn't find anything."

"Well, that's good at least."

Christine shrugged. "Mom called. She said she'd bring him over some food and coffee."

Hunter grunted. Were they enabling Chad? Allowing him to wallow in his destructive, self-pitying ways? Or were they keeping him from descending into a pit that he might never be able to climb out of? Indecision warred inside him. He just didn't know.

His phone rang. He looked at Christine. "Sorry, let me grab this."

"Sure."

Hunter pressed the button to answer the call. "Hey Brian, what do you have?"

"The video from the witness's phone."

"Yeah?"

"Not much, sorry. The man in the back had on a dark suit, but I couldn't get his face. With a little more work I might be able to get a good picture of the suit that you could match if you found one during a search or something."

Hunter blew out a sigh. "Thanks."

"Sure."

He hung up and turned back to his sister. "I can check on Chad later, before I head home for the night. I have to go talk to a family about their dead son."

"Devin?"

"Yeah." He studied her. "How well did you know him anyway?"

She shrugged. "We graduated together, of course, but I didn't hang out with him in high school. As for recently, I've come across him in the singles' group at the church. He seemed nice enough, I guess."

"Any sign of violence?"

Christine shook her head. "Devin? No. He was as meek as they come. I remember at a volleyball game, he missed a shot and some of the guys were ragging him about it. They were kind of mean too. His ears got really red and a muscle in his jaw started twitching. I remember thinking he was going to deck someone. Then he just shoved his hands into his pockets and walked away. A few minutes later, he was laughing with one of the ministers."

Devin had learned self-control in the past ten years? It wasn't impossible to believe. People changed. *He* sure had.

"Have you ever heard of him hitting anyone?"

"No." Her eyebrows pulled together at the bridge of her nose. "I told you. He was one of the most gentle souls I've ever met."

"What about a girlfriend?"

Christine gave an uneasy laugh. "What is this? An inquisition?"

"No, but when you mentioned Devin's name, it occurred to me that you guys were the same age, graduated high school together, and went to the same church. It stands to reason you might have some information I might find helpful in the investigation."

Her brow relaxed. "Huh. Well, I know he was interested in Marcie Freeman. They hung out a lot, looked like they might be more than friends. Guess you could start with her."

Hunter left his spot by the mantel and walked over to plant a kiss on his sister's forehead. "Thanks, Chrissy-mine."

She laughed. "You haven't called me that in forever."

"I know. You grew up on me. I miss the little squirt who used to follow me everywhere I went."

Christine lifted a brow. "You miss her?

Sorry, I'm not buying it. I used to drive you crazy."

Hunter laughed. "Yeah, you did."

"Get out of here." Her expression sobered. "I'll take care of him for a while, then I've got to go. We're having a reunion committee meeting tomorrow night at Lori's, and I haven't written the first note about what we need to talk about."

"You working tomorrow?"

"Yeah. I'm off Friday, though. It'll be nice to have a long weekend."

"Tell Rick hello for me."

A flush crept into her cheeks, confirming something he'd suspected for a while now. She was definitely interested in the man.

"Shut up," she said in a voice sweet enough to give him serious cavities.

Hunter left, his heart heavy with thoughts of his brother. But also with an anticipation at seeing Alexia again that was so sweet it rivaled his sister's tone. He pulled out his phone and punched in Katie's number.

Voice mail. "Hey Katie, I've got one more thing for you to run down for me, if you don't mind. Marcie Freeman. She and Devin were an item, according to Christine. Can you see what you can find out about her? Thanks."

He hung up, then dialed the number of the person he really wanted to talk to.

Still jumpy from her threatening phone call, Alexia jerked when the doorbell rang.

Hunter. She glanced at the clock. 7:18. Hurrying to the peephole, she looked out. Yep. Her heart thudded a little faster.

Opening the door, she gave him a smile. "Thanks for letting me go with you."

"Katie's working another angle of the case. I told her you would fill in for her."

Alexia raised a brow. "I'm sure that went over well."

One side of his mouth lifted. "Katie's not so bad. You just have to get used to her way of thinking and doing things."

Hunter's phone rang just as he pulled out of Serena's drive. "Hello?" He listened. "What?"

At his harsh tone, Alexia's ears perked up. She looked at him.

"I'll be there in ten minutes." He snapped his phone shut.

"Chad again?"

"Katie. Her house is on fire." The car lurched as Hunter's foot pressed the gas. He flipped the siren on and they sped toward the west side of town.

Alexia felt herself pale. Then the hunger

struck her. The urge to be suiting up, slipping on the gear. Fighting the flames that would destroy, greedily grasping at anything in their path. "What happened?"

"Not sure," he yelled over the siren.

"Is she all right?"

"Sounded furious, but not hurt."

Alexia held onto the side of the door as they screeched around a corner, then raced past the cars pulling over to get out of the way.

Soon, she could see the smoke in the distance. Then they were turning into the neighborhood. Fire trucks and police cars lined the street. One of the officers turning away traffic waved Hunter on through.

Alexia absently noted that Katie lived in a neighborhood similar to Serena's. Nice houses, manicured lawns. The kind of neighborhood she'd always dreamed of living in.

They pulled up next to one of the police cruisers and Alexia took in the scope of the fire.

"Wow." She breathed in horror, yet couldn't squelch the surge of fascination she always felt when confronted with the roaring monster.

Hunter's stunned expression said it was worse than he'd imagined. "She'll lose everything."

Alexia saw Katie standing back in the street, hands on her hips, expression hard as stone.

"At least she's alive," she said, compassion for the detective filling her in spite of their rocky relationship.

He nodded. "True enough."

They climbed from the vehicle and Alexia continued to watch the firemen battle the blaze. They'd already saturated the two homes on either side of Katie's and so far the fire hadn't spread.

But Alexia could tell this was going to be a long, hard fight. She wanted to join in, offer her expertise, beg someone to let her hold the hose.

But she couldn't. Because someone had taken that away from her.

Fists clenched, she realized she might have made a mistake in coming home. Maybe she should have fought to clear her name, find the person responsible.

"What are you doing here?"

Alexia spun to see Katie standing next to her. Her pale, soot-streaked features said she wasn't happy with Alexia's presence.

"I was with Hunter when you called. He drove straight here."

Hard eyes assessed her — then dismissed her.

Katie walked over to Hunter and he placed an arm around her shoulder.

A flame of jealousy fired through Alexia and she turned so she couldn't see them. What was she doing? The woman was his partner. Of course he'd want to offer her comfort. It didn't mean anything.

A car pulled up and parked. A man got out, flashed something at the officer in charge of keeping the crowd back. The officer let him through and Alexia gulped. Chad, looking ragged and hungover, approached her. "Are you all right?"

"What are you doing here? How did you know —"

"Chad?" Hunter called to his brother.

Chad looked up and gave a halfhearted wave. He looked stunned at the sight of Katie's house.

Hunter waved the man over and Chad patted her shoulder as he passed. "I'm here for you, Alexia. Whatever you need, okay?"

"What?" Where had that come from? She didn't want him to be there for her. She wanted his brother. The one with his arm around his partner.

"I'll be right back," Chad reassured her.

She ignored him, blinked and stared at

the flames. Memories of her life in Washington swept over her. She missed her job. Missed the camaraderie she shared with most of the other firefighters.

Her jaw tightened. And something shifted inside her.

Time to clear things up. She would find out what really happened the night of the fire so many years ago. She'd either prove her innocence or she'd own up to it and find a way to deal with it.

Then she'd go back to Washington and fight for her good name and get her job back.

Already, peace from making the right decision flowed through her. She saw Chad frown, say something, then shake his head. Hunter looked like he wanted to argue, but didn't have a chance before Katie turned on her heel.

The detective marched up to Alexia and her peace evaporated. Hunter pushed past Chad to follow Katie, frowning, the lines between his brows furrowed deep.

Something in the woman's eye made Alexia tense.

"Do you know something you'd like to share with us?" Katie spat. "First Devin's murder, then that attack in the hospital garage that you could have set up. Now this.

Come on, you have to know something."

"That's enough, Katie. You need to watch yourself." Chad defended Alexia, his eyes narrowed.

Alexia stared at the woman. "What are you talking about?"

Hunter gaped at his partner. "Katie?"

Shame appeared briefly on the woman's face. But then she shrugged and said, "She's not the little innocent you think she is. Your own father said —"

"I get it." Alexia interrupted her with a raised hand. Barely holding on to her temper, she glared at the two of them.

"Alexia . . ." Hunter's protest bounced off her ears as she turned her back on both of them.

Then she realized she couldn't storm off in a snit. She didn't have a vehicle. She'd come with Hunter. A quick glance at Chad and she decided against asking him for a ride. No sense in encouraging him in that area.

With as much dignity as she could, she looked only at Hunter. "I'll be in the car when you're ready."

She took two steps in the direction of the car when the explosion rocked her backward.

24

Wednesday, 7:32 p.m.

Hunter watched in disbelief as his car lit up the sky while Alexia hugged the ground. Bolting toward her, he snagged her arm and yanked her to her feet even as the fire chief barked an order to turn one of the hoses from the house to the car.

Pulling her with him to a safe distance, he felt her sag against him. Realizing her legs had given out, he let her sink to the curb. Shock twisted her features and he thought he saw tears standing in her eyes.

Fortunately, she'd been far enough away from the car when it had exploded that she wasn't hurt, but it didn't change the fact that if she'd started for the car less than a minute earlier, she would be dead.

His heart jolted at the thought as he wrapped his mind around the fact that someone had gotten close enough to his car to plant an explosive.

When? Who? How?

Katie stood apart from them, her eyes darting between her house and his car.

"I'll be right back," he told Alexia.

She simply nodded.

He went to Katie, watching her face twist with fury as hot as the flames that licked at her house. Leveling her gaze on him, she planted her hands on her hips. "She did this."

"Who?"

"Her!" An accusing finger pointed in Alexia's direction. "Somehow, she managed to do this." She snapped her head toward Alexia. "Where were you between two this afternoon and seven tonight?"

Alexia shook her head in disbelief, pulled herself to her feet, and approached them, ignoring the chaos rocketing around them. Mimicking Katie's stance with her hands on her hips, she demanded, "What do you have against me, Detective?" She flung a hand in the direction of the burning car. "I'd be dead if I'd been any closer! What makes you think I would do something like this?"

"Because Dominic told me all about you." With that flat statement, Katie spun on her heel and stormed away, leaving Hunter gaping after his partner while Alexia recoiled, stumbling back.

"Katie!"

"Leave her alone."

Alexia's dull voice pulled him to her side. Cupping her shoulders, he asked, "What did she mean by that?"

"I have no idea." Her eyes narrowed as shock fell away to be replaced by stiff-jawed determination. "But you can bet your badge I'm going to find out."

Alexia slumped in the passenger seat of the car that had been delivered to Hunter. They were now pushing ten o'clock. "We're not going to make it to the Wickhams' tonight, are we?"

Hunter gripped the steering wheel, brow furrowed, jaw tight. "Probably not. I'll call and ask them if we can make it tomorrow morning."

She asked him, "Will you pick me up in the morning or should I meet you there?"

"I'll give you a call and let you know what my schedule's like and if I even get in touch with them."

"Okay."

Hunter dropped her off at home with orders to get some rest.

Right. As if.

First thing in the door, she set the alarm.

Then she kicked off her shoes and scratched Yoda's head. As she went through the routine of feeding the animals and watering the plants, Alexia thought about the day. She was exhausted.

She'd almost been in Hunter's car tonight. She shivered as a wave of nausea coursed through her.

All right. Someone was after her. Who?

Grabbing a pen and a pad, she sat at the kitchen table and wrote at the top of the paper: People who might want to kill me.

My brother.

Person from Washington — whoever set me up to die in the fire. Paul Sanders?

Someone who thinks I know where Jillian and Serena are.

Katie?

Well, probably not Katie, but the woman sure acted like she couldn't stand Alexia for personal reasons having to do with Dominic.

One more person came to mind.

As though her fingers didn't want to write the words, they hesitated. Then she wrote:

My father.

She lay the pen down on the paper and stared at the last person on the list.

Was it possible?

The man had been severely burned in the

fire. He'd spent most of her senior year at a burn unit in Georgia.

When he'd come home, shortly before her graduation, still weak and scarred, his eyes had followed her everywhere. Promising retribution. And she knew she was on borrowed time at home. Because she'd known as soon as he regained his strength . . .

Even now the memory made her shudder.

And so she'd left. With her mother's harsh "encouragement" to do so.

Then two years later, her father had disappeared. Never to be heard from again.

Right?

Unless somehow he'd heard she was home and had decided now was his chance to get her. To get even.

For something she couldn't even remember.

And where was Jillian?

She thought about the phone call. Someone wanted to know where Jillian was. Shivering, she made her way into the guest bedroom. Yoda followed her and Chewie disappeared in the vicinity of the kitchen.

In the bedroom, she flipped on the light and stared at the surroundings. King bed with a mint green comforter, the attached bathroom done in matching green and tan colors. All the comforts she would have loved as a child. For the majority of her years, she'd slept on a mattress with a sleeping bag.

A lump formed in her throat as she envisioned her mother handwashing that sleeping bag, then hanging it out to dry in the backyard. Where had that memory come from?

"The washing machine was broken," she whispered. And Alexia had been sick with the flu. Tossed her cookies all over that sleeping bag.

And her mother had washed it. By hand.

Yoda lifted her head from her paws and cocked her ears toward her.

Alexia blinked and got ready for bed, but the image of her mother working to clean her bedding never left her. As she settled under the blankets, her eyes fell on the nightstand.

A Bible, with several pieces of paper stuck inside. She'd seen it last night, but tonight, she was curious. She placed it in her lap and let it fall open to the first piece of paper. A note from Serena.

"I was hoping I'd get to hang out with you some, but I guess it wasn't meant to be. I know you're having a hard time with everything and I want you to know I'm praying for you. You're a great friend,

Alexia, and a wonderful person. I've marked ten different passages that I think you'll find comfort and meaning in. The first one is John 3:16. Know that you're loved. That you're worth being loved. And that you're loved so much that someone died so that you could live."

Alexia studied the notes and wondered how much time Serena had taken to do that. Time she should have spent getting ready to leave the country. First Hunter, now Serena. Both had said, "You're worth the time and trouble."

Her heart warmed and she read the verse aloud. "For God so loved the world that he gave his one and only Son, that whoever believes in him shall not perish but have eternal life."

Shutting the Bible, she placed it back on the nightstand. And started to believe that maybe Hunter and Serena knew something she didn't.

Senator Hoffman yanked on his tie and let it fall to the bedroom floor. Another late night of campaigning, smiling, pretending all was right with his world.

November would be here before he blinked and the people would make their way to the polls. He intended to be the majority's choice. Right now, polls showed he had the lead.

His phone rang and he snatched it before Elizabeth woke up. "Hello?"

"We still have a problem."

"You've got to be kidding me. How hard is it to grab a woman?"

"Harder than you may think. She's become real buddy-buddy with Hunter Graham. All of the attempts to grab her have made her extra cautious. She's almost never alone. And when she is, she's barricaded in a house with an alarm system better than yours." A pause. "Any more notes?"

"No. And it's making my blood pressure go crazy wondering when the next one's going to arrive. I've instructed Ian that if I'm not home to get the mail, he's to make sure he gets it. I told some story about expecting a surprise for Elizabeth and not wanting her to see it."

"And he won't question that?"

"Ian?" The senator barked a laugh. "No. He's as faithful as a lapdog. I gave him a job when no one else would after his stint in prison. Trust me, he'll do whatever I need him to do." He sighed. "All right, maybe we need to turn our focus elsewhere. Lay off Alexia for a while and let her get comfortable. But keep an eye on her."

There was a slight pause from the voice. "I'm not sure that's a good idea . . . but we'll play it your way for now. I'll inform my contact."

"You do that."

25

Thursday, 8:17 a.m.

Alexia awoke to Yoda's nose in her ear. The dog was snoring. After pushing the dog off the bed three times last night, Alexia finally gave in and let her stay.

Rolling over, she groaned and punched the pillow. Yoda protested the sudden movement and hopped to the floor.

Her thoughts turned to what she needed to do today. Her mother was the first thing on her mind. Hunter, the second, and Devin and the Wickhams, the third.

She grabbed her cell phone and checked it. Two messages. One from her mother, who wanted to let her know she'd be speaking with the doctor in a short while but would call again later. A surge of guilt came over her. She really needed to make more time to be with her mother at the hospital. But her mother had Michael and didn't really need Alexia. Right?

Still . . .

The second was from Hunter.

"I can't get ahold of the Wickhams. I'll keep trying and let you know what's up. In the meantime, I'm going to be talking to Marcie Freeman. Talk to you soon."

She frowned. Why couldn't Hunter get in touch with the Wickhams? That didn't make sense. Their son was dead. An idea formed. It was probably a really bad idea, but once it was there, Alexia couldn't shove it away. The little voice in her head screamed she was crazy. The stubborn part of her said she didn't care. She wasn't going to live her life in fear. Alexia punched Hunter's number in and let it ring.

Straight to voice mail. She left a message. "Hi, Hunter, I got your message. I'm going to go over to the Wickhams' and see if they're home. Maybe they took the phone off the hook or something. It's better than sitting around here all day staring at the walls."

Within fifteen minutes, she was ready.

Ten minutes after that, she pulled into the Wickhams' driveway. The house looked exactly like she remembered, just a little more worn, like upkeep wasn't a priority. The garage door was open and an older model Buick made itself at home inside.

Frowning, Alexia put the car in park and stepped out of the vehicle. Nothing odd about the Wickhams' car being parked in the garage, but if they were home, why weren't they answering the phone?

She walked up to the front door and rang the bell. No sign of life inside. Alexia pressed it again, then tried to see in the side window, but the small white curtain blocked her view. She stepped off the porch and walked around to the garage.

Maybe they'd taken a second car. But where would they go? And why would they leave the garage door open?

She made her way inside the garage to the kitchen door.

Their son was dead, but no funeral arrangements had been made yet. The investigating detective wanted to speak with them, and they'd rushed home to do that. Something just didn't feel right.

Alexia rapped her knuckles on the door.

It swung inward.

That little voice inside her cranked up the volume. *Get out. Leave. Wait for Hunter.*

But she couldn't.

Her heartbeat doubled and the adrenaline kicked in. Just like it did when she was about to enter a burning building and walk right into danger.

Her gut said she was being stupid as she stepped inside. Just like it did when she found Devin.

"A smart girl would run, Alexia," she whispered to herself.

You've been running all your life. When are you going to stop?

Not today.

She spun to leave and slammed right into a hard chest. Hands gripped her upper arms and her scream turned into a smothered gasp.

Hunter tried the Wickhams' one more time. He looked at Katie. "Busy."

"Again?"

"Yeah. After we talk to Marcie, let's head over there and see what we can find. The Wickhams probably took the phone off the hook once the press got wind that they were home." Changing the subject, he asked, "What did you get on the phone call to Alexia? The one who threatened her?"

Katie looked at her notes. "I pulled her records. And there was a call to her cell phone just like she said."

"Let me guess. It's from a prepaid cell?"

"Yep."

"So, another dead end." With a sigh, he pulled into the parking lot of First Bank of

Columbia, Marcie Freeman's place of work, and climbed out of the car. Katie followed him up the walk.

Before they went in, she laid a hand on his arm. "You know she could have made that call herself. Bought the prepaid cell and simply called her number. Ran through the conversation to make it look like she was on the phone with someone for a while and then called you."

Hunter stared down at his partner.

"You are really determined to lay all this at her feet, aren't you?"

She snorted and removed her hand. "No, Hunter. I'm trying to wrap my mind around every possible scenario so I don't get sucked in by a pretty face and wide, innocent eyes."

Biting his tongue against what he really wanted to say, he growled, "And that's what you think I'm doing?"

She shrugged. "I don't know."

"And in the four years that we've been partners, has that ever been an issue."

She blinked and her shoulders drooped a bit. "No. You're right. It never has."

Slightly mollified, he shot her an irritated look and pulled the door to the bank open.

The blast of cool air-conditioning felt good after being out in the blazing heat. Summer in the south. You'd think he'd be used to it by now.

As he and Katie walked into the bank, several tellers worked their stations. He zeroed in on the one who matched the picture on the driver's license he'd pulled that morning. Five feet six, one hundred forty pounds, green eyes, blond hair. And a pretty smile with white teeth that made her stand out.

Approaching the woman, he waited until she finished with her customer, then flashed his badge. Her eyes widened. "Can I help you?"

"Is there someplace we can talk?"

"Um. The break room?"

"Sure."

Marcie moved her "next window" sign in front of him and said, "It's behind you to the right. Down the hall. Second door on the left. I just need to tell my manager that I'm stepping away from my window."

Hunter nodded and motioned for Katie to precede him.

A minute later, they all took a seat around the conference table. "What's this all about?"

"Devin Wickham," Katie said.

The color left Marcie's face. "Oh. What about him?"

Hunter frowned. "You did hear what happened to him, didn't you?"

She swallowed. "Yes." Tears filled her eyes and she looked away. "I did."

"I'm really sorry we have to ask, but do you know who would want to kill him?"

Her eyes rose to meet his. "No."

"Were you dating him?"

"Yes." She flushed. "I think he was going to ask me to marry him. I think." Marcie crossed her arms in front of her and shifted her eyes to the door. Then to the table.

Hunter exchanged a look with Katie.

Katie leaned forward, her gaze intense. "What is it you want to tell us, Ms. Freeman, but are unsure about saying?"

The woman fidgeted, froze, and looked up. "Nothing. Why would you ask that?"

"Your body language."

Hunter tapped his chin and studied the woman. "Were you afraid of him? Of Devin?"

Now she met his gaze. "No, not him."

"Then who?"

"Whoever else he was seeing. I don't want to believe it, but . . . I'm not sure what to think, to be honest."

Katie threw up her hands. "Okay, now I'm thoroughly confused. Do you mind explaining?"

Marcie drew in a deep breath. "Hold on a

241

minute. I'll be right back." Hunter rose and she looked at him. "I promise. I need to get something from my purse to show you. I'll only be a minute."

He nodded and Marcie slipped from the room and returned with a piece of paper. She handed it to Hunter, who read it out loud. " 'Stay away from him. He's mine.' "

"Any idea who wrote this?"

She shook her head, her face finally crumbling as her stoic posture gave way to grief. "No. I really wish I did, but I can't for the life of me figure out who could have written it. Devin never ever gave me the impression there was someone else."

Katie sighed and took the note by the corner. "We're probably not going to be able to get anything off of this, but we'll send it to the lab to try. When did you get this?"

"It was in my mailbox about three weeks ago. Someone came by my house and put it there." She shrugged. "I almost threw it away, but I kept it thinking I would ask Devin about it."

"Did you ask him?"

She shook her head. "No. I just . . . I don't know why I didn't." Marcie sniffed. "Maybe I was afraid of what he'd tell me."

Hunter leaned forward. "Could you make a list of Devin's friends for us? Anyone you know for sure he had contact with?"

"Sure, but I know I won't cover them all. I didn't know a lot of his co-workers before he was laid off, and then he was doing odd jobs for people around their houses and stuff. He was very handy that way. But I'll give you what I can."

"That'd be great." Hunter handed her a card. "Just email it to me as soon as you can."

"Chad!" Alexia gasped. "What are you doing here?"

Clear blue eyes, very much like Hunter's, stared down at her. "I thought I'd come check out the Wickhams. Christine said Hunter was going to question them. I thought I'd see what they had to say too."

"Are you crazy?"

"Probably."

She stared at him. He looked like a different person. Sober and well put together. Professional. It was a new look for him, and she was glad he seemed to be making the effort to help himself.

A suspicion nipped at her. "What do you do, Chad?"

He looked at her. "What do you mean?"

"What's your occupation?" That suspicion grew . . .

"I'm a cop. A detective, to be precise." He flashed her a grin.

She wasn't even surprised. She'd already taken note of his professionalism when he'd rescued her from the speeding van. For some reason, she'd had a feeling he was a cop. "Of course."

He lifted a brow at her. "What's that mean?"

"Nothing. But I don't think you should be here. This is Hunter's case."

The grin morphed into a sneer. "Yeah, well, I have some questions of my own that I want answered, and I don't want to wait on Hunter to ask them."

She'd let the brothers hash this out. "The kitchen door was open."

He blinked. "What do you mean, 'open'?"

"When I got here. I spotted the car in the garage and figured someone was home. Nobody answered the front door, so I decided to try this one. When I knocked, the door cracked open."

His hand went to his gun, his eyes to the stairs behind her.

Alexia swallowed. "I got this really creepy feeling I shouldn't go in."

"Well, let's find out. You stay out here and let me check it out."

Alexia nodded.

Chad eased the door open a fraction more and stepped inside. "Mr. Wickham?" he called. "Mrs. Wickham? This is Detective Chad Graham with the Columbia Police Department. Your back door is open. Is everything all right?"

No answer.

Alexia bit her lip. Were they being paranoid?

Maybe.

A flashback to the masked intruder at her mother's house made her shiver.

Better paranoid than dead.

She stepped over the threshold, keeping her eyes on Chad's back.

As he crossed the kitchen and entered the den to the left, he came to an abrupt halt. Then bolted forward. "Call 9-1-1, Alexia! We need an ambulance."

Alexia grabbed her phone and punched in the numbers even as she ran into the den to see what was wrong.

As the operator came on the line, she saw Chad drop to his knees next to a body.

"What's your emergency?"

She caught sight of gray hair. "Oh no," she whispered.

Chad moved to the next person laid out on the floor in front of the couch. "She's still alive."

"Ma'am?"

Alexia rattled off the address. "Someone tried to kill them," she whispered.

The operator's voice sharpened. "Kill who, ma'am?"

"They need help. Please send help."

"Help's on the way. Just stay on the phone with me."

Alexia set the phone down and rushed forward to help.

Devin's parents.

Sorrow welled up and she swallowed hard. Then went into first responder mode. Just like she'd done when she'd found Devin bleeding to death on her mother's basement floor.

Moving quickly, she noticed the blood from a wound in Mrs. Wickham's chest.

Alexia rushed into the half bath she'd seen off the hall from the foyer. She grabbed a towel, ran back to Mrs. Wickham's side, and pressed it against the wound.

The woman's grayish color didn't bode well. "Come on, hang in there." Alexia hadn't been able to save Devin, but maybe she could save his mother. She looked for other wounds, but didn't see anything.

Chad said, "I need to look around. Whoever did this may still be here."

Her head snapped up. "You need to wait

for backup."

"I need to get the guy that did this and I can't have you sitting here as a target. Now get up and come with me. I need to make sure you're not a sitting duck if the killer is still here."

Sirens reached her ears. "Some of this blood has dried — it looks like she's been bleeding awhile." She kept pressure on the wound. "I'm not going anywhere. If she loses any more blood, she'll die for sure."

He looked torn.

Footsteps sounded in the hallway, and he pivoted, gun pointed straight at Hunter's chest.

Hunter froze. "Chad?" He looked beyond his brother. "Alexia?"

Katie strode up behind Hunter. "What's going on here?"

"The guy may still be here," Chad snapped as he pointed his weapon at the floor. "Ambulance is on the way for Mrs. Wickham. The husband didn't make it. I'm going to check out the back."

Hunter and Katie immediately drew their weapons.

"I'll go with you," Katie said to Chad.

With that, they disappeared, weapons ready. Hunter strode toward Alexia. "How's she doing?"

"Not good."

"What are you doing here?"

She glanced up at him. "I woke up and got your message this morning. Thought I'd come pay my respects. Tell them how sorry I was that I couldn't —" She stopped and looked away.

He thought he caught a sheen of tears in her eyes, but when she glanced back up, they were gone.

Katie reentered the room. "All clear in the house, I told the paramedics to come on in."

Paramedics made their way inside. Hunter slid his weapon back into his holster and watched as they took over the work on Mrs. Wickham.

Alexia held her hands out in front of her and stared at them. Once again, she had someone else's blood on her hands. Hunter placed a hand under her arm and gently propelled her out of the house where he helped her wash them off in the back of the ambulance.

As he dried her hands, she looked at him, eyes red, yet dry. But the emotion in them nearly tore him in two. "What's happening, Hunter?" she whispered.

After a moment of hesitation, he pulled

her to him and she rested her head on his chest. "I don't know, Alexia, but you sure seem to be caught in the middle of it."

She let out a humorless laugh. "I didn't ask for this."

"I know."

A van and two other vehicles pulled up next to the house, and Hunter stepped back. "CSU's here."

She nodded. "All right."

Chad stepped out of the house and Hunter met him halfway between the front door and the ambulance. "What are you doing here?"

Chad shrugged. "I was bored."

Anger swelled up in Hunter's chest, and with effort, he shoved it down. "Bored, huh?" He swallowed the words he would regret if he let them pass his lips. "I see. Well, how did you know to come to the Wickhams'?"

"Christine may have mentioned you planned on questioning them this morning."

Hunter nodded and gazed at the house. "This is my case, Chad. I don't need you messing with it."

Hurt crossed his brother's face and Hunter wondered if it was real or affected. Chad said, "Thanks, bro. I try to support you and this is what I get?"

Drop it, he ordered himself. He sighed. "You look good, Chad. Glad to see you back on the job."

A grin that most ladies couldn't resist replaced the hurt. "Yeah. It feels good."

"What brought on this change?"

A nonchalant shrug, but his eyes were on Alexia. "It was time."

Alexia watched the action in the room. Katie ignored her as she discussed the case with Chad and Hunter.

When CSU arrived, Hunter and Chad filled them in. Finally, the two brothers were distracted. Alexia walked up to Katie and asked, "What do you know about Dominic?"

Katie simply looked at her. "What do you care?"

"I care, okay? Is he all right?"

The detective shrugged. "I guess. Last time I heard from him."

"When was that?" Alexia gritted her teeth. What she wanted to do was grab the woman and give her a good shaking until everything she knew spilled out of her.

"About three years ago, okay?"

"No, not okay. Where was he? What was he doing?"

"I don't know. He called to check on your mother. I haven't heard from him since." She clicked her pen shut. "Now, are you done with the questions? I've got a case to solve."

"Wait." She placed a hand on the detective's arm. "Please. Did he say anything about our father? Did he —" she swallowed — "did he ask about me?"

"No. To both questions."

Hunter turned back to Alexia, his eyes darting between his partner and the woman he was falling for. Something had just gone on with them and he wondered what it was. He walked up to Alexia. "Are you ready to go home?"

Yes. "No. I need to go to the hospital to see my mother. She's already called me like five times since I stumbled on the Wickhams. I need to see what she wants. I also need to tell her about Devin — and now, his parents."

"Come on, I'll give you a ride."

"I can take you if you want." Chad's voice rang between them.

Alexia looked surprised. "Well thanks, I appreciate that. But I have my car here, remember?"

"Sure, no problem." Chad gave another

one-shouldered shrug, but Hunter thought it looked forced. As did the smile.

She looked at Hunter. "I want to talk to you about what you learned this morning when you talked to Marcie Freeman."

He nodded. "I'll meet you at Serena's house. You can drop your car there, and I'll drive you to the hospital to visit your mother."

"Okay. Give me a little time. I —" she looked at the house that contained the crime scene and shuddered — "need a shower." Alexia turned and walked to her car.

Hunter noticed Chad's eyes following her until she climbed in. Then Chad looked back at Hunter and gave an odd little smile.

"What?" Hunter frowned at him.

"May the best man win."

26

Thursday, 11:42 a.m.

Back at Serena's house, Alexia took a long, hot shower and thought about the incidents of the morning. She couldn't believe Devin's father was dead and his mother close to it. Who had wanted them dead and why? Sheer coincidence that they were attacked so soon after their son was murdered? No, she wasn't buying that one. There had to be a connection. But what? None of it made any sense.

She dressed and made ready to meet Hunter. He still had some things to take care of at the Wickham house, but he should be here soon.

As she walked down the hall to the kitchen, Yoda followed at her feet. Scratching the faithful animal behind the ears, she couldn't help but wonder what Hunter had learned from Marcie. And why did that name sound so familiar?

She poured out the morning's coffee, rinsed and refilled the coffeemaker, then filled the animals' bowls.

The knock on the door made her jump. Yoda padded over to it and sat on her haunches as she waited for her to look through the peephole.

Her heart stuttered and her pulse jerked. Hunter was here. Placing a hand on her stomach, she waited a few seconds to give the butterflies time to settle.

Opening the door, she pulled in a deep breath and smiled.

"You ready?" he asked.

"As I'll ever be, I suppose."

They climbed in the car and Hunter glanced at her. "I got a call from Chief Granger."

"Who?"

"The guy investigating the fire at Katie's house."

Wariness filled her. "What'd he say?"

Hunter's fingers tapped the wheel. "It was arson. The person used paint thinner as the accelerant."

Alexia froze. Paint thinner. The same kind of accelerant that had been used in the fire that had burned her home to the ground as a teenager.

More tapping. "My car had C-4 in it.

Traces of paint thinner were also found there."

She gulped, unsure what to say, how to respond. She looked at him. Did he think she had something to do with the fire? She'd been all alone when it was set — she had no alibi. And as for his car . . . "Hunter —"

"He also said they found something at the fire."

Apprehension coursed unabated now. "Come on, Hunter, quit tiptoeing around whatever it is you're trying to tell me." She looked up and blinked. "And why are we back at my mother's house? I need to get to the hospital."

He parked in the drive and sighed. "They found a piece of jewelry that belongs to you."

"Me?" she squeaked. "How would they know my jewelry?"

"They don't. I did." He pulled out his phone. "Katie texted me this."

She looked and gasped. The letter *X* on a silver chain. "What? That's not possible." Alexia exploded from the car and hurried up the front walk. Jamming her key in the lock, she twisted it and raced to her room. Heart pounding, pulse racing, she stood in the doorway and forced air into her lungs.

She heard Hunter calling her name even

as his footsteps charged after her. Her gaze landed on the desk. The necklaces all lined up in perfect order.

Except for the one that was missing.

Hunter watched her walk toward the necklaces as though in a trance. One by one, she checked them, then turned to him in disbelief. "It's really not there."

"Who else has access to this house?"

"I have no idea."

"Then I suggest we visit your mother and get a list."

Still looking a little dazed, she nodded. "Right."

Back in the car, Alexia was silent for the first few minutes.

"What are you thinking?"

"That I should be ashamed of myself," she whispered.

He blinked as her words sank in. "Excuse me?"

"I've been a selfish brat."

"What brought that on?"

"I've been trying to think of who might have a key to my mother's house and realize I don't have a clue. I should have at least a clue."

"It's been ten years, Alexia." He kept his

voice soft, nonjudgmental. At least he hoped he did.

"I should have made more of an effort to get in touch with her. Leaving those stupid messages —" Her voice caught. "She apologized to me. For being a lousy mother."

"Hmm."

She looked at him. "I guess it's my turn to apologize to her for being a lousy daughter."

He glanced at her from the corner of his eye. "You've grown up, Lex."

Silence filled the car until she blew out a soft breath and asked, "What did you learn from Marcie Freeman?"

"That she and Devin were dating. But it looks like he was also seeing someone else and that someone didn't particularly like the fact that Marcie was in the picture."

She blinked. "Really? How did Marcie know that?"

"Marcie got a note telling her to back off from Devin."

A frown pulled her brows down. "But that doesn't make sense. Devin is the one who was killed."

"I know. You're right. It is weird."

"Unless Devin did something that made his killer mad."

"Ya think?"

She rolled her eyes. "Well yes, of course, Devin did something to get himself killed. But that still doesn't make sense because the person on the phone specifically said, 'Next time I won't kill the wrong person.' "

Hunter blew out a breath. "Yeah. And with Devin's father being murdered, his mother barely hanging on . . ."

"Can you find out who sent the note to Marcie?"

"I sent it to the lab. My guess is the person wore gloves, and it looks like it was written on standard white copy paper. I doubt we'll get anything off of it. Our best bet is asking around to see if anyone knows who else he was seeing — or someone who was interested in seeing him. Could be some kind of stalker thing going on here."

"Try the church."

"Yes. That's our next step. Apparently he was pretty active. Knew lots of people. I'm hoping someone will have something to tell me that will lead me somewhere besides another dead end." He smiled. "You're starting to think like a cop. Good job."

He pulled into a spot near the entrance to the hospital reserved for security. "But first, let's see who has access to your mother's house."

They walked through the lobby doors and

headed for the elevator. The ride to the fourth floor was a quick one. Once off the elevator, Alexia led the way to her mother's room. "I wonder if she has company."

She got her answer as soon as she approached the cracked door. Voices from inside the room grabbed her attention. As did the mention of her name.

"I can't ask her that."

"You have to. Right now, she's pretty much your only hope."

Alexia frowned at Hunter, who lifted a hand to knock. She motioned for him to stop. To listen.

He raised a brow and shook his head. Alexia felt shame creep up into her cheeks. Right. Eavesdropping wasn't exactly very ethical. Alexia turned to knock.

"She'll think I only want to make amends so she'll help me out."

She let her knuckles come into contact with the door as she processed the words. Her mother needed her help? With what?

"Come in."

Alexia pushed the door open and stepped inside. Hunter followed and she nearly jumped when she felt his hand at the small of her back. His touch shivered through her, but the silent gesture of support meant so much more.

Her mother lay in the bed, looking frail and wan. But at least she was awake and talking. Michael Stewart sat in the chair beside her, holding her hand. Alexia nodded at him and he smiled his welcome as he stood and held out a hand to Hunter, who shook it.

"I'm Hunter Graham, a friend of Alexia's."

Friend? She looked at him in surprise. She would have thought he'd introduce himself as the detective on the case. Then she remembered. No one had told her mother about Devin yet.

"Hi, Mom."

"I've gotten your messages."

"Great." Could the conversation get any more stilted? She sighed. "How are you doing?"

A weak smile crossed her face. "I've been better."

"What is it you think I can do to help you out?"

Her mother flinched, then lifted a brow. "What makes you ask that?"

"I was in the hall and heard part of your conversation."

Uneasiness flickered on the pale features. "It's nothing."

"Tell me."

"Not right now." The sharp words stung.

Alexia stared at her for a few seconds, then shrugged. "Fine then." She'd drop it for now. Maybe her mother didn't feel comfortable talking in front of Hunter. "Um . . . I need to give you some bad news." Her gaze landed on Hunter, who gave her an encouraging nod.

Michael moved closer to her mother, his hand tightening protectively around hers.

"Devin's . . . dead."

Her mother's harsh gasp echoed in the room. Then she asked, "How? What happened? When?"

"He was killed Monday night." Should she give her the details? "Um, Mom? He was killed in your basement. I . . . found him when I got here from Washington. It's one of the reasons I've been so scarce around here. I'm . . . sorry."

The woman gaped at her. "Oh Lex. Oh no," she whispered.

"I . . . understand you were helping him out." Alexia hoped her mother would fill her in, but she didn't want to press her or put any stress on her.

"Yes. I was." Her mom breathed out, closed her eyes, and leaned her head back against the pillow. "He was having a hard time. I let him move in the basement apartment."

"Mom, Hunter is a detective, trying to find Devin's killer. He needs to ask you some questions."

Eyes still shut, her mother nodded. "All right."

Hunter asked, "Is there some reason he didn't move back in with his parents?"

Faded green eyes opened. "He didn't get along with them."

"Why not?" Alexia asked.

Her mom looked at Michael as though asking permission for something.

He nodded. "I think you need to tell them as much as you know. It might help them find out who killed him."

Her gaze turned toward Alexia. "I got to know Devin through a Bible study at church. He was a very confused young man at first, but as he started to realize God's love, it was amazing to watch him change, to become confident in himself, in who he was created to be."

"What?" Alexia stared, dumbstruck. Who was this woman? Her mother talked about God like he was a friend or something.

Kind of like Hunter did. And Serena.

"Anyway," her mother continued, "throughout Devin's childhood, his father was very abusive toward his mother — and still is. I didn't want him going back there. He and his father had had some pretty bad . . . incidents, and I told him he didn't need to put himself back in that situation."

She motioned for the cup of water on her end table. Alexia reached for it the same time as Michael. He withdrew his hand with another smile. Alexia held the cup so her mother could sip.

"Thank you."

"So you let him live with you."

Her mother's eyes met hers once more. "It was a temporary arrangement. Just until he could get another job and get back on his feet. He had decided to save his money and open his own lawn care business. Living rent free was helping him do that faster." She shrugged. "And he took care of things around the house that I couldn't do."

"He didn't have any other friends he could have stayed with?" Hunter asked.

A frail shoulder in a half shrug. "He said no."

"Do you know anyone who might want to hurt Devin?"

A frown creased her mom's forehead. "No. Certainly not."

"What about his parents? You know anyone who would want to hurt them?"

"His parents? No." Confusion rippled across her face. "Why?"

"Someone tried to kill them too," Alexia whispered.

Shock held her mother speechless. Michael made a sound in his throat and Alexia looked at him. Wrinkles pinched his forehead and his face had paled to the color of parchment.

"His father's dead and his mother is in critical condition."

After a few seconds of processing this news, Alexia's mother said, "I'm not sure anyone knew their family secret other than Michael and the few people in our Bible study. And none of us wanted to do them harm. We just wanted to help them."

Hunter said, "Can you tell me anything about a woman Devin was dating? Marcie Freeman?"

Her mother raised a shaking hand to scratch her nose. Her eyes closed and she swallowed.

"Mom?" Alexia frowned and touched the soft hand lying on top of the blanket. "Are you all right?"

The concern she felt for the woman who'd basically thrown her out of the house ten years ago surprised her. But this was her mother. And Alexia cared.

"Just tired." Her grimace said it was more than just fatigue bothering her. After a deep breath, she opened her eyes. "Marcie's a young woman in our church. She and Devin had been dating for about a year. I think he was planning on asking her to marry him."

"Really?" Hunter looked to the silent pastor standing by, watching the interactions. "Did you talk to him much? Did he say anything about the women in his life?"

Michael shook his head. "Women? There weren't any women as far as I know. As for Marcie, she's a great girl. And while Devin and I talked extensively about his childhood and his plans for the future, he never mentioned dating anyone else."

"A secret life?" Alexia suggested.

"No." Michael shook his head. "Not Devin. He was an open book."

Alexia noticed her mother had fallen asleep. She stood. "I guess we'd better go and let her sleep. I think this visit wore her out."

Hunter looked at Michael. "Do you think you could give me a list of people who have access to Mrs. Allen's house?"

The pastor scratched his head. "I'll be glad to try."

Hunter handed him a piece of paper and a pen.

A knock on the door made Alexia swivel.

Lori Tabor stuck her head in and smiled. "Hi. I hope I'm not interrupting."

"Not at all." Alexia motioned her in. "She just fell asleep."

Lori entered, a vase of flowers clutched in her right hand. "Oh well, that's okay. I had told her I'd come by sometime today."

Hunter took the flowers and placed them on the counter next to the sink.

Lori smiled. "Thanks." She looked at Alexia. "How's she doing?"

"She's hanging in there."

"I came yesterday too, and we had a nice chat, but she seems to get tired very easy."

"She does."

"Well, I won't stay. Tell her I'm thinking about her. And see you tonight, right?"

The reunion committee meeting. Right. Alexia swallowed a groan and forced a smile. "Right. See you then."

Lori wiggled her fingers and headed out the door.

Alexia smacked her forehead.

"You okay, Alexia?"

Hunter's question brought her head up. She met his gaze. "I agreed to help with the reunion committee. We're having the first meeting tonight and I just don't know if I'm up to it. That's all."

"Here." Michael held a sheet of paper out to Hunter.

Ten minutes later, armed with the list of names, Hunter and Alexia walked out of the hospital and toward his car. The sun beat down and she broke into a sweat. Her nerves tightened as she glanced around. Staying hyperalert was getting tiring, but she couldn't relax her guard.

Beside her, Hunter glanced at the list. "Okay, we have a ton of information but no real leads. I need to sit down and process all of this."

"I want to look at that list and see if I recognize any of the names."

He handed it to her.

She frowned. "Michael, her pastor, has a key. What does he need a key for?" Without waiting for him to respond, she continued. "A couple of her friends from church. A Mrs. Love and a Mrs. Hardy. Devin had one."

"And yourself."

Alexia snapped her gaze up to his. "Yes, and me." She gave a fake smile. "Thanks for pointing that out."

"Anytime."

"I don't know Mrs. Hardy, but I remember Mrs. Love." Alexia frowned. "She lives one street over from Mom. She would bring food over every Christmas Eve. And she was the one woman my father couldn't intimidate. She was one of the reasons I started standing up to him." She blinked. Where had that memory come from?

But once she opened the door on it, she remembered more. The time her mother had been so sick and in excruciating pain, Alexia had been scared to death. Her father had refused to get her help. Alexia had snuck out of the house and run to Mrs. Love, who had promptly called for an ambulance. Her mother had been in the hospital for six days after her appendix ruptured on the way. The doctor said if she hadn't gotten into surgery when she did, she would have died.

Mrs. Love's voice echoed in her mind even now. "You saved your mom's life, Alexia. Good job, hon."

Alexia saved the memory to dwell on later.

"I'm going to call Katie and give her these names," Hunter said. "She can do a background check, a little digging, and see what she comes up with."

"Okay. I'm going to call a locksmith and have the locks at Mom's house changed." She waited while Hunter made the call to Katie. When he hung up, she said, "Anyway —" Her foot caught on a piece of cracked cement and she stumbled.

Hunter moved fast and caught her arm.

She looked up to thank him but startled when a puff of dust blew up right in the very spot Hunter had been before moving to grab her.

Then she found herself facedown in the hospital parking lot. Heart thudding, she rolled with Hunter as he grabbed her and pulled her back toward the building. A bullet slammed into him and he spun backward, jerking her with him.

27

"Hunter!"

"Keep going!" He gave her a shove.

She looked. The door to the hospital was much too far away. She'd be exposed. The only cover available was the short brick wall that surrounded the nearby fountain.

And Hunter was hurt.

People screamed and scrambled for cover. Hunter had his phone in one hand, his gun in the other. The blood pooling on his shirt didn't seem to bother him. But it bothered her.

He'd been shot.

But how bad?

Not bad enough to slow him down. A slight comfort.

Alexia made it to the back of the brick wall and scrunched behind it. Two and a half feet tall, it was the best choice for protection at the moment. As long as the shooter didn't move and angle for a better shot from a higher elevation. Her back felt exposed, like it had a big red target on it.

Hunter slammed into the small space beside her, his pained groan reaching her ears. "Officer needs assistance." Vaguely, she heard him bark the location. "I've got a shooter."

He screamed at a couple exiting the building across the street. "Down! Down! Get back inside!"

They froze and ducked back into the office just as another bullet zipped over the wall to dig into the post next to Hunter's head. Alexia swallowed a scream and scuttled forward next to him. "He's shooting at you!"

"Looks like it," he muttered as he adjusted his gun in his hand. "I can't get a location on him. He's hiding pretty good."

"How bad are you hit?" Concerned, she eyed the circle of blood that seemed to grow with each passing moment.

"Just a graze, I think." He grimaced. "Burns like fire." He rotated his arm and hissed. "But no major damage. That's good."

"Let me take a look at it."

"Later. I'm all right."

Alexia studied the surrounding area. Tops

of buildings. Parked cars. Nothing. "Where is he?" she whispered.

"I don't know. Stay down."

Sirens rent the air. Help was on the way. Alexia pulled in a shuddering breath. "He stopped shooting. That's good, right?"

"For now." His gaze met hers. "Just because he's not pulling the trigger doesn't mean he's not there."

Alexia dropped her head into her hands and closed her eyes. With danger coming at her from all sides, she was beginning to think she should have stayed in Washington.

But someone had tried to kill her there too.

Hunter peered around the edge of the wall and waited. His arm hurt like crazy, but he didn't think the wound was too bad. Ignoring it seemed like the best idea for now. He knew a SWAT team would be deployed. But until they got here, he needed to do something.

From what he could tell, everyone had taken cover. A few cries and screams still reached his ears. But he didn't think anyone else had been hit. So far, only three shots had been fired. All at him.

He glanced at his watch. Three minutes had passed since the last shot.

Alexia huddled beside him. A fierce anger shifted through him. Who was doing this and why?

Slowly, he lifted his head. And caught sight of someone running across the top of the doctor's building just across the street, heading for the parking garage. Hunter grabbed his phone and spoke into it. "The pediatric office on Forrest Drive. Tall, thin, dressed in black. Has a mask on."

"Got it."

"Where's the SWAT team?"

"On the way."

"That's not fast enough," he muttered under his breath as his eyes tracked the possible destination of the shooter. The parking garage. Lots of places to hide — or grab a hostage.

Hunter nudged Alexia's arm, and she looked at him with such rage in her eyes, it almost froze him for a nanosecond. He understood it wasn't directed at him, but still . . .

He looked at the hospital door thirty feet away. "You need to stay put until I tell you to move, got it? The door's too far, you'd be exposed too long."

She narrowed her eyes. "Where are you going?"

"I'm going to catch this guy. Wait here."

"Hunter —"

"I'm serious, Alexia. Don't move until you get the all clear."

Without another word, he popped up to race across the street.

Alexia sat there, fury churning in her gut. Not to mention a healthy dose of fear. She watched Hunter weave across the circular drive, keeping behind parked cars and as much cover as possible as he made his way closer to the building where he'd seen someone on the roof.

Gunfire erupted, bullets popping around him, hitting the ground in front of him. One ruptured the window of the car he now hid behind. She wanted to scream at him to stop. She knew he was determined to get to the shooter. But at what cost?

More terrified screams renewed in pitch and volume at the onslaught of the bullets.

Please don't let him die.

Was that a prayer? If God was listening, definitely.

Hunter had pinned his badge to his shirt in plain view. Her eyes flicked from one spot to the next. Everyone still kept out of sight. Cops in protective gear swarmed the area, yelling commands and doing their best to stay out of the line of fire.

Hunter disappeared around the edge of the building and Alexia waffled. Did she just sit and wait?

Another shot rang out and she ducked instinctively. More screams echoed all around her. But the shot hadn't come from the roof this time. The parking garage?

A young woman to her left screamed and broke free, racing toward the parking lot to the left.

The older man with her yelled, "No, Jeannette! Come back."

But the woman was beyond reasonable thought, her fear propelling her.

Another shot sounded.

Jeannette staggered and fell to the ground.

"No-no-no-no-no," Alexia whispered. "Don't do this. Why shoot her? You're not after her. You want me. Or Hunter."

And she knew she had no choice. Alexia narrowed her eyes and tried to see how bad the woman was hurt. The woman's left hand grabbed at her wounded shoulder as she rolled toward a parked car, trying to get cover. But the angle was all wrong. If she rolled under that vehicle, the shooter could still see her from the garage. At least she thought that was the case.

Maybe not. Maybe she would be just fine. Maybe.

Alexia calculated the distance between her and the woman and the nearest shelter.

More shots fired in rapid succession. Another person screamed and Alexia knew someone else had been hit. But the bullets weren't coming her way this time, so she dashed across the exposed area and grabbed the woman by her uninjured arm. "Come with me!"

Hysterical sobs ruptured from her, but she didn't fight Alexia's propelling grip. She staggered to her feet and allowed Alexia to steer her toward the security guard's box in the parking lot.

Stumbling, shoving the woman along, Alexia slammed her way into the box to find the security guard on the floor. The man looked up and scuttled back against the wall. Alexia pushed the woman inside, crawled in after her, and snapped the door shut.

A bullet shattered the glass above her head.

Hunter ducked into the parking garage and spoke into his phone. SWAT had finally arrived and knew he was there. His boss knew he was there. Both had ordered him back as they swarmed the doctor's office next to the garage.

"He's not there anymore!" Hunter gritted into the phone. "I saw him run across the top of the roof. Get the parking garage covered."

"We've got it," his boss's bass voice echoed in his ear. "Now get back and let the SWAT guys do their job."

"Yes sir. I'll do my best." But by this time, Hunter was already in the garage. To leave now would possibly expose himself to the shooter. He was safer in the garage.

A car door slammed and Hunter froze.

An unsuspecting innocent who'd arrived after the shooting? Or the shooter trying to get away? Hunter couldn't believe the person would be so stupid as to actually park in the parking garage. But you never knew.

Keeping his weapon in front of him, ignoring the fire shooting down his wounded arm, Hunter moved in the direction he thought the sound had come from. His black rubber-soled shoes made no noise on the concrete floor. Then he saw the SWAT team enter the area. The lead man pulled up short when he saw Hunter and slammed his rifle to his shoulder, the barrel pointing at Hunter.

Hunter flashed his badge and the man gave him a short nod, turning his weapon to the right. A finger to his lips, Hunter then gestured toward the sound, indicating the men should head that way.

Another nod and a signal to the team behind him.

And another sound behind them.

One SWAT member bolted to the man exiting the stairwell. "Freeze!"

The man dropped his briefcase and lifted his hands into the air. "I . . . I'm just trying to get to my car. I need to get out of here." Sweat ringed his armpits, terror made him shake.

The SWAT member took care of him as the rest of the team fanned out in different directions. Hunter scooted to the next pole and fell to the floor, his eyes scanning every corner, crevice, and shadow under the cars. Then above the cars.

Back under the cars.

A pair of legs. Crouched beside the car. Looked like nice linen pants. His guess was another innocent bystander, but he took no chances.

He crept in that direction, taking silent, measured steps. He rounded the back end of the car and pulled his badge with one hand and kept his weapon ready. "Ma'am?"

She whirled and opened her mouth to scream. Then saw his badge and managed to swallow her fear and part of her scream.

"Where's your car?"

"This one."

"What's your name?"

"Sandy Sanford." She swallowed hard but kept her eyes on him.

"Get in the car and lock it. Lie down on the floorboard and don't move until some-one comes to get you."

She nodded. Two quick jerks of her head. Then she opened the door and did exactly what he said.

Into the phone, he let his captain know about the woman in the vehicle along with the license plate number, make, and model. A quick check would be made on her.

He stayed near the car. Looked under it. Around it.

Nothing.

The garage was well-lit but contained more hiding places than he was comfort-able with. It wouldn't be hard to ambush him or the SWAT team. However, Hunter felt like the shooter had hightailed it out of there. Escape would be his number one priority right now.

Weeping reached his ears.

He swung his head in the direction of the sobs and picked up the pace. Two rows over he saw another woman huddled against her car.

Several SWAT team members surrounded them while still others branched off to continue the search of the parking garage.

"Ma'am?" Hunter asked. "Are you hurt?"

His gaze flicked to the lead SWAT member. The man studied the surrounding area, alert and ready for a trap.

Hunter saw the woman's hands shake as she lifted her head. Recognition hit him in spite of her disheveled, tearful appearance. "Lori?"

She nodded, her skewed ponytail bobbing on one shoulder. Sweat dripped from her forehead. "He was here. He — he had a rifle. He shoved me down." She swiped a hand under her nose, then scrubbed her eyes. "He said he was going to kill me. Then he heard you running and he made me sit here. He told me not to move or he'd kill me. I . . . I didn't move, I promise." The last word squeaked out on a sob.

Once again Hunter felt the rage well up in him. He patted the terror-stricken woman's shoulder as his eyes scanned the parking lot once more. Where had the shooter gone? His gut tightened. They'd covered the area and nothing. How was that possible?

She started to stand and he motioned her

back down. She immediately slid back down the side of the car to crouch on the garage floor.

"Stay there," he said. "If you stand, you might expose your head."

He watched as she gripped her purse to her stomach. Her eyes darted, probing, looking for her attacker. Her fingers twitched as she pulled in a hitching breath. Her gaze came back to him. "So, is he gone?"

"I think so. I don't know how, but yeah, looks like he managed to get away."

Hunter could tell his words had an immediate calming effect. Her shoulders slumped in relief.

"Did you see his face?" he asked her.

"Not really. He had a mask on."

Of course he did.

Hunter gestured to the car. "Is this yours?"

Lori shook her head and pointed behind her. "It's over there. He came up on me before I had a chance to get to it."

The SWAT team returned from their search. Hunter looked at the man in the lead. "Anything?"

"Nothing." The ferocious frown said he wasn't happy about it either. "I don't get it. It's like he disappeared into thin air."

"Clear over here," a voice to his left.

"Clear on the bottom level."

And so it went until the parking garage was declared safe. Free of the shooter.

Who had disappeared.

Hunter itched to get back to Alexia and make sure she was all right. He said to Lori, "These guys will take care of you. Okay?"

She nodded. "I'm fine. Now that I know he's gone."

Hunter signaled to the lead SWAT member that he was leaving. The man tilted his head in acknowledgment and Hunter took off toward the last place he'd seen Alexia.

He had to flash his badge and shove through officers, medical personnel, and another SWAT team before he arrived at his destination.

The fountain. And of course she wasn't there.

He whipped his head to the right, then the left. "Alexia!"

It was impossible to see through the crowd.

"Hunter!"

Behind him.

He whirled to find Alexia exiting the security booth. An injured woman stumbled with her. Hunter jogged over and did a visual inventory of Alexia while an EMS worker took over and began assessing the injured woman. Hunter zeroed in on Alexia. "Are you in one piece?"

She lifted a brow and even offered a slight smile. "I'm in one piece. You?"

"For now." When his boss got through with him, he might need a whole roll of duct tape to put the pieces back together. But he couldn't get out of that garage without endangering himself. His boss would understand.

He hoped.

"Did they get whoever was shooting at us?" Alexia asked.

"No." He couldn't help that the word came out clipped, hard, angry, frustrated. Which was fine. It was how he felt about the fact that the shooter got away.

Surprise lit her eyes. "I would have thought he would have been easy to pin down in the garage."

Hunter shook his head. "I don't understand it. We had him right there. And he got away clean." He rubbed his jaw with his good hand. The brief thought that he ought to get the wounded shoulder looked at crossed his mind.

"How? Did he leave the weapon?"

"No. There wasn't a trace of him."

"But . . ." She trailed off, her brow furrowed.

Hunter shook his head. "I know. We'll get him, though. He's going to mess up eventually."

Frustration stamped itself on her pretty face. "Eventually? Before or after he hurts someone else?" She gestured toward his arm. "You need to get that taken care of."

He understood what she was saying. Unfortunately, he couldn't offer her any reassurance. However, he could try to pull some strings in a few areas. "Come on. Let's do everything we've got to do here. Then we're going to do some digging into some things."

"Like what?"

"Like your family members who have grudges against you."

"Oh. Right."

As Hunter walked with her to the area where she would give her statement, he used his phone to email his contact at SLED, the South Carolina Law Enforcement Division, and asked for an update on Dominic and Greg Allen, Alexia's brother and father.

And then he might get someone to look at his arm.

It hurt.

28

The senator closed the drawer to his desk, sat in his leather chair, and shut his eyes. He longed for a good night's sleep again, but felt quite sure that such a blessing was not in his immediate future.

He looked at the gun collection on the wall. A collection he'd taken pride in for a long time. Like the 1894 Colt Bisley. Or the .44 caliber Wild Bill Hickok "Dead Man's Hand" 1851 "Aces & Eights" Black Powder Revolver. His antique revolvers — all thirty-four of them. He'd invested a small fortune in the guns and now wished he could get rid of every single one.

Instead, he was stuck looking at them every day. A reminder of his skeleton in the closet. The one Jillian seemed determined to unveil. The one Frank Hoffman was just as equally determined to keep buried.

Then again, maybe God had decided it

was time for Frank to fail. That it was time for the senator to reap what he'd sown.

Frank shuddered. "Stop it. Paranoia will only get you in trouble."

And he'd been able to skirt the edges of trouble all his life, never getting caught, never being blamed for the mischief he caused. Only this time, it wasn't mischief. This was serious stuff.

Frank sat up and blinked. This situation wasn't his fault. It was Jillian's. If only she'd accepted the social boundaries and knew her place, none of this would be happening.

Yes indeed, he thought as his anger grew. If Jillian had just stayed on her side of town, everything would be fine.

Only she hadn't and now she was taunting him, mocking him. Threatening him.

No one threatened the senator.

It was time to get a little more involved. If the people he paid good money to couldn't resolve this problem, then he would have to take matters into his own hands.

Hands that he'd managed to keep fairly clean.

Hunter clicked the mouse and the screen lit up with the information he was looking for. His arm throbbed, but he ignored it. He had more important things to worry about.

Like crimes reported graduation night ten years ago. Out of the twenty-three, Hunter was interested in four of them.

A breaking and entering.

An armed robbery at a convenience store.

The murder of a homeless man.

And a shot reported in one of the nicest neighborhoods in town. When the police arrived, they could find nothing amiss. They'd even gone door to door, questioning the residents. Nothing.

Could Jillian have seen one of those? Been a part of one? But why run? Why not report it? Unless she'd been the one to instigate it or was involved in it somehow.

But he didn't get that from Alexia's story. Jillian had been scared. Terrified, as Alexia put it. Seen something she shouldn't have seen.

He studied the details of each crime. Nothing stood out to him. Except maybe the shooting. But nothing had been found at the time ten years ago. And nothing of that nature, in that neighborhood, had been reported since.

Hunter glanced at his phone, wishing his contact would get back to him about Dominic or Greg Allen. He frowned, wondering what was taking so long. Usually Brian was much faster than this. How hard could it be to locate someone? Unless they were dead or in the CIA, Brian could find anyone.

Dead.

The possibility had occurred to him. But if they were dead, he was back at square one looking for other suspects. And Alexia wasn't on the list. His list anyway.

Katie's? Well, that was probably another story.

As though thinking about her conjured her up, Katie stepped into the office.

Hunter waved her over with his good arm. "Hey, I want to run something by you."

Katie pulled up a chair and settled next to him. "What are you doing?"

"Going over everything with this case. Will you be my sounding board?"

"Sure. I've got some news, though."

"What's that?"

"Mrs. Wickham just died."

Hunter winced. He figured it would happen but had prayed the woman would live long enough to at least be able to tell them who attacked her and her husband. He would have to tell Alexia.

He focused on something he *could* make a difference in. "We've got a dead body in Hannah Allen's house."

"And a suspect with bloody hands."

Hunter shot her a look. "She didn't do it, Katie."

Katie rolled her eyes and shrugged. "I think she had reason to."

"Why? Because the guy was living in her mother's house and she was jealous?"

Katie lifted a brow. "Was she?"

"I don't think so."

"Well, I think so, and I also think you're attracted to her and are blinded by your hormones."

He blinked. Felt anger stir. "And I think you've held a grudge so long against a woman you never met that you're grasping at any opportunity to stick it to her. Accusing her of murder without any solid evidence? How can you justify that?"

Katie bolted to her feet and planted her hands on her hips. Outrage spit from her gray eyes. "No solid evidence! We walked in while she still had his blood on her hands. You found that box with Wickham's blood on it and the knife inside it. My house burned to the ground and she doesn't have an alibi, but her necklace is at the scene. Your car blew up just minutes after she rode in it. What more do you need?"

"More than that." He kept his tone even. "Her story checks out. She couldn't have hidden that knife. There was no time. And how do you know she doesn't have an alibi?"

"I asked her where she was. She says at home. Alone. With no one but a couple of pets to verify she was there. I need more than that. Sorry."

He had to admit when she laid it all out like that, the trail led right to Alexia. However — he blinked. Trail.

"There was no blood trail to her room," he said.

"What?"

Excitement filled him. "There was no blood trail. From the basement, all the way up to her room and under the bed. Not a spot of blood. If she'd killed Devin and raced upstairs to hide the knife, she would have left evidence behind."

Katie frowned and for the first time, doubt flickered.

"Then how did the knife get in the box under her bed?"

Hunter ran a hand over his jaw as he considered her question. A question he'd already asked himself a dozen times. "I don't know. I just know she didn't put it there." He clicked his pen. "She has a theory, though."

"Of course she does."

"She says the killer had the box in his hand when she saw him run from the basement. He took it, put the knife in there, intending to frame her."

"And you just happened upon him putting the box back in her mother's house."

He nodded. "Sounds crazy, doesn't it?"

"Yep."

"But not impossible."

She shot him a sad look. "She's gotten to you. You've fallen for that little-miss-innocent routine too. Well, she tried that back in high school and look where that got everyone in her family. She turned her own brother in to the cops and she burned her house down. Not to mention the fact that her sister committed suicide because she couldn't live with the way she looked after the fire."

Hunter held up a hand to stop her. "Look, I knew Alexia back in high school too." He felt a flush creep up the back of his neck. "Trust me, I watched her my entire senior year, wishing I had the guts to tell her to dump Devin and take a look at me. But I didn't. And then when she finally did dump him, I couldn't get her to give me the time of day."

Katie's jaw dropped. "You're kidding. You had a thing for her back in high school?"

Hunter rolled his eyes at her shock. "Look, I'm only telling you that to make my point.

She's not like you're making her out to be. She wouldn't do the things you're accusing her of. She was a gentle soul in high school. And a wounded one."

"Which makes her all the more likely to commit a crime as an adult."

Hunter stopped and raised a brow. "You just made that up."

"Yes, I did, but I still think she knows more than she's letting on."

His phone rang, saving him the trouble of arguing with his partner any more. "Hello?"

"Hey Hunter, Brian here."

Now maybe they'd get somewhere. "What you got for me?"

"Okay, I've got nothing on Dominic Allen."

"You're kidding."

"Nope. My guess is he's either living on the streets, dead and his body never found, or he's unofficially changed his name. Could really be anything. His trail ran out about eight years ago. He was arrested for drugs at the age of seventeen here in Columbia. Never served a day."

"What?" Now that was news. "What happened?"

"Dunno. Charges were dropped."

"Weird." Hunter thought. "Who was his arresting officer?"

"Cop by the name of Marcus Porter."

Hunter wrote the name down. "What about Greg Allen?"

"Now he was a challenge. I managed to trace him for a couple of years after he left Columbia. He was working under the name Greg Adams. Then he got into a fight with a guy in a bar. Killed the guy with a broken beer bottle. Slashed his throat. Was found guilty of manslaughter and served about nine years. He got out three months ago and was employed at a gas station. His last known address — Winthrop, Washington."

Shock rippled. "Washington?"

"Yeah. That mean something to you?"

"It might." Might mean more to Alexia than him, though. "What's his most recent address?"

Brian gave it to him. "Do you know how many Greg, Gregory, et cetera, Allens there are in the country?"

"Not a clue. You sure this is our guy?"

"I'm sure. He finally confessed his real name to his cell mate. The cell mate told a guard and the information filtered up to be put into the system. It just took me awhile to follow the trail."

"Good job. I appreciate it."

When Brian hung up, Hunter looked at Katie and filled her in on the conversation.

Then he asked, "Have you found anything on Jillian Carter yet?"

She frowned. "No. And that's kind of weird. I know she took off the night of graduation. I trailed her to a hotel about a hundred miles away where she used a credit card. Then the trail ends. It's like she dropped off the face of the earth."

Hunter blew out a frustrated sigh and looked at Katie. "Something happened ten years ago in this city. Something that Jillian Carter witnessed. Something that had to do with Alexia and Serena. I'm finding it really interesting that as soon as Alexia comes back to town, she's a target." He thought it through and said, "And the man in her mother's basement was stabbed in the throat."

"Not exactly a beer bottle," Katie said, "but yeah, I can see why you'd want to look at Greg Allen."

"A grudging admission, but I'll take it."

Katie wrinkled her nose and rolled her eyes.

He shook his head, unable to put everything together. It would help if he had all the pieces. "I've got an errand to run. I'll catch up with you later."

Alexia sighed as she pulled the brush

through her hair. Everything in her wished she hadn't agreed to be at the reunion committee meeting tonight. Then again, she wondered if she might find out some more information about Devin and his parents.

Sadness filled her as she thought of the small family. Her initial attraction to Devin had died a quick death back in high school, but she'd always liked his parents well enough. Especially his mother. And the woman had seemed to take a liking to Alexia. Maybe because she hoped Alexia would be the daughter she'd never have.

Who knew?

Regardless, their deaths impacted her in a way she hadn't expected.

Tossing the brush onto the dresser, she grabbed her purse and headed out the door. And pulled up short.

An unmarked cop car sat in front of her house.

She walked to the curb and he rolled the window down.

"Hello, Alexia."

"Chad? What are you doing here?"

He smiled and flashed a dimple. Her heart lurched. He looked a lot like Hunter when he did that. "I'm keeping you safe."

"By following me wherever I go?"

Chad shrugged. "With all of the crazy

stuff that's happened over the last few days, Hunter asked for a few volunteers to keep an eye on you. I'm off duty today so I volunteered."

Alexia didn't know whether to be touched — or creeped out. "Oh. Um . . . thanks."

"I'm on duty until ten."

"And after ten?"

"Jackson Mann will be here."

She stared at Chad. "But . . . why? Why would they volunteer to do that?"

His lips thinned. "Because Hunter asked. And when Hunter asks for something, he always gets it."

Chad's jealousy made her shudder. "Chad —"

He held up a hand and his features lightened. "Look, it gives me something to do other than sit at home pondering whether or not I'm going to go to my favorite bar and toss a few back. I can't drink if I'm doing this." He flashed her a weak grin. "You're doing me a favor."

What could she say to that?

The ten-minute drive to the meeting passed without incident. Still, she couldn't keep from looking in her rearview mirror the entire drive to see if someone other than Chad was behind her.

She pulled into her old neighborhood,

drove past her mother's house, and pulled up to the curb in front of Avery Tabor's home. Chad parked behind her. Three cars were in the drive. Two others were parked on the curb like hers.

And that's when the nerves hit her. What would these people think of her? Would they just remember the girl accused of setting fire to her family home, or would they be willing to know who she was today?

She had a feeling she might be in for a rough night. All of a sudden she wanted some comfort. Someone to tell her it was going to be all right.

God? Are you there, God?

Never mind then. She could do this herself.

Lifting her chin, Alexia stared at the well-lit house. She had nothing to be ashamed of, nothing to hide. They could take her as she was or she'd leave.

A longing for Hunter pierced her in spite of her silent reassurances. She wanted him by her side. She wanted the security he represented to her. And that made her even more determined. She'd gone this long without a man in her life, she sure didn't need one now.

But I want one.

Climbing from the vehicle, Alexia did a

scan of the area, checking for anything that made her feel uncomfortable, uneasy. She had to admit Chad's presence eased her nerves quite a bit.

When nothing jumped out at her, she walked up to the front door, took a deep breath, and rang the bell.

Footsteps sounded and within seconds the door swung open to reveal a little girl in a pink sundress. Blond curls tumbled around her shoulders and a shy smile hovered on her lips.

Alexia felt her heart melt. "Hello. I'm Alexia. Who are you?"

"I'm Mary Ellen. I'm seven. My brother, Bradley, is nine. He's with my daddy doing a 'guy thing.' " Alexia choked back a laugh when the little girl wiggled her fingers as though putting quotation marks around the last two words. Then she shrugged. "Whatever that means."

The smile widened into a grin and Alexia could see the child was missing her two front teeth.

"Very nice to meet you, Mary Ellen. I'm here for the committee meeting with your Aunt Lori."

Mary Ellen stepped back. "Come on in. Everyone's in the den."

Alexia followed the little girl through the

foyer, down a short hall, and into a nice-sized den already filled with chattering people. Most of whom she recognized. Chairs made a circle within the space. Toys lined the shelves near the fireplace. Little army men surrounded a fort made out of popsicle sticks.

"Alexia!" Lori called as she headed over. "Come on in. I think you know everyone."

A hush fell over the group as all eyes turned on her.

She ran down the names in her head. Harry Chumley, Carl Standish, Erin James, Patricia Hammond, Leslie Monroe, Christine Graham, Lori Tabor, and herself.

And one person in the corner she didn't know. Or didn't remember.

Lori took her arm and faced the group. "Y'all remember Alexia."

Cautious smiles appeared. Christine, former senior class president, rose and walked over to give Alexia a hug. "Glad you could make it, Alexia. Hunter's talked a lot about you."

That seemed to break the ice.

One by one they greeted her. The one person she didn't know was from another graduating class and the spouse of Harry Chumley.

In the back of her mind, though, Alexia

couldn't help wondering exactly what Hunter had said to his sister about her. Must have been good if the girl was offering her a hug. Apparently the Graham children didn't hold their father's opinion of her.

Then she had no more time to ponder. Lori handed her a bottle of water and opened the meeting. Alexia found herself in charge of the food. She would contact different catering companies and get prices.

The meeting passed in a blur as she tried to remember if any of these people had had a relationship with Devin. But for the life of her, she couldn't put his face with any of them. Being on this committee might just be a huge waste of time for her. And yet, surprisingly, she found herself laughing and reminiscing a bit as talk turned from business to socializing.

Alexia nodded to a picture of Lori and two men dressed in army fatigues. "I didn't realize you served in the army."

Lori picked up the photo. "Yeah. Right after high school. I didn't have a clue what I wanted to do with my life, so I enlisted."

"Who're the two men?"

A soft expression covered the woman's face. "This one is Avery, my brother. He was a medic with the special ops team. This one was Jackson Peters. He was special ops too and was killed right before I got out."

"I'm so sorry."

"Avery and Jackson. The two of them were inseparable until I came along." She replaced the picture and shook her head, sadness etching lines along her mouth.

"How are you doing after the excitement at the hospital this morning? Hunter told me you were caught in the parking garage."

Lori shuddered. "That was awful. I think I finally quit shaking about an hour before people started getting here. Of course if I'd had to stay at the police station any longer, I would have had to call it off."

"That might not have been a bad idea."

The woman shook her head. "No. Having to rush home and get ready for this took my mind off of it." She gave a small shrug. "It's not like I've never heard gunfire before or been in a dangerous situation, but that was . . . intense."

"Yeah. I can't believe he got away."

Lori looked like she would say more, but excused herself to address the group. "I think we have a great start on everything. When would be a good time to get together again? Next week same time?"

Everyone agreed and Alexia made her way over to Christine Graham. When she touched the woman's arm, Christine turned and gave Alexia a smile. "Hi. It's really kind of you to help out with the reunion when you have so much going on in your own life right now."

"Thanks." Alexia gave a rueful smile. "When I agreed, I didn't have quite so much going on."

They chatted a couple minutes about the careers they had pursued after high school.

Then Alexia paused. "Speaking of what all is happening in my life, I'm sure you know that Devin's parents were killed."

"Yes, I saw that on the news. Just crazy. I wonder if there's a connection there."

"I'm sure there is. The police are working on finding it. Did you keep up with Devin much?"

"No." A slight shake of her head dislodged a few curls. She pushed them out of her eyes and said, "Hunter's already given me the third degree about Devin. The only person I know that might know anything about him is Marcie Freeman."

Alexia nodded. "He's already talked to her and didn't get much from her." She sighed. "Thanks anyway."

"Sure."

The other women had already left, and Lori came up beside them. "Thank you, guys, for coming. I appreciate it. This

302

reunion is turning out to be more work than I planned."

Alexia smiled. "It's no problem. I'll start pricing the food and get back with you soon."

"Well, I'd better get Mary Ellen heading for bed. Her dad and brother will be home soon."

Christine patted the woman's shoulder. "It's so great that you can help him like you do. Not all sisters would be willing to help out like that."

Lori shrugged. "I love those kids like they were my own. When Melissa died in that car wreck and Avery needed help, I couldn't say no."

"That must have been a horrible experience. I'm so sorry." Alexia felt her heart go out to the little family and admiration for Lori welled. What would it be like to have a family so committed to each other that nothing, not even the death of a loved one, could tear them apart?

Grief for her brother, her dead sister, her relationship with her mother blindsided her and she gasped.

Fortunately, neither of the women seemed to notice.

"Well," Lori pursed her lips, "Melissa was a tormented soul. She was bipolar and refused to take her medication. She caused Avery and the kids so much grief with her ways that —" She shook her head and bit her lip. "You get the idea."

Christine looked troubled. "I admire everything you're doing. With everything you have on you, are you sure being in charge of the reunion committee isn't too much?"

"No." Lori shook her head. "This is fun. I need this."

Christine nodded, then sighed. "I've got to run. I have a brother that needs help too." She gave a tight smile and headed out the door.

Alexia watched her go without saying anything about Chad sitting outside. If he wanted his sister to know what he was up to, he would tell her. She said to Lori, "Thanks so much for doing all this. It is nice to get together. Kind of lets you put all your troubles aside for a little while."

"I know."

Alexia could tell she did. "Well, it's getting really late. I've got to go too."

As Alexia headed to her car, a black Mercedes turned into the drive to pull into the garage.

29

Thursday, 10:15 p.m.

Hunter's phone rang for the second time that night. The first time was Marcus Porter, Dominic Allen's arresting officer. He listened to Hunter's plea for help, asked for some time, and promised to call him back.

Walking into his den, Hunter grabbed his cell phone from the coffee table where he'd tossed it thirty minutes ago. "Hello?"

"So you think I need babysitters, hmm?"

His phone beeped indicating an incoming call. He pulled the phone away and looked at it. Chad calling. He could wait.

Right now, he had Alexia on the line. At least she didn't sound mad. "You're in danger. I'm just covering all of our bases."

"You must have some really nice friends or co-workers who owe you a lot."

He paused. "You talked to Chad?"

"Yes."

"Are you angry?"

"No. Yes." She paused. "No."

Hunter kept quiet hoping she'd tell him more.

She did. "I'm not angry at the protection detail. I'm angry because it's a necessity. I don't like the fact that my life is spinning out of control. I don't like feeling helpless."

Hunter took a deep breath. The phone beeped again. Again, he ignored it as he focused on what Alexia had just told him. He couldn't imagine what it took for her to admit that. "You're not helpless. You're being proactive. Making sure whoever's causing all this trouble can't get to you."

"Hmm. I suppose that's one way of looking at it." Another pause. "Hey, you need to tell your guy who's following me to back off."

Hunter frowned. "What do you mean?"

"I mean his headlights are blinding me. He's following way too close."

Hunter clicked through the schedule he'd set up. Jackson Mann was on duty at ten. A chill hit him. Following too close? That didn't sound right. "Okay. Let me give him a call. Hold on."

Hunter walked into the kitchen and picked up the handset for his landline number. He dialed Jackson's number and waited through three rings. Finally, "Hello?"

"This is Hunter. Are you following Alexia?"

"No, man. I called Chad and told him I'm in bed with a stomach bug. He said he would cover for me."

"Thanks." Hunter hung up and dialed Chad's number.

Chad answered on the first ring. " 'Bout time you picked up."

"Back off Alexia. She said you're following too close."

A flash of silence. "I'm not following her at all. That's what I've been calling you about for the last ten minutes. I've got a flat tire."

Foreboding made his gut clench. Into the other phone, he said, "Alexia, I don't know who's behind you. But don't stop."

"What is it? What's wrong?"

He could hear the fear in her voice. "Maybe nothing. Could be you just have an impatient driver behind you. Could be something more."

In his other ear, Chad said, "I've already called backup and gave them the direction she's headed, but I don't know if they've found her yet or not. She's probably already at Serena's. I sent a car over there."

To Alexia, Hunter said, "Where are you?"

"Almost to Serena's subdivision."

"Drive past her house and tell me if you see a police car. If not, find a place to turn around and come here."

"Where?"

He rattled off the directions to his home. "Chad, you got that tire changed yet?"

"Almost," his brother grunted. "Tightening the last lugnut now."

"The person turned off." Alexia's voice came through the line.

Relief claimed Hunter.

"No, wait." He could hear the fear return. "The car's coming back."

Relief fled. "Do you see any other police cars? Backup should be there."

"No. Yes. I see someone. The officer turned on the blue lights."

"Is the car that's following you still there?"

"No. It's gone." He could almost picture the tension leaving her.

"Okay, do you have somewhere you can stay tonight?"

"I can't stay at Serena's?" She sounded befuddled.

"Alexia, you just led the person to where you were staying."

"But I didn't turn in the drive. Maybe . . ." Now he could hear the tears in her voice. "I don't know, Hunter, if I can't stay here . . . I guess I can go to a hotel . . ."

He'd offer her his couch but didn't think she'd go for that. And a hotel wasn't a good solution. No alarms, too easy to break into. No way.

"You don't need a hotel. I'm going to contact the cruiser. You park your car in the driveway."

"Okay." More confusion on her part.

"I'm on the way. Wait for me to get there, okay?"

"Sure."

"Hey bro, you there?"

Chad.

Hunter had forgotten the man was still on the line. "Where are you now?"

"Climbing back in my car." Hunter heard the door slam. "Heading to Serena's."

Chad hung up. Keeping Alexia on the line, Hunter grabbed his keys from the kitchen counter, went out the door, and down the steps to his vehicle. In the background, he could hear Alexia talking to someone he prayed was the police officer.

Hunter grabbed his radio that would allow him to speak to the officers in the cruiser. "Officers in the vicinity of Hartford Road, please respond." The appropriate code came back to him. Then he heard a familiar voice. "Alpha-304 this is Alpha-501. We've got your friend here."

"Don't leave her alone. Wait for me to get there."

"10-4."

Hunter switched back to his phone. "Alexia, are you okay with me hanging up? I'm on the way."

"That's fine. I've invited the officers in just in case my stalker is still hanging around." She sounded subdued. Resigned. Tired.

He said goodbye and hung up. However, he placed the blue light on his dash and let his foot rest a little heavier on the gas than he normally did even as a plan formed. He grabbed the phone again and called Chad.

The mesmerizing sweep of blue strobes from the street washed the neighboring homes.

"How many cops is this woman friends with?" It was getting almost ridiculous. The cell phone on the seat buzzed. "What!"

Silence. "What was that stunt at the hospital? That was not part of the plan." The voice was calm. An awful calm that did not bode well.

"I wanted to get rid of the detective. He's in my way. I need to take him out to get to her."

Another pause. "Thanks to your shooting" — the voice sharpened like a razor — "her protection detail will be even more difficult to get around."

"Don't you think I've thought about that?"

Silence. The sound of a slow, deliberate exhale.

Sweat began to drip into bleary eyes. The headaches, the fatigue were getting worse. *Should have taken more meds.* "Sir, I'm sorry. I . . . It won't happen again."

"Not if you know what's good for you." The tone changed slightly. "We're backing off. Let her get comfortable."

"What? But you said —"

"I know what I said. Now I'm telling you to lay low right now. Understood?"

"Yes sir."

"Good."

Click.

The front door of the house opened and two officers moved quickly toward the street. Then the happy couple exited. She'd changed clothes, put on a ball cap. Odd getup.

The police car peeled away from the curb and shot down the street. The couple climbed into the detective's car and pulled out of the driveway, heading slowly in the opposite direction.

Back off? No way. Not now.

■ ■ ■ ■

"So, what do you think of my plan?" Hunter asked.

Alexia gaped at him. "Are you insane?" She turned her stunned gaze from the man to the nice middle-class house. "This is your parents' house. There's no way I'm staying here."

"Sure you are. Christine is living with them right now and she said she'd appreciate your company." She felt his gaze rove over her and an appreciative gleam entered his eyes. "Have I told you that you look awesome in a uniform?"

"Yes, you did." Exasperation filled her. Alexia honestly didn't know whether to laugh or cry. Crying sounded pretty good. "Hunter, we've been over this. Your father hates me. He believes I burned down my parents' house. I'm not staying here!"

Finally she seemed to get through to him. His brow furrowed and his lips turned down like a two-year-old who was told no. Then those lips thinned. "Look, you can't stay at Serena's tonight. Swapping places with Pete and Maria allowed us to get away without being followed. If nobody was watching, fine. But if someone was, hopefully, we've thrown them off. Now you can get in there and get a good night's sleep. We'll figure out what you're going to do tomorrow." He paused. "And besides, my parents aren't home tonight. They'll be gone until Saturday, home in time for the dinner."

Right. The dinner.

He continued. "The dinner you still haven't said you'd attend. With me."

Exhaustion and fear pulled at her. "I'll give you an answer on that tomorrow."

He looked away, but not before she saw a hint of disappointment. And why was she hedging anyway? She knew she was going to say yes. The thought of spending that time with him, going on an actual date, was exhilarating. In spite of the fact that she was feeling scared, irritated, and frustrated at the moment.

"Great. Now, let's go in and find Christine. She can take care of anything you might need. Including a clean toothbrush."

"Hunter . . ."

He climbed out of the car. Grudgingly, she followed. What choice did she really have? What if he was right and the killer was watching Serena's house? Did she really want to be there alone tonight?

Of course not.

"What if my staying here puts your family

at risk?"

He didn't even flinch at her question. Which meant he'd already thought of that. And come up with a good enough reason not to be concerned. He said, "The alarm system is awesome here. Plus there are two dogs that roam the yard at night. Everything will work out fine. Come on." His hand grasped her upper arm in a gentle grip. He propelled her toward the front door. "For the record, I have someone watching your house — Serena's house — tonight. If anyone tries anything, I'll be notified."

Chad opened the door. "Christine's not here yet, but come on in."

The words were no more out of his mouth than Alexia heard a car turn in to the driveway. Christine parked and climbed out. She looked disheveled and upset.

Hunter frowned at his sister. "Are you okay?"

"Just fine. Just great. I'm wonderful."

Alexia lifted a brow as the woman walked past her and into the house.

"Chris?" Hunter asked.

The woman's shoulders lifted, then fell. "I'm all right. Just a little perturbed with your friend Rick."

"Ah." Hunter's knowing drawl earned him a scowl from Christine.

"Shut up and get in here." Her words may have sounded harsh to an outsider, but Alexia could hear the love behind them.

Hunter kept his hand on her arm and a shiver danced up her spine as she entered the foyer. Class and good taste greeted her. And she felt as out of place as a mouse at a cat family reunion.

Christine's smile looked forced, but she looped her arm through Alexia's and looked back at the men. "Let me just show Alexia her room. We'll be back in a minute. Try to behave, please." With that, Christine pointed her toward the staircase. But instead of going up, her host led her around. "We have something of a mother-in-law suite back here. My parents added it on when my grandmother came to live with us. She died a couple of years ago and now we use it as a guest room. It'll be the perfect place for you. All the comforts of home, but you won't be disturbed unless you want to be."

And then she was inside a small apartment. Alexia looked at Christine. "Why are you doing this?"

Christine didn't bother to act like she didn't understand. "Because Hunter believes in you and that's enough for me."

A wave of longing for her big brother hit her. *Dominic, where are you?*

Biting her lip, she studied the girl she'd known in high school, but hadn't really *known.* "Well, thank you."

"Sure. Do you have a bag or anything?"

"She'll need the works until I can get her bag from Maria and Pete," Hunter said from behind her.

Alexia spun to see him and Chad vying for elbow room in the narrow doorframe.

Good grief. "Have you two always been this competitive?"

Chad raised a brow like he didn't know what she was talking about.

Christine gave a snicker. "No, it's been a more recent development."

Hunter flushed and moved back. "Not that recent. I've got to meet Pete and give him his car back before he gets in trouble for missing a call or something."

Alexia stopped him. "They risked a lot to help me, didn't they?"

One strong shoulder lifted; however, she caught a glimpse of a small smile playing around the corners of his lips. "I think under the circumstances, the captain would be fine with what we did."

So many people helping her. Opening their homes to her. Putting their lives and jobs on the line.

For her.

Hunter she understood. He was a cop. He wanted to catch the bad guy and she seemed to be the magnet that drew the bad guy out. But the other two cops agreeing to Hunter's crazy scheme, Serena letting her live in her house, and Christine's friendly acceptance. Why?

But she couldn't ask that. Not right now.

The bed in the middle of the room looked so inviting. A glance at the bedside clock made her swallow a groan. 12:32. She was an early morning person, not a night owl.

"Okay, everyone out," Christine ordered. "And that includes me. Alexia, you'll find a pair of my pajamas in the bathroom along with a toothbrush, toothpaste, and anything else you might need. We'll have breakfast at seven thirty, but feel free to sleep in if you wish. The food will wait on you." She flashed an ornery grin at her older brother. "Although, if you're on time, I'm guessing you'll have company for breakfast."

She'd see Hunter first thing in the morning.

Somehow the idea didn't bother her in the least.

30

Friday, 7:12 a.m.

Alexia rose early to find her bag sitting on the chair in the corner of the room. She unzipped the bag and pulled out her clothes. After she showered and dressed, she reveled in her surroundings even as they stirred sadness and regret. Hunter could never be with someone like her.

She and Hunter didn't match. She, a poor girl from a dysfunctional family. And Hunter, the son of the fire chief, soon to be mayor? She would wind up embarrassing him at some point, and he would see the error of his ways and dump her. And if he didn't, his parents would surely want someone "better" for their firstborn.

And his father thought she was an arsonist. Yes, that could definitely be a relationship killer right there.

But she was still going to the dinner with him. And then she'd let him finish the investigation and send him on his way. After all, there was no sense in developing any more feelings for the man when she was just going to turn around and go back to Washington.

Right?

Maybe. Assuming she lived long enough for him to catch the person after her.

She started toward the door. Then stopped, glanced at her watch, and retraced her steps back to her bag. She reached in and pulled out Serena's Bible. Moving the bag to the floor, Alexia settled herself in the chair and opened the Bible to the next entry Serena had marked.

Romans 8:38–39. "For I am convinced that neither death nor life, neither angels nor demons, neither the present nor the future, nor any powers, neither height nor depth, nor anything else in all creation, will be able to separate us from the love of God that is in Christ Jesus our Lord."

Really.

Was Serena serious? She really thought nothing could separate her from God's love?

Yearning ignited inside Alexia. What would it be like to be the recipient of such love? To know that there was nothing she could do to turn that love off?

With a sigh, she placed the Bible back into

the bag, then stared at the opposite wall. *God, if you really love me, I need to see it. Guess that kind of doesn't do much for the faith thing, does it?* She paused, thought about it, then prayed, *Okay, so help me have faith. Faith that you are who Serena and Hunter seem to think you are. Who I want to believe you are.*

Leaving her meager belongings on the chair, she followed the delightful smell of bacon and cinnamon. In the kitchen, she found all three of the Graham siblings sitting around the table sipping coffee and putting away a good amount of food.

Chad saw her first and jumped up. "Hey, grab a plate and sit here."

The food sat on the counter behind the table.

"We don't do this every day," Hunter said.

Alexia jerked, turned, and stared at him. "What? Are you a mind reader now?"

He laughed. "Your face was an easy read."

She flushed and shrugged. "So, what's the occasion this morning?"

"You're here."

The simple words floored her and she frowned. "Excuse me?"

Christine let out a little laugh. "Sure. Anytime we have guests, we bring out the big guns." She took a bite of bacon, then scooped up a forkful of hash browns.

The bowl of fresh fruit in the center of the table beckoned.

"Sorry we started without you, but we wanted to make sure you slept as late as you wanted." She grinned. "Now that you're here, dig in."

"But . . . but . . ." All she could do was sputter. She hated it when she did that. Biting her tongue, Alexia pulled in a deep breath and said, "You mean if I hadn't been here, you wouldn't be eating like this?"

"Exactly," Hunter said with a nod. He lifted his coffee cup in salute.

She simply stared. "Y'all are nuts."

Christine giggled. Chad barked a laugh. And Hunter smiled with such a tender look on his face that Alexia nearly melted into a puddle on the floor. But what did it mean? That look? The breakfast? Their acceptance?

"Fill your plate and have a seat," Hunter said.

The amusement in his voice should have spiked her anger. Instead, she shook her head at the wonder of it. A five-star breakfast had been prepared.

Because of her.

For her.

She couldn't fathom it. Alexia held her tongue, suppressed her amazement, and filled her plate. She turned back to the table.

Chad rose, walked to her, and took her plate. "Let me help you with that."

"No, it's fine. I can —"

"I insist."

She relinquished the plate without further argument. Hunter had a small frown between his brows, but said nothing.

Unwilling to appear rude, Alexia sat in the chair next to Chad.

Which gave her a perfect view of his brother. Hunter sat opposite her, an empty chair to his right and Christine to his left. She had a feeling Hunter wanted her in the empty chair next to him.

Chad looked at Hunter. "Well? Aren't you going to fill Alexia in?"

Hunter's glass thunked on the table as he glared at his brother. "Now's not the time, Chad."

"Honestly, Chad." Christine sighed. "Why do you have to be such a pain?" With that shot, Christine got up and looked at Alexia. "Just leave everything on the table when you're finished. I'll take care of it."

She left after one last disgusted look at Chad. Chad managed to look slightly chagrined.

Alexia ignored him and lasered Hunter

with her gaze. "What do I need to be filled in on?"

He looked at her. "I got some news this morning. When we're finished, let's go into the den and talk."

Alexia lifted a forkful of scrambled eggs to her mouth. Her eyes landed on Chad, who lifted his shoulders in a nonchalant shrug. "Sorry, thought you'd want to know as soon as possible." He finished his breakfast and stood. "I've got to run. Duty calls." He looked at Alexia. "Wish you'd stay another night. Mom and Dad will be home tomorrow. I'd love to see the fireworks."

"That's enough, Chad." Hunter's voice rang soft. And lethal.

Chad lifted a hand in salute and left without another word.

Alexia forked another bite of eggs. After she swallowed, she asked, "What kind of news?"

"You don't want to finish your breakfast first?"

"Why? Is your news going to ruin it?"

Hunter sighed. "Probably."

"Just give it to me straight."

After a slight pause, Hunter nodded. "All right. I found your father. Or rather a friend of mine found him."

She froze. Then took a bite of hash

browns. Chewing methodically, she tried to buy some time. Did she even want to know any more?

Then realized she didn't have a choice. "Where?"

"Winthrop, Washington."

She choked, the hash browns lodged against her windpipe. Hunter thrust her glass of water in her hand and she gulped it.

Finally, when she could breathe again, she stared at him. "What?"

"I'm sorry. I didn't mean to make you choke." He looked troubled.

Alexia waved a hand, her lovely breakfast forgotten. "Forget it. How did you get that information and is it reliable? Is he still there or . . ." She bit her lip. Did she really think her father could be behind all of the problems that had happened to her this past week?

Yes. She did.

"Is he here?" Hunter finished the question for her, compassion softening his eyes.

"Yes," she whispered. "Is he here?"

Another maddening pause, then he nodded. "It looks like he might be."

Alexia pushed away from the table and walked into the den.

Too restless to sit, she paced in front of

the fireplace. "So where is he? What is he doing?"

"He just got out of prison not too long ago."

"Of course he did." Fury burned in her gut. And a desperate fear that she would never be free of her past. "Why do you think he's here?"

"He bought a one-way train ticket from Winthrop to Columbia."

"When did he buy it?" she whispered.

"A week and a half ago."

"How long would it take him to get here?"

"A few days."

Her knees felt weak. She crossed to the sofa and sat, staring at Hunter. "You think he could be the one behind all of this?"

"I don't know, Lex. His train arrived Monday. Devin died on Monday."

Lex. The nickname rolled from his tongue like smooth honey. She decided she liked the sound of it. It soothed her, calmed her. "And my life spiraled out of control on Monday too. Okay. So, he may be around here somewhere. Watching me, trying to kill me."

Hunter shook his head. "You know, I don't think they are trying to kill you. They're trying to get to you."

"Well, if that's the case, then why is he

planting evidence to suggest that I'm involved in Devin's murder, the fire at Detective Isaac's house, and who knows what else that we haven't come across?"

He sighed and a thumb caressed her knuckles. "I haven't figured that out yet."

"I might know," she muttered. She shivered at his touch and at the thought coursing through her mind.

"What?"

"If it's my father, I'm sure he wants me to suffer as much as possible before he gets his hands on me and extracts his revenge." The thought made her stomach hurt. What had she done to deserve his hatred?

Maybe she really had burned the house down.

She looked at Hunter. "My sister killed herself. She OD'd on her pain medication."

He blinked at the blunt words. As soon as they left her mouth, she wanted to snatch them back. Why, oh why, did she let that out?

"I know," he said.

The soft compassion in his voice made her eyes sting. She blinked because she didn't cry. She wouldn't.

And the fact that he knew how her sister, Karen, died shouldn't have surprised her. "I guess you read the story in the newspaper like everyone else."

"Yes. And my dad wasn't exactly quiet about his thoughts on the matter."

She nodded. "Right. And you want me to go to that dinner tomorrow night with you. Why?"

He pulled in a deep breath. "Because —"

His phone rang and she jumped.

Snatching it from his pocket, he barked, "Hello?" Then listened. For about three minutes. Then his eyes darted to hers. "Thanks, Brian, good work."

When he hung up, he just stared at her for a few seconds. Alexia wanted to squirm. "What?"

"Well, we're on a roll. I think we've found your brother too."

Alexia paused, prepared herself for whatever Hunter was going to say. "Okay. And where is he? What's he been doing all these years?"

"He's a cop."

It was a good thing she was sitting down. "A cop?" Disbelief shuddered through her. "A cop?" They were the only two words left in her vocabulary.

A small smile curved his lips. "What did you think I was going to say?"

She shrugged and managed to find more words. "I don't know. A drug addict? A mob boss?" She tried to smooth her hair, fingers tangling in the curls. She'd meant to pull it up in a ponytail this morning and couldn't find a tie. The mundane thought allowed her to gather her scattered wits. "Anything but a cop."

"Well, he's not just any cop. He's a special agent with the FBI. He's been undercover for years. That's what made it so hard for Brian to track him down."

Could she be any more stunned? "Wha . . . how . . . ?" Alexia clamped her teeth together. Pulled her thoughts together. "How did Brian finally find him?"

"Dominic just renewed his driver's license yesterday in Florida."

She nodded. "Okay, so now what? If he's in Florida, I guess that means he's not the one after me."

Hunter gave her a patient smile. "He works for the FBI. Just because the paperwork says he renewed his license in Florida doesn't mean he's really there."

"Oh. Right."

"I've got a call in to the bureau requesting to speak with him. I'm hoping he'll get the message soon and will call me."

Alexia gulped. "Okay. And if he does? What does that mean?"

"I don't know. Do you want to see him?"

Did she?

Desperately. She wanted to tell him she was sorry she was such a rotten sister. She wanted to tell him she shouldn't have called the cops on him. She wanted to hear him say she was forgiven.

But what if he wouldn't accept her apology? What if he still hated her? What if he was behind everything going on with her?

What if her father and brother were somehow in it together?

Okay, now she was officially losing it. "No. I don't want to see him." She was more afraid of his rejection than the chance that he might have forgiven her long ago.

Of course if he'd forgiven her, he would have gotten in contact with her. Wouldn't he?

The frown on Hunter's face stopped her. "What is it?"

"I just . . . nothing." He looked at her and smiled. "I'll tell him you don't want to meet with him if he asks."

"You think I'm wrong, don't you?"

"I don't know. If he's not the one causing all of your problems, then I think you two should try to resolve your differences."

"Like you and Chad have?" He winced and she sat forward. "I'm sorry. That was a low blow."

"It's okay."

"No." She got up and walked over. "I'm lashing out because I suspect you're right. I do need to see him." The words came out soft, low . . . honest.

He sighed and wrapped an arm around her shoulders to bring her close to him. "You may be lashing out, but you're not wrong. Chad and I need to find a way to stop acting like a couple of losers every time we're around you."

"You don't act like a loser."

"Sure I do. He likes the girl I like. I like the girl he likes. It's in our genetic makeup to act like cavemen whenever we're in the same room with you."

She laughed. "Cavemen?" Then his words sank in. She looked him in the eye. "You like me?"

"Yeah," he whispered. "Just a little."

Then he leaned over to cover her lips with his, gently, questioning, exploring, then deepening until she pulled away. Heart thrumming like a wild thing, she pushed back and slipped out of his arms even while she longed to stay there. A quivering smile curved her lips while her insides trembled. "Yeah. I like you a little too."

Once again his phone rang and she left him to answer it as she processed the news

330

he'd just delivered — and the kiss they'd just shared.

He'd found her father and brother. Both of whom might be somewhere close by. Both of whom might want her dead. Or in their hands for reasons she could only guess at. Both certainly had reason to want revenge.

Hunter said goodbye and she turned her thoughts to the handsome man in front of her. The one who seemed to support her no matter what happened.

"Why haven't you arrested me?"

He blinked as he pocketed his phone. "Arrest you?"

"Yes. With all the evidence that says I'm the one that killed Devin and started the fire at Katie's house, you haven't arrested me. The knife was found in my house. My necklace was found at Katie's. Paint thinner was used for the accelerant, the same thing that was used when my house burned down in high school . . ."

A memory rose up and flashed from nowhere . . .

"He's going to kill me," Karen sobbed. "Don't let him kill me."

The end of the rifle looked huge. She shuddered, expecting to feel a bullet rip through her at any moment.

Hunter strode across the room and took her hands. She gasped as she returned to the present.

He was saying, ". . . You didn't do it. The evidence is circumstantial. CSU covered your house right after the murder. No knife. I have proof that you didn't leave Serena's house that night. The necklaces were in your room. I saw them. Someone managed to get in and get one. As for the paint thinner . . ."

"What?"

"It's someone who knows you," he said as he narrowed his eyes in thought. "Someone who's close to you. Someone who knows the details of your past."

She stared at him. "Someone who still has a key to the house, the same way I do." Her voice came out in a low whisper. "You think it's my father or my brother, don't you?"

He sighed. "From what you've told me, I think it's a good possibility."

Alexia nodded and bit her lip. "I was afraid of that." She looked at him. "But which one?"

31

Friday, 4:46 p.m.

The rest of the day passed in a blur as Hunter found two off-duty detectives willing to put in a few hours to cover Alexia.

Knowing she had a competent protection detail made him feel slightly better about leaving her. It didn't stop him from missing her. From wanting to kiss her again.

He couldn't believe how much he was looking forward to the dinner tomorrow night. Usually, he dreaded the things but went to support his family. With Alexia by his side, he knew there wouldn't be a dull moment.

Part of him wondered if he should give his father a heads-up on the fact that Alexia would be accompanying him. Then decided against it. His father told him to bring a date, so he was. End of story. He knew his dad would be on his best behavior at the dinner. He wouldn't embarrass Alexia or himself by saying or doing anything to make him look bad.

He parked in his usual spot at the office, determined to make headway on this case. Be productive. His phone rang as he pushed open his door. Grabbing it from his pocket, he barked, "Hello?"

"Hey, this is Rick."

"What's up?"

"I just got a vehicle over here to finish processing. They think it's the van used to try and run your girl down. We got a partial plate off the video, put out a BOLO for it, and thirty minutes later, we have a hit."

"Where'd they find it?"

"A cop spotted it parked in a convenience store parking lot. Called it in. I sent my team over to process it. They did what they could do there in the lot, then had it towed over here."

"You find anything yet?"

"A set of clothes."

"Male or female?"

"Hard to tell. Could be either. It's a guy's pair of jeans and a muscle T-shirt. So, if I had to guess, I'd say male. But women wear this kind of stuff all the time, so it could fit a tall woman or a shorter man . . ."

"Yeah, I see what you're saying."

"We found a few hairs, but we'll have to

test and rule out the owners of the van. Then I can try and see if we have a match in the system, but no guarantees."

Hunter nodded as he walked up the front steps. "I know. Just keep me posted and I'll send you any new info as I get it."

"Deal. See you later."

Hunter hung up and said a short prayer that Rick and his team would find something in the van that would help lead them to the person responsible for terrorizing Alexia.

Walking into the precinct, he spotted Katie by the coffee machine. She looked tired, worn down. He watched her pop a pill and frowned. What was she taking?

"Hey, partner."

She started and her coffee sloshed over the side. Swallowing, she lifted her gaze to his and frowned. "Hey."

He handed her a paper towel. "Sorry about that."

She sniffed and dabbed her nose. "No problem."

"Are you okay?"

"Just a cold. I'll try not to breathe on you."

He looked at her flushed cheeks, then lifted a hand to her forehead. "More than a cold, I'd say. You've got a fever. Go home before you infect us all."

"I've got to solve this case," she protested. "I promise, I'm not that sick. If I feel worse, I'll call it a day."

"Give me access to your files and any information you've acquired that you haven't told me about and I can read through it."

She paused. Then nodded. The fact that she gave in so easily told him she felt worse than she let on. She said, "All right, I guess I could catch a nap and see how I feel when I wake up. I also want to run something else by you before I leave."

"What's that?"

"CSU found a little book in a box of things in Devin's apartment. It has names and dates and monetary amounts in it. Looks like customers for a lawn care business. The money's not that much and it doesn't look like he was doing anything illegal, but you might want to run the names of the people in the book. Maybe one of them knows something."

She walked over to her desk and opened the drawer. She pulled out a 4 × 6 spiral-bound notebook and handed it to him. "I'll keep my cell on. Let me know if you come up with anything."

"Sure. Feel better."

"I will. I just took some ibuprofen. Hopefully that'll kick in pretty quick."

She left and Hunter said a quick prayer that he'd be spared whatever she had. Then he sat down with the book and started going through it.

A lot of names including Hannah Allen, Alexia's mother. The pastor, Michael Stewart; the girlfriend, Marcie Freeman; Lori's brother, Avery Tabor. All with a set amount beside each name.

So, Devin was going to branch out and go for his own business. He was working hard, saving his money . . .

Money. How much did he have in his account?

Hunter shuffled the papers on his desk until he found what he wanted. Devin's last bank statement. "Close to three thousand dollars."

He blew out a sigh. Not much. Seemed like the man should have more than that, but he'd just lost his apartment. No other debts that Hunter could find.

So everything he earned in the yard business he could sink into an account. Very little went out in the way of expenses. So in about eight weeks' time, he'd accumulated three thousand dollars. Fifteen hundred a month? Yeah, that was very possible.

Nothing weird there.

He glanced at the clock. Five o'clock. He wondered what Alexia was doing for dinner. His gaze went to his cell phone acting as a paperweight.

Call her? Or not?

His hand reached for the phone. He pressed the button for her number.

"Hello?"

She sounded breathless.

"Hey, this is Hunter. Are you all right?"

"Yep." A grunt, a muffled utterance.

"Um . . . what are you doing?" he asked.

"Trying on dresses. If I'm going to this dinner thingy with you, then I'm going to do my best not to embarrass you."

His heart thudded. "You could dress in jeans and I still wouldn't be embarrassed."

Stillness on the line. "Thanks, Hunter. I appreciate that." Then another grunt and a long sigh.

He frowned. "What's wrong?"

"Nothing a little dieting won't take care of."

Hunter chuckled. "Ah, let me guess. You tried on a dress a size smaller than you normally wear."

Silence.

He waited.

More silence.

He shifted. "Alexia?"

"That was not a smart thing to say to the woman you're having dinner with tomorrow." Her voice was low, her words deadly.

He gulped. "Sorry. It's just that Christine —"

"I'm *not* your sister."

Totally uncomfortable with the foot in his mouth, he searched frantically for the right words. "No. No, you're definitely not my sister. Thank God for that."

A muffled chuckle? *Please, God, let that be a laugh.*

"Hunter?"

"Yeah?"

"I'm going to go now."

"Okay. I'm going to go wash out the taste of shoe leather."

A giggle. That was definitely a giggle. *Thank you, Lord.*

Alexia's phone rang within five minutes of hanging up with Hunter.

With a critical eye, she gave herself the once-over in the mirror and had to admit the one-size-larger dress fit much better than the last one she'd tried on. Rats.

Absently she reached for the phone and brought it to her ear. "Hello?"

"What's the pretty dress for? Dinner with Hunter?" the voice hissed.

"Excuse me?" She froze.

"I saw you take it off the rack."

Alexia darted from the dressing room, still in the fancy black dress, looking for the detective who had been her shadow most of the day.

He stood talking to the security guard.

"It's not like you're going to be around to wear it to the dinner with your detective boyfriend."

A frantic wave at the detective brought him rushing to her side. She clicked the phone on speaker. "Who is this and what do you want?"

"Tell that pretty boy detective that I could have grabbed you while he was yakking it up with that old has-been cop wannabe near the cash register."

Alexia's gaze shot to Detective Hudson. His lips thinned and his eyes darted around the store, to the big window at the front.

The voice continued. "No need to look for me, Detective. I'm long gone now. But I'm never very far away."

Click.

Her heart stuttered, fear engulfed her. And anger bubbled closer than ever at the surface.

Already Detective Hudson was on the phone requesting a search of the street and surrounding stores.

But who would they be looking for?

Her hand shook as she curled her fingers around the cell phone.

"The voice on the phone," Hudson said, "did it sound weird to you?"

She frowned, focused on his words, shoved the fear down. "Weird how?"

He shook his head. "Weird, as in I couldn't tell if it was male or female."

Alexia thought. "I . . . no. I couldn't tell."

"The person disguised his — or her — voice," he muttered. "The caller used a voice changer device. You can attach them to your cell phone. That one was high end — good quality."

She shuddered. "All I know is that it sounded the same as the one who called and threatened me last time." She looked around. "Whoever it was is watching me. Following me, knew I was trying on dresses." She shivered and crossed her arms to grip her elbows. "I don't like this."

Alexia began to pace, her gut churning, while Detective Hudson spoke into his phone. The door opened and she turned to see Chad enter the boutique. As her heart deflated, she realized she'd been hoping to see Hunter. Still, getting such immediate protection helped calm her nerves.

She could see Chad was looking for her. Lifting a hand, she waved him over, studying him as he walked toward her. He looked good. She could see the family resemblance now that he was sober and . . . not pitiful. But she felt nothing for him, not one little zing of attraction. Not like she felt for Hunter.

"Guess you heard all of the excitement on the radio?" she asked.

"I heard." Concern for her drew his brows together as he settled his hands on her shoulders. "I had to come make sure you were okay."

His touch made her uneasy. She gave a subtle twist, using the pretense of ducking back into the dressing room to tuck her phone into her purse.

When she resurfaced, she said, "I'm fine. Nothing happened other than another creepy phone call."

Chad began questioning the customers. The front door dinged and she turned to find Hunter making his way toward her. He reached her and placed his hands on her shoulders. She had no desire to move away from *him*. "Are you all right? What happened?"

Alexia forced a smile. "I'm fine. It was just a phone call."

"Right. Like the last one?"

She nodded.

"Okay," his hands gave her shoulders a light squeeze, "we'll pull your phone records. Maybe we'll see where the call originated from. I feel sure it's the same prepaid cell that called your home, but it's worth a shot."

She bit her lip and nodded. "Okay."

The officers who'd scanned the area came up empty.

Chad walked over. "No one saw anyone unusual in the store or lurking outside. One lady said she saw a woman and two children peering in the window. Another saw an older man sitting on the bench talking on a cell phone."

"Could be him," Hunter said. "Are there any cameras along the street?"

"I'll check." A young officer hurried off.

Hunter finally looked at his brother. "Are you working this case now?"

Chad had the grace to flush. "Hey, it's my day off."

"You've had a lot of those lately, haven't you?" Hunter muttered.

Chad's flush deepened into a dark red as he narrowed his eyes at his brother. He pulled in a breath. Then let it out and ignored Hunter's comment. Chad turned to the nearest officer and asked him a question that Alexia didn't hear.

In other circumstances, the look on Hunter's face would have made her laugh. Instead, she felt a pang. Was she the reason the two of them butted heads so often?

No, the tension between the brothers had been there long before she entered the picture. At least Chad looked like he'd sobered up and was staying that way. If that was because of her, then fine. But it was Hunter she was attracted to. It was Hunter's arms she wanted around her, comforting her.

She blinked. What was she thinking? She was tough, she could handle whatever was thrown her way. She'd never leaned on a man who hadn't let her down.

And yet . . .

"Okay, I need to change." She whirled and went back into the dressing room. She needed to get away from the circus the store had become.

Alexia just wanted to go home — to Serena's house — curl up in bed, and pull the covers over her head.

She eyed the dress and firmed her jaw.

So her caller didn't think she'd have a chance to wear it, huh?

The bubbling anger seethed. "Oh yes I

will," she whispered to her unknown harasser. "You're always watching? Then watch this."

She hung it back on the hanger and belatedly checked the price tag. After a wince, she shrugged. She liked it and hadn't bought anything like it since . . . well, she couldn't remember when.

And if the person determined to get her *was* successful, at least she'd die looking her best.

32

Friday, 5:58 p.m.

Senator Hoffman stared at the latest note as he took deep breaths in a futile attempt to lower his blood pressure.

TELL WHAT YOU DID AND I MIGHT GO AWAY.

Tell? "Not likely."

"Talking to yourself, dear?"

Frank jerked, the paper rattling in his already shaky hand. Elizabeth stood in the doorway. "Just trying to figure something out." He laid the note on the desk, not attempting to hide it. Elizabeth would catch on and demand to see it. Then what would he do? He could feel his blood pressure rising with each passing second.

As long as she stood in the doorway, she couldn't see what was on the paper.

"Any luck?"

"Not a bit." At least he could tell the truth about something.

Elizabeth waved a hand. "I have no doubt you'll succeed. You have the Midas touch, don't you?"

"Did you need something?"

Her eyes cooled. "I just came to tell you that I'm going out to look for a birthday present for Carmen. I'd like Ian to drive me so I don't have to worry about parking. You don't need him, do you?"

"No. I'm fine. You go on. If I need to head into the office, I'll take the Beamer."

Carmen. Their daughter. He looked at the calendar. She'd be twenty-four next week. The one thing in his life that he felt good about right now.

Elizabeth left without another word.

Working at home was becoming a habit. He felt like he needed to be on guard, to be the first to get to the mailbox. What if he wasn't here and Elizabeth or one of the hired help decided to open the mail? It had happened before. And he sure didn't want to bring the subject up and ask them *not* to get the mail. That would just incite questions he wasn't interested in answering. Then again he might need to come up with something, a good reason to keep Elizabeth from getting the mail.

He glanced back at the note.

Telling wasn't an option.

■ ■ ■ ■

Alexia didn't want to go home and she didn't want to go to Serena's. She would have to go later to feed the animals. For now, she forced herself to face another necessary task.

Visiting her mother.

She'd left the little boutique on Main Street with Katie Isaacs right behind her. Of all people to volunteer to protect her, it had to be Katie. Frankly, Alexia thought the woman looked sick and needed to be in bed, but Hunter said she'd insisted on helping.

Alexia headed east for about two miles. Then pulled over into a fast-food restaurant parking lot. She needed to make a phone call.

He answered on the fourth ring, just when she was about to give up. "Hello?"

"Hello, Pastor Stewart, this is Alexia Allen, Hannah's daughter."

A slight pause echoed over the line before he said, "What can I do for you, Ms. Allen?"

"Please, call me Alexia."

"All right. Why don't you call me Michael? I'm very informal with my congregation."

But she wasn't part of his congregation. "I'm on my way to see my mother. You seem to be . . . close . . . to her. I just . . ." This was harder than she'd thought it would be. "I just wanted to know . . ." Again, she faltered.

A light laugh came over the line. "Are you calling to ask what my intentions are toward your mother?"

She flushed, grateful he couldn't see her discomfort. "Maybe." Yes. "I mean I know it's not really my place, I don't have the right, but I just —"

"You do have the right. You're Hannah's daughter."

"Michael, I haven't been her daughter for ten years." She couldn't seem to find her filters. The words tumbled from her lips and she waited to see what this man would say. How could he not lambast her for being a lousy daughter? She hadn't even made regular trips to the hospital to see her mother.

But he didn't. He simply said, "To Hannah, you've always been in her heart. You and Dominic, both. She's prayed every day for your return and the return of your brother."

Alexia drew in a deep breath and shuddered.

A car pulled up beside her and she jerked, ready to throw the vehicle in gear and speed off. However, it was just her shadow. Katie Isaacs. She rolled her window down and motioned to her phone.

Katie rolled her eyes, but nodded and backed off. Alexia grimaced her dislike of the woman but figured she'd do her job. If she let Alexia die on her watch, Hunter would point the finger right in Katie's face.

Small comfort. She'd still be dead.

"Ms. Allen? Alexia?"

Alexia blinked. "Sorry, I was . . . distracted."

"My intentions toward your mother are honorable. My wife died six years ago. Since then, I've carried on, but it's been lonely. Then your mother joined the church and she just brought a whole new dimension of joy to my life."

"My father was an abusive man," she blurted. "A horrible, selfish, awful man."

"I know."

"She told you? Everything?"

"Everything. At least I think so."

Alexia swallowed hard. "She sent me away. Practically pushed me out the door."

What was she saying? She didn't want to do this on the phone.

"You were in danger." His voice was soft. "Ask her."

"What? In danger? How?" But she knew.

350

"From my father." The words came out flat.

"Just talk to her. Really talk to her. And listen."

The compassion in his voice made her want to weep. And it made her want to see her mother. "All right. I'll try."

"Right now, your mother's having a few more tests run. I'm not telling you not to come to the hospital, but you might have quite a long wait. They came and got her about fifteen minutes ago."

"Oh. I think I'll go on home then. Will you call me when she's finished?"

"I'd be happy to."

"Thank you."

She was scared. No doubt about it. But she couldn't stay at the Grahams' tonight, not after finding out they would be home early tomorrow morning. Seeing Hunter's father at the dinner was one thing; facing him in their home was another. Hunter hadn't liked it, but had given in to her stubbornness with the understanding that she would have someone on guard and he would check in with her on a regular basis. She didn't argue with him on those points.

Alexia peered out the window and felt her tense shoulders tighten even more. Katie had followed her home and waited for her replacement before leaving, and Chad had called twice to check on her. The unmarked car sat at the curb. The pretty black dress hung on the hook on the door of Serena's closet. Everything was as it should be.

The female officer, Marty Howell, had been assigned to her inside the house. She spent her time pacing between the French doors leading to the deck and the back door leading to the garage, and on her radio with her partner on the curb.

Walking into the den, Alexia turned on the TV, settled in the recliner, and stared at the flickering screen. Annoyed with it, she flipped the television off.

Chewie jumped in her lap and Alexia grunted. "You're a heavy thing, aren't you?"

The cat kneaded Alexia's right thigh before perching to wash a front paw. Yoda's nails clicked on the hardwoods as she joined them. With a weary groan, Alexia leaned her head back against the chair and gazed at the ceiling. Her thoughts ran wild. Fear was now her constant companion.

The other human body in the house helped, especially since she knew how to use a gun. But Alexia's nerves jumped and her heart thudded.

"Are you all right?" Officer Howell asked from the kitchen doorway.

Alexia nodded and forced a stiff smile. "I'm fine."

"Okay." The woman flashed a friendly smile. "Just checking. I'm going to walk to the back of the house and look out those windows, all right?"

"Sure."

Alexia glanced to her right.

The Bible lay on the end table where she'd put it. More pieces of paper stuck out from the end. She reached around Chewie to pick up the Bible and flipped to one of the pieces of paper and read the note aloud.

Hey Alexia, I'm so glad you're reading this. Just know that I'm praying for you. Praying for you to come to terms with your past. Praying that you find the God you're searching for. (Hint: He's not hard to find. It's not like he's hiding.) And I'm praying that things work out for you and Hunter if that's what God's got in mind. (Don't think I didn't notice the way he looked at you.) He's always been a little in love with you. Yeah. I noticed. Anyway, keep reading, Lex. Sending you hugs from China. Serena.

The lump in her throat grew. Serena. The one person who'd stood beside her through everything. The one person who hadn't given up on her or tossed her aside.

Serena loved God and wanted Alexia to understand why. For that reason, Alexia would read every word Serena left her. She'd read the Bible cover to cover if that's what Serena wanted.

It was the least she could do.

She opened the Bible. And paused.

It was awfully quiet.

Yoda paced to the front door then back. To the window, then in the kitchen.

"Yoda? Come on, girl, what's wrong?"

The dog came to her side and sat, cocked her ears. Turned back to the front door.

Uneasy, Alexia set the Bible back on the end table and stood. Chewie meowed in protest, but Alexia ignore her. She walked to the window, pushed aside the curtain. Her watchdog was still there.

So what was her problem?

She checked the alarm. Armed and ready. Cop on the prowl inside, cop on guard outside.

Alexia sighed and looked at Yoda, who had followed her every step. "I need to relax."

If only.

Her cell phone rang and she jumped. Heart thudding, she wondered again how her stalker had found her number. She glanced at the caller ID and felt her pulse slow.

Hunter.

"Hello?"

"Hey."

His warm voice flowed over her, soothing her agitated nerves with that one word. "Hi there."

"Are you settled in for the night?"

"I think so. You?"

"Hmm. Not really. Working on this case is keeping me wide awake." He paused. "Is Jimmy outside?"

"Is that the cop in the car on my curb?"

He chuckled. "That's the one."

"Then yep, he's there. And Officer Howell is doing her job prowling the house," she said before he could ask. She settled back into the recliner. Yoda had made herself at home on her bed in front of the fireplace.

"I'm looking forward to tomorrow night," Hunter said.

Alexia smiled, her earlier nerves calming as she talked to this man she was coming to really care about. She yawned, then said, "I am too."

"The dinner starts at seven o'clock. I'll pick you up at six thirty. Is that all right?"

"I'll be ready."

"Great. Here's the other thing. I'm off

tomorrow. What would you say to spending the morning on the lake? Just you and me and a couple of bodyguards in a separate boat."

"Oh, that sounds lovely." She frowned. "But you have to get me back here in time to get ready for the evening."

He laughed. "I can handle that."

"Then sure, I'd love to."

"Great, I'll see you in the morning around eight?"

"Okay. See you then."

The conversation lagged, seemed stilted. Because neither of them wanted to hang up? Possibly. "Hunter?"

"Yeah?"

"I'm . . . scared."

She could almost see him sobering. "I know, Lex. I promise I'm working hard to find the person doing this to you."

"I know you are." She sighed. "I just . . . I'm afraid."

"Can I give you a verse?"

"A Bible verse?" Him too? Seriously? "Sure."

"Psalm 56."

"Psalm 56 what?"

"The whole chapter, but the first few verses often bring me comfort when I feel like the bad guys are winning."

He felt that way? "What's it say?"

"Hold on a sec, let me get my Bible and I'll read you the whole passage." She heard his footsteps retreat, then come back. "Okay. You ready?"

"Shoot."

He read, " 'When I am afraid, I will trust in you. In God, whose word I praise, in God I trust; I will not be afraid. What can mortal man do to me? All day long they twist my words; they are always plotting to harm me.' "

"Boy, is that accurate or what?" she breathed.

He gave a light chuckle. "Yes, it goes on with David asking God not to let them escape and for God to bring down the nations. And that when he calls out to God, his enemies will turn back. That's how he knows that God is on his side. Verse 13 says, 'For you have delivered me from death and my feet from stumbling, that I may walk before God in the light of life.' "

For some reason she felt a lump in her throat. Maybe God did care about her. Maybe he cared enough to put two people in her life who wanted to steer her to him.

Something to think about. "I like those verses." She climbed out of the recliner, still holding the Bible, and made her way to the guest bedroom. "I'm going to look them up."

A pause. Had she shocked him speechless?

Then he said, "Good, I'm glad."

"Hunter?"

"Yeah?"

She curled up on top of the comforter and opened the Bible again. "Will you stay on the phone with me until I fall asleep?"

His husky voice came through. "Sure, just put me on speakerphone. I'll do the same."

"Thanks, Hunter."

33

Hunter held his cell phone to his ear and heard Alexia's soft, even breathing. He smiled as he put the phone on mute and laid it on the charging pad. Then he stood and began pacing. His mind worked the case, going over it point by point.

Something bothered him, something he was missing. The nagging at his subconscious wouldn't go away, so he worked on trying to bring it to the forefront of his mind.

He grabbed the file folder from the end table and opened it before him. Just as he started to read, his doorbell rang. Frowning, he checked his weapon, then walked to the front door. A quick glance out the side window made him relax.

Katie. Opening the door, he said, "Hey."

She stepped in and shut the door behind her. "We need to talk."

"How are you feeling?"

"Lousy, but I can't sleep and I can't get better as long as this case has me by the throat."

"I was just going through some of my notes. Want to join me?"

"I thought you'd never ask." She pulled out a tissue and blew her nose.

Hunter rolled his eyes. "But if you get me sick, you forfeit your vacation days. I get them."

"Dream on. What do you have?"

Together, they read through his summary:

Monday:

- Devin Wickham found dead in Hannah Allen's home.
- Alexia attacked in the hospital parking lot.

Tuesday:

- Someone shoots at Alexia with darts. Chad shows up to offer help, to see how she's doing.

Wednesday:

- Someone broke into Hannah Allen's

home and planted the knife in Alexia's bedroom.

- Took knife to the lab. Found a print of a list of possible matches. No names recognized by me or Alexia.
- Alexia is almost kidnapped outside the restaurant. (How did they know she'd be there?) Chad shows up and rescues her.
- At the hospital, watched the videos of the attack on Alexia. No help there. Van was stolen.
- Alexia got a threatening phone call.
- Katie's house burns and my car explodes. Chad shows up.

Thursday:

- Alexia goes to Wickhams' and finds them murdered (or close to it). Chad shows up.
- Questioned Marcie Freeman. Got the note from someone interested in Devin and wanted Marcie out of the picture. (So, why kill Devin? Are the two related?)
- At the hospital, got list of people with keys to Allen house. Questioned each person who said they hadn't used the keys.

361

- Got shot at outside the hospital. (Again, how did shooter know we were there?)
- Brian calls with information that Alexia's father served time in prison for killing a man in a bar. Got out three months ago and bought a train ticket to Columbia a week and a half ago. History of family abuse — suspect?
- Someone followed Alexia to Serena's house from the reunion committee meeting. Chad's car has a flat tire.

Friday:

- Alexia finds out her brother is also alive and is a cop. Possibly has a grudge against her. Is he in town? *Call Marcus Porter.*
- Alexia goes shopping. Gets another phone call that she's being watched. Chad shows up.

Hunter stopped. Focused in on the last three words he'd written.

Chad shows up.

A cold chill settled in the pit of his stomach. Chad?

Did Katie catch that pattern? He looked at her and saw the concentration on her features. Hunter glanced back at the paper.

"Hunter? I'm a little concerned at what I'm seeing here."

"What's that?" He played innocent.

"You keep insisting Alexia had nothing to do with what happened to Devin. I have to admit, after studying everything, I'm inclined to agree."

"Yeah?" That was a surprise. After her adamant stand that Alexia was behind it all, Hunter didn't figure she'd change her mind anytime soon.

"Yeah. After finding Alexia's necklace at the fire, I knew it was her. But you're so sure it's not." She glanced at him. "And I really do trust your judgment. So, I started going through everything. Combine that with your belief that she's innocent . . ." Katie shrugged. "It looks like someone might be setting her up. I'll give you that and try to help you prove it."

"Thank you."

"But you must subconsciously suspect Chad. You mention him in almost every notation." Accusation shot from her eyes. "What are you doing, Hunter?"

His head felt like it might explode. "I'm trying to solve this case, Katie."

"By blaming your brother?"

"No! I don't think he's involved. He

couldn't be. He was drunk and passed out when Devin was killed. He wasn't anywhere around there, but after he saw Alexia . . ." Hunter raked a hand through his hair. "After he saw her, he just sort of fixated on her. And then the incidents started happening."

"And Chad's always conveniently there."

"Coincidence?" Hunter shook his head. "I don't know. One thing I *do* know is that he's not a killer."

No, Chad wasn't a killer. But he kept appearing whenever something happened. And the fact that he was the one rescuing Alexia . . .

But Chad hadn't been at the hospital when the shooter had tried to kill Hunter. Had he?

Could Chad do that?

Slowly, Hunter stood and walked to the window to stare out, unseeing into the dark while Katie kept quiet, lost in her own thoughts.

He hoped hers were better than his. Those shots at the hospital had been aimed at him. Not Alexia. Would Chad —

No, he wouldn't even go there.

Chad was a crack shot. If he'd been trying to kill Hunter, Hunter would be dead. But the doubt now niggled at the back of his mind.

Was it possible the shooting at the hospital had nothing at all to do with the other incidents involving Alexia? He looked back over the list. Then at Katie.

She said, "We need to figure out a way to prove Chad has nothing to do with the stuff happening to Alexia. And we need to figure it out fast, because if someone else looks at this file and puts it all together like we did . . ."

"I know. I know."

Together, they brainstormed a plan, and by the time Katie left thirty minutes later, Hunter felt the rock of dread in his gut expand, making him wonder if the decision he'd just made would be the end of him.

Alexia drifted between that state of waking and sleeping, not quite asleep, but not awake. Images flickered through her mind. Devin laughing. Devin's fist shooting out and catching her in the jaw. Her father's laughter, low, deep . . . evil. Her brother begging her not to say anything about the drugs she knew he was dealing. Her mother yelling at her to get out of the house and never come back.

Then Hunter's comforting touch. His

sweet kiss. The look in his eyes when he told her, "You're worth it, Lex."

Her heartbeat slowed. Her tense muscles relaxed. She drifted.

The house was quiet. Still. The light in the back bedroom went off.

The cop had parked on the curb, back far enough from the house to allow him a view of the front and one of the sides. He would be doing his next perimeter check in about two minutes.

The seconds ticked by. His door opened.

Right on time. The cop vanished around the corner. There was less than a minute to act.

The killer slunk to the back of the car, made quick work of the locked door, and slid into the backseat. The door closed with a soft click.

The meds had kicked in, and complete calm settled like a cloak over the killer's shoulders.

A piercing sound jerked her awake, heart pounding. Sleep still fogged her brain and the thundering of her pulse blocked any other sound. Sitting up, she clicked on the bedside lamp. "Yoda? Officer Howell?"

Where was the dog? Where was the cop?

Stilling, she closed her eyes and forced herself to control her breathing. Her pulse slowed. She listened.

All was silent.

What had she heard? Had she been having a bad dream?

She rose and walked to the window, the very edge, and pushed the curtain aside just enough to peek out. Hunter had drilled it into her that she was to stay away from windows and keep the lights low so as not to make herself a target for a sniper. She could see the back of the unmarked car from her angle at the window.

"Yoda? Where are you? Officer Howell?"

Uneasiness crawled through her. When she was in the house, the dog usually stayed nearby. And why didn't Officer Howell respond? Of course if she were at the opposite end of the house, she wouldn't have heard Alexia.

The air conditioner clicked on and began to hum. The blast of cold air from the vent at her feet made her shiver. Turning from the window, she eyed the bed, wanting nothing more than to slip back between the covers.

But something felt wrong. Yoda's absence bothered her more than she wanted to admit. And Officer Howell hadn't shown herself.

She leaned toward the phone. "Hunter?" she whispered. "Are you there?"

No answer. But the phone was still connected. Maybe he had walked out of the room for a minute. She picked up her phone — the battery was almost dead. She laid it back down and quickly plugged it into her charger, annoyed that she'd forgotten to do it earlier. She tugged a pair of sweatpants over her pajama shorts and padded barefoot from the bedroom into the hall. The nightlight spread enough light that she could see clearly. She looked left, then right.

Nothing.

When the alarm sounded for that brief second, the dog entered the kitchen and came over to investigate. The killer held out a hand. The doggie treats disappeared immediately.

"Good boy. Have a nice nap."

Hurried footsteps sounded from the hall.

The killer's blood surged, excitement pounded. The anxiety was gone now, but anticipation made for slick palms and a fast heartbeat.

"Alexia?" The one word whisper echoed in the foyer. The cop. Being cautious. Not sure who was lurking in the kitchen.

"I'm in here," the killer whispered.

"Oh," the officer said in a normal voice. "It's pitch black in here. Let me find a light." Rustling sounded. The officer was running her hand along the wall, looking for the switch. "I thought I heard the alarm —"

The wire passed over the cop's head and landed underneath her jaw, tightening immediately.

After a brief, silent struggle, the officer surrendered and went slack.

"Now, Alexia. Your turn."

Her stomach jumped and twisted.

Alexia thought about her cell phone on the bedside table. She should have brought it with her anyway. Assuming Hunter was still on the other end. Somehow she knew he was. However, if someone was in the house with a gun, Hunter wouldn't be much help. And she might need both hands.

Alexia continued down the hall and into the den. Shadows danced, caused by the nightlights and the moon shining through the window blinds.

And still no sign of Yoda or Officer Howell.

Nerves humming, shoulders tensed, Alexia

made her way to the kitchen where she found Chewie under the table. Now she felt the first stirrings of real fear. At night, Chewie liked the recliner in the den. And Officer Howell wasn't responding. Her eyes fell to the counter where Serena's phone should have been. The handset was missing from its cradle.

Her breath caught in her lungs. Something was definitely wrong.

As she hurried from the kitchen into the foyer, the green light on the alarm pad caught her eye.

Green? It should be red. Meaning it was armed. She'd punched in the numbers before she'd walked to her room.

And now it was green. Meaning it was unarmed.

Full-blown panic exploded within her. She raced for the front door, her one thought to open it and get out of the house.

"Hello, Alexia."

Her fingers froze on the doorknob.

Slowly, she turned. And came face-to-face with her black masked intruder.

Her breath stopped, terror seized her. *Think. You have to think.*

But all she could process was that she was trapped. There was no way she'd be able to get a door open fast enough. Her only hope was the cell phone in the bedroom.

"Where's . . . Yoda?" she blurted. She almost asked about Officer Howell and stopped herself at the last minute. What if the woman was hiding somewhere, waiting for a chance to disarm the intruder? Over the pounding of her heart, the rushing of her blood, she strained to hear, to really listen to the voice.

A low laugh came from the black form. "The dog? You're worried about the dog? Don't worry, the mutt's just sleeping. I don't kill animals."

But killing her wouldn't be a problem. She got the unspoken message. Her eyes darted. Where was the officer?

"What do you want? Why are you doing this?" she whispered.

"Where's Jillian?"

"Why do you want to know where Jillian is?" Alexia inched away from the door.

The knife in the intruder's right hand lifted. "Where is she?"

Unable to think of anything else that she could say that would save her, Alexia turned and darted down the hall, her goal the bedroom where she prayed Hunter was still on the line.

Light footsteps followed behind her, the unhurried pace mocking her, chilling her with the knowledge that her attacker was very confident in how this night would end.

Silence came from the phone. Was she asleep or just lying there thinking?

"Lex?" he whispered.

No answer.

Asleep. He smiled and started to hang up. Then hesitated. If she woke up, she might want to know he was still there. With a shrug, he set the cell phone on the end table and turned back to finish writing out the plan he and Katie had come up with. He still didn't like it, but it would definitely be effective.

After using his home phone for three more calls to line everything up, he decided to call it a night.

A resounding crash came from his cell phone still on speaker. A muffled scream froze him even as his adrenaline spiked.

Alexia!

"Hunter! Help me!"

34

Friday, 10:58 p.m.

She had nowhere else to run. Her attacker had easily kicked the bedroom door in and made a beeline toward her. Alexia picked up the bedside lamp and swung it.

She missed.

Trapped. She was trapped. "Stop! Leave me alone!"

Fear beat a steady rhythm within her as did a rage that began to consume her.

The masked person lunged, grabbed at her as Alexia did her best to dodge the outstretched hand.

The hand that snagged a chunk of hair.

White pain streaked through her as she froze. "Please," she whispered.

A sickly sweet aroma wafted toward her and she turned her head from it. The knife flashed in front of her face, but it wasn't aimed to cut her. Instead, it was held behind a cloth.

The cloth that she instinctively knew was supposed to drug her.

Terror shot through her as it closed in and slapped over her mouth and nose. She held her breath and jerked. But he was stronger than she was — and she was in good shape, strong enough to pass the rigorous training of a firefighter.

She needed air.

Another twist pulled her face free. The knife clattered to the floor. The cloth slipped away long enough for Alexia to draw breath.

And then she heard his voice. "Lex! Are you there? What's going on? I'm on my way!"

The fingers gripped her hair, yanking. The pain seared through her.

Lashing out, she avoided the cloth once more even as panic made her breath come in quick pants.

Where was her help? Where was the detective watching her house?

Her attacker moved once more, strong fingers never slacking. Alexia felt herself weakening. She wanted to cry out. Instead, she kicked, squirmed, resisted, and fought with everything in her.

Until something slammed into her stomach, paralyzing her for a few seconds as her lungs emptied.

The cloth slapped back over her face, she breathed in once, twice, and knew no more.

Hunter snatched up his landline and called Jimmy, worry for Alexia eating at his gut.

No answer.

He grabbed his car keys and punched in dispatch's number. He rattled off the address, gave her the short version of what was happening, and listened to the struggle going on over his cell phone.

"Leave her alone!" he yelled into the device. He knew his order would do no good. A fact that was confirmed when a light chuckle rang out. It sounded distant. The person must be standing on the other side of the room from Alexia's phone.

In the car and heading down the road, he prayed.

The cell phone sat in the cup holder in front of him, mocking him with its sudden silence.

Ten seconds later, heavy breathing filtered to him. A grunt.

"Who are you?" Hunter growled. "I've called for backup and I'm on my way to find you." He kept his words low, controlled, not expecting an answer, but hoping the person had stopped to listen.

Where were Jimmy and Marty? Why

hadn't either answered their phone?

"Then I'll just have to move a little faster, won't I?" The hissing voice startled him and he almost froze.

Then he gunned the car. "Hang on, Lex, I'm coming!"

The next six minutes were the longest in his life. Finally, he rolled up to the curb to see that red and blue lights had taken over the neighborhood.

At the sight of the ambulance, his stomach dropped.

At the sight of the draped body on the gurney, he nearly lost his dinner.

"Lex!" He bolted from his car.

And skidded to a stop.

Chad hovered over Alexia as the paramedics worked on her.

Jerking from his stunned lethargy, Hunter raced to her and dropped to his knees. "What's wrong with her?" he demanded. Then fixed his gaze on his brother. "What did you do to her?"

Chad recoiled. "What?"

"Every time something bad happens, you're there."

His brother flinched, then drew back. Hunter told himself to shut up, but in his mind, he could clearly see his notes — as though he had them in front of him.

Chad shows up.

Not now, he told himself. Later. "Where's Jimmy?"

"He's dead. So's Marty." Chad's voice was tight, angry. But controlled. "Both Jimmy and Marty were strangled. The person was watching and ready to strike when the opportunity presented itself. Probably came in from the woods behind the house."

"Marty was supposed to be watching those woods." Hunter wondered if Jimmy and Marty had died before or after Chad arrived on the scene, then shuddered at the thought. No, it was a coincidence. Chad wouldn't . . .

Focus on Alexia. Ignoring his sibling, Hunter looked down at the woman he was falling for. She looked pale, yet peaceful. And no blood that he could see. He looked at the paramedic who released the blood pressure cuff from around Alexia's upper arm. Her name badge read Sheri Morris. He asked, "What is it? What's wrong with her?"

Ms. Morris's eyes met his. "It's like she's in a really deep sleep. My guess is some kind of drug. Her vitals are slow, but nothing dangerous. We'll get to the hospital and let a doctor check her out."

"And she was just lying out here in the

yard when you arrived?"

The paramedic helped her partner lift Alexia onto the second gurney. Thank goodness the sheet was only drawn to her chin.

Ms. Morris grunted as she rolled the gurney toward the back of the ambulance. "No. That guy you were arguing with was carrying her toward his car. When he saw us, he waved us over to help."

Hunter whirled to face Chad. "Carrying her toward your car?"

Chad exploded. "I was getting her to a hospital, man!"

"What about Jimmy and Marty? Were you going to try to get them to a hospital too?" Hunter yelled back.

Chad's fingers curled into a fist and Hunter prepared himself for a blow.

Instead, Chad took a deep breath and said through clenched teeth, "They were dead when I got here. At least Jimmy was. Officer Cortez found Marty in the kitchen pantry. They couldn't revive her."

Hunter swallowed a groan as Chad said, "I checked Jimmy, called it in, and then this person comes out of the house carrying Alexia like a sack of potatoes. I hollered at him and went after him. He dropped her and took off." His brother swiped a hand down his face as though the action could get rid of the tension he obviously felt. "I had to either chase him or make sure Alexia was okay." His eyes drilled into Hunter's. "I checked on Alexia. When she wasn't responsive, I picked her up and figured it might be faster to drive her to the hospital myself. Then these guys showed up."

"We were right around the block up at the diner. Took us less than a minute to get here," Ms. Morris said. "Now, we're ready to roll. Bye, guys."

She started to shut the door when Hunter stopped her. "I'm going with you."

"You can ride up front or meet us there."

Hunter debated for about three seconds. He might need his car. "I'll meet you there."

"I'm right behind you," Chad said.

"No, you're not." Hunter held up a hand, halting his brother's movement. "You're the only one that saw the person trying to snatch Alexia. You need to write up an incident report."

"I can do that later."

Hunter felt his jaw go rigid. "Do it now, please. You want to help Alexia? The sooner we have all the details, the sooner we'll catch the creep that did this."

It took all of his self-control not to plant his fist on Chad's nose. Instead, he took a deep breath and let it out slowly.

Self-control.

Right.

He didn't want to argue with Chad. He wanted to be with Alexia. But he was a professional and had an attempted kidnapping to investigate. With regret, he watched the ambulance pull out of the drive and head toward the subdivision's exit.

First things first. Protection for Alexia.

He called his captain and filled the man in. Then asked who could be spared to cover Alexia. The captain promised to have someone meet the ambulance at the hospital, then ordered Hunter to solve this case yesterday.

"I'm working on it, sir. Every cop within twenty miles is now on this scene ransacking the neighborhood looking for the perp and asking questions. We're doing all we can do."

"Do more. This is getting ridiculous. This perp is making us all look like idiots. And now we have two more murders. Killing Jimmy and Marty was a big mistake." Grief filled the man's voice. He'd lost two of his own tonight. They all had.

"The media's going to be all over this. In fact, I think I see a truck pulling up now."

"Use them. Get the word out. We don't have a great description of the killer, but maybe something will filter in."

"I'll put Chad on it if that's all right."

"Do it. This woman, Alexia, she either knows something or has something this person wants. Find out what it is."

"Yes sir." Relief filled him, glad he had his captain's permission to pull out all the stops to protect Alexia. Although, short of using a safe house and hiding her away, there wasn't much more that he could do.

He pulled Chad aside. "All right. Run it by me again."

Chad did, leaving out no detail. And Hunter had to admit his brother was a good cop with great observation skills.

Chad rubbed his head and frowned. "You know, there's something about the way the perp moved."

Hunter lifted a brow. "What do you mean?"

His brother shook his head. "I mean, the dude was strong to be able to carry Alexia the way he did. What do you think she weighs? A hundred twenty? Twenty-five, tops?"

"Yeah. Probably." He had a glimmer of where Chad was going with this. "So, our intruder was someone who works out a lot?"

"Definitely. But not just that. It was the way he ran after he dropped Alexia to the ground. It was more like *he* was actually a *she*."

Hunter considered Chad's little bomb-shell. "Are you serious?"

"Yeah. In fact the more I think about it, the more I'm not liking it."

Because you're the one who's actually after Alexia and are trying to throw me? Or because you are truly on to something?

Chad swallowed hard. "She . . . uh . . . kind of reminded me of . . . someone."

"Who?"

"Well, it was just the build, the way the person ran . . ."

"Who, Chad?"

"Christine."

35

Saturday, 9:04 a.m.

Alexia got tired of waiting on the paperwork that would allow her to leave the hospital. Instead of sitting in her room twiddling her thumbs and watching brain-numbing shows on the little TV, she decided to get up and visit her mother. For the most part, she felt fine after her terrorizing ordeal from the night before. A tender scalp from where her hair had almost been yanked out, some lingering fatigue, and a slight headache. The side effects of being drugged with chloroform.

She opened her door and walked into the hall where she found an officer sitting with his back to the wall. He stood when he saw her.

"Ma'am? Is everything all right?"

"I'm just going to take a walk, Officer —" she leaned forward to read his name badge — "Pickens."

"Then I'll walk with you."

Alexia nodded, not minding the watchful eyes. In fact, she was grateful for them and knew that she could thank Hunter for the protection.

Officer Pickens was quiet as she made her way to the nurses' station to let them know where they could find her should they need to.

Five minutes later, she found herself on her mother's floor in front of her door. Officer Pickens planted himself at attention to one side of the door.

Alexia knocked, then pushed into the room slowly, not wanting to wake the woman should she be sleeping. Peering around the edge, she saw her mother propped up in the bed. A bowl of soup sat in front of her.

"Hi, Mom."

At Alexia's voice, the woman's eyes brightened. "Alexia, come in, darling."

Alexia made her way to the empty chair beside the bed. "You look better today."

"The medicine they gave me seems to be working. For now."

Interesting comment. "Where's your sidekick?"

"Michael?" Her mother took a sip of the soup from the silver spoon. "I told him he

384

couldn't stay by my side the rest of his life. He has a job and needed to go do it."

"He cares a lot for you."

Her mother paused and studied Alexia for a moment. Then she gave a slow nod. "Yes. He does."

Alexia fidgeted. Then blurted, "I figured after Dad, you wouldn't want another man."

The woman blanched, then grimaced. "I didn't for a long time. Then I met Michael. He's . . . special. I like him."

"Do you love him?"

A frail shoulder lifted in a slight shrug. "I don't know. I'm not sure I even know how to love a man."

The honest confession threw Alexia for a moment. Then she asked, "Why did you send me away after graduation?" She hadn't meant to be so blunt, but she had to know.

Her mother drew in a deep breath and let it out in a slow, shallow stream. "You were so anxious to leave, to get away, I didn't blame you."

"But you practically forced me out the door. Did you hate me that much?"

An agonized cry escaped the dry lips. The spoon clattered to the tray. "No, no, Alexia. I *loved* you that much!"

Alexia blinked at the passionate words. Her heart trembled and she felt short of breath. "How can you say that?" Anger churned. "How *dare* you say that?"

A single tear traced a zigzag path down her mother's cheek. "I had to send you away. My precious child. Your father was so bitter, so angry with you. He blamed you for the fire, for his burns and his pain. He was so full of the desire for revenge that I knew as soon as he regained his strength, he would do something to you. Something horrible." Another tear slipped from beneath her lashes. "I had to send you away. I had to make you hate me enough that you would leave. It wasn't hard," she finished with a whisper, "you already had no respect for me for staying with your father. Turning that to hate didn't take much."

Stunned, Alexia stared at the woman she'd resented, maybe even hated, for the past ten years. For years, she'd hung onto the memory of her mother telling her to get out and never come back.

It was that memory that fueled her desire to succeed, to show her mother she wasn't a loser, that she was lovable. To prove she was somebody. Her fingers went to the ring on her left hand. Twisting, turning, worrying it.

And all along, her mother had loved her? Had sent her away because she feared for

Alexia's life? It was almost too much to take in.

Alexia pulled in a shuddering breath. "What about after he left? Why didn't you tell me? Why wait until this past year to start trying to get in touch with me?"

Her mother shrugged a sad, slow lift of her shoulders. "It was only recently that I've felt safe enough to try to contact you. I was so afraid he'd come back," she whispered.

Alexia swallowed hard. Yeah, she still had that nightmare too.

Her mother's gaze fell to Alexia's hands. "You still wear the ring?"

"What?"

"The ring I gave you for your twelfth birthday, remember?" A smile softened her features.

Alexia stared at the piece of silver jewelry. "Yes. I remember." The ring had brought her comfort in the last ten years. She never took it off. Swallowing hard, she was hit with the knowledge that it was the connection with her mother she'd longed for. A connection she never allowed herself to openly admit. Until now. Confused by her conflicting feelings of love and hate for the woman before her, she asked, "What is it you need me to do for you, Mom?"

"What?" Confusion knit the woman's

brow then cleared. "Oh. The conversation from the other day."

"Yeah."

"It was . . . nothing, Alexia. All right? Just forget you heard what you heard. Really, it's nothing."

"It's not nothing and I can't forget. Just tell me what Michael wants me to help you with."

A shaky hand brought a tissue to press them against her dry lips. A sigh escaped and she closed her eyes for a brief moment. "I need a bone marrow transplant."

Surprise slugged her. "What?"

"I have aplastic anemia. Michael —" She paused, then sighed and closed her eyes. When she opened them, more tears swam, threatening a deluge. "Michael told me I needed to ask you to be tested as a possible donor."

Alexia froze as she took in her mother's words. Her mouth moved but nothing came out. Then she started laughing. A hysterical laugh void of humor. The laughter turned to tears, but she wouldn't let them fall. She clamped a hand over her mouth, unable to figure out why she was reacting this way.

Finally, she calmed enough to swallow. "You want me to be tested."

Tears flowed down her mother's cheeks,

freely, like a river with a broken dam. "No. No, I don't."

That stopped Alexia. "What?"

"I don't. I told him I couldn't ask that of you. Because I don't want you to think . . ." She pressed her lips together. "No. I don't want you to be tested. You weren't supposed to find out, to know about this. I didn't want you to know." Her voice trailed off into a whisper. Then she gathered some strength and said, "I've been added to the transplant list. I'll find a donor another way."

36

Saturday, 9:58 a.m.

Hunter flashed his badge to the officer seated outside of Alexia's room. The man nodded and motioned him to the door. Hunter rapped his knuckles on the wood, waited until he heard her call "Come in," and pushed the door open.

He stepped into the room, a bouquet of flowers clutched in his fist. Alexia sat on the bed fully dressed. She looked tired and stressed, but other than that, he couldn't see any obvious side effects from the night before. And she looked beautiful to him. Her red curls dangled over her shoulders, just begging him to run his fingers through them.

He cleared his throat. "Hey, how are you feeling this morning?"

She shrugged, but her emerald eyes flashed with gladness at seeing him. "I'm doing all right. Other than a little bit of a

headache, I'm fine. The doctor said someone used chloroform on me."

Hunter winced. "Yeah. I got the criminal
report. It came last night, but you were
really out of it. I just ran home to grab a
shower and get back over here."

Her gaze flicked to the floor, then back to
him. "What happened to the officer watching the house? And Officer Howell?"

Hunter swallowed. "They're . . . dead."

She nodded, no emotion showing other
than a shuddering indrawn breath. "I'm
sorry," she whispered and closed her eyes.
"I'm so sorry."

"We are too."

Alexia lifted her eyes to his. Dry eyes, he
noticed, although her upper teeth were sunk
deep into her lower lip. After a minute, she
said, "How did the person get in the house?"

"With the alarm code."

Another short nod as she considered this.
"And how did this person get the code?"

"That one I haven't figured out yet. Or
how he got the drop on Marty. She was
killed, then hidden in the kitchen pantry
with the dog." He took a step closer, then
another.

Finally, he reached the bed and sat beside
her. In a smooth move, she turned and
wrapped her arms around his waist, burying

her face in his shoulder. Fortunately, it was his good arm, not the one that still ached from the recent bullet wound.

"Why is this happening, Hunter? What did I do to deserve this? Am I such a rotten person that God has to come after me this way?" she whispered.

He squeezed her shoulders a little tighter and leaned over to place a kiss on her head. "It's not God doing this. He loves you and wants the best for you whether you can believe that or not." He paused. "I don't know what's going on, but I promise, from now on, I'm not letting you out of my sight until we get this figured out."

"Thanks."

They sat there for the next fifteen minutes, not moving, not talking, just . . . being. And Hunter prayed. Without ceasing. For Alexia, for justice, for peace, for wisdom. For God to show Alexia he loved her and was there for her.

She finally stirred and stood. "I'm ready to get out of here." A pout formed on her lips. "You know, this person is really getting on my nerves. I can't handle anyone else dying because of me."

He thought she might let the tears fall at this point, but she blinked them back.

"Nobody died because of you. Two good

cops died because there's a sicko out there."

He could tell she wanted to argue. Instead, she said, "I want to leave."

"Have you been released yet?"

"The doctor came by a little earlier. I'm just waiting on the paperwork."

"Sure." He lifted a hand to rub circles on her back. "What's wrong, Lex?"

She raised a brow. "You have to ask?"

He simply stared at her and a frown furrowed her brow.

Finally she said, "I'm not sure anything is actually wrong — other than the obvious. I had a conversation with my mother this morning that I need to process."

"Want to share?"

Alexia was silent for so long after his question, he wondered if she was going to answer.

Then she said, "My mom needs a bone marrow transplant."

"And she wants you to get tested to see if you're a match."

"I'm not sure if she does or not. I can't tell if she's playing me or if . . ." A sigh slipped out and she grimaced. "I hate being so suspicious. Why can't I just take things at face value?" She told him the rest of the conversation. "So, part of me is hurt, thinking she only wants to make nice to get me to have the test and see if I'm a match. But part of me wants to really believe her when she says I wasn't supposed to find out because she doesn't want me believing exactly that." A shrug. "I do know that she was trying to get in touch with me before she found out about the need for the transplant, so . . ." She stood and paced to the other side of the room, then turned back and waved a hand dismissing the topic. "I'll think about it and figure out what to do."

"Would you like to pray about it?"

She froze. "Pray about it? Like . . . with you?"

"Sure. I've been praying *for* you — now, if you want, I'd be glad to pray *with* you."

He waited while she thought about it. "I don't know, Hunter. That might be a little weird. I wouldn't know the first thing about praying with someone. I'm just now figuring out how to pray inside my head."

Her words lifted his heart. So, she'd been praying on her own. He was glad to hear it. "Come here and I'll show you."

After another brief hesitation, she stepped over to him and placed her hands in his. He bowed his head and closed his eyes. He could feel her watching him. Not letting it distract him, he focused on the prayer, tuning his heart to the God who would listen.

"Lord, thank you for your unconditional love and your interest in even the smallest details of our lives. You know what's going on here. You heard the conversation. Alexia has some choices to make. Could you just open her eyes to the truth and lead her to the right decision?" He prayed just a little longer, ending with a request for Alexia's protection and justice for the one after her. "In your name, Jesus, we pray. Amen."

When he opened his eyes, he found Alexia staring at him. He smiled. "What?"

Her lips curved into a smile and some of the stress seemed to be gone from her face. "That wasn't so weird."

Hunter laughed and pulled her into a hug. Then he sobered. "You'll know what to do, Lex. Trust God."

"Hmm."

Now for the hard part. "I need to ask you something."

"What?" she mumbled into his chest.

Hunter gripped her upper arms and gently pushed her back. "I need to know if you saw anything last night. If you had any impressions about your attacker. Anything."

Alexia sighed. "Somehow I figured we'd get to this."

"Yeah, you need to tell me exactly what happened."

Hunter watched her gather her thoughts. She said, "I was in bed asleep. Then the alarm went off. I think. Just for a split second, like when you enter the door and hurry to punch the numbers in."

He frowned.

"At first I just laid there, wondering if I'd heard right or if I was dreaming."

"I must have been in the bathroom when that happened. I didn't hear it go off. But Marty did and probably went to investigate."

Alexia eyed him. "And when she did, the person was waiting for her?"

He nodded his approval. "Marty was garroted."

A pained groan escaped her. "That's horrible." She blinked her shock. "How can someone *do* that?"

"It's a brutal way to kill a person." Hunter felt the anger claw at him. He controlled it and said, "Jimmy was killed the same way. The killer managed to crawl into the backseat of his car and get him."

"And I was drugged. So, it's still pretty obvious that this person doesn't want me dead. Yet."

"Right. But he's not afraid of killing. In fact, he's quite skilled at it." Hunter paused. "Anything else?"

She filled him in on the rest of it, ending with waking in the hospital with the doctor standing over her.

Hunter took her hand. "I need you to think about something."

"What?"

"The person who attacked you . . ." He paused, wondering if he should even bring it up. Finally, he said, "Could you tell if it was a man or a woman?"

She lifted a brow. "I . . . don't know. I mean . . . I think it was a man. But I suppose it could have been a really strong woman. Maybe." Doubt crossed her face. "I don't know, Hunter. I'm pretty strong for a woman. I mean, I work out all the time. Becoming a firefighter isn't physically easy. I'm stronger than a lot of men. So for a woman to overpower me . . ." She shrugged. And wondered at the relief on his face. "Why would you ask that?"

He shook his head and pursed his lips. "Just something Chad mentioned."

"What was that?"

"He seemed to think the person he saw carrying you out of your house was a woman."

"And how would he know that? The person was dressed completely in black. I mean from head to toe. And I struggled and fought against him . . . her . . . whoever." A light pink stained her cheeks. "And I didn't notice any . . . uh . . . female attributes during my struggle."

He smiled. "Were you in any kind of state of mind to notice?"

She grimaced. "No, all I was thinking was that I wasn't ready to die yet. I know the person is taller than I am. That I'm sure of."

He stood and pulled her up beside him. "I'm six feet tall, exactly. How tall are you? Five six? Five seven?"

"Five seven. And a half."

His hands rested on her shoulders as he stepped closer. The top of her head came to just below his chin. He liked being this close to her. Memories of their shared kisses surged to the surface.

"Okay," he said, clearing his throat, "five seven and a half. Now, tell me where you think you might measure against the person who attacked you."

"About your height. Maybe a little shorter."

He frowned. "Anything else? Any smells?"

"Just the smell of my own fear." Alexia shook her head. "No, nothing really. Except . . ."

"Yeah?"

She still stood in his arms and he found he wasn't in any hurry to let her go. She said, "Maybe . . . fabric softener."

"Fabric softener?"

"Maybe. But then I was smelling the chloroform and was doing my best to avoid it." She grimaced. "Only I failed."

His fingers started a slow motion on her shoulders, offering a light massage. She leaned into it and he felt her muscles start to relax.

"How's your headache?" he asked.

"Fading by the second," she murmured as her eyes closed.

Hunter covered her lips with his, pulling her closer, his hand now rubbing circles on her shoulder blade. She kissed him back and Hunter silently thanked God that she was alive and well. Holding her, his senses tantalized by her nearness, the scent of her freshly washed hair, nearly had him on his knees.

And then she pulled back. Wide-eyed, she stared up at him. The red flush on her cheeks said she'd enjoyed the moment as much as he.

The door opened and he turned to face the nurse, who handed Alexia the papers that would spring her. As she signed, the woman rattled off instructions finally ending with, "Call your doctor if you have any problems. And be sure to get some rest."

"Rest. Right."

Knuckles rapped on the door. Hunter looked up to find Chad's large frame standing in the doorway. He smiled at Alexia, then frowned when he spotted Hunter. "Morning."

"Good morning, Chad." Alexia's body language shifted. Hunter thought she might not want Chad here. Which he thought was odd, since he'd probably saved her life last night.

She said, "I hear I owe you a big thank-you."

Chad's shoulders lifted in a modest shrug. "I was just in the right place at the right time."

"Speaking of that," Hunter said, "how was it you were at Serena's house that time of the night anyway?"

Chad's eyes narrowed in anger at his brother's tone. "What are you implying, Hunter?"

Innocence radiated from Hunter. "I'm not implying anything. I was just curious how you came to be there."

Another shrug. "I had a call out that way and decided to drive by." His lips tightened. "I saw Jimmy kind of slumped over the wheel and pulled up next to him to blast him for sleeping on the job." Chad's eyes flickered and grief twisted his face for a brief moment. "Then the front door opened and out comes this person dressed in black carrying Alexia over his shoulder." He shook his head. "It was so weird. So blatant. Like the person didn't think anything about kidnapping someone from their home and just walking out the front door."

"You're right," Hunter agreed. "It is weird."

"Anyway, I yelled at him to freeze. He took two steps, then threw Alexia to the ground and took off."

"And the way he ran was weird too, you said."

Chad sighed. "Yeah, it was."

"What do you mean?" Alexia asked.

"I mean . . . women run differently than men. When the person took off, it looked like a woman running."

"He said it looked like Christine," Hunter said.

Alexia stared at the brothers. "Christine? Really? Have you two lost your minds?"

Hunter finally allowed a smile to crack and he saw Alexia relax as she realized he didn't believe it one bit.

Chad flushed and shot Hunter a disgusted

look. "I said she ran *like* Christine, not that it *was* Christine."

Alexia let out a little laugh. "No, it definitely wasn't Christine." She frowned. "And I don't think it was a woman. If it was, she was awfully strong."

"There are a lot of strong women out there," Chad muttered defensively. "Those who stay in shape, lift weights." He crossed his arms. "Firefighters, for example."

Alexia nodded. "You have a point."

Chad glared at Hunter. "You know this as well as I do. What about that woman who nearly took you down two years ago? It took you and two other cops to subdue her — and she wasn't on drugs."

Hunter grimaced. "Yeah. I remember that."

"Uh, you guys ready to go?"

All three of them jerked at the orderly's quiet question. He'd come up without a sound.

"Sure." Alexia settled herself in the wheelchair, too tired to argue that she could walk out on her own just fine.

Hunter and Chad followed behind.

Hunter's cell phone rang and he snatched it.

"It's all in place," Pete said. Pete was a fellow detective and occasional racquetball buddy. But Pete wasn't happy about Hunter's latest request.

"You're sure?"

"I'm sure, Hunter. You better hope Chad doesn't find out about any of this."

"Yeah. All right. I'll be there shortly and we'll discuss that."

Hunter caught Chad's satisfied gleam and knew that he was thinking he was going to get to take her home.

He looked at Alexia. "I've got to go. Katie's got some information she wants to share with me." His eyes flicked to Chad. "You can take her home, right?"

"Sure." Surprise flashed across his face. "It would be my pleasure."

Hunter looked back at Alexia and she motioned for him to go. "I'll be fine. I'll see you tonight around six thirty, right?"

He lifted a brow in disbelief. "What? You're still planning on going?"

"Well, of course." She frowned. "I mean if you still want me to."

"Of course I still want you to. I just wasn't sure you'd feel up to it. You've had some pretty rough days."

Alexia firmed her jaw. "I'm not letting this creep mess with me any more than I can help it. I'll go to Serena's and get some rest and be ready for you to come pick me up."

"What's tonight?" Chad asked, the frown pulling his brows to the bridge of his nose.

Hunter lifted a brow. "The dinner. Aren't you going?"

Chad's eyes flew upward and he groaned. "Aw man . . . no, I'd forgotten all about that." He gave them a puppy dog look. "I hate those things."

Hunter slapped his brother on the back, the first gesture of real camaraderie in a long while. "I know, bro, but it's gotta be done."

Chad grumbled, "Maybe I can get the flu between now and then."

This time Hunter gave a genuine laugh. "No way. If Christine and I have to go, you do too."

"And you're going with him?" Chad asked Alexia.

"Yes."

A sigh slipped out of Chad. A long, mournful sigh.

Hunter turned serious and lasered Chad with a deadly look. "Don't let anything happen to her."

37

It was all Hunter could do to let the elevator door shut behind him. It had taken everything in him to leave Alexia with Chad. But . . . it had to be done.

Was he out of his mind leaving her alone with a man he had doubts about?

But this was Chad. His baby brother. Sure, he was a little messed up because of his wife's desertion, but Chad wasn't a murderer. Besides, he had no connection to Devin other than graduating with the man.

Hunter had checked. And felt guilty for doing so. But couldn't deny he was relieved when nothing turned up. There was absolutely no evidence to suggest Chad was the one after Alexia.

Except that he kept turning up almost every time there was trouble. And he had the nerve to suggest the attacker was a woman.

Who reminded him of their sister, Christine.

Lunacy.

A chill shot through him. What if that was Chad's way of throwing suspicion elsewhere?

Because if they started looking for a tall woman who worked out and was able to carry another woman the size of Alexia over her shoulder . . . well, that would take all eyes from the men in Alexia's life, wouldn't it?

And Chad definitely appeared to want to be a man in Alexia's life.

And Hunter had just asked him to take her home.

But he had to know.

As Alexia and Chad exited the hospital, she couldn't help but flinch as memories assailed her from the last time she'd walked out these doors. The orderly had let her out when the elevator doors opened and hadn't bothered to argue when she claimed that she could make it out the doors unassisted.

Chad's hand on her arm pulled her attention to his concerned eyes. "What is it?"

"Just some bad memories."

"Ah yes, the shooter on the roof." A muscle jumped in his jaw. "Good thing the guy was a lousy shot."

She paused and looked at him. "I thought you thought it was a woman."

He shrugged. "Well, yeah. I do. But Hunter thinks I'm crazy."

Alexia decided not to touch that comment and climbed into the car. A sleek black Corvette. "Nice ride you have here."

He flashed her a grin. "I've had this car since I graduated from the academy. A present from my parents."

A pang shot through Alexia as she remembered her own graduation. High school graduation. All by herself. No family. No one to celebrate with her.

Except her two best friends.

"Have you heard from Jillian Carter?" she asked.

Chad jerked. "Jillian?"

"Yes. I know you remember her." A memory dawned. "Didn't you date her for a while?"

A red flush crept up his neck and into his cheeks. "We did. For about three months before what's his name moved in on me."

"Right. Colton Brady."

"Yep. Colton."

"What's he doing now anyway?"

Chad barked a laugh. "You wouldn't believe me if I told you."

"Seriously. What's he doing?"

A snort escaped Chad. "He's an agent with SLED."

Alexia lifted a brow. "Did everyone in our graduating class go into law enforcement?"

Chad let out a laugh as he made a right turn. "Kind of seems like it, doesn't it?"

Then Chad pulled up in front of a beautiful brick home in one of the nicest neighborhoods in Columbia. She simply stared.

"Come on inside." He smiled and a hint of a dimple dented his cheek.

She hadn't been paying attention as he was driving. She'd been focused on the conversation. "Chad, I'm tired, I just want to go home. Please."

"I know. And I'm going to take you there, but first I want to show you something."

With a sigh, Alexia opened the door and climbed out. "What is it?"

"Follow me."

She did. Reluctantly.

He opened the front door for her and she stepped inside an amazing foyer. Wood greeted her. Wood floors, wood paneling. Wooden staircase leading up to the second floor balcony. To her left was the den area. To the right, the kitchen. She looked at Chad. He seemed to be waiting for her to say something.

"It's beautiful." And it was.

Chad let the storm door close silently behind him as he stepped over the threshold. "It's my refuge."

She could imagine him leaving the front door open to the wide wraparound porch, sitting in the kitchen, listening to the night sounds through the screen door. "Why did you bring me here?"

"I wanted to share it with you."

She sighed. "Look, Chad. I appreciate you want to share it with me. I do. But maybe another time. It's been a rough day."

Chad left the heavy wooden front door open and stomped across the open foyer and into the den. He turned and glared at her from across the room. "What is it about Hunter that makes him so special?"

She didn't like the turn of this conversation. "What do you mean?"

"I mean, he always gets the promotion first, he always solves the case first, and he always gets the girl I'm interested in. What is up with that?"

She threw her hands up in frustration. "What do you want me to say?"

"It's not so much what I want you to *say* as what I want you to *see*. I want you to see what I could give you, that I'm not a loser just because I drink a little too much sometimes. I'm not an alcoholic." He frowned. "Although I can see why you would have that impression."

She clenched her fists at her side. "No one ever said you were a loser."

"But your actions say you believe it."

"What actions?" she cried.

"The mooning over Hunter, for crying out loud! And ignoring me. What's wrong with me?" She felt quite sure he hadn't meant for the words to come out so petulant.

Alexia eyed the man and felt a twinge of sympathy for him — and maybe a smidge of fear? Warily, she backed up. "Nothing's wrong with you, Chad. You're a great guy. I just happen to be . . ." She searched for the right word, not wanting to use the first ones that came to mind — in love with. ". . . attracted . . . to your brother. It's nothing personal. Nothing I could necessarily control. It just is."

He stared at her and she blinked. The rage on his face sent shivers of real fear through her.

"Nothing personal?" he hissed.

Alexia backed toward the kitchen. She'd seen the back door as they pulled into the driveway. If she couldn't get out the front, she'd settle for the back.

Chad took two steps toward her.

She held up a hand. "Stop. You're scaring me."

He froze. Then threw up his hands. "I don't want to scare you. I want you to understand."

"Understand what?" Frustration bit at her. How should she handle this?

The case of beer on the counter nailed home the fact that in spite of Chad's attempts to get it together, he was still a man who needed help.

"Understand that I'm just as good a man as Hunter. I can give you all this and more. I did great in the stock market, pulled out before it crashed. I have enough money to set you up so you never have to work again." His eyes pleaded with her for something. Something she didn't have to give him.

"Chad . . ." She tried to sound soothing, but her heart stuttered in fear. He looked too much like her father in this moment. "There's someone out there for you. Someone who'll be lucky to get you. But it isn't me," she whispered.

A fist slammed down onto the mantel and she jumped, her mind flashing to her father, gun in hand, held against her sister's head.

"Stop it!" she screamed at Chad. "Stop it! Don't hurt her!" Her fingers curled around a beer can and she lifted it.

Time stopped and whirled back to that awful day. The smell of paint seared her nose. Drop cloths lined the floor to protect it from her father's rare attempt to do something constructive around the house.

"Get me a beer, girl," he ordered around the cigarette.

Alexia didn't move.

He dropped the paintbrush into the little plastic tray and eyed her. "I said get me a beer, you useless twit."

"Get your own beer," she said, her tone defiant, scared, shaky, unsure about what she was saying.

The world stopped.

He stared at her, the cigarette dangling from his lips, forgotten. She hid her shaking hands behind the counter. The den opened up into the kitchen. Standing at the sink, she could see every move he made. "What did you say?"

"I said, 'Get your own beer.' " Repeating the words fueled her courage. His shock surprised — and delighted — her. "You've treated me like a slave all my life. Well, I'm sick of it. And I'm sick of you."

"Alexia, no," her mother whispered from the basement door.

"Get me a beer! Now!" her father screamed at her.

Her heart pounded. With fear or what, she wasn't sure. All she knew was that she wanted out from her miserable life. Maybe if he killed her, he would go to prison and her sister and mother would finally be free.

"No." She kept her head up, her eyes locked on his.

"I'll get it, honey." Her mother scurried to the refrigerator. "I've got it right here." She rushed to the now raging man and held the can out to him.

He whirled on his wife and knocked the hand that contained the can. Almost as an afterthought, he punched her in the face, sending her to the floor beside Karen.

Alexia flinched, dread creeping up on the courage.

Her mother moaned, "No, Greg, please don't."

Then Alexia felt her own rage building, like a fire that would consume her. Hate licked through her and her breathing grew ragged. She vaguely wondered why she wasn't afraid. Just filled with loathing for the man in front of her.

She continued to stare him down, gaining courage from the hate. If this was the day she was to die, he was going with her.

Her fingers reached for the block of knives beside the sink. Wrapped around the largest one, but didn't pull it out.

Yet.

He stalked her. Moved toward her, slowly, like a leopard after prey, his eyes blazing with some emotion she couldn't define. "Well, well," he hissed. "Is one of my sorry kids trying to grow a spine?"

He came within touching distance. Then he paused as though trying to figure out who she was. She saw the moment his eyes changed. That crazy wild look replaced the puzzlement and his fist pulled back.

In a flash, she slid the knife out of the holder and held it in front of her. "Hit me and it'll be the last thing you ever do." Alexia didn't raise her voice. She just stated a fact. And noticed the shakiness was gone from her. The knife didn't even tremble.

Stunned, he stumbled back from her. She still didn't move, didn't breathe, didn't blink. Felt the coldness sweep through her. Freezing her. Her emotions, her feelings, everything she was. And she knew she wasn't lying. If he took one step toward her, she would plunge the knife straight into his evil heart.

Something of what was in her must have shown on her face.

Fear flashed across his features. Then anger. Then more fear as he took another step away from her. And another step until he was on the other side of the kitchen.

Satisfaction filled her.

Elation made her nearly dizzy.

She'd fought back and beaten her father.

He turned his back on her and walked toward the basement stairs. And disappeared down them.

The hate still buzzed inside her, and for a moment, she was tempted to follow him and finish what she'd threatened.

But her mother and sister needed help.

Dropping the knife into the sink, she rushed to them.

Karen sat against the sofa staring at Alexia, stunned with awe, and something she thought might be respect, in her eyes. "I can't believe you just did that."

She looked at her sister. "You need to get out of here now. Go somewhere, anywhere. You don't want to be here." Karen simply sat like a rock. "Go!"

Not waiting to see if Karen obeyed her or not, she turned to focus on her mother.

The woman had passed out. Alexia shook her shoulder. "Mom?"

The first bullet shattered the window above Karen's head. The second plowed the floor beside Alexia and her mother.

Karen screamed and Alexia whirled to see

her father standing at the top of the steps, his hunting rifle held in his hands.

His eyes were on her.

"Get. Me. A. Beer."

The cold words sent shivers darting up her spine, terror clawing at her soul.

She didn't move, her only thought was that she should have kept the knife instead of throwing it in the sink.

He stomped over, kicked the paint can out of his path, and aimed the rifle at her head.

The shakiness returned.

Fear now took hold of her, but it was a fear laced with something more, something she couldn't define. But she wasn't moving. Even as her eyes dared him to shoot her, she couldn't stop staring at the cigarette still hanging from his mouth.

Her father moved the gun and placed it against her sister's head. He looked her in the eye. "Get me a beer."

Alexia shot to her feet.

The fear faded.

A strange buzzing filled her ears. She nodded, never taking her eyes from his. Her sister sat frozen to the spot, her face bleached white. Alexia said, "Okay, Daddy, I'll get you a beer."

A cruel smile pulled his lips apart.

Some silly part of her wondered why,

when he smiled like that, he never lost the cigarette that still burned.

Like a robot, Alexia turned on wooden legs and walked into the kitchen. The buzz grew louder. Her pulse hammered. The hate intensified.

She went to the refrigerator and pulled the case of beer from it, turned and set it on the bar.

When she looked back, her father had the strangest look on his face. An expression she couldn't explain, but one that sent horror straight to her heart.

He lifted the gun, sighted her sister's face, and wrapped his finger around the trigger.

"No!" she screamed. Reached into the case and pulled out a can. With all her strength, she fired it at her father.

The can slammed into his shoulder.

He jerked the gun in her direction. "I'll kill you! I'll kill you all!"

She threw another can. And missed.

But it made him flinch. He pulled the trigger and the bullet splintered the cabinet above her head. She ignored the wood falling into her hair, stinging her cheeks.

And fired another can at him.

She caught him in the face. He screamed and the cigarette finally fell from his lips as his foot knocked the can of paint thinner over.

The cigarette landed on top of the old tarp.

She glared at the man with murder on his mind. Her chest heaved, her hands shook. She had to get him to put that gun down. Blood dripped from the gash on his forehead where the last beer can hit him.

A soft whoosh sounded and she looked at the floor. The cigarette had sparked a flame. And the flame quickly multiplied, devouring the tarp and heading straight to the paint thinner.

Then toward the couch and her mother and sister.

Alexia took in the sights, the smells, the sounds. Her sister huddled against the couch, weeping. Her mother was still out cold. "Karen, get Mom and get out!"

Her father lifted the gun and took aim at her once more. She hurled another can in his direction while she ducked behind the counter. The bullet screamed above her to plant itself in the wall behind her.

And still she felt no fear. "Karen! Do it!"

Another scream rent the air.

Smoke filled her lungs and made her choke.

Alexia raised up to see the living room on

fire, the flames burning straight up, reaching for the ceiling.

And her father running like a madman in circles in the midst of it, his pants on fire, turning the gun in her direction every so often.

Karen beat at the flames now licking along her sleeve.

Horror now filled Alexia as the buzz faded and left her gasping. Racing to her mother, she grasped the woman by the shoulders. And pulled her toward the door. Heat enveloped her. Smoke again invaded her lungs.

Her father's screams echoed in her mind. Or were those Karen's?

"Karen," she screamed, "come on! Get out of the house!"

"It's burning me!"

"Get out!"

"Alexia, where are you? Alexia! I'm gonna kill you!" Her father's hoarse scream exploded her hate into a rage she'd never felt before.

But she ignored him. Her mother and sister needed her help. This was her fault!

She pulled her mother across the lawn to the street where people were already racing from their homes to see what was going on.

"Alexia! Help me!"

Karen's cries echoed through her. She turned. And tackled her burning sister. Rolling her in the grass until the fire was out.

"It hurts," Karen whispered, then mercifully, she passed out.

Alexia blinked, her vision clearing to see Chad's shocked expression. She looked around to find herself back in his kitchen, where he stood watching her, his eyes puzzled, curious, slightly scared.

"Alexia?"

She stared into his eyes and whispered, "I remember. It was my fault." With the beer can still clutched in her right hand, she sank to the floor, never taking her eyes from Chad. "Oh no. It was my fault."

She buried her head in her knees, felt the tears push at the back of her eyelids. She refused to let them fall.

Then strong hands gripped her upper arms and she looked up.

Chad helped her move to the leather couch in his den. "You want to tell me about it?"

She shook her head. "No. I want you to take me home. Now."

His eyes narrowed and anger flitted briefly across his face. "You remembered something about the fire at your home, didn't you?"

Alexia stood. "Yes. And now, I'm ready to leave, Chad. So, will you please take me home?"

"Not just yet."

She felt another flicker of fear. "You're refusing to take me home?"

"I'll take you home when I'm ready."

Alexia gulped. "Are you the one who's been causing me all this trouble?"

Confusion stopped Chad for a moment, then a burst of humorless laughter erupted from him. "Me? You think I've been trying to kidnap you? Kill you?" Without giving her a chance to answer, he raked his hands through his hair and shook his head. "Man, all I wanted was for you to give me a chance to beat out Hunter just one time in the woman department." Regret twisted his face. "No, Alexia, I'm not trying to hurt you or kill you or kidnap you. I just wanted you to —" He broke off with a snort. "Never mind. You can leave if you want." He pulled his keys from his pocket. "Come on."

He walked back to the front door and Alexia followed him. Then he stopped and turned. "Before we go, though, would you mind telling me what you know about the fire? The one at your house?"

"Why?"

After his incredulous response to her

question as to whether he was the one after her, she felt herself relaxing. He wasn't out to hurt her. He was being a jerk, but he wasn't a dangerous jerk.

"Because —" he paused and rubbed a hand over his mouth — "even my father admitted to me he wasn't really sure what happened that day. It's been one of those things that's haunted him, still bugs him to this day. If I could find out the true story . . ." He blinked and broke off. "Your father was his friend. They grew up together."

"I know."

"Well, do you know the reason why my father was so loyal to yours?"

She shook her head. "No, why?"

"Because your father saved my father's life."

Surprise shot through her, chasing away the initial squiggle of fear. "What? How?"

"Back before you were born, your dad was going to be a firefighter."

Alexia jerked and she gave a short laugh of disbelief. "No, it's not possible."

"Yep. He and my dad went through the training together."

"How do you know all this? You're the same age I am."

Chad nodded. "My dad filled me in on

most of it. Plus, I was there when my dad went to see yours in the burn unit in Georgia right after the fire. I overheard the conversation. Your dad was still barely lucid, in and out of consciousness. But one thing he made abundantly clear was that the fire was your fault."

"And it was." She still saw the flash of the beer can hitting her dad's face, the cigarette flying through the air. The flames leaping, grasping.

All in slow motion.

"No, it wasn't, Alexia."

Alexia froze at the familiar voice. Whirling, she saw Hunter standing on the other side of the screened door. And a stranger standing next to him. A stranger she'd longed to see for years. A stranger who wasn't really a stranger.

"Dominic?" she whispered.

38

Hunter saw the shock, longing — and wariness — flicker one by one over Alexia's distraught face.

Chad simply looked furious at the interruption. And yet, he'd passed the test. He wasn't the one after Alexia. Hunter had pulled more strings and called in more favors than he really had to prove it, but it was worth it.

Thankfully, while Chad's actions hadn't been exactly gentlemanly, he hadn't done or said anything to lead Hunter or the ones on Chad's tail to believe he was the one after Alexia.

Guilt momentarily blindsided Hunter. He'd put a GPS on his brother's vehicle, tapped his phone, and bugged his house. Had fellow officers in on the plan. Officers who couldn't believe what Hunter was doing but were willing to help — if only to prove Hunter wrong.

But, in Hunter's opinion, it had all been necessary to clear Chad of Hunter's awful suspicions. Alexia couldn't have played along more perfectly. She'd asked Chad the question that had been burning in the back of his mind, haunting his dreams and kicking his denial button for a while now.

He wondered how Alexia would feel if she knew he'd basically used her for bait. That awful feeling in the middle of his gut said he might not live to share another kiss with her if she ever found out.

But she was never in danger. Never.

At least that's what he told himself.

What if Chad had been guilty and decided to just kill her and be done with it?

It had been a calculated risk. One he'd been reluctant to take but was relieved had paid off. And he'd be honest with Alexia about what he'd done. Soon. He winced at the thought.

Then saw Alexia moving toward Dominic and pushed all other thoughts out of his mind as he watched the reunion of brother and sister.

She came to the screen door.

Dominic pulled it open.

Hunter could see the family resemblance. Both tall, athletic, with emerald eyes and fiery hair.

They stared at each other for a brief moment. Then Dominic made the first move and pulled his sister into a tight hug. "I've missed you."

Hunter thought he saw Alexia's shoulders give a shake. A spasm. Something. But she didn't make a sound.

Alexia couldn't find her voice. She was being hugged by her big brother. And hugged. And hugged.

Finally, she pulled back and looked up into his eyes, drinking in the sight of him. "You look older, harder."

He smiled and nodded. "You don't."

A surprised chuckle hiccupped from her. She couldn't believe he wasn't disowning her, refusing to have anything to do with her.

But no. He was looking at her with love in his eyes. She gulped. "Why aren't you furious with me?" she whispered.

From behind her, she heard someone clear his throat.

Chad.

He said, "Y'all want to come in and sit down instead of standing in the foyer?"

Dominic nodded and led a still-reeling Alexia to the couch. She slumped onto it and Dominic sat beside her.

"I'm sorry I didn't get in touch with you."

Alexia bit her lip. "I guess I understand. I'm sure you hated me for a long time."

Dominic sighed. Alexia vaguely noticed Hunter motioning to Chad to leave them alone. The brothers left the den and walked into the kitchen.

Alexia focused on Dominic. He was saying, "I owe you a huge apology."

What? First her mother and now Dominic? Had the world spun off its axis?

She simply stared at him, once again searching for words in a brain that was pretty close to shutdown mode.

Dominic took a deep breath as though trying to figure out where to start. She decided to help him along. "Where did you go when you left home? After you were arrested because I called the cops?" There. She got the words out.

"Marcus Porter was the officer who arrested me. Lucky for me."

She lifted a brow.

Dominic nodded. "I'd met Marcus a couple of times. You remember Mom used to call the cops on Dad occasionally when he got really bad. Marcus just happened to be on duty the last three times."

Alexia wondered at the way he said the

words "just happened." But she didn't want to interrupt him. She knew Marcus well. He was the one she'd called to inform him of her brother's impending drug sale. He said, "When you called him, he set up a sting. I walked right into it."

"I'm sorry," she whispered and hung her head. His hand came out and lifted her chin.

"Don't be. You probably saved my life."

Dumbstruck, she met his eyes. "How?"

"I didn't realize it until much later. I was a pretty angry guy for a while. But Marcus managed to talk me into working with him. He finagled a deal with the DA and got the charges dropped, but only if I followed a few of his rules."

"Rules?"

"Yep. I had to keep my nose clean and go to church with him and his wife."

Alexia stared in disbelief. "Seriously?"

"Yeah. Marcus became like a father to me. But I'll admit, I hated you for a long time."

She winced, then said, "But you don't hate me now?"

"Nope. Like I said, you saved my life. I ended up moving in with Marcus and seeing how a father was supposed to treat his children. I went to the police academy, got my life together, then went on to join the FBI."

"Is that why you didn't contact me?"

"Yeah. I figured you were better off not involved in my life. For the past ten years, I've been mostly undercover. One assignment after the next. If I'd contacted you and the wrong person found out about it . . ." He shook his head. "That would have been ugly."

She understood. Sort of. Still, it seemed like he could have at least let her know he was alive. "I just figured you hated me," she whispered.

He grimaced and pulled her into a hug. "I'm so sorry, Lexi." She almost smiled at his little pet name. Lexi. "But I need to make something really clear here. That fire was not your fault." He swallowed hard.

"But I remember everything. It was my fault. I threw the beer can and it hit —"

Dominic was shaking his head. "About five years ago, I tracked Dad down to the jail in Washington State."

"But he's out now."

"I know. But before he got out, I went to see him."

A pang hit her in the heart. He went to visit their father, but couldn't contact her? Anger wanted to bud, but she refused to let it. "What did he have to say?"

"A lot." His lips twisted and regret filled

429

his eyes. "Keep in mind, I had no idea you were blaming yourself for the fire or I would have . . ." He looked away and shook his head.

"What, Dom?"

"Aw man, this is hard."

Impatience flooded her, sparking the anger. "Just spill it, will you?"

He barked a short, humorless laugh. "Dad finally talked. He refused at first, then admitted that if you hadn't thrown those beer cans at him, he was going to kill everyone that day."

Alexia lurched to her feet and stumbled from her brother. What was he saying?

Dominic waited until she turned to face him once again. "What?" she whispered.

"He said he had it planned. He was going to wait until everyone was asleep, then kill all of you. Mom, Karen, and you."

"I . . . I . . ." She couldn't find any words. But she began to shake. A chill swept over her.

"Because of the fire, Mom and you are still alive."

"Karen's dead." Alexia felt her emotions start to freeze. It was all too much.

Hunter walked in and pulled her into his arms. But even his warmth wasn't enough to chase the chill invading her.

Dominic continued. "Dad blamed you for the fire, and I suppose if you hadn't thrown the beer cans, the fire wouldn't have started, but if you hadn't started the fire, you'd be dead."

She didn't know what to think. In fact, she was having a hard time thinking anything. Pulling out of Hunter's arms, she turned to find Chad staring at them.

Ignoring him, she looked at Dominic. "What was Dad doing in Washington State?"

Dominic's throat bobbed and he exchanged a look with Hunter. Something passed between the two men and she planted her hands on her hips. "What?"

"Dad was coming after you."

She felt the blood drain from her face and her knees went weak. She stumbled back to the couch and sat. Hunter hovered nearby.

"After me?"

"Yeah. He found out where you went and was coming to get you, but he said he lost track of you. He was in a bar one night and killed a guy. He's been in prison until a few months ago."

"If he hadn't landed in prison, but instead found me —" She shuddered at the thought.

"Exactly."

Alexia rubbed her arms to ward off the chill.

Dominic reached out and stroked her cheek. "I'm sorry I went off and left you and Karen in that house to deal with Dad."

"It doesn't matter now." She looked into her big brother's eyes. "You forgive me. That's all that matters."

"I'll admit, that took awhile, but if you hadn't called Marcus, I don't know where I'd be today."

"And you forgive me? Just like that?"

"Just like that. Just like God does."

"God?" She nearly squeaked the word. "You too?"

Puzzlement pulled his brows together. "What do you mean?"

She shook her head and muttered, "It seems like every time I turn around, I'm running into God."

A strange-sounding snort came from Hunter, who had moved into the kitchen, and she turned to glare at him.

Dominic laughed. "Then I suggest you give in. He always wins in the end."

Somehow she thought he might be speaking from experience. "You ran too?"

"As far and as fast as I could. It didn't matter. God was always waiting for me when I had to stop for a rest."

Alexia simply stared at him. "Have you talked to Mom?"

"No." Pain flashed in his eyes. "She's next on my list."

"Why now?"

He blinked. "Huh?"

"Why are you here now? Telling me this."

"Oh." Dominic cleared his throat and glanced in the direction of the kitchen. "Your boyfriend tracked me down." A respectful gleam appeared in his eyes. "And trust me, I'm not easy to find."

Boyfriend? She let that slide. "I know. I tried."

Another anguished look. "The average person would have run up against a brick wall. I'm sorry. I should have . . ."

He sighed and Alexia squeezed his fingers.

"Don't." She paused. "Has Hunter filled you in on anything going on right now with me?"

His jaw hardened and his eyes narrowed. "A little. That's one reason I'm here. I'm going to be unofficial, but I plan to help find out who's after you."

"That's what we're all here for, Lex." Hunter stood in the door, Chad behind him.

She gulped. And then silently thanked God for placing these people in her life right when she needed them. The thought hit her that maybe God didn't hate her after all. Maybe it was possible that he did love her. Something she promised to discuss with him the next chance she had.

Alexia glanced at the clock. "Will someone please take me home so I can get ready for tonight?"

Hunter laughed and held out a hand. "Come on. I'll take you. We'll stop by Serena's house and get whatever you need, then we'll go by my parents' so you and Christine can get ready together. Dominic's heading for the hospital to visit your mother."

"Wait a minute." His parents'? "Uh, I think I'll just get ready at Serena's if that's all right with you."

"My parents won't be there, Alexia."

"Oh." She shrugged. "Then that's fine."

Chad snickered and Hunter glared at him. Dominic's gaze ping-ponged between the three of them.

When nobody bothered to explain, he said, "Right. Then I guess I'll see you all at the dinner. I have a feeling Alexia's tormenter will be there too."

He stood and so did Alexia. Her heart swelled when Dominic leaned over and gave her a hug.

"Good to see you again, Lexi."

"You too, Dom."

Dominic left.

She eyed the brothers, then looked at Hunter. "We need to talk."

39

Saturday, 2:30 p.m.

"You knew what Dominic was going to tell me, didn't you?" she asked.

"That the fire wasn't your fault?" Hunter lifted a brow. "Yes. I talked to him earlier today."

A frown flickered on her forehead, then he had to look away and back at the road. "How did you know I was at Chad's?"

He paused, not wanting to lie, but not wanting to tell her exactly the truth either. "No one answered at Serena's. Chad didn't answer his cell phone. Process of elimination."

"Oh. And I don't have mine. I guess it's still at Serena's."

"We'll get it." His fingers tapped the wheel. "Anyway, I'd already talked to Dominic's supervisor once. When I explained the situation, he had Dominic call me immediately. We had a long conversation last night while you were still snoozing in the hospital. He arrived in town via FBI helicopter shortly before you were released from the hospital this morning."

"And you didn't think you should tell me all this earlier?"

He felt his jaw tighten. "Not until I saw him face-to-face."

She didn't know whether to be grateful or annoyed. He'd been protecting her physically, doing his best to keep her from harm from her attacker practically from the moment they'd met.

Now, he was doing it on an emotional level.

A man protecting her was a new concept. One she hadn't totally come to terms with. Or was even sure she was comfortable with.

He pulled into Serena's drive.

She started to open the door when she felt his hand on her arm. He said, "Wait. Not yet. Give me the key, would you?"

"Why?"

"I'm going to open the garage door and pull in when the guys get here."

She felt the frown on her face. "Guys? What guys? And Serena's car is in there. She took a cab to the airport."

It was his turn to frown. "It's a three-car garage. What about the other two spaces?"

Now she fought a grin. "Her boat and jet ski."

"Seriously?"

"Yep. And you just punch in the code for the garage door. You don't need a key."

Still frowning, he said, "Okay. We'll just have to form a wall around you." He sighed. "You wouldn't consider leaving the city, would you?"

She stared at him. "Are you crazy? After all we've already been through? Absolutely not." She paused. "I think we both know that if I leave, he'll just follow."

"Or she."

Alexia tilted her head. "You really think it could be a woman?"

"I suppose we have to take it into consideration, although I don't know if I believe anything . . ."

When he stopped, she looked at him. "You don't believe Chad when he says the person ran like a woman?"

His jaw firmed. "I didn't say that."

"Yeah. You kind of did. Anyway, I still think it's my father," Alexia murmured as a car pulled up to the curb. Then another in the drive next to them.

Puzzled, she asked, "What's going on?"

"Your protection detail. The guys." His lips tightened. "They want this perp off the street just as bad as we do."

Her throat tightened and she realized it was doing that a lot these days. "I can't believe they're just willing to give up their personal time to help someone they don't even know."

He nodded. "These guys are the best. They're also working security detail tonight at the dinner. They're our escorts. Then after the dinner, I want to know if you'll be open to a safe house."

"A safe house? Like a comfortable jail?"

Hunter sighed. "I don't want you to think of it like that. Try to think of it more along the lines of doing your best to stay alive. It will only be until we catch the guy."

Alexia groaned. "I don't know. If I disappear, the person after me isn't going to know where to strike next. How will you catch him?"

"We should be getting some DNA information back on everything processed. The knife, the van, Serena's house. Hopefully, we'll get a hit on something. If we don't . . ." He shrugged. "Yeah, it'll take a little longer."

Alexia watched Hunter as the guys cased the house. "Maybe I shouldn't go tonight. I don't want to put anyone at risk because I show up at a dinner."

Hunter nodded. "I thought about that,

but the security there is going to be top-notch. If there's any place in Columbia that you would be safe, it's at the dinner tonight. And since that's where I'm going to be . . ."

She smiled and he continued, "I really think you need to consider it. Let us put you in a safe house."

Her smile turned south. "I still have some things I need to take care of back in Washington. If my father is out here and I go back there, I should be fine."

"You're contradicting yourself now. You just said he'd follow you if you left the city."

Alexia groaned. "I know."

An officer appeared in the doorway of the house and signaled the all clear. Hunter turned the car off. "Let's get inside and get what you need. We can finish this conversation on the drive to my parents' house."

She nodded. "All right."

Then Hunter organized a human wall of Kevlar-vested officers who escorted her from the car to the house.

Once inside she expressed her thanks to the men and quickly fed the animals, watered the plants, and gathered her things. All of her things.

And Serena's Bible.

Hunter watched over her. Or rather hovered over her. She decided that was all right.

For now.

With the bag slung over her shoulder, her dress folded neatly across her other arm, she walked back into the den. "I'm ready."

Hunter took the dress from her and nodded to one of the four men scattered at various positions around the house. "Let the boys know we're ready to roll."

The man, whom Hunter had introduced as Erik, spoke into the air and got an immediate response. If she squinted, she could see the microphone in his ear.

Just as they entered the house, they made their exit, the men surrounding her, one big wall of bulletproof. Erik hung back and rearmed the alarm system with the new code. Alexia wondered if the new four-digit number made any difference at all. Whoever had gotten the first one probably already had the second one.

The thought chilled her.

Back in the car, Alexia asked, "Has anyone been able to locate Jillian?"

Hunter shook his head. "Nope. I've got Brian and Katie working on it and so far nothing. The guy who bought the phone said he lost it."

Alexia pondered that. They'd finally been able to contact Serena again, but accessing her phone records didn't help. The phone number was a prepaid cell phone no longer in service — a dead end. If Jillian wasn't ready to be found, she didn't need her old friends sending someone after her. And if the person after Alexia was also after Jillian . . . it was a good thing no one knew where she was.

Hunter drove, following behind one of the vehicles driven by his friends and co-workers. The second car followed on Hunter's bumper. Close enough so that another car couldn't get between them and far enough to allow Hunter to stop quickly if he needed to.

Everything seemed rather surreal to Alexia all of a sudden. Was this really happening to her? Was it possible her father had been waiting ten years to extract his revenge on her?

It sounded like it. "Has anyone located my father?"

Hunter shook his head. "We tracked him to a homeless shelter not too far from your mother's house. I've got a couple of guys watching the place. I've also got a guy on the inside who'll call me if your dad shows up."

"My father. He's not a dad."

Hunter reached over and squeezed her hand.

Swallowing hard, her heart hurt. How she longed for a loving dad.

"If God loves me, why is he letting this happen to me?"

Hunter glanced at her, then back at the road. She saw his throat work. Then he said, "Lex, bad stuff happens. It's a fallen world. Like I told you back at the hospital, God's not picking on you and letting bad stuff happen. But he wants to be there for you to get you through it."

She blinked and looked out the windshield.

Could that be true?

He thought so. Serena thought so. And, wonder of wonders, Dominic even spoke of God as though he were a friend. A companion. Someone he revered.

And her mother was a changed person. Or so she claimed.

The conversation from the morning echoed through her mind. She claimed she was tired of being a spoiled brat. That she wanted peace in her life.

Maybe the only way to do that was to forgive her mother. Like Dominic seemed to have forgiven her.

The thought hit her hard. She didn't have any trouble accepting Dominic's forgiveness, but wasn't so gracious in extending forgiveness to her mother.

That seemed wrong.

It was wrong.

Being on the receiving end of forgiveness was an amazing thing. Did God forgive like Dominic? If so, could she forgive like God?

She wanted to. And the fact that she wanted to made it seem like it might not be the impossible task she'd once thought it was.

God, I believe in you. I believe you're there. I just never really believed you cared. But I'm starting to think you do. Thank you for putting Hunter in my life right when I needed him.

When Hunter pulled into his parents' drive, for the first time since she'd left Washington, her heart felt lighter. Freer.

Once again, she had the human shield escort her to the front door. Christine opened the door and gave them a welcoming smile. There was no surprise on her face, so Hunter must have filled her in beforehand.

"Hey, come on in."

Guilt pierced her. Did she have the right to infringe on people this way? What if she was putting them in danger in spite of Hunter's reassurances? And yet, if she tried to leave town or steal away, how would she protect herself?

She knew fires, not killers.

Christine looped her arm through Alexia's. "I gave you the room you had before. I hope that's okay."

Alexia smiled. "Sure. Thanks for letting me invade your space again." As they walked to the back room, Hunter following behind, Alexia couldn't help notice how tall Christine was.

Taller than Alexia, but not quite as tall as Hunter. Isn't that how she'd described her attacker this morning in the hospital?

Chilled by the thought, she shoved it aside. If Christine wanted to get to her, she could have done it the night before last when Alexia lay vulnerable under her roof.

Now, back in the room, she forced herself to focus on getting ready, not worrying about who might be after her. Tonight, she wanted to enjoy her time with Hunter — and maybe prove to his parents that she wasn't the loser they thought she was.

Part of her wondered if she should tell Hunter's father what she remembered. Then decided against it. Why stir it all up? What was in the past was in the past. She was going forward.

Taking a deep breath, she hung her dress on the closet door, then turned and looked at the bed. Fatigue tugged at her. She'd had a crazy, impossible-to-believe week. Other than the drug-induced sleep of last night and into the morning, she'd had very little rest.

Alexia decided she had time for a nap. She had a feeling she was going to need it.

40

Saturday, 6:04 p.m.

The senator tugged on the tie and made sure it was perfect. There'd been no more letters, but he didn't kid himself — he felt sure more were coming. His lips tightened. Fortunately, Serena was out of the country for the time being. One less thing to worry about. But Alexia was still walking around. Available for Jillian to spill her guts to.

Frank was almost convinced that Alexia didn't know where Jillian was. Unfortunately, he'd come to that conclusion too late to help Alexia. She knew someone was after her. After all the things that had happened to her in the past week, she wasn't just going to go away.

"Are you ready?"

Elizabeth's question jerked him from his thoughts. "Almost. Has Ian brought the car around?"

"Waiting on you. As usual, dear."

Frank tried to figure out if there was something in the undertone of her words. If there was, he couldn't put his finger on it.

Then she smiled and turned to leave.

"Elizabeth . . ."

She stopped and looked back, one brow arched. "Yes?"

"Is . . . everything all right?"

She tilted her head. "Of course. Is everything all right with you?"

Frank forced a smile. "Yes, I was just checking. We haven't had much of a chance to talk lately with all of the campaigning going on."

Her face softened. "It's all right. You know I understand this life. After the election, maybe we can go somewhere for a few days. Just the two of us."

Relief relaxed his tense shoulders. "That sounds wonderful."

"Now come on, we're going to be late."

This time she left without looking back.

Unfortunately, the senator couldn't look forward without looking back. "I'm going to find you, Jillian. Wherever you are, I'll find you."

His phone rang. When he saw the number on the screen, his gut tightened. "Hello?"

"I got the phone records for Serena Hopkins and have been cross-checking the calls from the last month. One was really interesting."

"Which one was that?" Ever since the first letter, he'd made the call to keep tabs on Serena's phone. They pulled her records twice a week. He wished they'd tapped it.

"She got a call from Los Angeles, California. I've never seen that number before. My sources tracked it back to a guy who sold his phone to an investigative reporter by the name of Julie Carson."

"Julie Carson, Jillian Carter. She's been living under an assumed name?"

"Looks that way. I'm still looking into it, but yes, I think we've found her."

"Then we don't need Alexia or Serena anymore, do we?"

"No. I've already got plans to take care of Alexia tonight. But I don't know what Jillian and Serena have talked about. I think it best that Serena have an accident before she gets home from China."

Frank felt satisfaction flow. Finally. "Make it work."

He hung up the phone.

Now, he could go enjoy the party.

Alexia felt the butterflies awaken in the pit of her stomach. Again. The first time was when she emerged from her bedroom, ready for the dinner.

She knew she looked good, but when Hunter's eyes went wide and his mouth dropped, she decided all the extra effort and time spent putting herself together had been well worth it.

Now, they were here. In the ballroom of the Grand Hyatt Hotel.

In just a few minutes, she'd come face-to-face with the man who thought she'd burned down her parents' house.

And in a sense he was right.

As she fit her hand in the crook of Hunter's arm, she lifted her chin. Hunter had asked her to be here. She wouldn't embarrass or disappoint him by acting like an insecure teenager.

"You look awesome tonight. Did I tell you that?" Hunter whispered in her ear.

She felt her face heat. "Yes, you did. Several times. And thank you."

"I'm glad you came with me. I don't feel so awkward with you beside me."

Her heart stuttered and warmed, even though she almost laughed. Hunter would feel comfortable anywhere. But his comment was sweet and she appreciated his attentiveness.

A band played in the background, a low jazzy tune that Alexia recognized but couldn't name.

Then Christine entered the room with the man Alexia had met at the lab, Rick Shelton. He'd picked up Christine about thirty minutes before Alexia and Hunter had left.

Alexia refused to have Christine ride with them in case the person decided to come after her on the way to the dinner. The threatening words the caller had said still echoed in her mind. "You'll never make it to that dinner."

Well, she'd made it, she just had to make sure she didn't turn her back on the wrong person.

"Hey, isn't that Lori Tabor over there? I'm going to go speak to her."

"Sure," Hunter said. "I see Katie talking to Chad. I'm going to go see if she's heard anything more about Jillian."

Alexia felt a pang of fear for her old friend. When Jillian was ready to be found, she'd make an appearance. She made her way over to Lori and the tall man at her side. "Hi, Lori, good to see you again."

Lori smiled, revealing her toothpaste-ad teeth. "Alexia! I didn't expect to see you here tonight." She gestured to the man beside her. "I don't know if you've met my brother, Avery, or not. He's a big supporter of Harper Graham."

451

Alexia shook the man's hand and suppressed a shiver. He stood about six feet tall, slightly taller than his sister, had blue eyes and sandy blond hair. He smiled. "So glad to meet you." Then his eyes narrowed. "Had a bit of trouble lately, haven't you?"

"A bit." Alexia shivered at the look in his eyes. He gave her the creepies, but she couldn't put her finger on the reason why.

Lori said, "Avery decided I needed the night off. Our mother came into town just in time to watch the kids."

Hunter came up behind her. "Everyone's sitting down. Are you ready?"

"Sure." She looked back to Lori and Avery. "Nice to see you."

Hunter led her to the table where he held the chair for her. She slid in and took note of her dining companions. Hunter's parents sat across the table from her. His father had the stunned look of a deer caught in the headlights. And with dread, she realized Hunter hadn't told them she was coming.

She shot him an incredulous look before pasting a smile on her face. "Hello, Mr. Graham. Mrs. Graham."

Alexia had to give the man credit. He recovered pretty quickly and his lips spread into a credible smile. "Hello, Alexia, glad you could join us."

Alexia was impressed. He almost didn't even flinch when he said that. Mrs. Graham simply smiled and sipped her wine. Alexia wondered if this was going to be a long night.

Senator Hoffman paused in the door to the grand ballroom. He glanced around, only vaguely aware of his wife on his arm. All that mattered were those who voted. He'd been invited to this dinner by Harper Graham, a well-liked, highly respected member of this community. Being seen in his presence might influence a few voters still on the fence. It was worth coming.

"Darling, there's Betty Ann. I'm going to go speak to her."

Frank patted his wife's hand and said, "All right. I'm going to make my way around the room and speak to those I know."

"And introduce yourself to those you don't," she murmured with a smile to the couple on her left.

"Exactly."

"See you soon."

She walked away, and Frank pulled in the first deep breath of the evening. Then nearly choked on it. He blinked, sure that his eyes deceived him.

Alexia Allen? Surely not. It was probably

someone who looked a lot like her.

Then the woman turned and smiled at the man seated next to her, giving the senator a full look at her face.

It was her.

Her eyes caught his and the smile wavered, then firmed back into place as she held his gaze.

She knows. That was his first thought.

But how? No. It was just his guilty conscience talking. There was no way she could know.

A hand slapped on his shoulder and he turned to find Elliot Darwin, his campaign manager. Keeping his smile as natural as possible, Frank shook the man's hand. "Glad you could make it."

"Wouldn't miss this shindig. Lots of voters in this room."

"Voters with big money."

Elliot flashed perfect white teeth and winked. "Those are the kind we like. Let's make this little party work for us."

Frank figured there had to be at least two hundred people in attendance. The large number helped him relax. All he had to do was keep out of Alexia's line of sight and keep his cool. Everything would be fine.

The man next to Alexia leaned over.

"Thanks for your help in proving Hunter wrong. You deserve an Oscar."

She frowned. "What are you talking about?"

"Lee," Hunter interrupted, brows furrowed, "don't you have something better to discuss than work?"

Lee froze, his gaze bouncing back and forth between Hunter and Alexia. "Um. Right. Sure."

"No, wait a minute," Alexia protested. "I want to know how I helped you prove Hunter wrong. Wrong about what?"

"Lex, I'll explain later, all right?"

Whatever passed between the two men wasn't pretty. She narrowed her eyes, ignoring the elegance surrounding her. "Hunter, tell me."

He shifted, obviously uncomfortable. Then sighed even while he shot Lee a black look. "All right, but not here. Let's find someplace quiet."

Worry gnawed at her gut, because he looked worried. What was it? What was he going to tell her?

As they excused themselves from the table, she felt eyes follow her. Refusing to turn around to see who was watching, she allowed Hunter to lead her down a short hall.

He opened the door to an empty conference room and she stepped inside. Shutting the door behind him, he turned and placed his hands on her shoulders. "I wasn't going to get into all of this tonight, but . . ." He pulled in a deep breath. "Look, I had my suspicions about someone being the person who was after you. I took steps to prove it. Instead, I was proven wrong. That's pretty much it."

The door opened and Chad stood there, fury on his face. "Only that's not all there is to it. The person he suspected was me."

Hunter could see the confusion on Alexia's face and his gut twisted. "Chad, I'm sorry. If you saw things from my perspective, you'd understand."

The fury didn't lessen, it blazed from his eyes, radiated from every pore. "You set me up?"

"What are you talking about?" Alexia demanded.

"You think you're so high and mighty." Chad ignored her, focusing on his brother. "The untouchable Hunter Graham."

Hunter knew Chad needed to vent, to heap his anger on Hunter's head. But he didn't want Alexia to get caught in the crossfire. "Lex, why don't you go on back to the table and make our excuses? I'll join you when Chad and I finish this."

She crossed her arms. "I think I'll stay."

"Yeah. Let her stay," Chad ground out as his nostrils flared. "Let her hear how you used her as bait to catch the bad guy."

"What?" Alexia let her arms drop to her sides as shock zinged through her. "Explain yourself, Chad Graham."

Hunter could see her anger rising by the second and knew he was going to be in for a rough patch trying to justify his actions.

Chad sneered. "What Hunter doesn't seem to realize is that I have friends in the department too. Not everyone is a Hunter worshiper."

Hunter shot his brother a warning look. "Chad —"

"So when I showed up for the dinner, I got an earful about how you set up this sting to prove I'm a killer. Isn't that why you asked me to take Alexia home from the hospital? Because you thought I was going to kidnap her or kill her or something?"

Alexia gasped and stared at Hunter.

He winced. "It wasn't like that. I didn't believe you were capable of anything like that, but Katie and I were working on the case and some evidence pointed toward you —"

"And you couldn't just ask me about it? Confront me?"

"No!" Hunter felt his own temper spike and fought to control it. "No, we couldn't. I needed irrefutable proof that you had nothing to do with any of the incidents against Alexia in case someone else got ahold of the file and started asking the same questions I did."

"You're a liar. You just can't stand the thought that I might actually win the heart of a woman you like."

"Oh, you two are ridiculous!" Alexia stomped her foot, fists clenched. Hunter winced as her glare landed on him, then Chad. "After tonight, I don't want to see either one of you ever again."

"Lex —" Hunter protested. But it did no good. She spun on her heel and exited the room.

Alexia was so mad, she thought she might literally shake apart, shatter into a million pieces. She had to get away from Hunter and Chad, and yet she couldn't return to the table in this state.

"Alexia, are you all right?"

Alexia whirled to see Katie standing in the hallway. "I'm fine."

Hunter came after her. "You can't be

alone, Alexia."

Still mad, Alexia looked at Katie.

Katie frowned, looking from Hunter to Alexia and back, and finally nodded toward Alexia. "I'll stay with her."

Chad appeared in the doorway and Alexia looked away from his red face.

"I need a restroom," she muttered.

Katie pointed. "There's one down this hallway, around the corner. The two near the ballroom are probably packed, with all these women here." She glanced at Hunter, then back to Alexia. "Come with me."

Without another look at either man, Alexia allowed Katie to lead her down to the restroom.

"You don't look fine. What happened?"

"Just a little too much excitement lately." Why was Katie acting so concerned about her? She stared at the cop, suspicion zinging all through her.

Katie nodded. "I know. And I've not been very nice to you. I'm . . . sorry."

Alexia's brows rose, but she said, "I understand. I suppose you were doing your job."

A rueful smile crossed Katie's lips. "No, not really. I wasn't very objective about it. I had a grudge against you and I let that affect my work."

Alexia turned on the water and washed her hands, then pressed them against her eyes. She'd have to redo her makeup, but right now, she didn't care. The coolness felt wonderful. Drying her face and hands, she asked, "And you don't have a grudge now?"

"No. All the evidence says you had nothing to do with Devin's death or the fire at my house. Hunter was right. Someone was trying to set you up."

Alexia felt some of the tension in her shoulders relax. A fraction. She was still spitting mad at Hunter and Chad, but Katie's words felt good. "Thank you for that anyway."

Katie shrugged and her eyes turned sad. "I saw Dominic in the crowd out there."

"Really?" Alexia hadn't spotted him. "I'll have to find him." She paused, then asked, "Are you okay?"

Katie shook her head. "Not really. I hadn't realized just how much I cared about him until . . ." She gulped. "Never mind."

Alexia bit her lip. "I'm sorry." And in spite of the way the woman had treated her, Alexia *was* sorry.

Katie waved a hand. "Are you ready to get back to the dinner?"

She blew out a breath just as the door opened again. Lori Tabor stepped inside, her face streaked with tears. "Oh," she started. "I didn't realize anyone was in here."

She dabbed at her cheeks.

Alexia stepped forward. "Are you all right?"

"Oh, I'm fine. Someone just said something that hurt my feelings." She waved a hand. "I'll get over it." She began digging in her purse.

Alexia said, "I'm going to use the facilities. I'll be out in a minute. You want to meet me at the table?"

Katie shook her head. "No, I'll just wait here for you."

Alexia entered the stall and shut the door. She didn't need to use the bathroom, she needed a moment to herself. Leaning her head against the door, she closed her eyes. She'd been gone a long time from the dinner and knew Hunter's parents were probably wondering where they were.

A scrape above her startled her. Looking up, she frowned at the white-tiled ceiling. Mice?

A muffled thud outside the stall made her jump.

Opening the door, she came face-to-face with a gun. A gasp escaped her as her eyes landed on the woman on the floor, the pool of blood spreading beneath her.

She stared into the face that didn't bother hiding behind a mask this time and asked, "You? But why?"

Another shuffle sounded above her, but she didn't dare take her eyes off the gun in front of her.

She heard a pop, felt a sharp sting on the back of her neck. As she felt the darkness descend, she wondered if she'd wake up.

Hunter!

41

"Where are they?" Hunter paced in front of the bathroom door. "Women," he muttered. Glancing at his watch, he frowned. It had been fifteen minutes already.

He and Chad had agreed to put on happy faces for their father and resolve their differences later. Now, Hunter wanted to talk to Alexia to see if he could salvage even a small possibility of a relationship with her.

He rapped his knuckles on the door. "Hey, Katie? Alexia? You guys all right?"

Silence echoed back to him.

His gut tightened. A bad feeling swept over him and he shoved the door open. "Oh no. Katie!" He dropped to his knees next to the woman and felt for a pulse. Slow and weak. Grabbing one of the hand towels from the sink, he pressed it against the wound and held it. With his other hand, he reached for his phone to call for an ambulance and bent low to check the other stalls. Empty.

"Come on, Katie, hang in there. Help's coming."

Where was Lori Tabor? He'd seen her crying as she entered. But now both she and Alexia were gone.

How?

How had she and Alexia gotten out of the bathroom without him seeing her?

He looked up. A displaced tile clued him in.

They'd taken her through the ceiling.

As she drove, she thought about how amazingly simple it had been. Of course it had been easier with the experienced help. But at least this time, the plan had worked. That was the problem before. There'd been no clear plan, no organization to how they would grab Alexia. It was just her looking for an opportunity to act.

But not tonight. Tonight the opportunity had been made. Her teary exit shortly after Alexia left the room was meant to play on Alexia's sympathies to support a distraught friend. Then they would find privacy in the quieter bathroom. But Alexia got there on her own, with just the detective to deal with. Finally, a plan that had worked almost all by itself.

And now Alexia slept in the back of the car, unaware that she'd been snatched through the ceiling of the bathroom with security crawling through the building.

It wasn't hard to admit he'd been right. Planning was everything. And the plan had worked. That dizzy, giddy feeling was addictive. Or was that the pill she'd popped before the dinner party?

Still riding that high, Lori Tabor wondered exactly how much longer Alexia had to live.

Alexia became aware of the sounds first.

Then the smells. Candles, freshly lit candles, burning. A musty smell. Mold.

The floor beneath her was cold cement.

The pounding in her head made her want to throw up. Some inner voice told her to be as still as possible. She cracked her eyes. Slowly.

And saw nothing.

Panic started. Was she blind?

No. She could feel something over her eyes. A blindfold? She tried to reach up to pull it off and realized she couldn't move her hands. They were tied behind her.

The panic morphed into terror. Her blood started pumping. Someone had managed to kidnap her. They'd finally succeeded. In spite of all the security at the dinner. In spite of Hunter not leaving her alone and Chad's diligent attention.

So. This is how it's going to end, huh, God?

Something nudged her foot.

She feigned unconsciousness.

A harder nudge. Then a jab in the ribs.

This time she couldn't hold back the gasp that escaped her.

"Wake up," the voice growled. Lori? The woman who'd kidnapped her? Where was she?

Alexia squinted, but could only make out a faint bit of light at the bottom of the blindfold. She felt tremors start in her gut and work their way up. She couldn't stop shaking.

The voice to her left laughed. "I see you realize you're in a bit of a bad situation here."

"What do you want? Why am I blindfolded? I already know who you are."

"I want to know where Jillian Carter is. Or should I say, Julie Carson?"

Alexia frowned, wishing she could see the woman. "I know Jillian. I don't know who Julie is."

"But you know Jillian's been in hiding these past ten years."

"Yes."

"And she's been in contact with you."

"No!" Frustration with the insistence that she knew where Jillian was nearly overshadowed the fear. "Why won't you listen? I haven't talked to her. I keep telling you I don't know where she is."

"That's too bad for you. If you don't know, then he doesn't need you anymore."

"He?"

"The reason for the blindfold. He'll be here soon."

Alexia felt herself drowning in the terror even as she felt the blade of a knife press against her throat. "And when he's done, I get you."

"What did I do to you? Why do you hate me?" Alexia whispered. "I haven't seen you since high school."

"Because you want the children," Lori hissed, and Alexia jerked at the change. She sounded . . . different now. "He said you'd take them away. That you were here to spy on me. That you knew I killed Avery's wife."

A chill settled between Alexia's shoulders. The woman was crazy. Insane. Psychotic. The list of terms ran through her mind even as her insides quaked.

"Well, you can't have them. They're mine now and no one, not you, not Devin, not even Marcie Freeman will take them away from me."

From somewhere, Alexia heard a small voice calling, "Aunt Lori, where are you?"

And Alexia knew exactly where she was.

Hunter thought he might very well lose his mind. He had no idea where Alexia was or how to find her. Chad stood beside him. Together they watched the video provided by the hotel security. Chad said, "There, they go in the bathroom. Katie and Alexia, then Lori."

"No one else went in there, just the three of them," a security guard said.

"No cameras in the bathroom," Hunter muttered.

"How did they know she'd use that bathroom?" Chad said.

Dominic entered the room. "Where are we?"

Hunter had called to let him know Alexia was missing. Dominic hadn't wasted any time in getting down to the security offices.

"We're not getting anything from the inside. Let's see the outside cameras," Hunter said.

After too much time scanning, they finally found the camera footage they needed. "Look. There." Chad pointed to the two figures leaving out a back door. They each had on black clothing and masks. The person in the middle didn't. Her back was to him, but Hunter could clearly see that it was Alexia and she was unconscious.

The two shoved her in the waiting car, then one drove off while the other returned to the building.

"Get the plates," Dominic ordered.

"See who's not here now that was earlier," Hunter told one of the officers. "Be discreet if you can. If you can't, that's fine. Just get the information we need."

The woman nodded and left.

The man in charge of security, Garrett Smith, sighed. "I can't get the plates. The car's angled away from the camera. They backed up and drove off."

"They scouted the cameras and parked out of range on purpose. Back it up and play it one more time," Chad said. "I want to see it again."

Mr. Smith complied.

Chad slapped the table. "I recognize that car. Or one like it."

"From where?" Hunter snapped.

"It pulled into the garage the night I was watching Alexia at the Tabor house."

Hunter pulled his phone out and dialed Brian. The man answered on the second ring. "Brian, I need a quick favor. Do you have access to a computer?"

"Sure."

"Pull up the DMV records for Avery Tabor, will you? I need to know what kind of car he drives and the license plate."

"Hold on."

While Hunter waited for Brian to come back on the line, he watched the video footage again. His heart thudded and fear roared through his veins, but he couldn't acknowledge it. If he did, he'd never be able to think through finding Alexia. And right now, she needed him.

Please, God, be with her. Keep her safe. Let me find her. Show me what I need to find her.

"Okay, it's a black Mercedes, license plate DOCTR A." Brian rattled off the information along with the address.

"That's definitely Avery Tabor's address," Hunter said. "He lives near Alexia's mother."

"What would he have against Alexia?" Chad asked.

"Who knows? Get a team over there and get Avery Tabor in here. We need to talk to him."

While someone went to find Avery, Hunter slapped his phone to his ear, putting together a plan to rescue Alexia. Backup should be on-site within minutes. A SWAT team and a hostage negotiator on standby.

Was Avery still at the party or had he left to take her to his house? Or was this a wild goose chase?

Hunter's phone beeped and he switched over to grab the call and put it on speaker so everyone in the room could hear. "Yeah?"

Dominic said, "I've checked the guest list against the people in attendance. Avery Tabor is here. His sister, Lori, isn't."

"Any indication that he left the party?"

"No."

"Lori was in the bathroom with Alexia and Katie. She must have shot Katie and somehow managed to get Alexia up through the ceiling."

Dominic broke in. "I'm going with the team to the house. I'll be in touch."

"Alexia wouldn't have just cooperated," Chad said. "She'd have fought tooth and nail and you would have heard the commotion."

"No, she had to be drugged." Hunter felt his heart clench. He prayed she was still out cold. As long as she was unconscious, she wouldn't be scared.

Alexia was terrified. Who was the "he" Lori referred to?

Her father? Had he set all this up?

"You killed Devin," she whispered when Lori returned from seeing to the child.

A hitched breath filtered to her ears. "Yes, poor Devin." A sniffle. Was Lori crying? "He wasn't supposed to be home. He was supposed to be cutting grass across town. But he was there and he moved wrong . . . and I . . ." A sob. Then a ragged breath. "I don't want to talk about it."

"And you were waiting for me in the basement?"

"Yes."

"And you planted the knife in my bedroom."

Lori laughed, all sign of tears and remorse gone. "Yes. Yes, it was all me. The plan was to have you arrested for everything. In jail it's much easier to get rid of someone. Unfortunately, the police didn't cooperate with us, so we had to find a different way to get to you."

We? All Alexia could think was that she needed to keep her talking. "Why kill Devin's parents? That makes no sense."

"They knew about me." She said it like the answer should be obvious. It wasn't. Really.

"Knew what?"

"That I wanted Devin. I was at his apartment before he lost it and moved in with your mother. His parents showed up and heard us arguing. Devin was interested in me before Marcie Freeman came into the picture." Alexia could hear the fury in the woman's voice. "He was going to ask me out, I knew it. I went to see him and . . . well, it doesn't really matter. As soon as he died, I knew they had to die too. I just had to get to them before the cops."

"Is that why you set the fire at Detective Isaac's house?"

"I knew Hunter would be the one to question the Wickhams, so I created a distraction. I figured he'd postpone questioning them to rush to his partner's side." A coarse laugh escaped her. "He did."

Please, Hunter, be looking for me. Please, God, show him where to look. Keep her talking. "How did you get in my mother's house? Steal my necklace?"

"Simple. When I killed Devin, I took his keys. Now shut up, I'm tired of talking."

Of course.

"Wait a minute. That was you watching me in the dress shop, wasn't it?"

A longsuffering sigh sounded from the woman. "Yes, I even gave the police a statement. Under a different name, of course. But it was so fun to watch all the action."

Alexia didn't know what else to say, to ask.

And then receding footsteps told Alexia that Lori was leaving the area.

The darkness was terrifying. Suffocating. Pressing down on her. She shifted, drawing her knees up and resting her forehead on them as she debated whether or not to slip the blindfold off.

Maybe not. If "he" came in and she saw his face, he might kill her on the spot. Then again, Lori wasn't about to let Alexia walk out of here alive, so did it really matter?

A different set of footsteps sounded.

42

Saturday, 7:56 p.m.

Avery Tabor looked nervous. "What's this about that couldn't wait until after my dinner?"

"Where's your sister?" Hunter demanded.

Annoyance chased the nervousness from his face. "I don't know. She said she was going to the restroom. I haven't seen her since. Now, if you don't mind . . ." He turned in the direction of the door.

Hunter stepped in front of him. "I do mind. There's evidence that says your sister and an accomplice kidnapped a woman tonight. One person drove off, the other came back to the party. Did you leave the table for any reason?"

Shock bleached the doctor's face white. "What? No. You can check with the people at my table."

"We will."

"Why do you think my sister — or I —

had anything to do with this?"

"We have it on video. Along with a black Mercedes. She used your car."

"My ca— what? Are you all crazy?"

Hunter's phone rang. He snatched it. Dominic said, "She's not here, but there's a nonresponsive woman on the couch. Looks like she's been drugged. We've called for an ambulance."

Hope deflated like a punctured balloon. He wondered about the woman, but right now, his only concern was Alexia. "Where is she then?" Hunter whispered, more to himself than Dominic. He started to panic. "I don't know where to look."

Hunter pointed to Avery. "She's not at your house. There's a woman passed out cold on your couch, but no Lori and no children. We called an ambulance for the woman. Now where would she go?"

He paled. "My mother. Is she okay?"

"Alexia! Where would Lori take her!" Hunter was just about out of patience with the man.

Avery flinched. "I . . . I . . . don't . . . Maybe her house."

"Her house?" Hunter frowned. "I thought she lived with you."

"No, she stays there most of the time because of my schedule, but she has a townhouse on the other side of town."

"Give me the address," Hunter snapped.

Avery complied and Hunter passed it on to Dominic. "Get over there. I'm right behind you."

"On the way."

Alexia tensed. She'd pushed the blindfold up a scant millimeter more, allowing more light in. The suffocating feeling dissolved a bit, the panic she felt ready to overtake her receded.

Think, Lex, think.

Pray, Lex, pray.

Please, God, I don't even know what to pray. Just let me say the right thing and don't let them kill me. Please.

"Hello, Alexia."

She froze. Strained to recognize the voice, but she didn't think she'd ever heard it before. But would she recognize her father's voice after all this time?

Definitely.

"What do you want?" she asked.

A hard slap to the side of her face sent her spinning sideways. Shock and pain radiated through her as she landed on the floor facedown, no way to push herself up with her hands bound behind her back.

A hand in the crook of her elbow yanked

her back into a sitting position.

"I'll ask the questions, thank you very much." The polite tone next to her ears was at definite odds with the man's actions.

Her head spun and her ears rang.

She wanted to cry.

And refused.

Clamping her lips shut, she remembered that little place she used to go in her mind when her father started his punches. The area around her heart that Hunter had touched had begun to thaw. It now chilled back over.

"This could get really painful for you — but it doesn't have to."

Alexia didn't answer.

She felt him move closer and breathed in, memorizing his scent. He smelled good, she noticed through the haze of pain. Rich. Like leather and cigars. She forced herself not to flinch. If another hit was coming, she'd take it.

"Now. Do we understand each other?" he almost whispered, the sound grating and terrifying all at once.

"Yes."

He moved back a fraction. "Good."

Alexia looked down through the bottom of the blindfold.

Expensive shoes.

She took a deep breath. *God, lead Hunter to me.*

"I'll get right to it. You've been a very troublesome girl to get ahold of. But I need to know where Jillian Carter is. I believe you know where she is."

"And why do you believe that?"

Another crack to the side of her head sent her sprawling to the floor. Pain ricocheted through her. Tears sprang to her eyes without her permission, and she squeezed her lids tight until the sensation passed.

Somewhere in the distance, a cry sounded. A young child. Alexia wondered how Lori could seem so normal and yet be so sick.

"Pay attention to me, Alexia. Tell me what I want to know or people close to you are going to start dying. Like your sick mother lying in the hospital needing a bone marrow transplant."

His words echoed in her head, freezing her blood in her veins. *What do I tell him, God?*

She drew in a deep shuddering breath. "I would tell you where Jillian was if I knew. I haven't talked to her since the night of the graduation party ten years ago." She spat the words along with a stream of blood. He'd split her lip.

"Let's talk about that night. Jillian was in

a place she shouldn't have been, saw something she shouldn't have seen. Did she tell you about it?"

"No." Alexia almost shook her head, then decided against it. "She just said she saw something, that her life was in danger, and if she told us, we would be in danger too. I haven't seen her since."

Silence greeted her words. Then more footsteps. Lori?

"She tell you what you wanted to know?" The voice came from her left.

"No. Kill her. But wait until I'm well away from here."

Her head and lip throbbed.

Where was Hunter?

The team surrounded the house. Hunter kept pushing the earpiece tighter into his ear. The minutes were ticking.

But they were in there. In Lori's house. A two-story townhouse in a cute little neighborhood.

Hard to believe it held such evil.

SWAT moved in, placed microphones and video surveillance in the windows.

Dominic shifted beside Hunter. "You ready?"

"Almost."

■ ■ ■ ■

Alexia had to figure out a way to get free. The man's cell phone had rung and he'd walked away from her, Lori's footsteps trailing behind. Up steps? Sounded like it.

And all was quiet once again.

Every bone and muscle in her body ached. Her head throbbed and her teeth had shredded her lower lip.

But she was alive. And determined to stay that way.

An idea formed.

Her forehead back on her knees, she shoved the blindfold up a little further and examined her prison.

Definitely a basement. Lori's house. Several windows lined the top of the walls, but it was dark outside so there was no help there.

Shifting, she saw what she was looking for.

The candles.

Worried she'd run out of time, and either Lori or her partner would return, Alexia scooted as best she could across the floor in her now ruined fancy black dress. Somewhere she'd lost her shoes.

Finally, she slid in front of the candles, her head pounding, mouth aching. With a grunt, she heaved up on her knees, backed up, and held her hands over the open flame. To her right were paint cans, a gasoline can.

And paint thinner.

Fury stirred in her gut as the flame worked on her bonds. Thank God, he'd used rope. If they'd been cuffs, it would be hopeless.

The flame singed her wrist and she jumped, her knee knocking into the gas can. Another idea formed as she listened for footsteps.

And then her hands were free.

She gasped as she pulled them around to her front to clasp and massage her arms. Her wrists had blisters, but she didn't care.

Footsteps sounded above, then began their descent.

It was time. The children were occupied. Another pill. She needed another pill. Killing Alexia would be the final act needed to ensure that the children were safe and would be with Lori forever.

No one was going to take them away. No one. Their own mother never loved them like Lori.

She stepped to the bottom of the basement and looked around. The concrete walls would muffle the shot.

Or maybe she'd use the wire.

She'd used it a lot in the army. They'd trained her well.

43

Alexia watched the woman from the corner of her eye. She'd ditched the blindfold. Now she held her hands behind her back. She wasn't sure where the man had gone, just knew that he'd left. Which was fine by her.

She also knew that Lori was stronger than she and there was no way Alexia could win a physical fight with the woman.

So she had a plan. A one-time effort plan. If she failed, she died.

Her only concern was the children. And Lori's mother.

"So," she said as Lori reached the bottom of the steps, "he left you to do the dirty work, huh?"

"You think you can take my children away? Oh no. No. No. No."

Alexia didn't bother arguing with the woman. She was loony tunes. She just needed her to come a little closer.

Lori took two more steps toward Alexia.

"You don't have to do this, Lori, we'll get you some help."

Alexia held her breath. Lori lifted the gun and stared at her with cold, emotionless eyes. "I don't want or need help. I just need for you to be dead."

And Alexia knew she had no choice.

She brought the old-fashioned gas can from behind her and threw the contents at Lori.

The woman yelled and gasped as the gas hit her in the face and down her front. Her finger twitched on the trigger and the bullet slammed into the wall behind. The candle on the table behind her rocked.

Lori thrashed, frantically wiping the gas from her eyes. She hit the table again and the candle landed against her.

The small flame lit the gas with a whoosh and Lori screamed as her skirt caught fire. Shrieking, she turned the gun on Alexia, who had darted for the steps.

Another bullet hit just above Alexia. Looking back, she saw the small rug catch fire, then a paint tarp. Horror hit her as the woman screamed in pain. Alexia paused, wondering if she should somehow help her. But those crazed eyes glared at her even as Lori frantically beat at the flames with an old rag. The gun cracked again and Alexia felt the bullet whiz by her head.

She didn't have much time before the entire room would be engulfed. She had no way to help Lori without getting herself killed. And she needed to find the children. She raced upstairs and looked for the children, first one room, then the other.

Finally, she found little Mary Ellen asleep in her bed. She shook the little girl. "Come on, we have to go. The house is on fire."

"I'm going to kill you!"

Alexia froze. The words came from the basement, but she could hear them even up on the next floor.

Mary Ellen looked up at her, blinking sleep from her eyes. "You were at Aunt Lori's party."

"Yes, sweetie, I was. Where's your brother?"

"Alexia!" Lori's frantic shout echoed through the townhouse.

Mary Ellen said, "He's probably in Aunt Lori's room. Why is she yelling?"

Had Lori managed to put the fire out?

It didn't matter. She had to get the kids out of the house.

"Something's going on," Hunter said into his microphone. "What is it? I can see activity through the windows."

"There's a fire in the basement" came the report from one of the SWAT members. He thought it was Harry.

Hunter frowned and shot a look at Dominic. "A fire?"

"The woman, Lori, is yelling she's going to kill Alexia," Harry said. "We've got to get in there. The fire's moving up to the main floor. Lot of smoke, hard to see."

Hunter shifted his bulletproof vest and nodded. "Go."

He and Dominic stood behind the two who rammed the door.

"No, Aunt Lori! Stop!" A child's cry pierced the heavy smoke.

"Put her down! Put her down!" Lori screamed the words as spit flew from her lips.

Alexia froze once again. She held the little girl in her arms and angled her away from the woman with the gun. She knew as soon as she put Mary Ellen down, Lori would fire the weapon.

Blood dripped from her scorched face and neck. She held the gun in her blistered hand that shook with each trembling word.

The woman had to be in horrible pain. She'd managed to put out the fire on her clothes, but not before it had done considerable damage to her. How was she even still functioning?

Mary Ellen kept a death grip on Alexia's neck and turned her face away from the grotesque image of her aunt, screaming her fear. "She's a monster! Don't let her get me!"

"It's okay, baby," she whispered, her eyes on Lori's.

Lori seemed shocked at Mary Ellen's cry. Then furious, the fire of hate blazing hotter than the fire now licking at the hot boards under Alexia's feet.

Trembling, heart thudding, Alexia made sure the child wasn't in the line of fire. But she had nowhere to go. Nowhere to run, nowhere to hide. Smoke swirled and she choked.

She had to get the kids out.

"Don't do this, Lori, think about the children. We have to get out of here!"

"You're not going anywhere!" Lori swayed and Alexia could tell she was weakening. But her finger was still on the trigger.

Alexia bit her lip. *God, please? Tell me what to do.*

Then before she could blink, Lori was on the floor, cuffs on her wrists. A swarm of officers descended on her, sweeping past her, searching.

Hunter appeared before her and she gasped. Relief nearly swept her to her knees, but she still had one more child to find. The smoke was getting thick.

She shoved Mary Ellen into Hunter's arms and said, "I have to find the little boy." She realized she didn't remember his name. She looked at Mary Ellen. "What's his name, honey?"

"Brad."

"Alexia, you're hurt."

She ignored him, desperate to find the other child. Thundering down the hall, she coughed, but pressed on. "Where are you?"

Lori's room. The master.

She turned right. And saw the little boy huddled on the bed. When he saw her, he jerked, fear written all over him. She held out her hand. "Come on, Brad, sweetie, the house is on fire. We have to get out now, okay?"

"What's going on? Where's Aunt Lori?"

"I'll explain on the way out. Come on."

Hunter reached around her and picked up the boy in his other arm. A child on each hip, he nodded toward the door. "Let's go."

44

Sunday, 12:36 p.m.

Alexia picked at the blanket on her hospital bed as she cut her eyes to Hunter. "I'm ready to get out of here. I'm fine." Hunter had insisted she get checked out because of the punches to her head and face. They'd kept her overnight for observation.

And frankly, she'd had enough of being observed.

"You've had a rough time. Let yourself be pampered."

Alexia chewed on her lip, then said, "I told them to test me. To see if I'm a match for my mother."

He lifted a brow. "And?"

"I'm not. I went to see her this morning to tell her." Grief twisted her insides as Hunter gripped her hands.

"I'm sorry." He paused. "I'll get tested too."

"Seriously? You will?" A lump formed in

her throat. Of course he would, he was that kind of guy.

"Seriously." He gave her a tender smile and she wanted to throw herself into his arms.

"Thank you, Hunter," she whispered.

"You bet." He leaned over and kissed her forehead.

"How's Katie?" she asked.

"She's doing all right. Should make a full recovery."

Her cell phone vibrated and she grabbed it. "Hello?"

"Hi, Alexia, it's Paul Sanders."

Taken aback, she fell silent.

"Hello? Are you there?"

"Uh, yeah. Hi, Paul."

"I . . . um . . . was given the honor of making this call." She could hear the wariness in his voice.

"Okay . . ." What was her nemesis from Winthrop, Washington, doing calling her?

"You've been cleared," he said.

"What? How?" Elation chugged through her.

"It's a long story, but evidence was found. The captain poked the holes in your mask hose."

"But why?" Confusion and a sense of betrayal flooded her.

"He confessed to the fact that someone contacted him a few weeks ago and asked him if he was interested in making a lot of money. Someone wired fifty grand to his account. You weren't supposed to live. After you died, he would have gotten rid of the faulty mask, replaced it with one that would pass inspection during the investigation, and no one would be the wiser. It would just be considered a tragic accident."

"Hold on a second, Paul, will you?"

She stared at Hunter. "Someone paid my captain to kill me. I wonder if it's the person who knocked me around in the townhouse."

His eyes narrowed. "It's a good possibility. I'm thinking this whole thing is bigger than we're seeing."

"You mean it's not over?" Dread threaded through her even as she asked the question she already knew the answer to.

"Unfortunately, no. Someone hired Lori."

"She wanted to kill me because someone convinced her I was going to take the children away from her."

"She's mentally ill. Avery said he prescribed her some anti-anxiety medication."

"She needs more than that," Alexia said, her voice flat, eyes narrow.

Hunter nodded. "I think this all started in Washington, but when you ran from Washington, you ran straight toward the killer. How convenient for him — or her." He rubbed his face and she could see his mind churning.

"That'll teach me to run from my problems," she muttered.

"Hey, I've gotta go," Paul said, and Alexia started.

"I'm so sorry, Paul, I didn't mean to be rude. I was telling someone what you said."

"No problem. I just wanted to let you know the good news. You can come back anytime."

She shot a look at Hunter, thought about her mother, wondered where her father was. "I don't think I'll be coming back. But thanks for everything."

"Take care."

"You too." He hung up and Alexia leaned back against the pillows. "So, it's really not over."

"Not completely."

She flinched, knowing what he meant. "They never caught the man who was in the townhouse with me, did they?"

"No." His jaw looked tight and she knew every time he looked at the bruises on her face, he thought about the man who put them there. "We'll get him, though."

"How did he get out?" she asked.

"There was an opening in the attic that ran the length of the townhomes. Someone went to a lot of trouble to make sure he — or she — had an escape route."

Alexia grimaced. "Sounds like something a paranoid person would do."

"And Lori definitely fits that description." Hunter said, "All your guy had to do was keep walking through the attic, find an empty home, come down through the attic opening in the ceiling, and walk out of the house."

"I'm worried about Jillian." Alexia looked away, then back at him. "I know she's not ready to be found. I don't know what's going on with her, but if she feels like she's in danger, I sure don't want to send the wrong people after her."

"I'm the wrong people?" His brows knit in confusion.

"No, of course not, but look what happened to me. The whole reason they came after me was to find Jillian. When they decided I couldn't help, they were willing to kill me." She paused. "And I'm scared Serena's next. This is all about the night of graduation and what Jillian saw." Biting her lip, she looked at Hunter. "What if they decide to go after her next?"

"We've warned her and we're ready to

have some kind of protection in place for her."

The doctor finally entered and declared her ready to leave. She stopped by her mother's room to find Dominic and Michael already there.

"Hi, Mom."

Her mother looked much better. Alexia had managed to do a little research into aplastic anemia and knew now that her mom had been accurately diagnosed, the drugs would help for a short time. But she really needed to find a donor.

"Hi, darling." She gave a radiant look at her son. "Dominic was tested. He's a match."

A thrill shot through her. "That's great, Mom."

"The procedure will be soon," Dominic said.

"Let me know what I can do to help." Alexia was amazed that she could feel this way. From hate to forgiveness to a resurgence of love for a woman she thought she never wanted to see again. She now agreed with Hunter. God was truly amazing. He cared, and while she knew she was unworthy of his love, she accepted that he found her worth loving.

Just as Hunter had said — and shown her

through his own actions.

Forty-five minutes later, Hunter pulled into the driveway of his house. His phone rang and he pulled it out. "Hello?" He listened for a few minutes. Then his disgusted sigh made her stare at him. "Okay, thanks for letting me know."

When he hung up, he closed his eyes and shook his head.

"What?" she asked.

"That was my captain. Lori Tabor was murdered this morning."

"What?" She nearly screeched the word. "How?"

"She was found dead in her hospital bed. Strangled." His fingers fisted on the wheel.

"By who?"

"Don't know yet."

Alexia swallowed. "And she never said who the man in the townhouse was, did she?"

"Nope."

"Great."

"Yeah."

They sat for a few seconds pondering the news, then Alexia asked, "The day of the shooting at the hospital, how did she manage to fool you guys in the parking garage?"

Hunter's jaw tightened. "Her car. Rick called this morning. Her trunk had a false bottom. In it were the mask, a long-sleeved black T-shirt, and gloves. She had time to stash everything before we got there, then she just hunkered down to play the part of victim."

"Very convincingly."

"She was sweaty and shaking and . . ." He shook his head in disgust. "I never thought anything about her being there." He reached over and squeezed her hand. "Come on. I want to show you something."

Alexia got out of the car and followed him. "Avery's taking Lori's involvement in all of this pretty hard, isn't he?"

"Yes. Finding out his sister murdered his wife was a stunning blow. And then add to that the fact that she killed anyone who got in her way." He sighed. "Yeah, he's pretty devastated. When she complained of anxiety attacks, he just prescribed some rather strong meds for her. Now he's kicking himself for not insisting on having her evaluated."

"At least he's got his kids to help him through it."

"They'll be all right."

Where was he going? He led her around to the side of his house, then down the hill to a small stream with a bridge. A bench sat off to the side, overlooking the water.

"It's beautiful here."

"Thanks. When I need to shut out the world, I come down here and sit on that bench and read or just think and pray."

Alexia settled herself on the bench. Hunter sat beside her and took her hand. She felt the butterflies take flight. What was he doing?

He said, "I can't believe it's only been a week since you've been back. I feel like we've lived a lifetime together."

She gave a shaky laugh. "I know what you mean."

He turned and pulled her to him. Leaning over he kissed her. A long, slow, sweet kiss. When he pulled back, his eyes were soft, a longing there that warmed her. "I want more time with you. I want to see where we're headed."

"I want that too," she whispered.

A satisfied smile crossed his lips. "Great."

She smiled. "Your parents' reaction to me at the dinner was surprising."

"I know." He laughed. "I guess my dad decided to let it rest." He fell silent for a moment, then said, "I told him what really happened with the fire. He said he wasn't terribly surprised, that he never really thought you started the fire on purpose, but that your father was so adamant and my dad felt like he owed him . . ." Hunter shrugged. "Anyway, he said the next time he saw you, he was going to apologize and ask your forgiveness."

Alexia grinned. "Really?"

"Yes. He's nervous you're going to tell him off."

Sobering, she stared out over the creek. "Last week I would have."

"But now?"

"So much has changed inside of me. Now, I'll tell your father that I accept his apology and hope we can start over."

Hunter hugged her and planted kisses across her eyelids. "You're amazing."

She shifted in his arms and looked away as she asked, "Will you help me find my father?"

He turned her back to face him. "We'll find him. Just like we'll find the creep from the townhouse."

"Thanks."

Hunter slid his hand through her curls and she felt his palm against the side of her head. The look in his eyes made her pulse kick it up a notch.

He said, "Alexia, I'm falling in love with you. I care about you more than any woman I've ever met before."

That silly lump formed in her throat. "I

know, Hunter. I feel the same for you."

He kissed her, a light, sweet kiss that left her wanting more. But another big obstacle stood in their way.

"I feel bad for Chad. Once again he's going to feel like he lost out to you." Trouble stirred inside her and she regretted it. This wasn't what she wanted to be concerned about when the man she loved told her he loved her. But she was genuinely concerned about Hunter's brother.

Hunter pushed her back to arm's length. "I told Chad how I felt about you."

She tensed. "What did he say?"

"He said that he wishes us the best."

"Really?" She was surprised. And glad. She liked Chad and hated the fact that he felt like he had to compete with Hunter in all areas of his life.

"Yep. I think he's doing a lot of soul searching."

"I'm glad. He needs to find peace."

Hunter sighed and pulled her back into a tight squeeze.

She giggled. "You're squishing me."

Loosening his grip, he said, "So, you're not interested in returning to Washington?"

"No." Alexia looked him in the eye. "I've got everything I need here in Columbia. Family. Friends. You. I'm not running anywhere anymore."

"Thank goodness for that. I'm too old to be chasing you across the country."

She smiled, and Hunter turned serious again.

"Can we take it one day at a time and see where it goes? Where we go?"

She nodded. "I'd love to do that. I'd love to see what God has planned for us."

Something wet splashed on her hand.

His thumbs swiped her cheeks for her. "You're crying."

"I am?" Startled, she lifted a hand to her eyes and found them wet. Giving a shaky laugh, she said, "I think God finally managed to knock down all my walls."

He pulled her to him in a hug. "No, you took them down to make room for him."

"Yeah." She sniffed. "I did."

He leaned over to kiss her again.

Joy surged through her and another tear slipped out.

EPILOGUE

The senator stared at the latest letter.

GOING AFTER *THEM* WON'T STOP *ME.*

How did these letters keep appearing?

Jillian was close by. Watching him. Dropping the letters in his mailbox. No postmark. Not even his name sometimes. But he recognized the writing. Even so, he now opened all the mail whether it was addressed to him or not.

He picked up the phone and pressed a speed-dial number.

When the voice answered, the senator nearly growled his frustration and fear. "I got another one."

A curse whispered through the line. "I have someone watching the mailbox. I don't understand."

"Then fire him because he's sleeping on the job."

"I'll talk to him."

"You don't understand. We must find Jillian. Today."

Silence. "I understand perfectly." The low, controlled words sent a chill up the senator's spine.

Softening his tone, he said, "Look. I admit it. I'm freaked. From what you said, Alexia doesn't know anything about that night. Jillian hasn't been in touch with her."

"But she has been in touch with Serena Hopkins." Another pause. "And now that we've failed rather badly in getting rid of Alexia, she and her detective boyfriend won't give up so easily."

"But you can monitor them. Right now, they know nothing."

"So we go after the one that does."

"Exactly. Serena's the one we need."

"I'm already working on it. She's on a job in China cleaning up after the earthquake." A sigh filtered through the line, then the voice hardened once again. "As long as she never makes it home, we should be safe."

We. The senator liked that. Was comforted by the fact that someone was looking out for him. For his career. For his very life.

"And if she does?"

"We get rid of her."

"Like we did Alexia?" He couldn't help the snide question.

"Alexia can still die."

The man on the other line refused to take the bait. Which was just as well. There wasn't time to argue.

It was time to act.

ACKNOWLEDGMENTS

Thank you to the incredible staff at Baker Publishing, especially Claudia Marsh, Barb Barnes, and Michele Misiak. You guys are amazing. And of course, a big thanks to my editor, Andrea Doering, who believed in the series and me.

Thanks to the original publisher's cover art department. This is the best cover I've ever seen! You guys did a fantastic job.

Thanks to my family, Jack, Lauryn, and Will, for putting up with me when I'm in deadline mode. I appreciate you and love you more than words can express.

Thanks to those who read the story and gave me feedback, especially my police officer buddy, Jim Hall. I appreciate you.

Thank you, Dee Henderson, for being willing to put your name on my book. I love you, my friend!

ABOUT THE AUTHOR

Lynette Eason grew up in Greenville, South Carolina. She graduated from the University of South Carolina, Columbia, and then obtained her master's in education at Converse College. Author of the Women of Justice series, Lynette is also a member of American Christian Fiction Writers (ACFW) and Romance Writers of America (RWA). In 1996, Lynette married "the boy next door," and now she and her husband and two children make their home in Spartanburg, South Carolina.

Visit Lynette at www.lynetteeason.com.

The employees of Thorndike Press hope you have enjoyed this Large Print book. All our Thorndike, Wheeler, and Kennebec Large Print titles are designed for easy reading, and all our books are made to last. Other Thorndike Press Large Print books are available at your library, through selected bookstores, or directly from us.

For information about titles, please call:
  (800) 223-1244

or visit our Web site at:
  http://gale.cengage.com/thorndike

To share your comments, please write:
  Publisher
  Thorndike Press
  10 Water St., Suite 310
  Waterville, ME 04901